Eloisa James
Say Yes to *the* DUKE

piatkus

PIATKUS

First published in the US in 2020 by Avon Books,
An imprint of HarperCollins Publishers, New York
First published in Great Britain in 2020 by Piatkus

3 5 7 9 10 8 6 4

A CIP catalogue record for this book
is available from the British Library.

ISBN 978-0-349-42370-8

Printed and bound in Great Britain by Clays Ltd, Elcograf S.p.A.

Papers used by Piatkus are from well-managed forests
and other responsible sources.

MIX
Paper from
responsible sources
FSC® C104740

Piatkus
An imprint of
Little, Brown Book Group
Carmelite House
50 Victoria Embankment
London EC4Y 0DZ

An Hachette UK Company
www.hachette.co.uk

www.littlebrown.co.uk

Say Yes to the Duke is dedicated
to Sharlene Martin Moore,
a wonderful friend and partner in running my
Facebook group, Lindow Castle. Its charming
atmosphere and flow of cheerful ideas and visitors
is largely due to Sharlene.
Thank you!

Acknowledgments

My books are like small children; they take a whole village to get them to a literate state. I want to offer my deep gratitude to my village: my editor, Carrie Feron; my agent, Kim Witherspoon; my Web site designers, Wax Creative; and my personal team: Franzeca Drouin, Leslie Ferdinand, and Sharlene Martin Moore. My husband and daughter Anna debated many a plot point with me, and I'm fervently grateful to them. In addition, people in many departments of HarperCollins, from Art to Marketing to PR, have done a wonderful job of getting this book into readers' hands: My heartfelt thanks go to each of you. Finally, my thanks go to a generous and knowledgeable Episcopal priest, the Rev. Lawrence N. Crumb, who was kind enough to explicate different aspects of the Anglican religion. Any mistakes are mine.

Say Yes *to* *the* DUKE

Chapter One

*M*iss Viola Astley, the stepdaughter of Hugo Wilde, Duke of Lindow, considered it the greatest misfortune of her life that she was the complete opposite of a Wilde.

She had realized as a child that she had no more in common with His Grace's offspring than a donkey to a dragon. As her mother, Ophelia, had married the duke when Viola was only two years old, her earliest memories were defined by feeling *not Wilde*.

Her half sister Artemisia, for example, was beautiful, bold, and audacious.

At the age of six!

Whereas Viola was timid, tongue-tied, and fairly useless.

Her older stepsister Betsy was famous in the family for being able to shoot arrows from horseback; Viola was afraid of horses, and didn't care for arrows either. Fear itself marked her as not a real Wilde.

Courage was a hallmark of the duke's other children. The oldest Wilde, Alaric, was a writer who wandered about foreign countries with his wife and children, fearlessly doing fearless things. Joan, whom Viola loved most of all, relished being in public, to the point of pining for a career on the London stage. And after Betsy put aside her bow and arrows, she triumphed in London society, rejecting nineteen suitors before marrying a future marquess.

Whereas Viola went to her first ball at the age of fifteen and disgraced herself by throwing up just outside the ballroom. Even worse, after that she lost what little courage she had. These days she could scarcely sit beside a strange gentleman without her stomach twisting into a knot.

No matter how many times her family reassured her that there was nothing to worry about, she didn't seem to be able to overcome the memory of her first ball, the Lindow ball of 1778.

Viola had been nervous, but Joan had floated down the stairs with a huge smile, thrilled to be old enough to join the festivities.

"Don't worry," she told Viola, with the supreme confidence of a Wilde. "We will be besieged by men begging us for dances."

Sure enough, they no sooner entered the ballroom than a friend of Alaric's—Lord Poplar, known at Eton as Poppy—bowed before them.

"Viola will dance with you, Poppy," Joan declared.

Lord Poplar burst out laughing and said, "I haven't heard that nickname in years. No one dares use it."

Joan rolled her eyes, and a minute later Poppy was leading Viola onto the dance floor. Viola concentrated on getting the steps right. The pattern of the dance ensured that she didn't exchange more than five words with Poppy, which was fine with her.

When the music drew to a close, Viola smiled at His Lordship, proud that she hadn't missed a step. She danced with one of her brothers, and after that, an uncle on her mother's side. If the experience wasn't comfortable, it wasn't unbearable.

Then one of her partners erupted into an uncontrollable fit of hiccups and reeled toward the door, leaving her marooned against a wall, peering through the shifting bodies of dancers for her family.

Where had everyone gone?

Aunt Knowe appeared at her side. "Didn't I see you dancing with Finrope?" Lord Finrope was a sixty-year-old neighbor, a kindly soul.

"He started hiccupping, and had to retire."

"Drinks too much," Aunt Knowe said, wrinkling her nose. "He's doing his belly no favor with all that whiskey."

Viola put a hand on her stomacher and whispered, "I feel ill." She had once retched before a maths examination at school, and she had a terrible fear it might happen again.

"Just give your nerves time to settle. Oh, rats, there's Lady Prunner arriving. Stay right here, Viola, and I'll be back."

Viola had no intention of going anywhere. Her hands were growing disgustingly clammy inside her gloves. She was breathing quickly too, and her gown wasn't helping; the point of her stomacher dug into her waist.

The dance drew to a close. People drifted past, glancing at her and looking away. It was humiliating to be standing alone by the wall. Yet in the press of over one hundred bodies, many of whom were wearing wide panniers, she couldn't see anyone she knew.

Stealthily, she began edging along the wall to the right.

There was a curtained alcove not far away, where the castle butler, Prism, stowed extra chairs when the ballroom wasn't in use.

A matron paused before her, and she forced herself to smile. The woman frowned slightly, likely thinking she ought to recognize her, and moved on.

Another way that Viola was different from her half siblings? She was short and nondescript, and people often forgot who she was.

No one forgot a Wilde.

Viola's heart had begun to pound so hard that she could hear it in her ears. Somehow she managed to get herself into the alcove, but that didn't help.

It was swelteringly hot in the tiny enclosure. On the other side of the velvet curtain, the musicians began a rollicking country dance. The floor of the ballroom actually shuddered under Viola's slippers from the pounding of feet.

The alcove had been a terrible idea. It was hot and smelled of varnish.

It would smell of vomit in a moment, Viola thought wildly. She had to leave, and quickly, before the worst happened.

She pulled back the curtain and hurried out, brushing shoulders with a gentleman and ignoring his startled exclamation. One violin was playing out of tune, and a woman's high laughter echoed in her ears.

In her panic, she had turned away from the ball-room entrance, but thankfully a servants' door not far away offered access to a corridor connecting the back of the castle with the public areas.

She hurtled through that door, never considering that someone might be on the other side.

Let alone two people.

Chapter Two

$\mathcal{V}$iola rebounded off a gentleman who stood with
his back to her. He rocked forward but withstood the
blow.

She fell back a step, an apology withering on her
lips.

He was huge, wide-shouldered, bewigged, with
one arm braced against the wall and the other wound
around someone she couldn't see. Her eyes skittered
over his back, registering yellow slippers that in-
congruously stuck out on either side of his waist. The
slippers disappeared, followed by a whoosh of skirts
falling to the ground before she realized what they
implied.

The man glanced over his shoulder for a second,
and then turned back to his . . . what was the word?
Paramour?

"You arranged for a witness?" His voice was raw
and hoarse—not with disbelief, but with a scalding
anger that jolted Viola's whole body. Her stomach
twisted tighter.

"No, indeed," the woman said, out of breath. "It's
merely a servant."

"Contrary to all expectation, a lady has invaded the servants' corridor. Your witness seems to have been afraid she might be late for the performance," he retorted, his voice cutting like a blade. "She's panting like a set of bellows. I gather you plan to use her testimony to force me to marry you?"

Viola was shaking all over. The servants' corridor was narrow, and he was blocking the way.

She took a sobbing breath. "Excuse me."

He didn't turn. "What sort of marriage do you think we'll have?"

The woman murmured something.

Viola edged to the side. Given that her panniers made her nearly the width of the corridor, she couldn't push past him.

"Do you imagine yourself a duchess, parading about town in a high wig and my mother's diamonds? I live in the country; I never attend Parliament; and I loathe polite society. My wife will, of course, be at my side. You might want to keep that in mind before you and your damned witness blurt out what happened."

"Excuse me," Viola said, her voice wavering. "I need to—"

She saw a flash of a strong jaw and bitter eyes before he slammed past her into the ballroom, revealing a woman in a mustard-colored dress who screamed, "You cow, you miserable bloody cow, why in the bloody hell did you come in?"

Viola stared aghast, unable to say a word.

"You've ruined everything!" the woman added, savage fury punctuating her sentence.

The door behind Viola opened, and another surge of panic flooded her body.

He was back.

She spun about and found a matron staring at her in bewilderment.

"You're too late," the woman in yellow snarled. "This fool interrupted, and he left in a fury."

Viola bent over and emptied her stomach, in the process splashing the woman in yellow and her witness.

She fled the shrieks that followed, ran to her bedchamber, summoned her maid, and huddled in a hot bath, trying to understand what she'd seen.

The act bore no relation to the placid marital relations her headmistress had described in hushed tones. To the best of Viola's recollection, Miss Peters had said that a lady relaxed on her back and allowed "relations" to happen in the dark. The event she had described was respectful, if uncomfortable.

The details magnified in Viola's brain, even as she tried to forget them: the breadth of his shoulders, the rasp of his breath, the way the woman's body thudded against the wall as Viola bumped into him, his sheer force.

The next morning, when no scandal broke, she realized that if she confessed what she'd witnessed, the man—apparently a duke—would be forced to marry the woman in yellow. Even if she was a widow, the woman's reputation would be ruined by gossip. Viola's stepfather, the Duke of Lindow, would be explosively angry to learn what his young stepdaughter had witnessed. There would be recriminations and the news would spread. Secrets were never private in a castle brimming with people.

An injustice would follow, and even though she loathed the man who would pay the price, Viola considered that she'd had a salutary glimpse into the darkness that gentlemen conceal with exquisite manners and elegant clothing.

He was a beast of a man, but he didn't deserve to be tricked into marriage.

She'd heard her stepbrothers joking about schemes intended to trap them, but there was an edge in their voices. They wanted to choose their own brides.

That man had sounded furious—and betrayed.

So Viola never told a soul what had happened at the ball. She did her best to forget it, never attempting to find out the names of the woman in yellow or the duke in question.

The following year she allowed her mother to talk her into coming downstairs to a musicale, and narrowly avoided vomiting on a young man, lunging toward a potted lemon tree instead. Her brothers teased her that the poor tree never bore fruit again.

Since then, her shyness had become uncontrollable. She couldn't stop thinking that she wasn't a real Wilde. The very idea of marital intimacies made her shudder with revulsion, and she was terrified of finding herself married off to a gentleman who would consider her second-rate, and possibly confine her to the country, or even to a garret.

Never mind how unlikely that scenario was; it had taken hold of her imagination and she couldn't seem to fight it off. She felt nauseated at the idea of flirtation, let alone marriage.

Marriage was inconceivable.

In the three years that followed, she became an on-looker to polite society, sitting quietly in the corner as the duchess welcomed guests, or in the back row while an opera singer entertained their visitors. She rarely joined the evening meal, but somehow she always managed to see enough of their guests to amuse the family with her observations—but only in private.

Unfortunately, private occasions were rare at Lindow. The powerful duke avoided Parliament, so ruling members of England came to him. The castle was often bursting at the seams with peers and politicians.

When the duke instituted a family dinner once a week, everyone knew it was so that Viola wouldn't have to retire to her chamber with a tray while everyone else entertained guests. Viola adored those nights, when Joan would leap up from the table and perform impromptu reenactments of scenes Viola had witnessed, until the whole family convulsed with laughter.

She was happy living in the country. She helped their elderly vicar, Father Duddleston, with his parish duties and spent time with the castle's beloved animals: Fitzy the peacock; her pet crow, Barty; and her two cows, Daisy and Cleopatra.

As a young girl, Viola had realized to her horror that the two adorable calves in the castle cowshed were being fattened for Easter dinner. She had begged her stepfather not to turn Cleo and Daisy into prime beefsteak.

The cowshed became her favorite refuge, the one place where beloved, brilliant, shining Wilde siblings came only if they were searching for her. She spent hours there, sitting on a stool, reading a book, and listening to the soft mooing of animals never forced into wigs and corsets and made to dance the quadrille.

When Father Duddleston passed away in his sleep, Viola gave up her dream of the vicar begging the duke to allow his stepdaughter to stay in Cheshire, and reconciled herself to the truth.

She would have to debut.

Viola's mother, Ophelia, put her foot down when Viola suggested that perhaps she could stay in the castle. In the long run, according to Ophelia, ballrooms didn't matter. However, a lady's presentation to polite society was not a choice, but a necessity.

Aunt Knowe, the duke's twin sister, agreed: The only way to surmount Viola's nerves was to put them to the test. Consequently, the 1782 Season would open with the Lindow ball in honor of Viola and Joan, to be held at the duke's townhouse in Mayfair.

"If you must throw up, darling, run toward a potted plant," Aunt Knowe advised. "I'll have Prism remove the lemon trees; they're too finicky."

The mere idea of the ball made Viola feel queasy, even though their debut had been delayed a year in hopes that her stomach would settle. From a distance of three years, she couldn't remember the lovers' features, but she still felt a wave of horror at the memory of the man's scathing voice and his brutal strength.

"I can get through it," Viola said to Cleo, stroking her smudgy, soft nose. "I can survive the Season."

Cleo didn't bother to moo.

Likely she knew as well as Viola that while survival was probable, success was unlikely.

Even Aunt Knowe had a tight look around her eyes when the subject came up. She had taken to dosing the footmen with dandelion potions and asking them if they felt capable of serving dinner without breaking plates. Unfortunately, when Viola tried a dose, she slept away the entire afternoon.

"It's only a few months," Viola told Daisy, who blinked her long eyelashes and chewed meditatively. Viola hitched her stool a bit closer and leaned her cheek against the cow's bristly, warm side. Inside she heard mysterious gurgling sounds. "But I'm a coward."

Acknowledging the fact didn't change anything.

Her pet crow, Barty, had been dozing on Daisy's back, but he woke up and gave a little squawk. She was doomed, and even Barty agreed.

That night at their family-only supper, the duke announced that he'd found a new vicar.

"His name is Mr. Marlowe," His Grace said. "He comes highly recommended by the Bishop of London. He'll have the living on a year's trial, as he's both inexperienced and unmarried."

"Is he handsome?" Joan asked, and squealed when ten-year-old Erik elbowed her.

"Children," Ophelia said placidly.

"It was merely a question. I don't want to marry a vicar," Joan said.

"Viola could marry him," Erik suggested.

"No, thank you," Viola said. Her grand life plan involved surviving the Season and gratefully lapsing into life as a spinster.

"Mr. Marlowe is betrothed," Aunt Knowe put in.

"He took an excellent first at Cambridge," the duke said. "He's young, though. Comes to us with only a few years as a curate."

"His entrée is his fiancée," Aunt Knowe added. She kept a close eye on polite society, by way of voluminous correspondence. "Miss Pettigrew is the granddaughter of an archbishop, daughter of a bishop, and reading between the lines, she means to push the man into a bishopric before he turns thirty."

A few days later, Viola and Joan were sitting in the drawing room when Aunt Knowe trotted in and announced that Mrs. Pettigrew, Miss Pettigrew, and Mr. Marlowe had unexpectedly come to pay a visit.

Viola and Joan sprang to their feet. They had spent the morning making paper flowers, and bright scraps of paper were scattered all over the carpet. Barty had been seated on the back of the settee, overseeing their work, but he startled, instinctively tried to fly, and flopped over the back of the settee instead.

"Barty!" Viola cried, peering over. Her crow managed to land on his feet and looked up at her crossly. From experience she knew that he would now spend an hour or two grooming each of his wing feathers into shiny perfection.

Barty was a pragmatic bird, as the duke pointed out: Having discovered that his wings didn't function, he focused on beauty.

"Join us whenever you wish," she told him, and got to her feet. When Barty wasn't embarrassed—as he was now—he was a sociable fellow who added companionable squawks to any conversation.

Aunt Knowe was greeting their guests at the drawing room door. Viola walked over to join her, leaving Barty to sulk behind the settee.

Miss Pettigrew was tall, with a superb bosom that curved like the prow of a ship. But nothing else about her resembled those jolly wooden women who plunge into the waves, breasts leading the way.

She wore a navy gown whose only ornament was a row of shiny buttons, a style that labeled the gown three to four years old. Viola had the strong feeling that Miss Pettigrew did not pay attention to frivolities of fashion. The pious look in her eyes suggested she considered herself above such earthly concerns.

Her mother was a taller version of the daughter, and her black gown, if not her expression, proclaimed that fashion was a trivial matter.

"He's very handsome," Joan whispered as Viola finished her curtsies. "I'd wager that all the ladies hereabouts begin attending services."

Viola always avoided looking at strange men, having perfected the art of dropping into a curtsy and murmuring a greeting with lowered eyes. She had registered only that Mr. Marlowe didn't tower over her the way the Wildes did. He wasn't much taller than she was, perhaps even shorter than Miss Pettigrew.

It wasn't until their new vicar was escorting his future mother-in-law to a settee that Viola dared to peek at his face.

Joan was right.

Squire Pretner's three young daughters would be lined up in the front pew after they caught a glimpse of Mr. Marlowe's profile. He was as startlingly handsome as an actor on the London stage. A lock of honey-colored hair fell over his bright blue eyes. He wasn't wearing a wig, nor had he powdered his hair.

She was so entranced that she forgot to look away when he sat down. When he smiled at her, she felt the shock to the tips of her fingers. His eyes were warm and caring. One knew instinctively that he would be kind to everyone, from a crotchety elder to a colicky baby.

He turned away to respond to Aunt Knowe's offer of tea, and Viola barely managed to keep her mouth shut. Her whole body was caught in a delicious, yearning warmth.

Joan, who always knew what Viola was thinking, planted a sharp elbow in her side. "He's betrothed," she hissed into Viola's ear. "And *short*."

"So am I," Viola breathed.

"I'm sorry about the untidy state of this room," Aunt Knowe was saying. "We've spent the last few hours making bouquets of paper flowers."

"Decorations for our little sister's birthday," Joan explained.

Miss Pettigrew brushed a paper scrap onto the floor before she seated herself opposite Viola and Joan. "A charming notion." Her expression suggested she would expect nothing less from indolent aristocrats.

"I could send a bunch of paper peonies to the vicarage, if you'd like," Aunt Knowe offered.

"I do not care for decorations that collect dust," Miss Pettigrew announced. Viola suspected that all her statements were announcements. "A tidy bouquet of fresh flowers is an acceptable adornment."

"I see," Aunt Knowe said.

Joan put her arm around Viola's waist and gave her a little pinch, signaling either delight or horror. Probably both, since Miss Pettigrew was proving to be a character, and thus likely to entertain the family at dinner, *in absentia*, of course. Joan loved to act out the foibles of more outrageous visitors to the castle.

Mrs. Pettigrew smoothed her skirts. "We just came from Mobberley. The vicarage needs complete refurbishing. I gather it suffered a fire a decade ago?"

Aunt Knowe nodded. "An unfortunate accident."

"We considered accepting His Grace's offer to stay in the castle while the building is being reconstructed to my specifications."

Aunt Knowe's eyelids didn't flicker at this news; not for nothing was she born and bred into the peerage. But Viola could tell that her stepfather would have an earful later.

"That will take some months. Upon consideration, I think it best that I return to London once I deem the building plans acceptable," Mrs. Pettigrew continued. "Bishop Pettigrew cannot do without me. Obviously, it would be unseemly for my daughter to remain in the castle with Mr. Marlowe, since they have not yet taken vows."

"Of course," Aunt Knowe said.

"Mr. Marlowe may remain here," Mrs. Pettigrew allowed.

Mr. Marlowe leaned forward. "I shan't be underfoot," he assured Aunt Knowe. "There is a great deal to be done in the parish, since Father Duddleston died some weeks ago."

"The parish is as disorganized as the vicarage," Miss Pettigrew put in. "Mr. Marlowe will need to catalogue the parish unfortunates."

Viola's mind was whirling.

Mr. Marlowe was . . . He was the man she had never dared to imagine. She hadn't the slightest hint of nausea in his presence. She had no wish to flee to the cowshed. Instead, she wanted nothing more than to listen and contribute to his plans.

Yet . . . he *was* betrothed. A daring and heretofore undiscovered part of her mind pointed out that betrothal was not the same as marriage.

She glanced back at Mr. Marlowe. The curve of his lower lip was remarkably appealing for a man. His form was slender. He would likely dance extremely gracefully. But no: Vicars don't dance, she reminded herself.

Joan elbowed her. "Stop ogling him," she hissed.

Viola looked down at her plate and discovered to her surprise that she'd finished her shortbread. She never ate among strangers and yet . . .

Her stomach felt entirely peaceful.

This must be love, she thought wonderingly.

Love.

Love is miraculous.

If she were a vicar's wife, she'd have no need of ballrooms, although at the moment she felt brave enough to dance a minuet. In fact, if she married Mr. Marlowe she might never have to enter a ballroom again.

Gladness flooded her body, and she barely stopped herself from gazing at the vicar again, her heart in her eyes.

Perhaps he would never be hers—although some steely part of her was determined he would be hers—but even if not . . .

She could still save him from this dreadful marriage.

He was like her beloved Cleo and Daisy. Like Barty, whom she rescued after he fell from the nest. Mr. Marlowe needed to be saved from the domineering Miss Pettigrew.

She had a *mission*.

And she was in love.

Chapter Three

The Duke of Wynter's townhouse
Mayfair

*D*evin Lucas Augustus Elstan, Duke of Wynter, was not the sort of man who wasted time. Or, rather, as he would have phrased it: not the sort of *duke*. He had grown up knowing that a duke (or future duke) was as different from the average man as a lion from a tabby cat.

He wasn't akin to the other lions either. He watched with bemusement as his peers gathered to circle a crowded dance floor, or met at the racetrack for the sole purpose—or so it seemed—of losing money in questionable bets. Being a mathematician, he had walked into a gambling house as a young man, spent precisely one hour there, and walked out considerably richer.

But also bored.

He had been educated in isolation by a series of tutors as befitted the future Duke of Wynter and an only child. Normally, a duke's son would have met other children at house parties, but due to his father's reckless propensity for dueling, such invitations had stopped by the time he reached the age of four.

His only acquaintances had been his cousins, especially the two closest to his age, Otis and Hazel. Even so, he saw them rarely, as his father didn't care to remain in the same house longer than a month or two.

Like Queen Elizabeth in the 1600s, the ducal establishment had moved from estate to estate as the duke's fancy struck him. While the duchess was alive—she had died when Devin was fourteen—she either engaged in pitched battles with her husband or disappeared for months, choosing to live in more congenial environs.

"The one thing you can say about marriage," she was fond of saying, "is that not even an idiot is allowed to challenge his wife to a duel."

Or, Devin might have added, challenge his son.

By the age of ten, Devin had realized that his father's adherence to that particular tenet of civilization was all that stood between him and a gravestone.

When he inherited the dukedom at age sixteen, it was too late to bother with Eton or Harrow, and he had no time to spare for Oxford. It was too late for friends.

People found him to be cold, arrogant, and uncaring.

He accepted that judgment with disinterest.

To go back to the image of the lions and tabbies, as Devin saw it, strange cats slept by each other in the sun, whereas a lion was only comfortable in the company of his blood relatives.

His pride.

Even the most frustrating ones, which in this case included his cousin Otis.

"Do you really mean to tell me that you're giving up your living, Otis? St. Wilfrid's, which I held open for you for the last two years until you *finally* graduated from Cambridge?"

Otis lounged opposite, looking entirely unrepentant. "It's easy for you to be so patronizing. As a second son, I'm supposed to find a genteel profession. The law is far too abstruse, and the military dismayingly violent. That left the church. I kept to the scheme as long as I could. My new plan is to move to the continent and woo an heiress."

"You've only been in the vicarage for two weeks. Why are you turning down St. Wilfrid's?"

"Not just Wilfrid's," Otis said. "I'm done with the clerical life, cuz."

Devin leveled a glance at Otis that had turned the current Lord Mayor of London into an incoherent apologist.

"No use looking at me like that," his cousin said, grinning. "You've known me from the cradle and there's no point in trying to shame me. It won't take. If you don't mind me pointing out the obvious, that should have been a sign that the clergy was never the place for me."

"Seven years of studying theology at Cambridge en route to becoming a priest, and you're throwing it away two weeks after ordination. Without trying to make a success of it. Even for you, that's remarkable."

Otis leveled a finger at him. "Careful, Dev. You're cold-blooded by nature, and if you don't watch yourself, you're going to become as prickly and mean-spirited as your father."

"St. Wilfrid's is an excellent post. With two curates in residence, you scarcely have anything to do other than marry the occasional parishioner and baptize a baby or two. You can't have given it a proper try."

Otis grimaced. "I did! I was going along merrily, ready to hand out wise advice to all those who asked, when Gerdsby—that's the curate who resembles a goat—hauled me along to someone's house yesterday morning. I'd had too much ale the night before and I wasn't paying much attention, but when I got there, it turned out I was supposed to give Last Rites."

"Didn't they teach you how?"

"There was a lecture that pointed out the right prayer. My tutor made me read it through twice. But it's not the same when a man is looking at you fearfully and his wife is crying. Even the kitchen maid was crying. I almost joined in."

"You'd get used to it," Devin suggested.

"That's easy for a duke to say," his cousin retorted. "If you stand around in silk holding a snuffbox, you've done the job. But if a man stands around looking like a vicar, people expect him to *save souls!*"

Otis had a point.

Even if Otis hadn't been wearing a canary-yellow waistcoat, Devin could see that his cousin would be unbelievable in the role.

"I can't do it. I won't disgrace myself by trying again either. Spare sons shouldn't be shunted into the church with the idea that it's suitable employment for a gentleman. I don't know how the rest of them get around the soul-saving part, but I'm not fitted for the role, and that's that."

Devin couldn't disagree.

"Your father will be very disappointed," he observed. His uncle, Sir Reginald Murgatroyd, had his
heart set on his younger son entering the church.

"He made that point repeatedly last night, but as
I told him, he's not the one who is supposed to be
clearing the way for people to line up at the Pearly
Gates. I don't know how you can stand it in here,"
Otis added, looking about Devin's study. "I haven't
been in this study for years, and it's even more
ghastly than I remembered."

The room was gloomy. It was a cavernous space,
mostly populated by Greek gods, thanks to his
father's mania for collecting ancient statues—as
well as wheelbarrows, Italian pottery, and wicker
chairs, among other things.

When Devin inherited the estate, he had ordered
his father's collections confined by room, and divided
between the townhouse and the ducal estates. The
pantheon thronged in the townhouse study, where
he had long ago learned the trick of ignoring them.
Forty-four chiming clocks stayed in an extremely
noisy bedchamber in Wales, while the wheelbarrows
had their own outbuilding in Northamptonshire.

"All those blank eyes," Otis said with a shiver. "Just
look at that one."

Devin glanced over his shoulder. "Perseus holding
up the head of Medusa. The triumph of good over
evil. It ought to be in your vein."

"Revolting," Otis declared. "If you don't mind my
saying the obvious, your father was as potty as a
cracked vase. You should clear these out. Give them
to a museum or something. Is that chamber upstairs
still crammed with dead birds?"

Devin shrugged. "Unless they flew away. I haven't opened the door in years, but Binsey told me recently that the housemaids are complaining about dusting. He wants to bring in some glass cabinets."

"Hazel and I used to goad each other into creeping into that room at Christmas," Otis said.

"What do you mean to do next?" Devin asked, having no interest in household arrangements.

"As I said, marry an heiress," Otis replied promptly.

"Do you have one in mind?"

"Not yet. I thought I might find one somewhere in Europe. Your solicitor paid out the living a year ahead—you might want to reconsider that with your next vicar—so I've got money to take passage."

Devin frowned. "Where in Europe?"

"Perhaps Spain," Otis said. "Actually, anywhere but here, because Father bellowed at me last night, pretending he counted on me to save his soul, which is absurd. He apparently thought that a cassock gave me magic powers, but damn it, he's known me my entire life. That would be like expecting *you* to empty the coal scuttle. It just ain't going to happen."

Definitely not, as regards the coal scuttle.

"Mind you, I'll miss England. I'll even miss these heart-warming talks of ours, Dev."

Devin didn't believe, on the whole, that expression of emotion was necessary. By the age of seven, he'd learned that a raised eyebrow could convey any number of emotions, and it was generally preferable to allow people to come to their own conclusions.

But Otis was irritating, cheerful, insouciant . . . *family*. Devin had kept the living in St. Wilfrid's open because he wanted him nearby, preferably down the street in the vicarage. If forced to articulate it, Devin would have admitted that his life was satisfying but somewhat cold.

Otis and Hazel darted in and out of his house like fireflies, shining with warmth and cheer, and he treasured that.

"I'd prefer you didn't leave for the continent," he said. "I will need you to help a new vicar settle into the parish."

"Help him with what?" Otis asked. "I was still mixing up the curates' names until a couple of days ago, when I worked out a system to keep them straight. Gerdsby, *goat*, thanks to that unfortunate beard. Habblety, *hound*, due to his hangdog look. I can leave the new fellow a note explaining my classification. No need to say it in person."

"I would be grateful if you would remain in England at least for the time being," Devin said, adding, "If I'd known you were set against the church, I wouldn't have encouraged your father when he steered you in that direction."

"I wasn't set against it until yesterday," Otis said. "And I'm not leaving directly; I have to talk to the bishop, for one thing. These things don't happen overnight, and I'd guess it will take at least three months for my request to be approved. I'm never putting on a cassock again, though. Wearing a gown doesn't suit my sense of self."

"I understand."

"Mind you, I'm not looking forward to moving back home. The place is a madhouse, with my sister's debut in the offing. My father imported a relic of an aunt from the country to act as a chaperone, and Hazel does nothing but complain that Aunt Elnora's ideas are antiquated. Well, of course, they are. The poor woman was born a million years ago."

"You could stay here. Or remain in the vicarage as my liaison," Devin suggested. "After all, we had it renovated to your taste. There's a fair chance that the next man won't appreciate all that blue velvet, so you might as well enjoy it."

"More the fool he," Otis said. "Blue velvet is *au courant*. I suppose that I could remain in the vicarage until I'm out of orders. It would give me a chance to follow through with some of the schemes I've put in motion in the parish. As long as someone else is doing the important parts."

"I understand," Devin said. "I'll find a vicar to give Last Rites."

"I actually don't mind the rest of the job," Otis continued. "The parish needs livening up. I've begun offering sherry after the service, which is very popular. Of course, I had to restock the wine cellar, or rather you did."

"I don't suppose you could wait to leave the church until after you conduct my wedding ceremony?"

Otis snorted. "You'll do your vows in Westminster Abbey, with a flock of bishops parading around like French cooks wearing Christmas hats. I must say, my father is beside himself about the idea that you're tying the knot. He had put your taking a bride in the same category as my being appointed a bishop: unlikely."

"I know my duty," Devin said. "I considered marrying one of the Duke of Lindow's daughters two years ago, but I was in the middle of something, and I never found the time to meet her."

"That the pi business?"

Dev nodded.

"Never understood why you waste time devising a scheme to compute something that's already been computed."

Devin didn't figure out a way to compute pi to 123 digits for any good reason other than that numbers made him happy.

Luckily, Otis didn't wait for an answer; no one else in the family had the faintest interest in mathematics. "There's a couple more Wilde daughters on the market this year, and you can make up for lost time."

"Do you know anything about them?" Devin asked.

"Of course I do. Hazel attended school with them. To call a spade a spade, they are my sister's prime competition. As I understand it, one of them is exquisitely beautiful, lively, and intelligent."

"Lady Joan," Devin said. "I heard as much."

"Illegitimate," Otis said. "Father was a Prussian count. The second duchess ran off leaving the baby behind. The girl has the count's yellow hair, by all accounts, and the Wildes are dark-haired. The other is the third duchess's daughter by her first marriage. Astley, I think his name was."

"I'll take the Wilde," Devin said.

Otis laughed. "'Take her'? It must be nice to be a duke. Maybe I'll offer you some competition. She *is* an heiress."

"As I recall, Uncle Reggie gave you an estate."

Otis waved his hand. "If I'm to live in the manner to which I aspire, I need a fortune. A large one. I likely won't find the right woman for years. Father will simply have to accept that."

In short, the heiress was a patent excuse for avoiding marriage for the next decade. Devin couldn't blame his cousin. He wasn't looking forward to it himself. But he'd promised himself two years ago that the next time a duke's daughter came on the market, he'd get the business over with.

"I do think it'll be better if I move here," Otis said. "In a few weeks, after I fix things up with the bishop."

"Will the bishop be surprised?"

"My expectation is that he'll be as eager to kick me out the door as I am to leave. Hopefully, I'll be out of the vicarage in time to supervise your courtship," Otis said. "I already have some advice as regards your marital ambitions."

"What?"

"You'll have some competition for the Wilde girl."

Wynter doubted that very much. He hadn't been to a ball in years, but the last time he attended one, it reminded him of a Scottish stream when the trout were running. Young ladies playing the role of shining, wriggling trout.

"I've got the title and money, I'm not lame or scarred, I don't drink to excess."

"Viscount Greywick is looking for a wife," Otis said. "He'll be a duke someday. Word is he almost landed the last Wilde, so I suspect he'll be on the lookout again. He's younger than you, and to be brutally honest, he's handsome to boot."

As Devin understood it, there were an infinite number of Wilde offspring. Greywick could wait another year or two if need be. He shrugged.

"You might want to try to appear less . . . *ducal*," Otis suggested.

Devin knew exactly what he was talking about, but his expressionless demeanor had saved his life many a time as a youth caught in the path of his father's rage, and it was too late to try to imitate Otis's cheerful smile.

"Lady Joan won't marry me for who I am," he pointed out. "She'll marry me because the duchy of Wynter is older and wealthier than Greywick's duchy."

Otis laughed. "Perhaps Hazel has a shot at Greywick."

"I wish her the best of luck," Devin said politely.

Chapter Four

The next day

$\mathcal{V}$iola didn't sleep more than a few hours that night, and by breakfast she had come up with a three-part plan to win Mr. Marlowe's hand and heart. She had to prove that she was worthy of his attention, bring him to London when the family moved there for the Season, and conquer her shyness.

That afternoon, the Pettigrews and Mr. Marlowe joined the duchess—whom they hadn't met the previous day—for tea.

Viola was trying to figure out how to prove her worthiness when Barty fluttered down from his perch, stopped at her foot, and let out a gentle caw. He could manage short flights, as long as he didn't overtax his wings.

"Oh, goodness me!" Miss Pettigrew squealed.

"This is Barty," Viola said, slipping her hand under the crow's round tummy and bringing him up to her knee. "He fell from the nest as a baby and now he lives with us."

Barty cocked his head and looked at Miss Pettigrew. He opened his wings and cawed again.

"He is wishing you good afternoon," Viola said.

Miss Pettigrew was clearly horrified. "I do not
believe in animals sharing human habitation."

"Insalubrious," her mother confirmed, frowning
at Barty.

Barty fluttered to the ground, picked up a piece of
bright red paper that had escaped the maids' notice,
and hopped to Miss Pettigrew. He spread his wings
again, bent his head, and laid it next to her slipper.

"It's a present," Viola explained.

"More likely payment. He tends to offer a gift before he pecks off a button, and yours are shiny," Joan
said, with a jaundiced air.

"Get that creature away from me," Miss Pettigrew
cried, shrinking back and slapping her hands over
her bosom to protect her brass buttons. Her mother
snatched up her saucer and held it like a shield.

Prism had been standing to the side supervising
the dispersal of lemon cake. He stepped forward.
"I shall take Master Barty," he said. The butler was
one of Barty's favorite people, since Prism had spent
hours feeding him as a baby, and he readily hopped
to his arm.

"Thank you," Viola said, as Prism walked away, his
arm held high at a right angle, as if he were dancing
a minuet.

"I never!" Miss Pettigrew said, dropping her hands
from her bosom.

Aunt Knowe stepped in before Miss Pettigrew
could elaborate on an opinion that was likely to prove
universally unpopular.

"How are your plans for the parish progressing?" she asked Mr. Marlowe.

"I have suggestions about how you might encourage parishioners to attend services," Viola said brightly.

Mrs. Pettigrew cast her a narrow glance. "Such matters are best left to the vicar."

But Mr. Marlowe was more polite, and for the next five minutes, they had a lively exchange about ways to bring people to the church, ranging from a harvest dinner—"expensive and unnecessary," sniffed Mrs. Pettigrew—to a Sunday school.

Mr. Marlowe was as delightful on closer acquaintance as he had appeared the day before. He was deeply kind and interested in the welfare of everyone in the parish. He listened respectfully to Viola's ideas, which was refreshing after Father Duddleston's invariable refusal to consider anything new.

"Our friend Lady Caitlin Paget began a Sunday school in St. Wilfrid's parish in London," Viola told him. "At first she had a hard time convincing mothers to send their children. Now she has a schoolmaster in the afternoons as well."

"I know Lady Caitlin, since I was a curate at St. Wilfrid's," Mr. Marlowe said, a smile lighting his eyes. "She is a remarkable young lady."

As Mrs. Pettigrew launched into a monologue about the poor's need to pull themselves up by their bootstraps, Viola began musing over her second problem. She couldn't leave Mr. Marlowe in Cheshire while she went to London. The Season began in April, but the family would leave for London in early February; it would take at least two months for *modistes* to create a wardrobe proper for Viola's and Joan's debuts.

Mr. Marlowe was planning to marry Miss Pettigrew in only eight months. How would he ever choose Viola over Miss Pettigrew if they didn't become better acquainted? He *must* come to London and be provided with opportunities for comparison.

Her shyness was a problem too. She couldn't be a true partner to Mr. Marlowe if she trembled every time she encountered a male parishioner.

That night she recruited Joan to help with her shyness, using their upcoming debut as an excuse.

"Aunt Knowe says that once you've met enough young gentlemen, you'll realize that they are mostly hopeless duffers, and not to be feared," Joan reminded her.

Viola had heard this bit of wisdom many times. "What goes through your head when you meet someone for the first time?"

"Do you mean an eligible young man?"

"Yes."

"I consider whether I find him appealing," Joan said promptly. "I like a firm chin and dark eyebrows. I can't abide sandy eyebrows. But looks are not everything. Does he have the faintest interest in what *I* have to say, or does he lecture me about his interests? Does he look like a gambler, a degenerate, or a fortune-hunter?"

"How would you know about the last?" Viola asked. She had a feeling she knew what a degenerate looked like, albeit a titled version, but she had no idea about fortune-hunters.

"Shifty eyes," Joan said, narrowing her own. "Versus lascivious ones." She goggled at Viola. "Like this. What do you think when you meet someone?"

"I—"

Joan waited, eyebrow raised.

"I wonder if they think I don't belong among the Wildes," Viola said in a rush.

Joan looked nonplussed. "Why do you think that?"

"I'm not *really* a Wilde."

"No more am I," Joan pointed out. Her mother had fled the country with a yellow-haired Prussian count, leaving her newborn (yellow-haired) baby behind. It was generally accepted by everyone in the family except for the duke that Joan didn't have a drop of ducal blood in her.

"But you . . . you're *you*."

"I won't make the obvious response," Joan said, looking suddenly very like Aunt Knowe. "You are as much a Wilde as I am. As is Parth, who is adopted. As well as your mother's other children, Erik, Artemisia, and Spartacus. All of us are Wildes, and that's the end of it."

"It's not that simple," Viola argued.

"Why?"

"You're all beautiful, for one thing."

"As are you," Joan flashed back.

Viola sighed. She had insipid brown hair, a pointed chin, eyes of an ordinary shape and an unremarkable color, and a small nose. In fact, she was small everywhere except her bosom.

Her stepsiblings were the result of years of breeding, and like the best racehorses, they showed it. Every single one was the very portrait of an aristocrat, with almond-shaped eyes, winged eyebrows, and an alabaster complexion.

Putting Joan's golden hair to the side, the older children had inherited the duke's dark hair, and the younger children had Ophelia's red hair. But all of them, including Joan, had finely wrought features that spoke to generations of noble birth.

It wasn't merely a matter of appearances. Over years of observation, Viola had realized that Wildes instinctively took on the mannerisms that defined the aristocracy. Even Erik at age ten excelled in raising one mocking eyebrow.

Viola had spent a whole summer squinting in the mirror before she accepted that her eyebrows were incapable of moving separately.

"When I meet someone, I imagine what they are thinking about me," she admitted. "Sometimes I can almost hear voices laughing about me not belonging among the duke's children, so loudly that I feel seasick."

Joan scowled. "You mustn't listen to that foolishness. The next time you meet someone, you should hold up your chin and silently repeat over and over, 'I'm a Wilde. *I'm a Wilde!'* We are your family, Viola, and we love you. You came to us as a baby, remember? You're as much a Wilde Child as I am."

"That's silly," Viola said, laughing.

"No, it is not. What if I succumbed to that sort of thinking? If *I* believed the worst that is said about me, I wouldn't dare to debut at all. As it is, you and I shall debut together, heads high."

"*I'm a Wilde,*" Viola mumbled. "I feel like an idiot."

"Please try it?" Joan asked. Her eyes were hopeful, and Viola couldn't say no. Besides, she was desperate. She had to conquer her shyness in order to be a true partner to Mr. Marlowe.

In the next few weeks, she practiced thinking, *I'm a Wilde* when talking to the housekeeper, when taking the pony cart into Mobberley to drop in on Mr. Marlowe and see how the vicarage renovations were coming, even when talking to her older stepbrother North.

Joan stayed at her side, and every time Viola faltered, overcome by a stab of shyness, Joan would hiss, *"Wilde Child!"* The phrase was so absurd that it made Viola smile—and somehow survive the moment.

It helped.

Absurd, unlikely, ridiculous as it was, the phrase helped.

In early January, two parliamentary lords and a visiting ambassador from France joined the dining table. Normally, Viola would have eaten in her bedchamber, but instead, she walked into the room clutching Joan's hand, *Wilde Child* beating over and over in her head.

One of the lords was sixty if he was a day, and Viola found herself discussing the nesting habits of gray herons with him. Before she knew it, she was talking to the other lord as well, even though he was a young man, and unmarried. She didn't feel even a tinge of nausea. Why should she? She had a mission.

The next morning she confided to Mr. Marlowe about her terror of the upcoming Season, hoping that he would volunteer to accompany the family to London. Instead he patted her hand, looked deeply into her eyes, and assured her that Providence would provide.

That wasn't particularly helpful.

At a family-only dinner that night, the conversation turned to the household's imminent move to London; Lady Knowe had decided that the household should depart in January, rather than February.

Viola felt a pulse of terror at the thought, but: "I'm a Wilde," she said to herself.

"I don't intend to marry until my third Season," Joan said. She waggled her eyebrows at the duke. "Any suitors who come your way . . . Reject them immediately, if you please. They needn't propose to me in person; it won't change my mind."

"I agree," Viola put in quickly.

"You can always live with me, Viola, if you don't want to marry anyone," Erik said. He peered at Viola owlishly. "There's something different about you lately. I hadn't noticed before, but you *are* pretty. I could marry you, if you don't mind waiting."

"That is a very kind offer," Viola said, smiling at him.

"Erik is right," Aunt Knowe said. "These last few weeks you've been less timid."

Viola's smile turned into a grin.

"What helped?" Aunt Knowe asked. The whole table gazed at her, and Viola froze. She couldn't admit in front of the duke that she hadn't considered herself a true Wilde. He thought of himself as her father. He would be deeply hurt, and her mother would be terribly sad.

"It's Mr. Marlowe," Joan said, coming to the rescue. "He's very, very calming. He's made all the difference, hasn't he, Viola?"

The sharp elbow in her side jolted Viola and she nodded. "Yes, he is. That is, he has. Made all the difference, that is."

"Perhaps we should bring him to London with us," Aunt Knowe said thoughtfully. "I think it would do him good to consult with older clergymen. He shared a plan to put on a cycle of plays depicting biblical events. I'm not sure that's a good idea, but better to hear it from a more experienced cleric than from me."

Viola twitched. Putting on plays drawn from the Bible had been *her* idea, but this clearly wasn't the moment to confess, not when the second part of her plan was miraculously coming true.

Lady Knowe nodded, having made up her mind. "Mr. Marlowe must come with us. His fiancée is in London, after all."

"I can't bear the woman," the duke said dispassionately. "I might let him go at the end of the year simply because of his future wife."

"My pity stems from his future mother-in-law," Ophelia said with a shiver. "I suppose it might be a good idea to bring him to London. Perhaps Mr. Marlowe will reconsider his marital plans."

Viola could scarcely stop herself from throwing up her hands in celebration.

Providence was indeed watching the fall of every sparrow. Mr. Marlowe was right! Now he would be coming to London, so all she had to do was make him fall in love with her.

How hard could it be?

She'd watched her older stepbrothers fall in love over the last few years. As she saw it, men denied their own emotions until they snapped and then pursued their future bride with a single-minded tenacity.

She could already picture Mr. Marlowe's blue eyes looking at her adoringly.

Chapter Five

The Duke of Lindow's townhouse
A ball in honor of Lady Joan Wilde & Miss Viola Astley
April 2, 1782

The Duke of Lindow's ball in honor of Lady Joan Wilde and Miss Viola Astley opened the Season of 1782. Within the hour, it was an acknowledged triumph.

The two young ladies were besieged by suitors, among them several noblemen. Queen Charlotte herself made an appearance, and only a bilious attack kept His Majesty from attendance. Equally important, given society's fascination with the Wildes, the family turned out in full force.

Attendees included the duke's heir, North, who was rarely seen in London, along with his wife. Even more exciting was the presence of Alaric, the famous writer just returned from a prolonged visit to India.

Lavinia Sterling, the wife of His Grace's adopted son, Parth, was exquisitely garbed, but no gown eclipsed the *robe à la française* worn by the duke's sister, the wildly fashionable Lady Knowe. Her skirts were "pale thrush eggshell color," scribbled a giddy fashion columnist for *The Ladies Gazette*, "trimmed with knots of roses and spangles fashioned from sunbeams."

In short, the ball satisfied every guest as well as curious bystanders. Even those looking for scandal were able to amuse themselves by making up reasons why Alaric's wife was not in attendance. The family kept to themselves the prosaic fact that (by her own description) Willa was as round as the full moon, and Lady Knowe had the idea that she might be carrying twins.

If truth be told, the Wilde family collectively breathed a sigh of relief as midnight rolled around without incident.

No one had fretted about Joan, but Viola?

Ever since Viola began throwing up from pure nerves, they had all worried that the pressure of a debut ball would be too much for her unruly stomach.

That very morning, His Grace had dispatched a constable accompanied by three burly grooms to confiscate hundreds of prints made by an enterprising stationer gambling that images of Vomiting Viola would sell like hotcakes.

Sometimes it felt as if all of England was collecting prints of the next Wilde escapade. Housemaids from Scotland to Cheshire waited with bated breath for the tinker's cart to appear with a stack of new prints depicting Lady Knowe dressing down an impudent knife grinder (fictional) or North knocking unconscious a man who had abused a dog (true).

When Betsy debuted two years ago and promptly began amassing marriage proposals the way children collect seashells, the printmakers of Britain had rejoiced.

Now, with *two* Wilde daughters to consider?

The family couldn't leave the townhouse without being besieged by reporters. Joan enjoyed blowing kisses to those she liked; Viola seriously considered refusing to leave her bedchamber until the Season was over.

Yet the debut ball was not proving as dreadful as she had feared. She had exchanged remarks with several young men and danced with two of them. Her wretched shyness had not disappeared, but it had receded.

Most importantly of all, her nerves hadn't gone to her stomach.

"Anyone who has heard you are incurably timid knows it to be a falsehood," Aunt Knowe had whispered in her ear after the first hour. "Brava, darling!"

What Aunt Knowe didn't realize was the reason for Viola's surprising change of heart. Her show of courage. Her cure.

It was love.

Love had changed everything.

Love kept her calm as she danced an allemande with a young squire, calm as an eligible earl lectured her on gargoyles, calm as she accepted gentlemen's compliments that would have made her squirm a month before.

She no longer worried whether her so-called suitors thought she didn't measure up to being a Wilde. If her dance partners were secretly as rough and unprincipled as the man she'd interrupted at that long-ago ball, it wasn't her problem. She could scarcely believe that she'd cared so much.

Every beat of her heart brought her closer to the part of the evening that truly mattered: a meeting with Mr. Marlowe in the library. At precisely twenty minutes past midnight, Viola slipped out of the ballroom, pretending that her hem needed adjusting.

To her horror, she arrived at the ducal library just in time to see Sir Reginald Murgatroyd, an acquaintance of her Aunt Knowe's, disappear inside. Surely a respectable widower in his fifties hadn't planned an illicit tryst?

Viola cautiously pulled open the door a crack.

"Found you!" Sir Reginald bellowed. He was standing with his back to Viola before an armchair set at an angle to the door. As Viola watched, he gave the pair of long legs stretched out before him a kick.

"That charming greeting can only originate from a member of my family," said a deep voice from the depths of the chair.

Not a tryst, thankfully. Viola would have fled a rendezvous, but family squabbling was old hat.

"Of course it's me, Nephew," Sir Reginald said, giving him another kick. "On your feet, you lazy laggard."

Viola slipped through the door and let it close silently behind her. Thanks to her bouts of shyness, she was an expert at concealing herself, and nothing could be easier than hiding in her own house.

The library at Lindow Castle was a comfortable room where the family lounged about, reading books and sipping tea. In sharp contrast, the library at the ducal townhouse was formal, with walls covered with brocade apricot silk and glass-fronted bookshelves designed to house works of great brilliance. Narrow, tall-backed armchairs were clustered around the room like stern matrons wearing whalebone corsets.

The windows were hung with silk curtains, heavy enough to conceal one small, if curvy, person. Over the years, they had proved useful for hide-and-seek—

and avoiding Aunt Knowe. No matter how beloved, she had always been the person most likely to push Viola into meeting strangers.

Viola slid quietly along the wall and nipped behind the nearest curtain, sending up silent thanks that fashion dictated modest side panniers this year. Then she sent up a fervent prayer that Sir Reginald would drag his nephew back to the ballroom, now that the fellow had been kicked awake.

"What are you doing in here?" His Lordship demanded. "I have picked out your wife, and I want to introduce her, since you were impolite enough to arrive after the receiving line had dissolved."

"I am thinking about a Persian king named Cambyses II who laid siege to the Egyptians," his nephew replied.

Viola felt a flash of envy. If a gentleman was tired of conversation and wanted to think of ancient battles, he could simply retire to the library. Whereas she'd be ruined if anyone found her doing the same. No one would believe her.

For good reason, she reminded herself fairly.

She hadn't left the ballroom to contemplate antiquity, and her mother would definitely not approve of her true goal. She edged along the window until she could peek through the opening in the curtains, curious to see the historian.

Retreating to a library to contemplate a Persian king was not customary, especially for a gentleman searching for a bride.

Unfortunately, she could see only Sir Reginald. He was a portly gentleman with a fruity accent, violet-colored pantaloons, and a wig powdered to match.

"What on earth are you talking about?" he demanded, scowling down at his nephew.

The man hadn't risen from the chair, perhaps thinking that a kick does not warrant a gentleman's greeting.

"The Egyptians revered cats. Cambyses II had all his men paint cat faces on their helmets, and he drove a herd of felines ahead of him. The Egyptians could not harm the cats, and therefore their soldiers retreated in disarray."

"Ridiculous!" Sir Reginald said. "Balderdash!"

"It happened, I assure you. As a result, Egypt became a province of the Achaemenid Empire."

"No one can herd one cat, let alone an army of them," His Lordship retorted, with some justification. "Help me to a seat, won't you? My lumbago is acting up and I made the mistake of attempting a minuet."

Viola agreed with him as regards the army of cats. In her experience, a cat wouldn't do anything unless a kipper was dangled before her nose, and only then if she felt like it.

Unfortunately, Viola didn't manage to get a clear look at the historian before Sir Reginald plumped down in an armchair. From her angle, she couldn't see either of their faces—but on the other side, neither could they catch a glimpse of her through the gap in the curtains.

"What do felines have to do with anything?" Sir Reginald asked. "You, Nephew, are supposed to be in the ballroom, hunting for a bride."

"I was contemplating the army of young women that rushed at me the moment I walked into the ballroom," the gentleman replied. "One of them had pinned a woolen cat atop her wig. I was struck by her counterpoint in Persian history, but not enough to marry her. In fact, she sent me into retreat, and you found me here."

"Lady Caitlin Paget!" his uncle said instantly. "I found it amusing that her wig ornament was a play on her name."

Caitlin was an old friend, and she wouldn't have rushed toward anyone below a viscount. But since Viola had never bothered to memorize the byzantine relationships that structured polite society, she had no idea who Sir Reginald's nephew might be.

"I disagree," the gentleman said. "I dislike cats at the best of times, and particularly when suspended in the air. It fixed its beady eyes on me while we were dancing."

He disliked cats?

Viola found that, on the whole, animals were far more enjoyable companions than people. In a better world, cows would be allowed in a ballroom and she could have leaned against Daisy's side while she conversed with suitors.

"That is ludicrous," Sir Reginald said. "One doesn't make decisions as regards matrimony on the basis of a woman's wig."

"Frankly, I didn't meet a single woman whom I could bear to see at the breakfast table, bewigged or no," the man said. "They all chattered as if conversation were a blood sport, although they had nothing to say. I retreated to this library, rather than to my carriage, because I have a dance with the Wilde daughter after supper. Until that appointment I see no reason to fight off the hordes."

Viola drew in a silent breath. He deserved that kick. His uncle should have kicked him harder.

"I told you, I've found you a wife," Sir Reginald said, ignoring his nephew's blanket condemnation of every young lady in London. "I can't think why it didn't occur to me earlier. You probably don't know this, but your father's best friend was a fellow called Astley, who died well over a decade ago."

Viola suppressed a gasp.

"Your father didn't make friends easily, it hardly needs be said," Sir Reginald continued. "Astley's daughter, Viola, is debuting at this very ball. I've met her several times and she's a lovely girl. What's more, your father would be very pleased if you married her. I think you should go out there and make a play for her hand."

"I hate to disappoint you, Uncle, but on his death-bed my father instructed me to marry the daughter of a duke. In fact, I believe those were his last words directed at me. He was primarily occupied by cursing at the doctor."

There was something very quelling about the man's tone. Of course, it didn't sound as if his father had been an affectionate parent.

"Miss Astley *is* a duke's daughter," Sir Reginald said. "Her mother is the third duchess. This ball is in her honor! For goodness' sake, Wynter, surely you knew that?"

Wynter?

Wynter.

He was a *duke*.

The Duke of Wynter.

Viola slapped a hand over her mouth to stop a nervous giggle. No wonder he had been besieged.

Caitlin's list of eligible men had Wynter's name at the top.

For a moment she wondered if he was *the* duke from the ball all those years ago—but no. Wynter was a recluse, rarely seen in society. Caitlin had been hoping he'd bestir himself to find a wife this Season.

Apparently, Caitlin's wishes had been granted, but it didn't sound as if she had made the impression she would have wished.

"No, it isn't," the man said flatly.

Isn't what? Viola had lost track of the conversation.

"Yes, it is," Sir Reginald insisted.

"The ball isn't for her, because she isn't a real Wilde," the duke said. "They stuck her in, of course, but the ball is in honor of the duke's daughter."

Viola lost all inclination to laugh as a wave of nausea went through her. She'd managed to put the question of being *not Wilde* out of her head, but there it was: evidence that the rest of the world agreed with her.

Hearing the words spoken aloud made her feel hollow inside, and for the first time that evening her stomach threatened to turn inside-out.

Joan would be furious if she had overheard Wynter. She would clench her fists and call the duke a fatheaded ass. But he was just voicing what they'd likely all been whispering behind her back.

Viola took a shaky breath and placed both hands on her stomach, trying to calm herself. It was absurd to feel hurt by a man whom she didn't know or care about.

Mr. Marlowe would be arriving soon, coming to meet her. When she returned to the ballroom, she would ignore Wynter.

She hadn't been introduced to the duke, which meant that the man was rude enough to come to her debut ball—because she and her family considered it hers as well as Joan's—and not even ask her to dance.

Aunt Knowe had taught them that eavesdroppers never hear well of themselves, and Viola didn't need the memory of her voice to realize it was true. She'd give anything to be able to leave the room.

In fact, she almost began to edge back toward the door . . . but her appointment. She couldn't leave the library.

What if Mr. Marlowe didn't wait for her?

"Your father would approve of Miss Astley," Sir Reginald argued. "The Duke of Lindow considers her his daughter, and that's all that really counts. What's more, Miss Astley has been dowered by her father *and* by the duke."

"I don't need money, and I want the real Wilde," the duke said flatly. "The other one, Joan."

He sounded as if choosing a wife was akin to selecting ribbons. No, like choosing between pickled herring or turnips.

Viola loathed both foods—and him.

"Joan is ravishingly beautiful, but if you want to be pedantic about it, she isn't a real Wilde either," his uncle argued. "Hasn't got a drop of Wilde blood in her veins. Hair is yellow as a buttercup, thanks to the Prussian who fathered her."

Viola scowled. She hated the fact that people maligned Joan due to her mother's infidelity.

"I don't care about that," the duke said, rather surprisingly. "She's a Wilde because her father says she is. She was raised a Wilde, ergo she is a Wilde."

"Miss Astley was raised a Wilde too, and her father was your—"

"It's not the same," his nephew interrupted, sounding impatient. "I need a woman who has been raised as ducal progeny, not just tossed into the nursery due to her mother's marriage. I don't have the faintest interest in training someone how to be a duchess."

His uncle guffawed. "Not that you'd know how!"

The duke didn't say anything, but Viola could imagine his well-bred upper lip curling. He really was awful.

"You're the oddest duke ever seen in the British Isles," Sir Reginald said, hooting. "All the rest of them went to Eton together, went to war together, went to brothels together, for Christ's sake. But you? You never go anywhere."

That explained why he'd never made his way to Lindow Castle. Viola had certainly never met him.

Imagining Joan leaping to her feet and declaiming, "I *loathe* cats," made Viola's heart ease. The Wildes enjoyed Joan's performances, but her mother made certain that they were never truly unkind, and no one other than family was ever invited to join the audience. All the same, a duke this arrogant would definitely have had a lead role at family dinner.

Her stomach steadied.

He was inconsequential.

"Exactly," the duke said now.

"Exactly what?" his uncle demanded.

"That's what it means to be a duke."

"Nonsense!"

"If the Duchess of Wynter wishes to waste her time at balls, she's welcome to do so," the duke stated. "I don't give a damn."

Viola believed him.

"I need someone who has a thorough, instinctive understanding of what a duchess does and doesn't do, so she doesn't bother me about it. I will certainly not accompany my wife into society. While I realize it is necessary to attend one to two public occasions in order to inform my choice of a bride, after marriage I shall not escort my wife to musicales, balls, or any other nonsense. She needs to be able to fend for herself."

Hopefully no lady would accept him, including Caitlin. He didn't deserve a wife.

"I didn't choose Miss Astley merely due to your father's friendship," his uncle said, persisting. "She's a little mouse. Perfect for you."

Viola winced. She didn't like the characterization, but she couldn't say it was unfair.

"Why would you think a woman of that sort appropriate for me?" the duke growled.

"She's pretty," Sir Reginald added hastily. "Not mousy that way. It's my impression that she doesn't even know how pretty she is, which is important."

Viola rolled her eyes.

"We can't have a vain woman as Duchess of Wynter," His Lordship went on. "Nor yet an overly proud one. But on the other hand, she can't be a dowdy girl either, because she will be a duchess, and she needs to hold her own once we get her portrait up there on the third floor."

"I'm sure I can find someone worthy of the gallery," the duke said indifferently. "Golden hair paints well."

Golden hair paints well indeed!

His chance of marrying Joan would be precisely zero after Viola recounted this conversation. Although she'd have to make up some excuse why she overheard his assessment. She couldn't reveal that she'd been hiding in the library waiting for an illicit rendezvous.

The reminder made her heart bound. Who cared if the horrid Duke of Wynter thought that she didn't belong at her own debut ball? If she had her way, she would have nothing to do with polite society in the future.

At this moment, Wynter stood up and reached a hand down to help his uncle to his feet, which finally placed him directly in Viola's eyesight.

His face was more angular than most gentlemen's; in fact, his features were as harsh as his voice. His heavy-lidded, arrogant look didn't surprise her, though.

She'd seen that her whole life. Her older stepbrothers were experts at wielding superiority like a hammer. They didn't mean it, but it was bred-in-the-bone.

He was as big as her brothers too. Rather than his coat hanging gracefully, it was snugly tailored to fit wide shoulders and powerful arms, as if he spent most of his time riding.

She preferred a willowy form.

And he was uncomfortably tall. Not like . . .

Not like the wonderful man with whom she would meet very soon, if they would *please* take themselves off! If only Sir Reginald would give up this useless argument and realize a ballroom full of ladies awaited his beastly nephew.

"I must be shockingly obtuse," the duke remarked, "but I fail to see why you think that *I* would wish to take a mouse to wife."

Viola made a note of that: "shockingly obtuse." Generally, Joan did all the impressions at the dinner table but perhaps she would do this one herself.

If the duke had a pair of horns, he could stand in for Beelzebub. He was wearing a wig, but given his dark eyebrows, his hair must be black. He'd stripped off his gloves—another mark against him, because no gentleman took off his gloves at a ball unless he was eating—and his skin was tawny.

She preferred the opposite.

Porcelain skin and celestial blue eyes.

And a sweet nature, she added, smiling despite the situation.

"You always were a stubborn lad," Sir Reginald grumbled. "The mouse is for you because she won't want to go into society, don't you see? Rumor has it she throws up if asked to dance, but that must be wrong, because I saw her circling the floor a while ago."

"A point in favor of matrimony," the duke said. "Able to dance without vomiting."

"My point is that she won't nag you to go to balls, and yet she's extremely well connected. She has powerful relations and an excellent dowry."

Sir Reginald's analysis wasn't entirely unreasonable.

But who cared? Even if Viola hadn't been in love, she would *never* marry anyone like Wynter.

An angel on one side and Beelzebub on the other: No one in the world would be surprised by her choice.

Except perhaps Beelzebub himself.

She had the distinct impression that His Grace planned to dance once with a lady and meet her next at the altar.

In fact, he thought he was the cat's meow.

Ha! She made a note of that: perfect for her dramatic rendition of the ducal terror caused by Lady Caitlin's beady-eyed wig ornament.

"I prefer the other one," Wynter said dispassionately.

Viola had no interest in him, obviously, but he still made her blood burn with annoyance. She'd like to stick him with one of her wig pins. She might not be a Wilde by blood, but knowing the truth herself, and being dismissed on those grounds, were not quite the same.

Not unrelated, but different.

It was very satisfying to realize that while His Grace could woo Joan all he wanted, Viola—the *not-Wilde* unworthy of his lofty attentions—would thwart his marital ambitions with a quiet word to her sister.

Or better yet, a lively performance of his arrogant disclaimers.

"You could try to push Otis onto the other one," the duke said now.

The other one? He meant *her*! And who was Otis?

"I'll come talk to you tomorrow morning about that boy," Sir Reginald said. "He was laicized yesterday. I am displeased that he has been released from Holy Orders, most displeased. For now, I'll nip into the retiring room and fetch you on the way back. I plan to introduce you to Miss Astley, whether you will or no."

Or no, Viola thought frantically.

Go back to the ballroom and find your own wife!

"Certainly," the duke said, suddenly amiable. "Take all the time you wish, Uncle. I'll be happy to await you here."

They moved out of Viola's eyesight but apparently stopped at the door.

"Your father was a difficult man," Sir Reginald said, a hint of regret in his voice.

The duke didn't respond.

"I believe Astley was the only friend he had whom he didn't challenge to a duel."

"A singular honor," the duke said. "One devoutly to be wished, given that the late duke killed at least one of those friends in a duel."

"The man died due to an infection," Sir Reginald said, clearly pained. "Your father didn't prick him in the lung."

"I doubt that was a consolation to his widow."

"Didn't have one," Sir Reginald said. "Good thing too. Otherwise there might have been a real fuss about the matter. Just think about the Astley girl, won't you?"

"Of course, Uncle," the duke said.

Viola didn't need her years of experience with Wilde males to translate his agreement into outright insubordination.

His uncle didn't reply. Maybe he kicked him a last time in parting.

One could hope.

The duke returned to his seat and stretched out his long legs again.

For two long minutes, there was silence as Viola tried frantically to figure out what to do. Before she could decide, the worst happened.

The door opened again.

"Your Grace!"

Chapter Six

$\mathcal{V}$iola couldn't stop herself from smiling.

She had sent a note to Mr. Marlowe, imploring him to meet her this evening. Although he hadn't replied, in a clear sign of his growing affection, he had obeyed her, even at this late hour.

As ever, Viola couldn't stop herself from delighting in his pure beauty. His profile was Grecian, and his eyes the color of the Aegean Sea.

Not that Viola had seen the Aegean, but her brother Alaric had said it was the bluest sea in the world. Mr. Marlowe's eyes were a tender, melting blue.

"Good evening, Your Grace," Mr. Marlowe said, dipping into a deep bow.

Wynter stood up and inclined his chin a fraction of an inch. "This is a surprise, Marlowe. One doesn't expect to see one's former curate at a ball."

"I currently have the pleasure of serving as vicar in one of the Duke of Lindow's livings," Mr. Marlowe replied, bowing again.

"You travel in lofty circles," Wynter said. "Forward-thinking ones too, if Lindow invites his vicar to circle the floor. I wasn't aware that clergy attended this sort of hell-begotten occasion. Though I suppose you have other ideas about Hades."

"I assure you that I am not attending the ball," Mr. Marlowe said, a touch of indignation in his voice.

Viola couldn't help smiling again. Mr. Marlowe's wife would never have to endure an endless conversation about the newest country dance, nor circle the floor anxiously trying to remember which way to turn.

"Luckily for you," the duke replied. "What are you doing here? Whether you are attending the ball or no, you are in the Duke of Lindow's library in the middle of the night. I hardly think that you are searching out a rare volume of sermons for inspiration."

An edge to his voice suggested there might be something nefarious about Mr. Marlowe's appearance in the library at this hour.

Viola's brows drew together. He was horridly distrusting. Just what sort of crimes did he think a man of God might commit?

"His Grace, the Duke of Lindow, brought me to London, or rather, his sister, Lady Knowe, asked me to accompany the family to London," Mr. Marlowe said. "There is a small chapel attached to the townhouse." He paused and added uncomfortably, "I am here to offer encouragement and support to the family."

Viola had a clear view of Wynter's face, and she knew that he was about to point out that the responsibilities of a vicar did not include midnight rendezvous.

Yet if Wynter made a fuss—or even a joke—about encountering clergy at the ball, her father might send Mr. Marlowe back to Cheshire.

As it was, she had counted it the greatest good fortune of her life that Lady Knowe had brought their new vicar to London. If Mr. Marlowe was sent back to Cheshire, he would be far away. An awful thought followed that realization.

What if the duke dismissed him?

Viola's eyes narrowed. She couldn't allow that to happen, not when the meeting was her idea.

This was her fault. After she had again told Mr. Marlowe how terrified she was by the ball—and the vicar had *again* promised her that Providence would provide—she had slipped a note under his door imploring him to meet her. She'd known perfectly well that he was too kind to refuse.

Quickly she slid along the curtain, ducked behind a tall-backed settee, and emerged as if she'd been seated against the wall, unobserved.

"Good evening," she called.

Mr. Marlowe jumped; their eyes met and she thought she saw a flash of happiness in his. Certainly, she was happy to see him; she couldn't repress a wide smile.

The duke, on the other hand, turned his head, and impatience crossed his face. "I came here for solitude, but this room is as crowded as the queen's antechamber," he said to Mr. Marlowe.

What a pompous fool. As if Mr. Marlowe knew or cared about the queen's antechamber! He had far more important concerns than the trivialities of polite society.

"Good evening, Miss Astley," Mr. Marlowe said, bowing as Viola reached his side. She dropped into a curtsy and beamed at him. She couldn't wait until they could greet each other the way her mother greeted her stepfather: with a kiss.

Out of the corner of her eye, she noticed that the duke hadn't responded to her name.

Mr. Marlowe looked from her to Wynter and visibly registered that they hadn't greeted each other. "Please allow me to introduce you," he said with a little gasp.

She'd have to teach him to be less nervous around the peerage. They were just people like anyone else, after all.

"Your Grace, may I present Miss Astley, the Duke of Lindow's stepdaughter? Miss Astley, this is the most noble Duke of Wynter."

A case in point: Mr. Marlowe should have presented the gentleman to the lady, not the reverse, because although Wynter was a duke, he wasn't an aged or particularly important duke. She nodded and dropped into a curtsy, giving the duke a wry smile that didn't hide either her amusement or her dislike.

"Your Grace," she said. "What a pleasure to meet a man who has such original ideas about courtship, not to mention the animal kingdom."

His face appeared completely indifferent, so much so that for a moment she thought perhaps he hadn't put her name together with the "mouse" his uncle had told him to marry.

"The pleasure is mine," he said, bowing. "A young lady of enterprise with such unexpected habits. My uncle would be astonished."

No, he had definitely caught her name.

Mr. Marlowe looked puzzled.

Viola patted his arm, and on better thought, tucked her hand into his elbow. Of course, he was not wearing a cassock—he only did that when he was actually in the chapel—but a lovely hint of incense hung about his coat.

The black fabric brought out his eyes, whereas the duke's ostentatious garb merely increased his satanic air.

In her opinion.

The duke's eyes rested for a moment on Viola's hand. In response she curled her fingers a little tighter and widened her smile. "Mr. Marlowe, did I understand that you used to be attached to one of the Duke of Wynter's livings as a curate?"

"St. Wilfrid's was my first posting after my ordination," Mr. Marlowe said, nodding. "A most pleasant parish."

"Yes, I agree," the duke said, his voice still unfriendly. "What I still don't understand is what you are doing here in the middle of the night."

"I came to offer support to Miss Astley," Mr. Marlowe said. "A debut is a taxing event for a young lady with delicate nerves."

"I requested that he meet me," Viola clarified, making it clear with a stare borrowed from Aunt Knowe that further commentary would be unwelcome.

Wynter treated her to a raised eyebrow—single, of course!—and proceeded to ignore her silent command.

"I suppose any young lady might be unnerved by a ball thrown in her honor. Though I'm not certain how that translates to a need for ecclesiastical counsel," the duke said, with the distinct air of someone who was about to insist that vicars ought not to offer said consolation, at least not in the middle of the night.

Viola felt dislike prickling all over her skin. She

rushed into speech before he could elaborate on his opinion.

"It is more difficult to enjoy a debut ball when some guests seem to believe that it is not thrown in one's honor," she said. "In fact, some people act as if my presence here is not only unnecessary but somehow fraudulent."

The duke nodded, apparently feeling no need to apologize. As if he were simply agreeing with her.

Fine.

Viola might not have learned to wield an eyebrow in the nursery, but as Joan often pointed out, she had her own ways of defending herself.

"Like myself, His Grace is discomfited by ballrooms," she said to Mr. Marlowe, putting on a sympathetic expression. "He retreated to the library because his nerves couldn't take the excitement. You might want to offer prayers that he grows more courageous, Mr. Marlowe. His Grace will never be able to find a wife while hiding in the library."

Wynter's eyebrow arched again, but she had stopped being intimidated by that particular weapon years ago. "I have learned to overcome my nerves," she said, pitching her voice to treacly comfort. "I'm certain if you put your mind to it, Your Grace, you'll be able to dance more than one measure without running to hide."

Mr. Marlowe patted Viola's hand encouragingly. "I assured Miss Astley that if she trusted in Providence, all would be well." He paused. "And it has been, has it not?"

"One gentleman uttered absurdities as could turn my stomach, but I managed to contain myself." She couldn't resist glancing at the duke to make certain he understood that he was the author of those absurdities.

"Excellent," Mr. Marlowe exclaimed.

"The duke has a more serious affliction than mine," Viola continued, noting with pleasure the way Wynter's jaw had tightened. "He apparently envisioned an army of cats rampaging about the ballroom on the verge of attacking him."

Mr. Marlowe's brows drew together. "Your Grace, if you'll excuse the presumption, did you visualize these cats or merely imagine them?"

"Oh, he saw them," Viola said. "He specifically mentioned the terror he felt on seeing beady eyes fixed on his face."

"I will pray for you, Your Grace," Mr. Marlowe said with the ready sympathy he showed everyone, even a duke.

"Thank you," Wynter said, his tone dangerously soft. But at least he was growling at her, not at Mr. Marlowe.

Viola was enjoying herself. "His Grace is somewhat . . . shall we say . . . *mature* to be attempting to find a wife," she continued, giving him an innocent smile. "I'm certain he could use your prayers in that regard as well, Mr. Marlowe."

The unfriendly glint in the duke's eyes seemed to worry Mr. Marlowe. He slipped his arm from her grasp. "I shall allow both of you to return to the festivities." He hesitated. "I am a stranger to the ways of polite society, but I can fetch the duchess, Miss Astley."

"We are of one mind," the duke said. "How did a fair young lady—the belle of the ball—find herself in the library unchaperoned at this hour? One might almost say *hidden* in the library?"

"There was nothing untoward about our meeting!" Mr. Marlowe said hastily. "I offer support to all members of the duke's household, though I did expect Her Grace to accompany Miss Astley to the library."

Viola felt slightly humiliated, because it sounded as if her darling Mr. Marlowe didn't care to meet her alone. He didn't mean that; he was merely responding to the duke's critical tone. She'd watched men make fools of themselves in front of her stepfather for the entirety of her life.

The word "duke" had a magic sound in England. People couldn't stop themselves from groveling.

Not that Mr. Marlowe was *groveling*. But he was flustered. Anyone would be flustered.

"There's no need to bother my mother," she said briskly.

"I am happy to escort Miss Astley back to the ballroom," the duke said.

"I promise not to jangle your nerves by meowing."

"The reassurance should be mine," the duke said. "My understanding is that mice are terrified of cats."

"It's too late to claim to be a feline," Viola told him. "All appearances to the contrary, we do have one thing in common. My nerves go to my stomach, and yours drive you to hide in the library. You too are a mouse."

Mr. Marlowe looked from Viola to the duke, and she was pleased to see that he appeared a trifle disgruntled. He'd probably looked forward to talking to her as much as she had to him.

"I look forward to seeing you tomorrow at breakfast, Mr. Marlowe," Viola said to him.

"Surely you will be resting after such a late night and much excitement?" To her delight, Mr. Marlowe seemed endearingly worried about her health.

"I am always up at dawn," Viola said. It wasn't precisely true, but ever since the vicar had told her that he rose every morning at five to say morning prayers, she had been asking her maid to wake her earlier than normal. She added, more truthfully, "Aunt Knowe is a great believer in breakfast and insists that the family attend no matter how late we went to bed."

"Marlowe," the duke said, inclining his chin the quarter of an inch that he apparently accorded those he considered beneath him.

Mr. Marlowe bowed again and walked quickly to the door, stopping to hold it open.

Viola sighed inwardly. She had to train him out of opening doors for . . . well, she hated the word . . . "betters." She may not be a real Wilde—not in her own eyes nor in those of the Duke of Wynter—but her father had been a lord.

Yet she didn't consider herself "better" than Mr. Marlowe.

Quite the opposite. She couldn't wait until she could help him with his life's work.

"You are no mouse," the duke commented, as they walked away from the library, heading down the long corridor that led to the ballroom, while Mr. Marlowe returned to the upper regions of the house.

Viola was trying to decide whether Aunt Knowe would allow her to retire before the repast offered to their guests. Now that she had no appointment with Mr. Marlowe to look forward to, she hadn't the faintest interest in a lavish meal that would last until two in the morning.

She shrugged. "I thought your uncle's assessment was fair as regards my character, though obviously he was mistaken about our suitability for matrimony."

"Because you were hiding in the library, waiting for the vicar?" His voice was velvety smooth and amused.

She cast him a look of real dislike. He was probably the sort of fellow who would go back to his club and make fun of her.

His opinion of her didn't matter, Viola told herself. What he said to his friends about her was unimportant as well.

Mr. Marlowe had been kind enough to meet her and to offer his support, although he had to rise with the dawn. Surely that was a sign that his affection for her was growing, if not turning to love.

"Perhaps you should return to the library and wait for Sir Reginald," she said, ignoring Wynter's question. It was self-evident that they would have been a wretched match, even if he hadn't already declared her unsuitable. "I shall be perfectly fine returning to the ballroom myself."

"My uncle won't be surprised that I didn't wait for him," the duke said indifferently.

"In that case, why did you promise to do so?"

"As you undoubtedly overheard while lurking behind the curtains, my plan was to wait in the library until it was time to dance with Lady Joan."

That was the final straw. It wasn't as if she had wanted to eavesdrop on his insults.

She came to a halt and drew her hand out of his arm. "Even for a duke, you are exceptionally rude," she informed him. "Your uncle sought you out in the library in an effort to help you find a wife, and you clearly need his assistance. Despite his kindness, you didn't wait for him."

"No, I didn't," the duke stated, looking down at her with a wry smile. "Will it give you an even worse opinion of me to learn that it didn't occur to me?"

"My opinion of you is irrelevant," Viola observed.

"Perhaps, but you are sharing it with such enthusiasm."

That was fair.

"If I left without dancing with your stepsister, I'd have to put on this ludicrous coat and go to another ball," the duke added.

She glanced at his coat. It was fashioned from lilac silk and embroidered up the front and waistcoat with cabbage roses. "Gaudy but not entirely tasteless. You *are* a duke. You need to dress to your station, enabling the army of ladies lying in wait to know instantly who you are when you enter a room."

"'Gaudy'?"

"Would you prefer 'extravagant'?"

"Apparently, I am a casualty of my lack of interest and my valet's questionable taste." His voice was deep—and amused. "Would you consider your gown its opposite?"

Viola and Joan were both dressed in white, their gowns explicitly designed to strike a balance between demure and ducal.

"The pearls could be said to be extravagant," Viola allowed.

"You could snip them off and buy yourself a country estate," the duke agreed.

Had his eyes lingered on her bosom? Viola's finest

feature had been shaped by a corset that hugged her curves and presented her breasts to the world in a manner that had almost distracted the young earl out of his obsession with gargoyles earlier in the evening.

Almost.

But no, the duke's eyes were fixed on her face.

"You will have to attend at least one more ball," Viola told him. "Joan is as unsuited to be your wife as I am."

"I hadn't met either of you before tonight," he said, sounding not in the least ashamed.

Was that supposed to be an excuse?

An explanation?

Music could be heard from the ballroom, but Viola could see guests drifting out of the door toward the dining room, where a supper was to be served before they all returned to their own houses. She began walking again, a little faster.

The duke kept pace with unhurried strides. "Miss Astley, may I have the honor of the next dance?"

"Certainly not," Viola replied. Then she realized that her response hadn't been precisely polite, although she had just criticized his manners. Hypocrisy is a sin, she reminded herself. Now that she meant to be a vicar's wife, she was trying to improve her personality.

Not just her shyness in public, but all her other faults as well.

The impulse to call the duke a fatheaded ass, for example. Not a sin, but an offense.

She stopped walking, flipped open her fan, and glanced at the names scrawled there. "Oh, dear. I'm afraid that I have promised every dance, and I cannot make room for you. If only you had asked earlier, when you first arrived."

"You could accompany me to supper. I believe that the supper dance is playing now, and obviously the gentleman to whom you promised the dance has been unable to find you."

She had promised the dance to her stepbrother Alaric, since his wife wasn't attending the ball. It was all planned beforehand so she wouldn't have to endure a meal with a stranger.

"Unless you're planning to run away, now that you've met with the vicar," the duke added.

That was too close to the truth to be comfortable.

Perhaps she could contrive to spill something on her gown, allowing her to retire for the night. Aunt Knowe would see through it, of course, but the ball had been such a success to this point that she wouldn't be too cross.

No, because a print would undoubtedly appear depicting Graceless Viola, the bumbling *not-Wilde*.

Speaking of which, she had to get rid of Wynter before anyone saw them together. He would draw far too much attention. She didn't want to be Graceless Viola, but she didn't want anyone to think that she had caught the eye of a duke either.

"You are waiting for Joan," she reminded him. "You must know what she looks like since you asked for a dance. Perhaps you can find her. There might be a seat free at her table. Or you could wait for her in the supper room and lunge when she makes an appearance."

"I would prefer to meet Lady Joan at the arranged time," the duke said.

"I understand," Viola said. "You don't want to

look desperate."

"No," the duke agreed. "Never that."

"Well, I will bid you good night, Your Grace."

"We might go to supper together," the duke repeated.

"No, thank you."

"You would be making my uncle happy, not to mention your father and mine," he said, looking down at her. He was absurdly tall. "That has to count for something."

"I didn't know my father," she said, nipping this ridiculousness in the bud. "He died before I was born. It sounds as if yours was not entirely affable, but all the same, he left you a direct command as regards marriage that should be respected. I am not a real Wilde, and certainly not a duke's daughter. You needn't waste your time with me."

"Sharing the meal will make my uncle happy. I scarcely knew my father and I am very fond of Sir Reginald."

She narrowed her eyes at him, but he somehow had managed to put on an expression that suggested filial duty. "You might well be barraged by women with stuffed birds on their wigs. I saw at least two or three." She herself was wearing a reasonably sized snowy white wig, ornamented only with pins topped with pearls.

"I would have you at my side."

"Yes, but I don't want you at my side," she said, resorting to truthfulness. "You will attract far too much attention and I don't care to be employed as a shield between you and your admirers. I have better things to do."

He looked faintly offended. "Better than hiding

behind the curtains waiting for a milksop?"

"Mr. Marlowe is not a *milksop*," she retorted, staying calm because . . . Wynter was an ass and that was that. No point in crossing swords with him. "Mr. Marlowe isn't vain, like the sort of aristocrat who boasts about his knowledge of the queen's antechamber. He is a *vicar*, and as such, he is . . . he is full of the milk of human kindness!" she finished in a rush, the phrase coming to her suddenly.

"Milky indeed," the duke said, a gleam of humor in his eyes.

"I didn't mean it that way."

"I imagine not, since the vicar has clearly been showering his milky kindness on the Lindow household, making himself available for pastoral counsel day or night."

Viola frowned at him. "Your Grace, I suggest you return to the ballroom and find another candidate to marry other than my sister."

"Why not Joan?"

"I won't have it," Viola said. "She won't have it either. You're not the sort of person whom . . . whom one would want to face over the breakfast table for years on end, to use your own criterion. Although," she added, "you must know that married ladies are allowed to eat from trays in their bedchambers."

Despite herself, envy leaked into her voice.

"Do you not care for the breakfast table, or are you simply a champion of breakfast trays?" the duke inquired.

"I can't imagine why you're interested, but the truth is that my nerves have often gone to my stomach, making a public breakfast an uninviting proposition,"

Viola admitted.

"More at breakfast than at supper?" he asked, looking as if he was actually interested.

"My aunt used to force me into the breakfast room to test my nerves," Viola said with a little shudder. "You can't imagine how many times I have come close to vomiting on a gentleman's shoes when he had no more temerity than to ask me if I was enjoying the sausage."

"Should I be worrying about my shoes?"

She frowned at him. "Don't think I haven't noticed the fact you're laughing silently, because I have."

"Not at your distress," he said immediately. "Perhaps at your phrasing. You are very funny, in a quiet way. What changed, Miss Astley? How were you cured? Because here you are, talking to an eligible duke, and you show no signs of gastric distress."

"You aired my opinion of me—that I'm not a real Wilde—before I had the chance to worry about whether you thought I wasn't a real Wilde. It was refreshing."

They were nearing the great doors to the ballroom.

"Goodbye," she said. "I should find my partner for the supper dance, even if I have missed it." She bobbed a curtsy.

He didn't bow. "You could take me with you. I am a fellow sufferer," he said instead. "Think of my nerves. You could support me, just as milky Marlowe supported you."

"No, thank you," she said cheerfully. "You'll get over it. Jangled nerves are not a life-long affliction. I can assure you that if you had met me last fall, I would have been miserably contemplating your shoes at this moment."

"What changed?" he asked. And: "Oh, bloody hell."

She looked around him to see Caitlin barreling toward them. "Hello!" Viola cried, waving.

Caitlin stopped before them, only slightly out of breath.

"Lady Caitlin, His Grace was just telling me of your graceful dancing," Viola said. "He has offered to accompany me to supper, but I'm afraid that I have torn my hem and I'll need to retire for repairs."

Wynter was staring down at her as if she were abandoning him to a conquering army.

"If you'll excuse me, Your Grace," she said, giving him a smile, "I'll find my mother and ask for her assistance."

"Her Grace is just inside the ballroom," Caitlin said, showing her eagerness all too evidently. Ophelia had emphasized that there was nothing a gentleman disliked more than being stalked.

But Cat was like her namesake in that.

"I'd like an answer to my question," the duke said. "What changed, Miss Astley? How did you conquer your nerves?"

Rather than answer, Viola dropped another curtsy. "Your Grace, it has been such a pleasure."

"You could join us," the duke said, showing remarkable persistence. "I would consider myself most fortunate to escort two lovely young ladies to supper."

Caitlin had attached herself to the duke's side like a limpet, and she gave Viola a direct look that begged her not to accept the duke's invitation.

The Wildes thought of Joan as the actress of the family, but Viola hadn't watched her perform all these years for nothing. She fluttered her eyelashes like a butterfly in a storm and said, "Would that I could, Your Grace! But . . . my gown."

"Your hem," Caitlin chimed in.

"Good evening, Your Grace, Lady Caitlin," Viola said, beaming at both of them before she walked off.

It wasn't until she was inside the ballroom that she realized she had given the duke a real smile.

Chapter Seven

*D*evin had taken Lady Caitlin into supper after he was deserted by Miss Astley—whose name was Viola, he'd discovered by striking up a conversation with her stepsister Joan while they danced later that evening.

Viola was right: Joan wasn't the wife for him.

Joan shone like torchlight in that bloody ballroom; all eyes were on them from the moment he bowed before her. If he married her, their every move would be catalogued in the popular press.

Exquisitely beautiful, yes. But one doesn't marry a woman for the sake of the portrait gallery.

The image of Viola practically baring her teeth at him as she informed him that she wouldn't allow him to marry her sister came to mind.

"What are you smiling about?" his cousin Otis asked. He had stopped by to let Devin know that he'd finally been officially released from the clergy, and his belongings were being moved from the vicarage in the afternoon. "You never smile."

Devin glanced at him. "You didn't attend the Lindow ball last night."

"I thought Father might break into tears if he saw his ungrateful son circling the ballroom floor," Otis said. "After we had an argument, I told him that I was thinking of heading to Spain to find an heiress, which led to a ruckus since Spanish women are Catholic." He was seated in a chair before Devin's desk, long legs stretched out before him. From his disheveled look, he'd been out all night, in livelier environs than the Lindow townhouse.

"No going to Spain until you find me another vicar. You took on the task months ago, and you haven't come up with a replacement," Devin said. "Luckily, I can point you in the right direction."

"That's your responsibility," Otis said. "Must be hundreds of them floating around. Some of the fellows I was at university with had five brothers, all of them taking orders. I'll give you some free advice, Dev: I don't think you should find another third, fourth, or fifteenth gentleman's son. We're not in the business for the right reasons, and that's me saying it. I say, don't you think we should celebrate my escape with a spot of brandy?"

"It's 10 a.m.," Devin observed.

"It feels later than that," Otis replied. "I've been out all night."

"I gathered as much from your attire. You have a distinctly nonclerical air."

Otis glanced down at his crumpled maroon coat, enlivened by a waistcoat embroidered with pansies. "A bit cheerful for the fellows in black," he acknowledged.

"I had the waistcoat made while I was at Cambridge, but I hadn't worn it since I moved into the vicarage. I couldn't even find it at first, until it turned out that my valet had tucked it away in the attic. He never liked it."

"Sherry?" Devin asked, moving toward the sideboard.

"Champagne is better for breakfast," Otis said, brightening immediately. "Here, I'll ring for that owl you call a butler. Now *he* would make a good vicar. You need a Bible thumper with a feeling for the business, a proper gospel grinder. You can tell that wearing black and brooding over people's sins comes naturally to Binsey."

Devin's butler, Binsey, pushed open the door with an alacrity that indicated he had been hovering in the vicinity of the door. And the dark look he threw at Otis suggested that he'd had his ear pressed to the keyhole.

"Champagne," Devin said, heading back to his chair.

Binsey narrowed his owlish eyes to indicate disapproval but took himself away.

"I hear you went to the Lindow ball last night," Otis said. "There was plenty of chatter about it from fellows who ended up at the club later. I don't know why people say that women are the gossiping sex; men love to blather on."

"What was the blather?"

"Did you see Viscount Greywick? Remember, I warned you that he would be competition?"

"I missed him."

"Well, apparently he danced with the Astley girl twice, and everyone says that he's decided that Joan's bad blood can't be allowed to dilute his family line.

Which means that the coast is clear for you to scoop up your Wilde. Except for the competition I offer, of course," Otis added. "It could be that Lady Joan will take one look at me and shrug off her ducal ambitions." He grinned.

"Greywick danced with Viola? He can't have her," Devin said, the words leaving his mouth without conscious volition.

Otis's mouth flopped open like a Scottish trout on the riverbank. "What?"

"What?" Devin was feeling disconcerted.

"He can't have her?"

"No," Devin said, committing to something that he hadn't even articulated to himself.

"I'm so glad I'm moving here, the better to enjoy every moment," Otis chortled. "A vicarage embellished with blue velvet is no competition."

"Are you comparing my future wife to upholstery?"

Otis's grin covered his whole face. "I wouldn't have missed this for the world!"

"I foresee no entertainment," Devin said in a quelling tone.

"I would be very surprised were that true," Otis said gleefully. "You *did* just say that Greywick wasn't allowed to 'have Viola,' otherwise known as Miss Astley?"

Devin frowned. "I didn't phrase that very well. I know Greywick. Look how he's decided Lady Joan won't do, merely because of the possibility that her mother was unfaithful. He's a decent fellow, but a prude at heart. He would trample Viola."

"A shrinking violet in the shade, is she?"

"No." Devin stopped, unable to express himself. Viola wasn't meek, though she was clearly retiring. She was funny and sweet. Brave.

In love with the vicar.

"Duke or no, young ladies are not yours for the having or taking," Otis said, his voice unexpectedly firm. "Any woman who marries you simply because of your title is not a woman with whom you should spend fifty years."

Devin thought about pointing out that matrimony was a matter of convenience and exchange of property—at least, that was clearly the kind of arrangement his parents had made—and decided against it. His uncle Reggie and aunt Margaret had had a very different union. The Murgatroyd family did not fit the mold.

"You're going to have to woo her," his cousin said, displaying a romantic streak that probably stemmed from his parents' unusual marriage.

"Dukes don't woo," Devin informed him. "We . . . don't."

"You haven't a chance of winning one of the Duke of Lindow's daughters without wooing her," Otis retorted. "Don't you know anything about the family, Dev?"

Devin gave it a moment's thought. "The duke has had three duchesses and an untold number of children. I met Horatius, the duke's eldest, before he drowned. I didn't like him. There was that ridiculous play, *Wilde in Love*. I heard about it, but never attended. I remember my father ranting that Lindow ought to horsewhip the second duchess for adultery, but Father died before the lady fled the country and Lindow was granted a divorce."

In short, just the sort of disorganized family structure that he most disliked. Lindow couldn't have anticipated his first wife's death, of course, but his second wife was an object lesson in choosing a duchess who understood the obligations that came with the title: to wit, marital fidelity.

Binsey nipped into the room with a bottle of champagne and two glasses. Otis accepted a glass and knocked it back as if he were dying of thirst. Devin took his and put it to the side. He didn't find that mathematics and wine were good companions, and hopefully at some point he'd get back to the equation he had been working on.

"The Duke of Lindow adores every single one of his daughters, including his stepdaughter," Otis said, getting up and pouring himself another glass. "He married for the third time specifically in order to give his children a mother. Of course, he had three more with the current duchess, but the fact remains that he puts family above anything else. He's famous for it."

"I am an excellent marital prospect," Devin pointed out, starting to feel somewhat testy.

"Next you're going to offer to show me your excellent teeth," Otis said, leaning back in his chair and balancing his champagne glass on his stomach. "What about when you have daughters, Dev?"

"What about it?"

"What if you managed to convince Miss Astley to take you, and the two of you had a daughter?"

"That's an absurd thought. I scarcely know the woman, and expressing concern about the fact that she wouldn't be an appropriate match for Greywick does not mean that I necessarily want her myself."

"You can delude yourself all you want," his cousin said. "Just do me the favor of imagining a daughter as shy as Miss Astley—not that I've met her, but that's her reputation."

Viola's child would have masses of hair, and beautiful hazel eyes. He could picture her anxiety at the idea of a debut ball. Perhaps a feeling that would curdle her stomach and lead her to hide behind curtains.

Viola seemed to be very familiar with the library curtains.

Without warning, a protective surge came over him, so strong that he clenched his jaw.

"See?" Otis said. "The duke isn't going to give his daughter away to any suitor who comes along, you ass. You're going to have to win Miss Astley's hand, and the only way you're going to be able to do *that* is if you listen to me."

"Listen to you?" Devin was reeling inwardly. He didn't *listen* to his younger cousin, or his uncle, for that matter.

But more importantly . . .

What the hell?

He'd only known the woman for five minutes. Perhaps a half hour.

"I don't want to marry Miss Astley," he said curtly. "It's merely that the ball was extremely crowded, and she was the only lady with whom I spent significant time."

Otis snorted. "Clearly you found time to chat with Lady Caitlin Paget, because at the club last night they were taking bets on the two of you. I leapt at the odds against, at one hundred to one, because I met her last year at one of my mother's afternoon parties. I wouldn't let that happen to you."

Devin raised an eyebrow. "You wouldn't let that happen?"

"Not even if I was still in the vicarage," Otis reassured him. "I've met Lady Caitlin at St. Wilfrid's any number of times, since she runs the Sunday school. The girl's potty about animals. Always talking about how adorable kittens are. I wouldn't let you make a mistake like that."

Devin had always thought—on the rare occasion that he considered the matter—that he was lucky to have been an only child. There was no one to say with a scowl, as Viola had said of Joan, *I won't allow you to marry her.*

It seemed he was wrong.

Otis threw back his second glass and got himself to his feet again. "I'd better take off. I have to go back to the vicarage and bathe before my man packs up my trunks."

"More than one trunk? How much clothing do you have?"

"My friends used to jest about me being a 'man of the cloth,'" Otis said. He was on his way to the door when he paused. "You'll need to put out a call for another vicar right away."

"I have someone in mind, but I'd prefer that you followed up with the man," Devin said. "Offer him an excellent salary."

Otis blinked at him. "Did I miss the moment when you turned into a churchgoing parishioner?"

"I'm not opposed to churchgoing."

"But you rarely do."

"I went to your ordination."

"Where in heaven's name did you meet a vicar?" Otis asked, abandoning the question of Devin's ecclesiastical attendance.

"His name's Marlowe, and he was a curate at St. Wilfrid's for two years," Devin said. "He left shortly before you moved in. I want him back. He's a good man."

He was.

Marlowe wasn't the right man for Viola, and he needed to leave the Lindow townhouse, where he was on tap to offer consolation for everything from a stubbed toe to an upset stomach.

Otis shook his head. "Here I thought you left the business of duking to your underlings, and all this time, you've been worrying about your parishioners. I underestimated you, cuz. I'll say as much to Father."

Devin thought for a moment about accepting the praise, but it didn't sit well with him. "Marlowe is currently living in the household of the Duke of Lindow," he said instead. "He's attached to the Mobberley living, but they brought him with them from the country."

Otis blinked. "I see?"

"He's . . . pretty."

"Your competition is a *vicar*?"

This was no bark of laughter; Otis was practically convulsing. "How the mighty are fallen!" he managed to say between paroxysms. That and a stream of disconnected words. "Pretty." And repeatedly: "A vicar!"

Devin waited. "Marlowe can succeed you at St. Wilfrid's," he said, when his cousin finally stopped hanging on to the door and straightened up. "That temporary fellow who succeeded you last November is as tedious in the pulpit as he is in real life."

"I suspect we need Marlowe today," Otis said, chortling. "Emergency, isn't it? After waiting two years while I was studying for the priesthood, now St. Wilfrid's can't survive a month without a vicar."

"I see you understand," Devin said, ignoring his cousin's glee.

"If you'd worried about your parishioners' suffering, you wouldn't have held the living for me."

"You're family."

"I'm a rotten vicar, and I always was headed that direction," Otis said. "You'll have to dispatch with your competition yourself, Devin. Marlowe is a good choice for St. Wilfrid's. One look at him and anyone would know that the fellow is not only picturesque but virtuous. A do-gooder to the bone. Ready to punt people into the next life with a prayer or twenty."

"I agree," Devin said.

"If I had any doubts about leaving the clergy—and I don't—this conversation would have turned the balance. This is going to be a marvelous Season. Just wait until my father—"

"Otis." Devin's voice cracked like a whip.

"Really?"

"No."

"I suppose," Otis conceded. "Father's going to see, though. People think he is too blunt to be perceptive, but they're wrong."

"There may be nothing to see," Devin said. "I merely had a brief conversation with the lady. I should make . . . I should thoroughly assess the field."

"You know, there are two ways of picking a horse, not that it's an appropriate comparison," Otis said. "You can check the teeth, the withers, and the gait of every steed for sale at Tattersall's or . . ."

"Or?"

"Or you can just look one in the eyes and start negotiating a price."

"Aren't you the one who just told me that I can't buy one of the Wildes? That my title and money aren't enough?"

"True," Otis said, pulling the door open. "I'm not saying that the negotiations would be easy or end favorably. I'm just saying that sometimes a man knows instinctively what he wants. And on that subject, not even a morning call to Miss Astley until I decide your next step."

Devin stared at the closed door for a long minute after his cousin left.

The door opened and Otis's head appeared. "Send violets, masses of them," he ordered. "No note, just your card." He disappeared again.

Devin had never done anything rash in his life. In fact, he couldn't think of a single impulsive decision.

As a child, his father's fits of uncontrolled rage had kept him from imprudent behavior. He had been educated at home instead of being sent to Eton, so that—in his opinion—his father could have the pleasure of exploding with rage and throwing his tutors out the door. Just when Devin turned sixteen and might have begun to rebel, his father died.

That huge, blustering life was snuffed out, and Devin stepped into the silence.

After that, there wasn't any time to rebel. He had to find people to advise him, as there was much he didn't know.

His father hadn't paid attention to estate management, and Devin had had no time to learn it. He needed to pay his father's debts, when he didn't even know how many there were. It was the beginning of a lifetime's practice of hiring the best and setting them to work.

In fact . . .

He froze.

Had he just enlisted his cousin to do his wooing for him?

Chapter Eight

The Duke of Lindow's townhouse
Mayfair, London
Later that morning

*L*ady Louisa Knowe, twin sister of the Duke of Lindow, followed the sound of women's voices to a small sitting room on the second floor. She hadn't expected to find her niece by marriage, Lavinia, along with Viola and Joan, but she recognized her laughter.

"Darling!" Lady Knowe cried, entering the room.

Lavinia Sterling, who was married to Parth, the duke's adopted son, looked up with a smile. "Forgive me for not rising, Aunt Knowe, but as you can see, I am buried in fabric." Her lap was piled high with an extensive selection of blue silks. In fact, the whole room had the look of a bazaar, with fabric samples separated by color.

"Just look at this beautiful lace," Joan cried. She had slung a length of violet lace edged with silver around her neck. "Don't you think I would look like a princess if I wore it to a ball?"

"The silver is giving your hair a metallic look," Lady Knowe advised, pushing aside a mound of fabrics to sit beside Lavinia on the settee. "You'd have to use very thick powder."

"That's just what I told her," Lavinia said.

Lavinia was a true original. Her husband was one of the richest men in England. One might expect that she would produce an heir and a spare, and spend her free time gadding about London going to balls and musicales.

Instead, she had turned into one of the most powerful people in English fashion—and that included the *modistes* who thronged London. Lavinia's pet project was Sterling Lace. Her husband had founded it, but she had pioneered the art of making colored lace. Moreover, she had informally partnered in a haberdashery known as Felton's, and built it into the most fashionable place to purchase fabric in all London.

"It looks as if you brought half of Sterling Lace as well as Felton's to the house," Lady Knowe commented, looking around the room.

"The presentation gowns are nearly ready, but Joan and Viola still need at least two morning dresses and a walking dress each," Lavinia explained. "The ball last night went very well, but we mustn't rest on our laurels. Have you read the columns raving about your gown, by the way, Aunt Knowe?"

"Absolutely not. You know I don't read that sort of flummery."

"You only stopped reading them once you began dominating the columns," Joan pointed out. She had discarded the violet lace and was experimenting with a swath of rosy silk instead.

Barty hopped along the back of the settee, paused at Lady Knowe's shoulder, and gave her a cheerful tap on the ear.

"Hello, Barty," she said, scratching Viola's crow on the back of his shining black head.

Barty cocked his head to the side and looked at her.

"No," she said firmly, "these are my favorite emeralds and you may not have them."

Viola was seated at a small desk to the side, writing a letter. She looked up. "Barty is in a naughty mood, Aunt Knowe. This morning Prism let him ride down to the kitchens on his shoulder and I'm afraid he is now in disgrace and banned from that entire area of the house under threat of being added to a soup pot."

Barty edged back along the settee until he could hop onto Lavinia's shoulder and lean against her cheek.

"That is quite adorable," Lady Knowe said.

"Lavinia brought Barty a particularly shiny sequin," Viola said, looking up again from her letter.

"Are you writing to Willa?" Lady Knowe inquired. "I promised I would send a note around describing the ball this morning, but I haven't found time."

"No, she is not," Joan said, lifting the rosy silk from her neck and dropping it onto a pile of fabrics. "Viola is writing the vicar, and never mind that the fellow could be found down the hallway. She and Mr. Marlowe are forever exchanging notes."

"Writing the *vicar*?" Lady Knowe heard her voice rising. "That would be quite inappropriate, Viola, and I trust that Joan is mistaken."

Viola looked up. "There's nothing inappropriate about the notes we exchange, Aunt Knowe," she said earnestly. "I spent considerable time with Father Duddleston in the past few years and I am able to help Mr. Marlowe with questions about the refurbishment of the vicarage. Since he's in London with us, he doesn't always know how to answer the dispatches sent by the builders."

Lady Knowe narrowed her eyes. "How long has this been going on?"

"Weeks!" Joan said, ignoring the scowl that Viola shot in her direction.

Since Joan and Viola were the dearest of friends and had been since infancy, Lady Knowe had no trouble interpreting this comment. Joan was not one to worry, but apparently she thought the correspondence had reached a dangerous state.

She was booting the problem to a higher authority.

"We are forever out of the house," Viola said. "I never see Mr. Marlowe, so how can I answer his questions except through an occasional note?"

Lavinia had been sifting through fabrics and held up a swatch of dark blue twill. "This would be perfect for a riding costume for you, Aunt Knowe."

For once, she was suggesting a subdued color. Louisa had enjoyed being in the forefront of fashion twenty years ago, but at her age she would prefer to be unremarkable. "An excellent idea," she said. "That is a very respectable blue."

Ever since Lavinia had taken to designing her wardrobe, "respectable"—not to mention "unnoticed"—was a fond fantasy. Lavinia's clothing sense ran more along the lines of "unexpected."

"We have not been corresponding for weeks," Viola protested. She paused. "Well, perhaps two weeks. I didn't notice. Anyway, it's not correspondence, because Mr. Marlowe is here in the house. We merely exchange notes because it's easier to share information this way."

"My brother would be very displeased to discover that you have been carrying on a clandestine correspondence with a young man," Lady Knowe stated. "*You*, Viola! Of all the hooligans who've gone through the Lindow nursery, I wouldn't have expected you to behave outrageously."

Lavinia held up a swatch of bright green lace. "I will pair the blue with this lace, Aunt Knowe."

"I knew the blue was too good to be true," Lady Knowe groaned. "That green is far too fashionable for me, Lavinia, darling."

The truth was that she had lost control over her own wardrobe. For the previous decade, she had scarcely left Lindow Castle, living happily in Cheshire and raising her brother's horde of children.

But the children began marrying and leaving the castle.

North and his wife lived not far from Lindow, but Alaric and Willa sailed in and out the port of Dover. Betsy had debuted in London, and her husband was often in the city. Parth had to manage his bank and all the rest of his businesses. Somehow Lady Knowe kept finding herself on the road to London.

Every time she arrived, Lavinia would have a new gown waiting for her, a garment she hadn't chosen, wouldn't have ordered, and would have never thought to wear.

Before she knew it, reporters had begun watching for her wherever she went. She couldn't attend the opera at Covent Garden without being besieged by newspaper correspondents working for *The Lady's Magazine*, or its French equivalent, *Galerie des Modes*.

"The green will clash," she said, trying in vain to regain some control over color, if not design.

"This is not mere green, but acid green," Lavinia corrected her. "I shall frame the bodice and large turn-back cuffs with an extravagant amount of this lace. And I mean to have some satin dyed to match for the lining."

Lady Knowe groaned. "Everyone will look at me."

"That's the idea," Lavinia said. "Viola and Joan must dress like perfect young ladies, albeit the best-dressed debutantes of the Season. But with you I can be creative!"

"Why can't you expend your creativity on your own clothing?"

"Because I'm married to Parth," Lavinia replied. "He's getting to be terribly powerful. Oh, no, Barty. Don't sit on that satin." She just managed to snatch the scrap of fabric away before Barty fluttered down and nestled next to her leg to take a nap.

"I don't see why that means you can't wear an acid green," Lady Knowe said.

"If Parth decides he wants to stand for the House of Commons, or accept one of those titles they keep offering him, I don't want the fact that he has an out-rageously fashionable wife to stand in the way," Lavinia said. "You know what people are like. I already attract far too much attention."

"Parth doesn't agree," Joan said. "He thinks *you* should be known as the most fashionable lady in London. He told me that last night."

"I am wiser to the ways of polite society than my husband," Lavinia said, even though her smile showed how much she appreciated Parth's unwavering faith. She clasped her hands and put on a beseeching look.

"Please, Aunt Knowe, allow me to design your riding costume. I promise that it will be flattering."

Lady Knowe bent over a pile of fabric to give Lavinia a hug, being careful not to dislodge Barty. "This family is lucky," she said, feeling misty. "The day you married Parth was one of our most fortunate moments of all."

"Does that mean you'll wear my blue and green riding costume in Hyde Park?" Lavinia's eyes were bright with excitement. "I promise you that the combination will be extraordinary."

Lady Knowe winced. But they both knew that she wouldn't refuse.

"Let's return to the question of clandestine letters," she said instead, looking over at Viola.

Viola stared back, fruitlessly wishing that she could raise a sardonic eyebrow. It would be so useful!

"There is nothing improper about our correspondence," she said instead. "Mr. Marlowe asked me if I knew the source of the unfortunate odor in the library. As it happens, I do. A weasel died in the attic and was undiscovered for some time."

"Disgusting," Joan said with a shudder.

"The smell seeped through the floorboards, and the only way to remove the smell will be to rip them out. I said as much to Father Duddleston before he passed away, but he thought the repairs would be too burdensome. His solution was to stop using the library altogether."

"Mr. Marlowe could have figured that out himself," Joan said, rolling her eyes. "He merely wanted an excuse to write to you, and never mind the fact that his fiancée is hovering in the background like a bird of prey. Wait until Miss Pettigrew finds out about these notes you're exchanging."

Viola felt a twinge of guilt and looked down at her letter. If the truth be told, she hadn't even mentioned the weasel. Mr. Marlowe's last sermon, preached in the townhouse chapel, had addressed marital love, and she was trying to compose an intelligent response to prove that she was worthy of being a vicar's wife.

Her lack of success was evidenced by the crumpled pieces of paper at her feet.

Miss Pettigrew certainly wouldn't approve.

Dear Mr. Marlowe, she'd written, *I wish to congratulate you on the perspicuity of your recent sermon on marital harmony.*

She wasn't quite sure what "perspicuity" meant.

I shall take to heart your point as regards avoiding using another human being as an instrument for one's own pleasure, thus making a spouse an object of indulgence.

That was as far as she'd got because, frankly, what did she know? Lavinia and Parth had joined them for the Sunday service, and she was quite certain that Parth had been laughing because she heard Lavinia hushing him. Her stepfather and mother had just looked straight ahead with mildly interested expressions.

Lady Knowe looked as if she might confiscate the letter, so Viola hastily folded the draft. It felt improper, even if it *wasn't* improper.

As if her aunt could hear her thoughts, Lady Knowe said, "The very fact you are corresponding is improper, perhaps even more so because you are abiding under the same roof. Darling, don't you see that it doesn't say much for Mr. Marlowe that he has engaged in, let alone encouraged, your correspondence? As Joan pointed out, he is betrothed.

Miss Pettigrew surely has no idea that you are exchanging missives, no matter how innocent the subject."

"He doesn't think in those terms," Viola explained. "Mr. Marlowe isn't attuned to the mores of polite society. He devotes all of his time and energy to helping parishioners." But she felt another pang of guilt.

"Here, do I look as peckish as Pettigrew?" Joan asked. She picked up a piece of black lace and hung it over her head.

"Don't be unkind," Lavinia said, plucking the lace away. "Whoever Miss Pettigrew is, she'd be lucky to find herself in that particular piece of lace. Do you know how hard it was to find a vegetable dye that results in a true black? We're having to reserve it for widows."

"I can't see how Miss Pettigrew could object to my notes," Viola said, not convincing anyone, including herself. "I'm merely trying to help."

"You're not the only one hankering after our local clergyman," Joan pointed out. "You do remember that in the week before we left for London, the church pews were fairly bursting? That wasn't the case when dear old Father Duddleston was preaching."

"You're being remarkably impolite," Viola retorted, leveling a frown at Joan. "Father Duddleston's sermons were excellent." She looked down at her folded letter. "I regularly told him what I thought of them, although he never agreed."

"That isn't what I meant," Joan said. She picked up some white lace and draped it on her head. "Here, now I'm saintly Viola."

"You're being horrid," Viola snapped.

Lady Knowe frowned. "The two of you rarely lowered yourselves to squabbling in the nursery, and there's no reason to do it now. Viola, I suppose I should be unsurprised that you would risk your reputation in order to share advice. You were the kindest child in the nursery by far."

"Except when she wasn't," Joan said. "Remember the scene she made when Father thought that Barty would be better off living in the woods?"

"He didn't understand that Barty's wings don't work properly," Viola said.

Lavinia looked up from the piles of fabric she was sorting through. "Do you have a hidden stubborn streak, Viola? I didn't know that."

"Of course I don't," Viola said. "Well, perhaps a little bit."

"Years ago she discovered two calves were being fattened up for Easter dinner, and she practically threw herself across their bodies to save them," Joan told Lavinia. "To this day, Cleo and Daisy live the life of queens. They have their own cowshed, and I'm surprised it isn't gold plated."

"No more letters to Mr. Marlowe," Aunt Knowe said, laying down the law. "If anyone found out, Viola, you'd be ruined, and never mind that you're sharing ideas for a Sunday school or whatever. It won't matter."

Viola nodded. She'd just have to find another way to impress Mr. Marlowe with her thoughtful appreciation of his sermons.

"Now we can talk of other things," Lady Knowe said. "What color will you wear to the Murgatroyd tea tomorrow, Joan?"

Joan sighed. "Lavinia has mandated that Viola and I have to wear pale colors. With white wigs. Ghostlike."

"Pale colors emphasize that this is your first Season," Lavinia said, looking unrepentant.

"I thought they both looked charming last night," Lady Knowe said, "but I didn't realize you meant to clothe them in white for the entire Season."

"Wildes set trends, we don't follow them," Lavinia said. "Our ball opened the Season. When Lavinia and Viola came down the stairs dressed in white, it changed the entire conversation. They'll wear pale tints for the Season, and I am expecting that by next year white will be *de rigueur* for a debut."

Viola knew exactly what she meant. A ballroom full of people speculating about Joan's and Viola's claims to being members of the Wilde family were being handed another subject of conversation. Rather than discussing the whole *not-Wilde* business, they could talk about fashion instead.

"You *are* brilliant, darling," Lady Knowe said, dropping a kiss on Lavinia's cheek.

"Everyone will be talking about you as well," Lavinia promised Aunt Knowe. "The color of this green lace has never been seen before. The clever man who creates our dyes made it from crushed beetles."

Lady Knowe groaned.

"That's horrible," Viola exclaimed. "Those poor beetles!"

Joan pointed at Lavinia. "You've done it now. She'll probably set up a beetle sanctuary outside the cowshed."

"Almost every dye comes from vegetables and weeds," Lavinia said. "I can't say that I feel true sadness for the beetles."

"I would wear the beetle lace," Joan said grumpily. "As it is, I'm going to spend all Season looking as if I'm being christened. I'd like to wear something that makes me stand out in the crowd. Scarlet, for example."

Viola rolled her eyes. "You always stand out in a crowd, Joan."

"You think you don't," Joan said, "but you certainly made an impression on the Duke of Wynter last night. The only thing he wanted to talk about during our dance was you! And if you'll forgive me, Viola, generally speaking, gentlemen at least ask me a polite question or two about myself."

"He isn't interested in me *that* way," Viola said quickly. "I overheard him tell Sir Reginald that he thought the ball was meant for the duke's real daughter and I was only included for practical reasons."

"Despicable!" Joan exclaimed.

"When he first arrived at the ball, he didn't even bother to be introduced, or to ask me to dance, because he is determined to marry a duke's daughter. A real one like you, Joan."

Lady Knowe narrowed her eyes. "Oh, he did, did he? My brother will disabuse him of that notion. You're not to dance with him again, Joan."

"His name is dead to me," Joan said. "I wouldn't have, anyway. I don't think he is handsome at all."

Viola didn't agree. The duke was not conventionally handsome but there was something very compelling about him. She was wrestling with a new twinge of guilt: After all, once they met, the duke had repeatedly asked her to dance with him.

"I think he's attractive," Lavinia said. "He's an acquaintance of Parth's, and I've met him a few times." She twinkled at Joan. "All that brooding masculinity."

"More importantly, Viola, what did you say to him in response?" Joan asked.

"How could she say anything, if she overheard the comment?" Lavinia asked, before Viola could answer. "Parth won't be pleased to hear of Wynter's comment. For obvious reasons, he abhors people who question whether His Grace is a true parent to all his children."

"I shared a nursery with Viola for years," Joan replied, grinning. "She doesn't need Parth to defend her, do you, V? May I remind all of you that the Duke of Wynter couldn't stop asking questions about Viola throughout our entire dance?"

"In fact, I was wondering if perhaps I'd been unkind," Viola confessed.

Joan laughed. "Out with it!" she demanded. "What did you say to him? Where were you when you overheard him making a fool of himself? Obviously, you tamed him within moments."

"I said that he was impolite, and I implied that he was too old to marry."

Lady Knowe nodded. "Wynter is not old, but it's the thought that counts."

"I asked Mr. Marlowe to pray for the duke's chances of matrimony," Viola said, uncomfortably. "I might have implied that His Grace was lacking courage and experiencing delusions. It's all a bit fuzzy in my mind because I was very cross, but I know that I told him his title was no justification for his opinion of himself."

Lavinia broke out laughing. "Oh, I wish I'd overheard the conversation!"

"I'm very sensitive about being a Wilde," Viola said, "but I am trying to be a better, kinder person."

By the time everybody in the room stopped screeching with laughter, Viola was feeling distinctly annoyed.

"One thing I don't understand," Aunt Knowe said, catching her breath. "Where was Mr. Marlowe that you were able to ask him during the ball, presumably, to pray for Wynter?"

Viola had never been any good at hiding her emotions. She knew perfectly well that guilt was written all over her face.

"I think that perhaps Mr. Marlowe should return to the vicarage and oversee the renovations," Lady Knowe stated.

Joan gave her a beseeching look. "Oh, please, please arrange it so that the man with blue eyes who can't talk about anything but good works—and is horrendously tedious as a result—returns to the country."

"That's mean," Viola said. "You simply don't like respectable gentlemen, Joan, and you never have."

Joan shrugged. "I don't like men who wear their virtue like a coat of armor, that's true. Father is virtuous, and he doesn't reek of holiness. Mr. Marlowe has no sense of humor and he is practically saintlike, except that I think saints have more ambition."

"Don't say that," Viola flashed. "He has done nothing to deserve such rudeness."

"Mr. Marlowe is good, but boring," Joan retorted. "He makes you boring too. All you do is sit around and gaze into his eyes. You may be shy, Viola, but you were always funny. Now if he's not in the room, you just sigh and look into space!"

"She'll get over it," Lavinia said. "When I first fell in love with Parth, I didn't know what to do with all that emotion."

"You gazed soulfully into the distance?" Joan asked skeptically. "I can't imagine that."

"Well, no," Lavinia admitted. "I spent my time making up insults about Parth. He wouldn't pay any attention to me, you see."

"Despicable Sterling!" Lady Knowe said, remembering that particular courtship with delight. "Appalling Parth!"

"I don't have the faintest inclination to call Mr. Marlowe names," Viola said.

"Parth thought I was an empty-headed bit of fluff," Lavinia said. "I couldn't make him like me, so I concentrated on the opposite." She shrugged. "I never said it was an intelligent plan."

"Maudlin Marlowe," Joan cried, brightening.

Viola scowled at her. "Stop that!"

"Mawkish Marlowe!"

Joan ran out of the room, shrieking with laughter, and Viola chased after her, trying to hit her with the folded letter.

Lavinia watched them leave. "What are you going to do about the vicar, Aunt Knowe?"

"I'm not sure. My instincts say that sending him to the country would be a mistake. Absence makes the heart, etcetera. He's a very good man, and an excellent vicar, but not the right husband for Viola."

"Ophelia will be here soon to discuss a new morning dress; perhaps she will have an idea," Lavinia suggested.

Barty woke up and squawked irritably, realizing Viola had left the room.

"Viola cannot marry a vicar," Lavinia stated, scooping up Barty and putting him on her shoulder. He settled down, stroking her hair with his beak.

"I wouldn't stand in her way if it was the right vicar," Lady Knowe said. "Marlowe is a good man with excellent ideas for improving parish life."

"But he wouldn't fit in with the men in the family," Lavinia said. "If you don't mind a bit of unasked-for advice . . ."

"From you, always," Lady Knowe said.

"Parth's courtship of me advanced at a snail's pace compared to some others in the Wilde family, partly because we had a history of disliking each other, but also because our relationship was not conducted under the same roof," Lavinia said. "Whereas Willa and Alaric . . ."

She cleared her throat. "Intimacy is easier to establish in close quarters. In this case, letters could easily lead to more clandestine meetings—even if only to discuss clerical arrangements."

"North and Diana were living together in the castle," Lady Knowe said, eyes narrowing. "Hell's bells, it was my idea to bring Marlowe to London."

"Send him back to Cheshire," Lavinia suggested. "Viola may have a bruised heart, but her virtue will remain intact. Either that, or invite Miss Pettigrew to stay here."

Lady Knowe shuddered. "I'd prefer to return to Cheshire myself than live with that woman. And

Ophelia would never agree. You know how amiable Ophelia is, and yet she's taken a strong dislike to the Pettigrews."

"Then you know what to do." Lavinia held up a bright square of printed red calico. "How do—"

"No," Lady Knowe said. "The crushed beetles are your triumph for the day. I'm sorry, dear, but I must speak to the housekeeper. I promised I'd join her a half hour ago." She stopped in the door and blew a kiss. "Where would we be without you?"

"Naked and ruined," Lavinia said, grinning.

"Precisely!"

Chapter Nine

*F*or the past two years, Devin and a German mathematician had been exchanging correspondence centering on the number 1,729, a number expressible as the sum of two cubes. They were looking for a new expression. Given the complexity of the problem, the months that passed between delivery of letters was a boon.

He'd barely settled back down at his desk after Otis left, when the door burst open and his uncle trotted in. "Your butler tried to keep me out, but I told him that in times of crisis, the head of the family must rally to the fore."

Binsey grimaced beyond Sir Reginald's shoulder.

Devin rose from his desk and walked toward him. "Uncle, I want to apologize for leaving the library last night after I told you I'd wait for you there."

"Champagne!" his uncle exclaimed, ignoring his apology. "I must say, Binsey, that I've never thought much of your butlering, but leaving a bottle open all night—and filthy glasses as well—is extraordinarily slipshod."

Behind him, Binsey puffed up like an exotic frog, his face turning ruddy with indignation.

Sir Reginald didn't bother to assess the effects of his reprimand. He picked up the bottle and examined the label. "It's a crime to allow this to go flat."

"It's not flat—" Devin began.

But his uncle had upended the bottle and was sampling the champagne himself. Devin returned behind his desk and sat down. He'd discovered that family members were more likely to leave quickly if he kept a distance.

"More of that mathematical business," his uncle commented, peering at his figuring. "I can't imagine why you aren't satisfied just being a duke, like every other man who has the title. Lindow complains about being up to his eyebrows in correspondence, and here you are, playing about with numbers all day long."

Devin could have answered that in a number of ways, most of which boiled down to: He hired other people to be the duke for him.

He went to Parliament only when his secretary—who was intelligent, politically adept, and happily took notes on every single speech—insisted that his vote was crucial. Even so, he generally remained in the parliamentary library until the vote was called, allowing him to escape prosy lectures on subjects that any fool could assess in a few minutes.

He had long since hired excellent managers for his estates in Northamptonshire and Wales, giving them plenty of leeway. Consequently, his estates were thriving. Or at least he wasn't being embezzled more than four percent, which he considered an acceptable margin.

The moment Parth Sterling opened a bank, Devin had moved all the family's investments there, which meant he didn't have to think about those either.

His uncle plunked the bottle of champagne back on the tray and smacked his lips. "Still nice and bubbly. Must be something to do with the design of the bottle."

He wheeled and leveled a finger at Binsey. "Not that it excuses your negligence in leaving a bottle of the best withering away in the night air. Any respectable butler would have drunk it himself rather than allow it to go to waste."

"We opened the champagne an hour ago to celebrate Otis's laicization," Devin said. He nodded at Binsey. "You may go."

His uncle watched Binsey scurry out of the room before he turned back, folding his arms over his chest. Since Sir Reginald had the approximate shape of a champagne bottle—narrower at the top, wider through the middle—this turned him from triangular to rectangular.

"*You*," he growled, giving the pronoun an ominous air.

"Indeed, it is me. Would you like me to find you a glass, Uncle, or do you prefer to continue imbibing from the bottle?"

"Don't change the subject! I see it now. I thought that Otis had been led astray by those friends of his from Eton, but now I realize the truth!"

Devin raised an eyebrow, knowing from long experience that said truth was about to be served up on a platter, with a sauce of righteous indignation.

"You led him astray," his uncle announced. "You turned Otis away from the church. You sopped up his best instincts with champagne and . . . and the lures of the flesh!"

Devin waited for a moment, since normally Sir Reginald's reprimands were composed of at least five sentences, but his uncle stopped short in order to glare at him, his dark eyebrows contrasting oddly with the butter-yellow powder he'd used on his wig this morning.

"I held the St. Wilfrid's living open for two years to give Otis the position," Devin reminded him.

"Just when Otis began the righteous task of saving souls, you lured him astray with French potions."

"Nonsense," Devin said. "I had nothing to do with Otis's decision to leave the church. He's not suited to the job, Uncle, and we both should have acknowledged that long ago. Actually, the fact that he put off ordination four times was a sign in itself. What was his excuse last time? That he lost a toe, wasn't it? He's walking very well for a man minus a digit."

His uncle scowled before he turned away to pick up the champagne bottle. "Otis faints at the sight of blood and always has," he said, taking a hearty swallow. "The injury wasn't as severe as he initially thought."

Devin waited.

"Otis is perfectly suited to the church," Sir Reginald insisted. "He was always a kind child, at an age when his older brother was pinning up butterflies and pummeling other boys. I can't imagine a better person to baptize babies. They wouldn't make a peep even if he drenched them with water. He's good with dogs too. No tears, no howls . . . He's perfect."

"There's more to baptism than preventing tears," Devin said. "Where do the dogs come in?"

"There's that day when all the animals are blessed," his uncle said vaguely.

"I've no doubt that Otis could shine when it came to blessing a baby goat, but would someone truly wish to leave a baptism in his hands?"

"He had all the necessary schooling," Sir Reginald said. But Devin could see a hint of doubt in his eyes.

"We should have given up when he kept failing that course on the New Testament," Devin said.

"He said the story was hard to follow," Otis's father said defensively. "I agree with him. Very complicated, all those different points of view, not to mention morbid."

Devin had always found it best to leave biblical exegesis to those with training—which wouldn't include Otis, and never mind all those years at Cambridge. "If I'm not mistaken, you gave each of your children an estate. Otis doesn't need the living."

"You don't understand. He's threatening to *move to Spain*," his uncle shrilled. "He told me that he plans to marry a Spanish woman. He failed Greek three years in a row, and he certainly won't be able to learn the Spanish language. That means my boy will have one of those marriages in which the husband and wife don't say a word to each other."

In short, a normal marriage.

But Devin didn't say that aloud because he was well aware that his parents' marriage had soured his view of such partnerships. In contrast, his uncle was still mourning his wife's death, some three years after the fact.

"I talked him into staying in London with the help of champagne," Devin said instead.

His uncle fell back a step and thumped the bottle down, causing yellow wig powder to fly into the air. "I always told my wife that there was a reason you were chosen to be the head of this family, and there it is!"

"Because I was born to it and had no choice?"

"No, because you always get your way," Sir Reginald said, his round cheeks bunching as he grinned. "I've been watching you quietly manipulate people since you were breeched, and I can always count on you."

"I am glad to hear it," Devin said. "If there's nothing else, I should return to work. You may take the bottle with you."

"As a matter of fact, there *is* something else," his uncle said. He sat down in the chair opposite Devin's desk. "We need to discuss Miss Astley. I noticed that you didn't dance with her."

"I did not," Devin agreed. "But I did meet her."

"Why didn't you dance with her?" his uncle asked.

"She refused."

"She did? I wonder if she hadn't heard that Lady Caitlin Paget had claimed you. I can't imagine what you were doing, going into supper with the gal after you told me that she drove you into the library. Now everyone thinks you're a match."

Devin didn't give a rat's ass what anyone thought. "We're not."

"I know that," his uncle said. "You wouldn't have fled to the library if you'd taken to her. More to the point, what did you think of Miss Astley?"

Devin was still trying to figure out how to answer that question when his uncle shook his head. "No need to answer." He cocked his head, giving Devin a sharp-eyed look.

"No?"

"You need more time to get to know her. She's quiet. Shy. You don't have an ounce of that sentiment in you, Nephew, but I can assure you that it's a difficult thing to grapple with if you have an abundance of it."

"Do you have an ounce of shyness?" Devin inquired.

"No, it's not part of the family makeup," his uncle replied. "Doesn't come down in the blood, as it were. The Wynters are the opposite of shy: always charging into battle and generally being cut off before the age of thirty as a result. Your parents, both of them, were prime examples."

Devin had never considered the pruning of his family tree in this light, but he had to admit there was some justification for it. His father had died after his umpteenth duel; his mother had died after eating stewed foxglove against the advice of the family doctor. She had been told that it might give her the art of prophecy.

It was kinder to think of that as a courageous impulse than pure foolishness.

"You see?" his uncle demanded, having apparently followed his train of thought. "I've had to rein myself in countless times, just to make certain that you and my children have one parent left."

This was obviously not the moment to remind his uncle that he was related by marriage, not by blood, to the Wynters. Nor of Sir Reggie's bet that he could get from London to Bath in a racing curricle. He'd been lucky to land in a hospitable hedge.

That was last year.

"What I'm saying is that you can't judge Miss Astley on such short acquaintance," his uncle said. "I've come over here to tell you that we're holding an afternoon tea with dancing for Hazel, and I want you to come. I told you that my cousin Elnora has joined us for the Season, didn't I? Had to have someone to chaperone Hazel."

"Otis told me," Devin said.

"You ignored my invitation."

"When is the tea?"

"Tomorrow afternoon. Very small, very select. The Wildes are coming," his uncle said. "And two other ladies, including Lady Caitlin. Ten or fifteen in all. I invited Caitlin before I knew that you were fussy about wig ornaments."

"A question of my nerves," Devin said, thinking with sardonic pleasure of the moment when Viola bade the vicar to pray for him.

"Poppycock," his uncle said. "You haven't a nerve in your whole body. I'll have some more of that champagne."

Devin came around the desk, poured champagne into a brandy goblet, and handed it to him.

"Have some yourself," Uncle Reggie said generously.

"No, thank you." Devin leaned against the desk in lieu of returning to his seat.

"You need to wear something lively to the tea," his uncle said, casting a disparaging look at Devin's black coat.

Years ago, Devin had come to the conclusion that his uncle's propensity for matching his wig powder to his pantaloons, together with Otis's penchant for brightly colored waistcoats, was best left to that side of the family. He had loathed roses on purple silk even before Miss Astley had informed him his coat was ostentatious.

"I am better suited to subdued clothing," he said.

"Black makes a man look sallow," his uncle said. "I suppose you could do with a light charcoal."

"I will keep it in mind," Devin said, accepting this sartorial dictate.

"That's one thing to be said for Otis dropping the church," Uncle Reggie said, his mouth compressing. "At least I won't have to see him around the house in black. I can't abide *black*."

Devin had the feeling that his uncle's abhorrence for the color stemmed from his wife's death. "I won't wear black," he promised.

"Not to the tea party," his uncle said. "Lively colors are the ticket."

"How was Hazel's first ball?" Devin had danced with his cousin the night before, but it was one of those dances with lots of to-ing and fro-ing, and no time to inquire as to her well-being.

"She thinks she's in love," his uncle said.

"After one night? Is it a respectable match?"

"No, and that's one of the reasons why I'm here. I want you to do something about it."

"What on earth can I do about it?"

"Dispatch the fellow."

Devin had a sudden thought. "Is he a vicar?"

"A vicar?" His uncle stared at him. "I should certainly hope not! He's an earl."

"Of course," Devin murmured. "It was just a thought."

"You're not talking about that fellow attached to the Wildes, are you?"

"Yes. Mr. Marlowe was the curate at St. Wilfrid's for two years, and now is vicar in one of the Duke of Lindow's livings."

His uncle snorted. "Last week Lady Knowe held an afternoon tea, not with dancing, merely for the young ladies who are coming out this Season. I went along with Hazel, and that fellow attended. The giggling sounded like the north wind coming down a chimney. He has all sorts of ideas, not the sort that I approve of either. Talking about orphanages and getting young ladies excited about going to church. It isn't proper."

Devin nodded. Mr. Marlowe's profile was a powerful lure. But Mr. Marlowe, the protector of small children, blue eyes glowing? All that virtue might rival a title, even that of a duke, the highest in the land.

"I think Marlowe would be a good vicar for St. Wilfrid's," he said to his uncle.

Uncle Reggie squinted at him. "You're up to something."

He looked back without responding.

His uncle guffawed. "When I haven't seen you in a while, I always forget that you move us around as if we were chess pieces. The pretty vicar will go to St. Wilfrid's to replace Otis, presumably?"

"It's a logical move to make certain that my parishioners aren't left in the lurch. There was a chance Otis would change his mind over the last few months since he first announced his reluctance to continue as a vicar, but no."

"I suppose I have to accept it," Sir Reginald groaned. "I was proud of the fact that this family had produced a man of God."

Except they hadn't.

But Devin kept that thought to himself.

"The Duke of Lindow obviously has a spare vicar," Devin said instead, "since he dragged this one up to London. Moreover, the man has already spent two years in the parish of St. Wilfrid's. Mr. Marlowe is an obvious choice to replace Otis."

"You do make it sound quite logical," his uncle said.

"St. Wilfrid's will be very good for his career. It's not every young man who's offered a living by a duke."

"That's true. I'm sure his fiancée will approve."

"Fiancée?"

"Miss Pettigrew. She attended Lady Knowe's tea. Can't say I care for her much." His uncle hoisted himself to his feet, leaving a patch of yellow powder on the back of the tall chair.

"You might invite Mr. Marlowe to your tea," Devin suggested.

"I'd rather not," his uncle said. "I can't abide all the foolish giggling without a good burgundy in hand."

"And Miss Pettigrew," Devin added.

"Want to meet the fiancée, do you? You're playing a deep game, Nephew."

"It will give me a chance to sound out Marlowe on the subject of St. Wilfrid's."

"I might invite them to dinner if you insist, but not tomorrow. Don't be late," his uncle ordered. "No running off to the library either. Even you can endure two hours of conversation and a dance or two. I've hired a quartet."

Normally the idea would have filled Devin with horror. Today it—didn't.

"I will attend," he said.

"I still think you're up to something." Sir Reginald peered at him.

"Very likely," Devin agreed. "Do you think that perhaps you need spectacles, Uncle? You seem to be squinting."

"I see perfectly well," his uncle reported. "One simply has to take a closer look at you than at most men. It's not that I can't trust you, but I don't always understand you." He gave a crack of laughter. "Not that I'm complaining. The family estates were trickling down the drain, paying off your father's more absurd peccadilloes, and now we're thriving."

"Hmm," Devin said. He knew quite well the amounts that the estate had to pay out, on a continuing basis, to widows and children orphaned as a result of his father's violent temper.

"I'll make my way to the butler's pantry and see how Binsey is doing with preparations for Hazel's ball."

Devin walked with his uncle to the door. "Didn't you just speak to him about it yesterday?"

"Binsey and I don't always see eye to eye," Uncle Reggie said, in a magnificent understatement. "I have to rehearse our plans on a daily basis to make certain that he doesn't undermine me. It's not easy turning a house this size into a fairy garden, but that is what Hazel wants."

Devin stopped himself from groaning, but it was a near thing.

"Lilac trees lined up all around the ballroom, draped in all manner of flowers and candles as well.

And a flowery arch leading to the dining room. I have to check every detail. Do you know that Binsey thought to serve collared eels for the supper!"

Devin steered his uncle through the door.

"I told him that we'll have fowls, lambs, lobster, and various meats. No fish and certainly no eels." He disappeared into the nether regions of the house in pursuit of Binsey, squaring his shoulders to take on the battle.

Devin went back to his chair with one idea foremost in his mind: He'd take a clear-eyed look at Viola Astley tomorrow. She was likely not worth the trouble.

All London knew her as a mouse, after all.

The very idea of an upset stomach was off-putting.

Then he thought about the way her eyes sparkled when she scolded him. It was an outlandish thing to find attractive.

There was plenty else to admire. She was just the size and shape that he would most prefer for his duchess, not that he'd given it much thought before.

But now that he had, his wife would definitely have to have a deep bosom. In fact, it was a requirement. And she had to be petite, with lush lips and thick lashes. It was hard to tell, given the fashion for panniers, but he had the idea that Viola's hips were round instead of lean, like those of taller women.

Joan Wilde was beautiful, like Venus or Helen of Troy.

But Viola was like a treasure box, hiding her sensuality and her intelligence and her sense of humor.

He had the feeling she shared it only with family.

Right. He'd always preferred a challenge. A woman who didn't share her thoughts? Who had no particular interest in going into society?

She was made for him.

All he had to do was get rid of the pretty vicar.

And somehow convince Viola that he was just as pretty—which he wasn't.

Ditto, as virtuous as Marlowe. Paying for orphans' maintenance didn't feel virtuous when one's father was responsible for their destitution.

Oh, and as malleable as Marlowe—no. He couldn't see himself obeying orders, even those handed out by a wife.

He shrugged.

Likely he would see Viola at the tea party, making eyes at the vicar, and realize that he'd suffered a bout of temporary insanity.

Chapter Ten

An Afternoon Tea with Dancing
The town residence of Sir Reginald Murgatroyd,
  in honor of his daughter Hazel
Hanover Square

$\mathcal{V}$iola was feeling glum as the Lindow carriage arrived at Sir Reginald's house. Mr. Marlowe wasn't invited, of course. When she saw him in the hallway as she and Joan were walking toward the front door, he merely nodded and walked briskly on.

She was fairly certain that Mr. Marlowe hadn't shared with Miss Pettigrew the fact they had been exchanging innocuous notes, but she had to admit that his fiancée would be unlikely to approve of such correspondence.

In short, she felt distinctly shaken by guilt, which was absurd, because hadn't she decided that Mr. Marlowe needed rescuing from his fiancée? But on the other hand, she had a strong feeling that she had been disrespectful of Miss Pettigrew, no matter how objectionable she might find her.

As if Aunt Knowe had been following her train of thought, she said out of the blue, "I'd be surprised if Mr. Marlowe isn't a bishop within the decade. Miss Pettigrew will ensure it."

Viola wasn't lost to the fact that her aunt had taken to mentioning Miss Pettigrew at every possible turn.

"I'm sorry," Joan whispered, as Aunt Knowe surged up the steps toward the Murgatroyds' butler, waiting at the front door. "Are you horribly cross that I told her about your correspondence with Mr. Marlowe?"

Viola felt a surge of affection meeting her stepsister's anxious eyes. "No, you were right. It wasn't proper to exchange those notes, no matter how innocent. I was just thinking that it wasn't fair to Miss Pettigrew."

"I'm sorry that I don't appreciate Mr. Marlowe the way you do," Joan said. "If you . . . if you are together in the future, I promise that I will make myself like him."

"On deeper acquaintance, you would certainly enjoy his company," Viola said. But inside, she wasn't sure. Joan, like most of the Wildes, had little tolerance for self-anointed sainthood, as Aunt Knowe put it.

The Murgatroyd drawing room was generously proportioned, with elegant plaster flourishes covering the ceiling. The walls were painted a pale green stripe down to the knee, with cream wainscoting to the floor. There were three seating areas, including one in front of a pianoforte, and tall windows at the far end opened onto a formal garden.

The first person Viola saw was the Duke of Wynter, seated to the left in a cluster of four young ladies. He looked like a bricklayer who'd been summoned to the parlor and found himself bored to death by elegant conversation.

No, that wasn't fair.

He wasn't a bricklayer, for all his features weren't refined nor delicate. The duke's nose had to be twice the size of Mr. Marlowe's, for example.

Mr. Marlowe had a trim nose, the kind that everyone admired. Viola had always wanted a stronger nose, like that of her sisters.

One couldn't overlook the Duke of Wynter's nose. Not that it was outsized. It fit the rest of his face: a bold nose. A patrician nose, like the rest of him, and like the noses of the Wildes too.

He was wearing a coat of a dark peach color without ornamentation, except where the collar turned over, showing a bit of cream satin. To the side of his leg, she could see his coat was lined in the same warm cream.

The costume was plain, but all the more elegant in its simplicity. Lavinia would approve.

He looked up, and she felt color surging into her face, so she quickly looked away.

As the butler announced their arrival, all the guests rose and moved toward them *en masse*. Viola already felt unnerved. She found herself falling back into her custom of curtsying with her eyes on the floor, though she registered the Duke of Wynter, not merely because he was tall but because he smelled marvelously like a pine forest.

And because he murmured, "Steady."

She almost glanced up, as it was a kind thing to say, but Sir Reginald had already moved on to the next introduction.

Joan was instantly surrounded by young gentlemen, and Aunt Knowe was chatting with Sir Reginald, so Hazel pulled Viola to the side.

"Why are you late?" Hazel hissed. "This tea party is a disaster. I have been desperately watching the door for your arrival."

"My little sister has a cold, and my mother decided to stay home," Viola explained. "My aunt had to change her dress to accompany us. The party seems very well attended."

"Naturally, because my father told most of London that Devin would join us." She nodded over to her left, where the Duke of Wynter was once again surrounded by eligible ladies. "He's looking for a wife, obviously. I do love Devin—he's my cousin—but he's frightfully superior and will scarcely attend any social occasion."

"That doesn't surprise me," Viola observed.

When Hazel looked at her inquiringly, she shrugged. "He's a duke. First on Caitlin's list, after all."

"Oh, I thought for a moment that you knew him." She lowered her voice. "Don't be insulted if he scarcely notices you're there, even if you're standing before him. He's all right around the family but haughty in public. Oh, and I should tell you that my father got an idea that you and Devin would suit, but it's only based on the fact that *your* father managed to put up with *his* father, who was a frightful beast. Devin is not the sort of man you would like at all, duke or no duke."

"I see," Viola said, feeling oddly disgruntled about Hazel's assessment. "What is the problem with the party?"

"All the girls are sighing over Devin, and you'd think that would leave the gentlemen to me, but instead they've been sitting about waiting for Joan to arrive. Now look, they're clustered around her as if she was handing out sweets."

Viola tucked an arm through hers. "You are beautiful and kind, Hazel. The right person will come along. Joan said last night that she hadn't danced with a single man whom she'd contemplate marrying."

"The Earl of Kimp asked me to dance twice, but his only subject of conversation is gargoyles," Hazel said. She lowered her voice. "As a joke, I told my father that I had taken a fancy to the earl, and he took me seriously."

"Whereas the only person whom Joan liked was Kimp," Viola pointed out. "She enjoys eccentrics."

Now she thought of it, that character trait might explain Joan's dislike of Mr. Marlowe. The vicar was not at all eccentric.

"I'm just glad you're here," Hazel said. "I want to introduce you to my brother Otis. He's over there, hiding from my father."

They were walking to the far side of the room, when a deep voice said, "Good afternoon, Miss Astley," from just behind her shoulder.

She startled, and let out a squeak as the duke stepped forward.

"Hello, Devin," Hazel said, glancing across Viola. "We're going to talk to Otis."

She kept walking toward the other side of the room, but Viola stayed where she was, if only to prove to the duke that she was capable of looking him in the eye.

"How's your stomach?" His Grace inquired.

"In no danger," she said, smiling because his straightforward question suggested that he hadn't the faintest worry about his shoes. That contrasted with her family members, who tended to look at her with apprehensive expressions.

She had been nauseated—just a tad—but now her stomach steadied. There was something very calming about Hazel's cousin.

Partly because of the whole *not-Wilde* business being out of the way, but also partly due to his calmness which stemmed, she would guess, from having nothing to prove to anyone.

In short, he was her opposite, because she constantly felt that she had to prove herself a real Wilde, and he was at home in his own skin. What's more, he knew she had an affection for Mr. Marlowe, and that took all the pressure away from their conversation. She didn't have to worry about whether he was courting her.

Hazel, having realized that they had not followed, trotted back and tucked her arm in Viola's. "Come along, V!"

"V?" the duke inquired, ambling along on Viola's other side.

"That's what we called her at school," Hazel said. And before Viola could elbow her, she said, "Because she's short. No need for a whole name."

"I didn't notice that she was short," the duke said, his eyes gleaming with an emotion that Viola couldn't quite make out.

Wasn't sure that she *wanted* to make out.

"You've gone blind from staring at mathematical formulas," Hazel said.

Viola was coming to the uncomfortable conclusion that perhaps the duke wasn't quite as fatheaded as she had thought. For one thing, Hazel clearly liked him. He couldn't be as stiff-necked as he first appeared.

For another, there was laughter in his eyes, though it didn't show on his face.

"Otis!" Hazel cried, when they reached a short gentleman in a bright yellow satin coat. "I want to introduce you to my dearest friend, Miss Viola Astley. I know you met a moment ago, but I mean a proper acquaintance. Viola, this is my brother."

Viola was somewhat surprised to find that Otis Murgatroyd had no resemblance to his cousin, the duke.

Before she thought of it, she turned to look up at His Grace.

"Absurd, isn't it?" Otis said. "Even Hazel is taller than I am, and given that she's a beanstalk for a woman, that makes me a shrimp."

"Mixed metaphors," the duke remarked. "If Hazel's a beanstalk, you are a bean. A yellow bean, as it were. I didn't realize that you liked such sunny clothing."

"My cousin is used to seeing me in black, as I used to be a vicar in one of his livings," Otis said to Viola. "Sartorial commentary to the contrary, my relatives are quivering with joy because I am returning to the embrace of the family."

"Now that you've stopped being such an ecclesiastical humbug, I shall introduce you to all my short friends," Hazel said, with a younger sister's brutal candor.

"I am one of those short friends," Viola admitted, smiling at Otis. "A white bean, given my attire this afternoon."

Otis beamed back. "I am looking forward to dancing with you. I can't tell you how awkward it is to find oneself eyeing a lady's bosom, when it's that or keep

my eyes turned to the sky like one of those languish-
ing saints about to be martyred."

"I think everyone agrees that you aren't a candidate
for sainthood," Wynter said dryly.

"It wasn't very sporting of you, Hazel, to draw the
biggest fish in the marital pond over here," Otis said.
"Devin, I suggest you return to all those damsels
throwing longing glances in your direction."

Hazel sat down and flapped her hands at the duke.
"I agree. Shoo, Devin. My father promised that you'd
be on display, not hiding amongst the family."

Viola thought she saw something in the duke's
eyes—heavens, couldn't the man just show expressions like everyone else?—that might have been hurt
feelings. His own relatives were tossing him onto the
battlefield.

She sat down on the settee opposite Hazel. "I have
a different suggestion, Your Grace," she said, patting
the cushion beside her. "You may compose yourself
among family, after which Hazel will introduce you
to just the right lady."

The duke settled down next to her, looking pleased
to be rescued.

Hazel shook her head at him. "Viola isn't that lady,
by the way. I've already warned her that the two of
you wouldn't suit. My father has a silly notion stem-
ming from the fact that your father actually restrained
himself from dueling with Viola's father."

Viola blinked. That sounded more serious than
merely a question of friendship.

One side of the duke's mouth rose in a lopsided
smile. "The late duke, my father, was prone to duels,"
he told Viola, "which were more acceptable at the
time than they are now. Since his friends were more

likely to be within shouting distance when he had the impulse, he challenged almost all of them."

"Killed one of them," Hazel said with relish.

"That is not for general knowledge," His Grace said.

"I apologize, cuz, but Uncle's dueling *is* general knowledge," Hazel said.

"We don't want to put off Miss Astley, if you're hoping that we two beans will become friendly," Otis said.

He was a born peacemaker. Not unlike herself, Viola realized. But not someone she had any interest in marrying.

"The real question is which of those ladies is right for our duke?" Otis continued. "I don't mind telling you, Miss Astley, that I've put in a bet against Lady Caitlin."

"She has to be tall," Hazel said. "A beanstalk, like me."

"Oh, I don't know," the duke said, glancing at Viola. "I am partial to beans. Whereas Hazel is partial to eccentric earls, according to my uncle."

"The earl plans to take a wedding trip to Paris," Hazel said, giggling, "and whilst he is there, arrange to buy a few gargoyles from the Cathedral of Notre-Dame."

"Less daring than doomed to failure," Otis observed. "He's a collector, I gather."

"Absolutely," Hazel confirmed. "If Notre-Dame refuses to sell him one, he means to make his way to the top and knock it off and take it away."

"I did meet him, but he didn't share his criminal tendencies with me when we were dancing," Viola said, laughing.

She was pricklingly aware of the duke's large body next to her. He was no beanstalk. He felt very muscled and solid sitting beside her. Like a stone gargoyle, she thought with amusement. She turned her head to see if she could imagine him glaring out over the city of Paris.

"What are you thinking?" he asked her, warmth deep in his eyes that wasn't the slightest bit gargoyleish.

"I was imagining you on top of Notre-Dame," she admitted, before she thought better.

"A noble gargoyle," Otis said, hooting with laughter.

Devin had promised himself that ten minutes' acquaintance would chase away the odd fascination he felt for the Duke of Lindow's stepdaughter.

Viola wasn't a real Wilde, as she herself had said. Not a likely prospect for a Duchess of Wynter, and Otis and Hazel agreed. Too shy. Too short. Too funny. Not to mention too fond of a vicar.

Ten minutes ago, he had been sitting in a near stupor, listening to a group of young ladies prattle on about the baby monkeys in the Royal Menagerie, when Viola walked in the door, wearing a confection that seemed to float around her and at the same time favor her bosom. When she glanced at him and turned pink, his entire body came alert.

The Duke of Wynter wasn't used to questioning his decisions. It was with a certain sense of satisfaction that he realized he had been wrong to doubt himself.

He had found a treasure in the Lindow library, and he merely had to win it away from a vicar. How hard could that be?

Even given the fact that his treasure had made it clear that she had no interest in his courtship, his title, or his person.

Lady Knowe strolled up. "Time to join us for tea, my dears. The fiddlers are tuning their instruments."

Viola rose when everyone else did, and somehow she found herself not only walking with the duke, but seated beside him as well.

"May I help you remove your gloves, Miss Astley?" he asked.

Viola glanced to the left and right and discovered that indeed, other young ladies were removing their gloves. Where a gentleman was available to help them, they had accepted his assistance.

"Very well," she said.

Her gloves went almost to her elbows, after all.

The duke bent over her hand and pulled gently at the tips of all five fingers. She stared down at his hair—thick, dark, and unpowdered, unlike many gentlemen in the room—and felt a strange qualm in her stomach, not at all like the warning of imminent gastric distress.

"I've never done this before," Wynter said, flashing a glance at her.

"There's nothing very difficult about it," she said. "Just pull it off, if you please, Your Grace."

He looked up at her again, his bare right hand holding her left. "It's the first time I will have seen your hand. You wore gloves at the ball."

Viola frowned at him. "Mine are perfectly normal fingers, Your Grace. You're making a spectacle of us."

"I don't mind," he said with a wry twist of his mouth as he picked up her other hand and began tugging each of her fingers free of her glove. "Very small," he observed.

"Oh, for goodness' sake," Viola moaned. "I shall

go sit elsewhere, if you don't stop it. We aren't suited, remember?"

His large fingers curled around her hand, hiding it from sight. "If you run away, it will cause more gossip."

"Stop it," she ordered, knowing that her cheeks were pink.

Slowly he unwrapped his hand from around hers. "Am I allowed to say that I think your hand is very beautiful?"

"Absolutely not!"

In the ensuing hour or so, Viola danced with every eligible gentleman at the party, including the Duke of Wynter. At one point her stomach began to clench, after a gentleman asked her too many questions about what it was like being "raised with the Wildes," but she caught sight of Wynter over the man's shoulder.

He was looking at her, not his partner. He nodded.

Her stomach uncurled and settled. "I wasn't raised 'with' the Wildes," she told her dance partner, and gave him a wide smile. "I *am* a Wilde."

Why hadn't she understood that? The most important thing was to know the truth herself. That was what Joan had tried to tell her. Joan's father was almost certainly a Prussian count, but she knew herself to be the duke's daughter, and she didn't need their father's assurance.

"Of course," the gentleman said respectfully. "I didn't mean to imply otherwise."

When Sir Reginald called the last dance, the Duke of Wynter bowed before Viola as if there was no question where he would be.

As if there was no question with whom he would dance.

Lord Poplar—Poppy—had been a step from her side, but he turned away with a rueful smile.

"What are you doing?" Viola asked Wynter in a whisper. "You should only dance twice with the lady whom you are planning to court!"

"I enjoy dancing with friends," he answered. A gleam of humor shone in his eyes. "I dislike dancing with strangers, and it's not as if I can dance with Otis."

"Surely one young lady took your fancy?" Viola asked.

"It is possible." There was a look in his eyes—

"Not me!" she said, frowning at him. He had an eyebrow raised, but when she looked at it, he stopped.

The duke had a brooding, rawboned face, but it transformed when he smiled.

Viola could feel her cheeks glowing, and she instinctively looked away, feeling flustered and uncomfortable.

And slightly mad, as if she were on the edge of a cliff, deciding whether to jump off. Of course she wouldn't jump. She was someone who was attuned to danger above all. Who avoided powerful men. Who was—perhaps not in love with a vicar, but—

Could it be that she had chosen Mr. Marlowe because he was unthreatening?

She looked back at the duke, and discovered that he'd stopped smiling, but he was still looking at her. Waiting.

She got the feeling he wasn't used to waiting for anything.

Of course, dukes never *waited*. That would imply that they put someone else before themselves: someone else's wishes or needs above their own.

Years of feeling that she was insignificant rushed into her mind and stiffened her backbone. She must be misreading the situation.

The music drew to a close, and she dropped into a deep curtsy. The duke bowed and bent to her ear. "May I pay you a call tomorrow?"

She gulped. Words fluttered around in her head and refused to line up in proper order. His eyes searched hers in the silence, and that devastating smile appeared again, crinkling the corners of his eyes and making him . . .

Irresistible.

"Or take you for a carriage ride?"

"I think it would be better if you spent time with a young lady whom you might woo," Viola said.

"Viola," Joan called.

She dropped into another curtsy, forgetting she'd already done so.

When Viola raised her head, the look in the duke's eyes made her feel as if her skin was too tight for her body.

There was a wordless moment in which they just looked at each other until Viola pivoted on her heel and hurried toward the door.

Chapter Eleven

$\mathcal{B}$y the end of the week, the Duke of Wynter had sent several bouquets of violets and paid two morning calls, both of which Viola had avoided by running up the stairs the moment his card was presented by the butler.

"You cannot avoid him at dinner tonight," Joan pointed out gleefully. She was absolutely delighted by the fact that the most eligible bachelor of the Season seemed to be making a determined effort to woo Viola. No matter how Viola protested that she would make a terrible duchess, Joan had begun dropping into deep curtsies at the slightest pretext, addressing Viola as "Your Grace."

In fact, to Viola's horror, the younger Wildes had taken up the practice, and she couldn't even pop her head into the nursery without Erik bowing until his head almost touched his knees while chortling himself sick.

Tonight they were bid to dinner at Sir Reginald's townhouse, an invitation that explicitly included Mr. Marlowe, and apparently Miss Pettigrew and her mother as well. Viola wanted to attend, of course, since Mr. Marlowe would be there. Viola's mother had promptly sent her regrets, and Aunt Knowe was again enlisted as chaperone, although she told them flatly that she meant to stay on the other side of the room from Mrs. Pettigrew.

"Once you're a duchess, you'll be able to refuse invitations with impunity," Joan said mischievously.

Viola turned away from the mirror and shook her head. "I've told you a million times that the duke isn't truly interested in me."

But she wasn't entirely sure.

"We wouldn't suit," she said more firmly. "Hazel agrees."

It was a warmish evening, and the first thing Viola saw was that Sir Reginald had opened the doors that led to the gardens. Outside was a line of tall torches, apparently warding off any evening chill. The fire danced against the darkening sky, making the garden look more intimate than the drawing room itself.

Viola was wearing one of Lavinia's designs, a gown made from pale rose silk with cream lace that wrapped around her bosom. Perhaps it was her imagination, but Miss Pettigrew's lips pursed, and her eyes seemed to fasten on Viola's chest as they greeted each other.

Were vicars' wives required to wear black, a version of a female cassock? Miss Pettigrew hadn't a hint of skin showing below her collarbone. She turned away with a final, condemning glance at Viola's bodice.

Joan dropped a curtsy and trotted over to Otis on the other side of the room, sitting in a group of young people that included Caitlin, but Sir Reginald caught

Viola's arm and steered her, the Pettigrews, and Mr. Marlowe to a group of chairs, calling, "Nephew, come with us and talk to Mr. Marlowe about that idea of yours."

Sir Reginald's matchmaking attempts were not subtle. Even if Viola hadn't overheard him urging his nephew to court the mouse, she could have guessed his intent from the way he bade Wynter be seated while pointing directly to the cushion beside Viola.

Aunt Knowe rolled her eyes and strolled off to join Joan.

The duke obeyed, sitting down next to Viola on the sofa, so close that their shoulders touched. "How are you, Miss Astley?" he asked.

"I am very well, thank you," she said, rearranging her skirts. It was surely imagination that led her to feel the warmth of his body next to her.

The butler appeared with a glass of sherry for Viola. "Would you like another glass, Your Grace?"

"Yes, I would," Wynter said. "Good evening, Miss Pettigrew. I believe I've met your father, the bishop, recently."

"My father counts among his acquaintances the highest in the land," said Miss Pettigrew, giving the duke a lavish smile with little relation to the pinched greeting she gave Viola. She sipped her sherry, frowned, and put it down.

"The Bishop of London is an excellent connection for you, Mr. Marlowe," Sir Reginald said. "My nephew tells me that you spent a few years as curate at St. Wilfrid's."

Viola had a strong feeling from the way Sir Reginald was eyeing Mr. Marlowe's golden hair that he felt a vicar ought to powder his hair, if not wear a wig. But Mr. Marlowe had once shared his equally strong feeling that flour that could feed the poor shouldn't be wasted to fabricate wig powder.

As Miss Pettigrew took it upon herself to confirm both her parentage and Mr. Marlowe's previous position, Viola turned to the duke.

"Shoo," she whispered. "Take yourself off, if you please."

"And allow you to make a cake of yourself ogling the vicar? Better you look at me, even if you are scowling at the moment."

"You are drawing attention," Viola explained.

Wynter glanced about, and Joan and her friends instantly looked elsewhere. A perfect storm of chatter rose.

"You see?" Viola asked. "Now they're talking of us."

"Why do you care?"

"Don't ask such a foolish question."

"I truly desire to know."

"They may come to the conclusion that you are courting me," Viola whispered. "We both know that isn't the case. Please don't encourage their attention. And while we're on the subject, why on earth did you send me flowers?"

"Let them talk," Wynter said, his lip curling in a truly ducal fashion. "I shall send you or any other woman in London flowers every day if I wish to."

"You should be across the room searching for a bride. I am not a real Wilde, as you yourself said," Viola reminded him.

"I was not in possession of essential information when I said that," the duke said. "Besides, I need to speak to Marlowe. I have a proposition for him."

A proposition?

Before she could ask what he meant, Sir Reginald pulled them into a conversation about the art of growing rhododendrons, a topic on which Miss Pettigrew seemed to have a great deal of information. Since Sir Reginald fancied himself an expert—said expertise gained by hiring the best gardeners—the conversation quickly grew animated.

Having no interest in shrubs, Devin sat silently beside Viola. He kept an eye on her to see if she was gawking at the vicar, but she was lost in thought. She was the sort of person who didn't have to be entertained at all times.

She appeared to be listening intently, for instance, but anyone who knew her could tell that she was far away, thinking of something else.

Rather more disturbing, to his mind, was the fact that Mr. Marlowe's eyes kept straying to Viola's gentle face, inspecting her thickly fringed eyes—at least, he did until Devin caught his attention and gave him a direct look.

"Wynter, you are not listening," his uncle complained.

"Please forgive me."

"Miss Pettigrew was remarking on my rhododendrons, which Miss Astley has never seen in bloom. You must escort Miss Astley to see them."

"They are remarkable, even at this time of year," Miss Pettigrew allowed.

"It's dark outside," Viola observed.

"My torches throw off more than enough light," Devin's uncle said proudly. "You should examine them, my dear. The pedestals are brass and highly ornate, made from my own design, I don't mind saying."

Viola had given Devin a few commanding glances in the time since he'd met her, but Miss Pettigrew's stare was extraordinary. She would be a natural governess for a royal nursery. No matter how entitled the children, she'd keep them in order.

She couldn't have said more clearly that Devin was to take the irritating young lady away with him. Apparently, Miss Pettigrew had noticed that Viola was offering some competition.

"Of course," Devin said, coming to his feet and holding out his hand to Viola. "May I escort you to the window, Miss Astley?"

"Oh, not the *window*," his uncle said. "Take her outside, Wynter. That's why I left the doors open to the garden. The torches are lit, as you can see, and there are wraps out there as well. As long as you don't leave the terrace, we'll consider you chaperoned." He airily waved his hand in that direction.

Viola put her sherry down and Devin took her hand, helping her to rise. He walked her past all the other guests. Viola was mumbling words under her breath, and Devin had the feeling they might be phrases considered improper for a young lady.

An unusual wish to laugh rose in his chest.

"We were as good as a circus exhibit, given the ogling we inspired," he said, once they neared the open doors leading to the garden. "Yet you don't appear to have turned green from the stress of entertaining an audience. Should nausea overtake you, we could duck behind a bush."

She darted a look at him. "Believe it or not, I am too irritated for nausea."

They walked out onto the terrace and she stopped. "Why, it's warmer outside than in!"

At even intervals down the terrace, tall brass oil torches warmed the air.

"My uncle saw these in India years ago, and had his own version fashioned here."

He led her around to the left, out of view of the occupants of the drawing room.

Viola peered over the marble balustrade at the shrubs below. "Are those rhododendrons?"

"One has to assume," Devin said. He leaned against the balustrade, which came to his lower hip, crossed his arms, and looked at Viola. He was very aware of how much he liked to look at her, especially in a gown that allowed a great deal of her to be admired.

"Are you chilled?" he asked, thinking that he ought to be more gentlemanly.

"Not at all. Now everyone is speculating about us," Viola burst out, in clear frustration. "I wouldn't have obeyed your uncle, except . . ."

"Miss Pettigrew," Devin said. "The lady does not appreciate your admiration of her fiancé. Or perhaps his of you."

She gave him a cool look. "That is an improper subject for conversation. Speaking of which, I want to apologize for my impoliteness the night of the ball. I was provoked, but I shouldn't have lost my temper. You didn't know I was eavesdropping, after all, and you have a right to your opinion about my parentage."

"I was mistaken," Devin said. "You are clearly a *real* Wilde."

"Why do you say so?"

"Because no one else would have dared rebuke me," he said frankly.

She smiled at that, and Devin had a queer feeling, as if he'd had a gulp of champagne straight out of the bottle.

"We can forge a friendship," she suggested. "After all, we both fled my debut ball, albeit for different reasons."

"Hmm," Devin said.

"There's something very reassuring about you," Viola said. "Have your friends remarked on your calm?"

"I have few friends," Devin said bluntly. "I was schooled at home, and I was already a duke by the time most men went to university. I hadn't the time to join them."

"No friends?" She looked appalled.

"I have cousins," he said, not liking the sympathy in her eyes. He patted the flat marble that topped the balustrade. "Otis and I used to sit here and play jackstones for hours." That would be when Devin had been dispatched to his uncle's house because his father was in a fit of homicidal rage, though he hadn't understood that as a child.

"I shall be your friend," Viola said, her voice so warm that he blinked at her. "I'm very good at friendship, although you'll have to try to be less haughty. For example, when I arrived here for tea a few days ago, Miss Belluce had a desperate expression and you looked bored."

"She had been talking about a baby monkey for at least fifteen minutes," he said flatly. "I *was* bored."

"You may feel that way, but you can't show it. It's impolite. I don't mean to lecture you as if I haven't personal failings," she added. "I am trying to better myself, but I am prone to jealousy, for example."

"Of the Wildes?"

"Well, yes. This *is* an odd conversation, isn't it? Were you jealous of your cousins since they had each other, and you are, I gather, an only child?"

Devin didn't care to think about his childhood; he said nothing.

"I wasn't jealous until I realized that I didn't belong in the family," Viola said, wrinkling her nose.

"You do belong." He didn't know why he was certain, but he was. "I suppose we could be friends."

He knew damned well that he didn't want to be merely friends with her. Not when lust coursed through him every time their eyes met.

She positively beamed at him. "I shall help you find a wife!"

"I can find my own wife."

"Now, there's an example," Viola said, poking him in the shoulder.

"Of what?"

"You almost looked human before you raised your eyebrow again."

"Eyebrow raising is not a sin," he said.

"It's lazy," she said, surprising him. "Easily done. Bred into the bloodline of dukes and the like. It's much harder to actually put into words what you are feeling. I gather you don't want me to choose your wife, and I understand your reservations. After all, your uncle knows you far better than I, and he made an obvious error."

Or not.

It was shocking, but Devin realized that his uncle—

the closest thing he had to a true father—had known precisely whom to choose for his bride. "I may not know much about friendship, but I believe it involves propinquity."

"What?"

"Closeness. Conversing on a regular basis. Rides in Hyde Park and a dance now and again. In short, people may conclude that I am courting you, and you seem to dislike that idea," he pointed out. "I called on you twice, and you pretended not to be home."

"How did you know I was pretending?"

He grinned at her. "Joan told me you were in hiding."

Viola turned a little pink. "We would have to disabuse people of the notion that your morning calls reflect more than friendship. You must find a lady to woo without further ado. The Season is only a few months long."

"Is this haste required by my elderly status?" he asked.

She wrinkled her nose at him. "You were irritating, and I couldn't resist saying that. But of course you're not elderly. Just a trifle older than the twenty-year-old gentlemen whom one usually meets."

"I've two more years before I'm thirty," he said evenly.

"Thirty or no, you don't want to attend another Season, any more than I do. We've scarcely been here a half hour, and my toes already hurt."

Devin glanced down. Peeking from under Viola's full skirts were pointed shoes with exuberant pompoms. Naturally enough, her feet were as neat and small as the rest of her. "They are very pretty," he said, meaning her feet.

"I should be rejoicing that I don't feel nauseated," she said, obviously following her own train of thought. "The fear of my debut terrorized me for years, and now I find myself annoyed instead of seasick." She threw him a helpless look. "You must think me a complete widgeon because I'm not even sure who I'm annoyed at: myself, Miss Pettigrew, your uncle . . ."

Everything in his belly tightened at the way her lips pursed. That, and the way she was treating him, not like an eligible duke, but something far dearer. He could feel desire settling in his spine.

He suspected it was a life-long condition.

"Since your feet hurt, would you like to sit?" he asked, noting that his voice had deepened, and trusting that she was too busy glaring at her shoes to notice.

"There aren't any chairs, and besides, we should return to the drawing room."

"You could sit on the balustrade," he suggested, patting the wide marble slab. He picked up one of the cashmere wraps that his uncle stacked about. "We used to sit on these to play jackstones if it was cold."

Viola's eyes searched his face. "It's hard to imagine you a boy. Were you any good at jackstones?"

"Not particularly, but I enjoyed the game," he replied. "I haven't played since my father died."

"How old were you?"

"Old enough to stop playing games. Sixteen."

Viola's eyes were hazel-colored, with green flecks, and at the moment they were full of sympathy. Devin couldn't decide how he felt about that. He was starting to think that Viola was prone to fits of pity. In fact, it was possible that her affection for Marlowe stemmed from pity due to his objectionable betrothal.

No, that was absurd. Viola had an infatuation for the man, one shared by most of the young ladies inside, as far as he could tell.

"I'm afraid I'm too short to hop onto the balustrade," Viola said. She cast him a rueful glance. "If there's anything that reminds me that I'm not a Wilde, it's my lack of height."

"I dislike tall women."

"You do?"

"Absolutely." It was a new opinion, but nonetheless firmly held. He moved a fraction of an inch closer. "I could easily lift you. We've only been outside for a few minutes. If we return directly, my uncle will consider me to have failed to make a proper attempt to woo you. That will lead him to push us together again. Stubbornness is a family trait."

"Somehow I am unsurprised to hear that," she said, giving him a grin. "At my ball, I thought you'd never stop insisting that you'd wanted to take me to supper."

"You had your revenge by handing me over to Lady Caitlin," he said. "May I?"

She glanced down at his hands, not touching her, but ready.

He thought there was a good chance that he would *always* be ready to hold her.

"Only because my toes hurt," she allowed.

His hands closed around Viola's waist and he lifted her to the balustrade in one sure movement. Her trim waist had no need of a corset. And she was as light as a feather.

There would never be that awkward moment when— He cut off that thought. She was a proper young lady. Marital relations took place in a horizontal position in the dark.

She gave a sigh of pleasure and wiggled her toes. "Your uncle is very amusing, isn't he? I can tell that he cares for you very much."

Devin nodded.

He was enjoying a heady bout of lust that a gentleman was never supposed to experience for a lady.

And he hadn't, even during that appalling *affaire* he'd had a few years ago. Now, looking at Viola's shining eyes, he couldn't imagine what he'd been thinking. A man couldn't be forced to marry a widow, of course. But Annabel had known perfectly well that as a man of honor, he wouldn't have allowed her reputation to be ruined. What if he had married her, and then met Viola?

The thought gave him a sense of what Viola must feel like when she described being "seasick."

Annabel had begun an *affaire* with him, presenting herself as a widow with no wish for a husband. But she'd entrapped him—or tried to—and after that he had even less desire to go into society than he'd had before.

"What are you thinking about?" Viola asked. "That was a fearsome scowl."

"A bad memory," he said.

"Where did it take place?"

"At a ball."

She wrinkled her nose. "Funny, my worst memory took place at a ball too. Well . . . not the worst. Worst would be the memorial service for my oldest stepbrother, Horatius."

"I'm sorry. I remember meeting him."

"You probably didn't like him," she said, resigned. "He was somewhat pompous. But he was lovely to all of us in the nursery. He would come up to play pirates, with costumes and an eye patch."

That was definitely the best thing Devin had ever heard about the stuffy heir to the Lindow duchy. "In that case, I'm doubly sorry that he passed away," he said.

"What happened to you at a ball?"

"I would prefer to hear what happened to you."

"You can guess," she said. "I threw up. Are you sure you want to be friends with me? I have a perilous habit of losing my breakfast."

"Yes, I am sure," he said.

Viola had powdered her hair, of course, but just around her face he could see little wisps of golden-brown curls. "You have freckles," he said.

"A few," she said, shrugging. "I know you're supposed to hate them, but I don't."

Devin discovered that he didn't hate them either.

Chapter Twelve

$\mathcal{V}$iola ought to be back in the drawing room, whispering *Wilde Child* to herself under her breath. But it was relaxing to be with Devin.

"Now what kind of wife should we find you?" she asked, beaming at him. "I have to tell you that there aren't many dukes' daughters in England, let alone unmarried and attending the Season. Are you prepared to stoop to the offspring of an earl?"

He was lounging against the balustrade, looking at her from heavy-lidded eyes.

She gave him a poke. "Stop that."

"What?"

"Looking at me like that. Joan would call those lascivious eyes," she said with certainty. "In your case, it probably means that you aren't horrendously bored, but you need to practice another gaze."

The edge of his mouth eased upward. "Like this?"

He gave her a look of foolish adoration.

"At least that's more respectful," she said, hooting with laughter. "Although if you give Caitlin that look, she'll take it as encouragement."

The duke grimaced. "Is she obsessed by cats, or was that just my impression?"

"She is very fond of felines," Viola said. "Perhaps her name led to her interest in them. I think she has two or three cats."

"I can answer that after the endless supper at your ball," the duke said. "She has three cats named Wynken, Blynken, and Nod after the nursery rhyme. She also has a collection of ceramic felines. I will never marry a person who collects objects of any kind." He frowned and looked at her. "Though I suppose I could be convinced. Do you have any collections?"

"No, but my pet crow, Barty, does. He has a terrible habit of stealing bright shiny objects."

"Hairpins?"

"Oh, hairpins would be fine," Viola said, laughing. "We found a diamond earring in his cage after a harvest ball at Lindow, and no one had the faintest idea whose it could be. He was terribly affronted when we took it away. He adores one of my sisters-in-law, Lavinia, because she has a ready stock of spangles and never fails to bring him a new one."

"Lavinia's husband is a friend of mine," Wynter said. "I can well imagine that she would share her spangles with your crow." He paused and then said, "My father was a collector, which means that he was more akin to a crow stockpiling spangles than to Lavinia."

His jaw had tightened, and Viola decided that he must have truly disliked his father. "I presume the late duke didn't steal other people's jewelry?" she asked. "The way the Earl of Kimp plans to steal a gargoyle, and the way that Barty steals buttons?"

"People were generally willing to hand over their wheelbarrow for a sovereign or two," Wynter said. "But I believe that if the late duke had seen an unusual barrow standing on its own, he would have absconded with it."

"*Wheelbarrow?*"

"We have fifty-five. I keep them in the country," he said.

"Why on earth would His Grace have wanted that number?"

"Some have a wheel in the middle and others have wheels at one end," he said. "One comes from China, and several from Rome. If you have a need for garden equipment, I could give you a wheelbarrow. Or five."

She gurgled with laughter. "I think the gardens at Lindow have no shortage of their own carts. Was your father's collection limited to wheelbarrows?"

"I have a large number of statues of Greek deities fashioned from marble, a room full of stuffed birds, and another filled with chiming clocks."

"You mustn't let your future wife know about the collections when you're courting her," Viola said. "A room full of stuffed birds?" She wrinkled her nose. "Next you'll tell me that he was collecting butterflies. I cannot abide people who think it is worthwhile to kill animals merely for display."

His eyelids flickered.

"He did!" Viola cried.

"My father wasn't a kindly man," the duke said, as casually as if he had remarked on the weather. "I'll take your advice, though, and rid the estate of his collections before I bring home a bride."

"You could keep a wheelbarrow," Viola suggested. "And perhaps one or two Greek gods, if they are the good ones. In the nursery, we preferred Roman gods."

"I've never looked closely enough to assess their characters."

"Where do you keep the pantheon?"

"In my library."

"You need a wife who doesn't bore you into retreating to the library to contemplate ancient history."

"I am the sort of man who is often found in the library by choice," he said. "Do you think that poses a problem to marital harmony?"

"It would for Joan," Viola said. "After our debut was delayed for a year, I thought she might spontaneously combust, since there is nothing she loves more than going to an event every night, if not two or three. She distracted herself by flirting with every unattached gentleman who walked through the castle gates, calling it practice."

"I am very glad that I didn't pay a visit to Lindow Castle in the last few years," the duke said.

The tone in his voice rang unmistakably true.

Which was reassuring.

It wasn't that Viola thought that Wynter had any real resemblance to the duke from her first ball, but like that gentleman, he was very large.

He said he liked short women—remarkable!—but *she* had always avoided tall men.

Yet there was something delectable about being lifted into the air with no more strain than she might lift Barty to her knee. The duke seemed to understand how much she disliked craning her neck to look up during a conversation.

"You planned to marry Joan," Viola reminded him. "You could have met her last year and never donned that rose-covered coat until your wedding."

"If I'd come to the castle last year, would I have met you?"

She shook her head. "Not unless you somehow found your way to the cowshed."

"The cowshed?"

She gave him a sheepish grin. "I have two pet cows, Cleopatra and Daisy. You like to be in the library; I like to be in the cowshed."

"A library smells a good deal sweeter," he observed.

"Daisy and Cleopatra live like queens," Viola admitted. "Fresh straw morning and night."

He laughed. "You'll be an expensive wife if every cow you encounter warrants the same treatment."

"Gowns and jewels are truly expensive," she said. "A cowshed is a modest expense. Not much more than the shelter for a collection of wheelbarrows."

Wynter was looking down at Viola in a way that made her feel peculiar in the stomach—but not as if she might throw up. Instead she felt warm and prickly.

He wasn't beautiful, the way Mr. Marlowe was.

But he was . . . he was something.

Grand, maybe. He was grand, in all the meanings of the word.

He was leaning one hip against the balustrade she was seated on, turned toward her. His features were far more rough-hewn than those of the men in the Wilde family—let alone Mr. Marlowe's—and yet she discovered that she was beginning to like them.

"Why is your nose crooked?" she asked. "It gives you the air of a boxer."

One side of his mouth hitched up. "Fell off my pony at age three."

"Three! Three is very young to be on the back of a horse, even a small one."

"I didn't ride; I fell off directly. My father was certain that I would manifest his riding skills early, since I was his only son. Only child, in fact."

"What does that have to do with it?" Viola asked. "My mother loves to ride, but I am a wretched coward and find myself clutching the horse's mane and squealing like a piglet."

"Somehow I doubt that."

His eyes smiled at her.

Viola pushed away the tingling response she had to that particular gaze. "Don't disbelieve it," she told him. "I'm a pathetic horsewoman. One of the many ways that I'm not suited to being a noblewoman."

"What are the others?"

"I can't sing. I can't embroider either. I can unpick knitting, mostly because my Aunt Knowe is good at tangling it, but I haven't much interest in making scarves, let alone complicated things such as mitts. I like to read, but that's a solitary pursuit."

"Are you any good at mathematics?"

"Absolutely not. The first time I threw up in public was when we had an end-of-the-year mathematics examination coming up."

"I'm no good at singing, embroidering, or knitting either," the duke said. "I don't read novels, but I do like mathematics." He leaned closer. "I like you."

Viola rolled her eyes. "Irrelevant."

"Why irrelevant? Because of the vicar?"

"No," she said hastily. "Because you're searching for a duchess, remember? Even if you can't find the daughter of a duke, you must marry a noble-woman who will be an appropriate match. I'm not a candidate."

"You could be."

"No, I couldn't. I'm short and ordinary. It's ridiculous that you thought golden hair qualified a duchess for the portrait gallery but—"

"I was being an ass," he interjected.

"I—" She cut herself off.

His eyes glinted with amusement. "Agree with me, do you?"

"Never," she said, unable to stop herself from smiling at him.

"I don't think you're ordinary," he said.

Viola's breath caught. If . . . if it had been Joan sitting on this balustrade, she might have thought that he was planning to kiss her.

Joan had described any number of kisses over the last three years. It was positively astonishing how often gentlemen stole kisses when a young lady's chaperone wasn't in direct view.

Aunt Knowe was nowhere in sight.

The Duke of Wynter was leaning closer to her, with a look in his eyes . . .

Viola had no idea how to kiss anyone. Joan had said there was more to it than pressing lips together, but she had never elaborated—and Viola had seen no need for more information.

She panicked, slid off the balustrade, and landed on her sore toes. "Time to go back inside," she said, as the duke's hand curled around her elbow to steady her. "Even Sir Reginald can't think that I am capable of admiring the rhododendrons for much longer than this."

Wynter murmured something, and she walked past him, her heart galloping. She must have been wrong. Why would the duke wish to kiss *her*?

The first thing she saw when she entered the room was Caitlin smiling at Mr. Marlowe with longing in her eyes. It was a little embarrassing, to be frank.

Surely she, Viola, hadn't displayed her affection so obviously?

She suspected that perhaps she had, which led to the sudden revelation that she wouldn't be happy if her husband had women hanging on his every word. Viola definitely didn't want to join the crowd around Mr. Marlowe. She felt a deep reluctance to sit at his feet, awaiting crumbs of wisdom.

If *she* were married to Mr. Marlowe, she would help him in his work. Not fawn on him.

Had Joan been betrothed to Mr. Marlowe, she would have swept Caitlin a look of Wildean disdain. But Viola? Short, inconspicuous Viola? She wouldn't be able to ward off Mr. Marlowe's admirers. For her entire life, she would have to get used to her husband smiling kindly at besotted women and assuring them that "Providence would provide."

After all, that was what a vicar did.

That was his job.

A hand took her elbow, and Wynter said, "Otis is sitting with Lady Joan. Shall we join them? I said that I have few friends, but I am proud to count Otis among them."

"Certainly," she said.

"I'll summon Marlowe to join us," he added, "because I do have a proposition for him, and it involves Otis as well."

She walked with the duke toward her sister, ignoring all the knowing eyes that followed them. Soon enough, the duke would begin courting a future duchess, and society would realize that the two of them were merely friends.

It was very friendly of him to create an opportunity for her to talk to Mr. Marlowe.

She wasn't sure how she felt about that, to be honest.

Was Wynter convinced she ought to marry the vicar? Obviously he hadn't been planning to kiss her. It was all in her imagination. Thank goodness, she hadn't humiliated herself by closing her eyes or leaning toward him.

"Were you introduced to a young lady with whom you'd like better acquaintance?" she asked him. "I know everyone here. Petunia is an earl's daughter. I can easily bring her to join us."

"No, thank you," Wynter said.

"Because she's an earl's daughter, instead of a duke's? You may have to lower your standards," she observed. "Or rather, your father's standards."

"Hmm," the duke said, steering her toward an empty settee next to Joan.

She'd noticed that he had a habit of avoiding questions that he didn't care to answer.

"You are somewhat irritating," Viola observed.

"My relatives tell me as much on a regular basis," His Grace said, smiling down at her. "Dukes are raised to be stubborn, perhaps because we have our own way most of the time."

"Aunt Knowe would say that one's upbringing was no excuse," she told him.

"Lady Knowe strikes me as a most formidable woman. I disagree with her. Parentage is irrelevant but upbringing is not."

His comment reminded Viola of the way he had described her as a stray child thrown into the Lindow nursery and tolerated for practicality's sake, but she kept her mouth shut. They were friends, but that didn't mean she could point out every idiotic notion the man voiced.

Or at least, not in the first forty-eight hours of friendship.

Tonight Otis was wearing a bright purple waistcoat with scalloped edging. Joan was seated opposite him, and somewhat to Viola's surprise, she had the jaunty look that she wore with family, instead of the seductive smile she wielded around eligible gentlemen.

"Thank you for joining us, Miss Astley," Otis said. "We are refugees from the lively battle going on between my father and Miss Pettigrew."

"About rhododendrons?" Viola asked.

"Actually, my father is currently engaged in a losing battle, trying to persuade Miss Pettigrew that private dramatics are great fun. Which they are, but she will never agree."

"She hadn't yet declared that they are the work of the devil," Joan said, "but it's a matter of time. I think the only reason she has restrained herself is due to our host's passion for them. Just look how pink her cheeks are."

"My father loves nothing more than putting on a play," Otis said. Then he brightened. "Now that I'm no longer a cleric, I shall tread the boards! Though our plays are performed only for close friends, needless to say."

"Last summer we went to a house party where we performed *The Man of Mode*," Joan said. "You would have made an excellent Dorimant."

"The rake? Not I," Otis said. "I'd have been Sir Fopling Flutter, the Man of Mode himself." He twitched the hem of his brightly colored waistcoat. "I have a weakness for fine clothing."

"Why are you biting your lip?" Wynter asked Viola quietly.

"I feel guilty," she said. "I suspect that Miss Pettigrew's high emotion stems from my suggestion that Mr. Marlowe stage a cycle of biblical plays."

She heard a choking sound, and frowned at the duke. "What is funny about that, pray?"

"You do realize that most vicars turn white at the very mention of a stage?" he asked.

"Mr. Marlowe considered it an interesting idea worth consideration," she said stoutly. "Your own cousin, Mr. Murgatroyd, was a vicar, and he just said that he takes great pleasure in private dramatics, which are certainly more improper than plays drawn from the Bible."

Otis grinned at her. "I was only a vicar for a few weeks, and my delight in dramatics was yet another sign that I wasn't suited to a cassock. Do you suppose that you could call me Otis? Mr. Murgatroyd is such a mouthful and it reminds me of my father."

"We should all be on a first-name basis, since we are friends," the duke said unexpectedly. He looked at Viola. "Don't you agree?"

"That would be scandalous," Joan said with obvious delight. "Otis, it's a pleasure to meet you. Your Grace?"

"Devin," he said to her.

Viola knew that her mother and stepfather were unusual in addressing each other by first names. And they were married! She didn't know what to say. Joan was always the first to leap into something improper, but Viola was wary of ending up in the scandal sheets.

"We *are* friends," the duke repeated.

"Just look at that," Otis put in. "Devin hasn't had to plead with anyone to get his way since he shaped his first word."

"All right," Viola said reluctantly.

"I can't wait to call you Devin in front of all those duke-hunting young ladies," Joan told the duke. "Oh, and in case you're worried, I am *not* interested in becoming your duchess. I won't use our apparent intimacy to force you to the altar."

"I'm grateful to hear it," he replied, looking supremely unconcerned.

"To go back to our original conversation," Otis said, "I've had some painful conversations with Bishop Pettigrew in the last few months, and can say with fair certainty that he won't approve of theatrics in the church, whether the plays depict biblical events or no."

"Miss Pettigrew doesn't even approve of Christmas pantomimes," Joan put in.

"For hundreds of years, people in local parishes performed plays depicting biblical events," Viola protested. "The plays depict the Bible in such a way that young and old can understand. What better way for children to learn?"

"Hundreds of years?" Devin asked, a distinctly skeptical note in his voice.

"They are called mystery plays. All the larger towns such as York had their own cycle of plays. We read some of them at school. The bakers would act the story of Jesus creating loaves of bread, for example."

"I remember a funny one about Noah's ark," Otis put in.

"I would love to play a queen," Joan cried. "The costumes would be marvelous."

"Alas, there are few queens in the Bible," Otis pointed out.

"There's always Bathsheba," Joan said mischievously.

Viola winced. She recognized the look in her step-sister's eyes. From time to time, Joan was prone to a fit of recklessness. At school, it would invariably lead to a scolding for nonladylike behavior, which would only drive Joan to be more provocative.

"Bathsheba, whom King David saw bathing, and fell in love with?" Devin asked.

"I think it would be great fun to put a lady in a bath on stage," Joan said, her eyes twinkling. "If Viola instructed him to do it, Mr. Marlowe would be out looking for a tin tub right now."

"I don't remember a cycle play about Bathsheba," Otis said, showing no signs of shock at Joan's suggestion. "Who would have staged it? The watermen?"

"Obviously, the ladies of the evening," Joan exclaimed, bursting into laughter.

Joan was being provocative for the sake of it, likely because she had been irritated by Miss Pettigrew. She adored private dramatics, and the family all knew that she dreamed of running away and joining a theater troupe.

Not that she would, because it was one thing to address a duke by his first name, and quite another to perform on a public stage. Joan would be ruined.

"There's a sweet play about the two shepherds who first saw the star," Viola put in, grateful that Aunt Knowe was out of earshot and didn't hear Joan talking about ladies of the evening. "A Christmas play would be a marvelous way to draw people into the church."

Otis grinned. "You're a revolutionary, Viola. Who could have imagined? You look so demure."

"What I am suggesting is traditional, and certainly not revolutionary," Viola said stoutly. "Many children never learn biblical history. Take the play of Noah's ark, for example. Who could possibly object to that?"

The duke's dark eyes were smiling, even if his face was as imperturbable as ever. "You might be surprised."

"A play could be performed for charity," she argued. "My family would come, and they would bring others. Tickets could be sold at a steep price too, perhaps making enough money to support orphans or do other good works."

"How will the poor children in need of education afford a ticket?" the duke asked.

"A second performance, the next night," Viola said, caught up in her vision. "Real animals could join Noah on the stage."

"One of your pet cows?"

"You have a pet *cow*?" Otis exclaimed.

"And a crow," Viola said, nodding. "I brought my crow, Barty, to London, but obviously London is no place for livestock."

"Not unless they're on their way to being made into beefsteak," Otis agreed. "Were I still the vicar, I could have a temporary stage built in St. Wilfrid's cloister large enough for the dramatic debut of one cow, though perhaps not two."

"Daisy and Cleopatra are not great travelers," Viola said, smiling. "Would you settle for a crow instead?"

"Absolutely!" Otis cried. "We just need a few more animals to put on Noah's ark at St. Wilfrid's. The parishioners would be thrilled."

Aunt Knowe swept in the circle and sat beside Viola, the feathers on her wig waving in the air like the plumes atop an outlandish chicken. "What are you all discussing?"

"My idea for a biblical play cycle," Viola said, moving closer to the duke, so that Aunt Knowe's voluminous panniers wouldn't crush her gown. "My stepfather was somewhat disapproving when I suggested it," she told the others. "Aunt Knowe wasn't entirely in favor either."

"I didn't know it was your idea at that point," her aunt reminded her.

"Noah's ark would have been a clue," Devin said dryly.

Lady Knowe shook her head. "Don't encourage her, Your Grace. People think that Viola is sweet-tempered, but sometimes I think she is the most obstinate of the children who grew up in the ducal nursery."

"A performance of Noah's ark, with the proceeds given to charity," Otis put in.

"I agree," Devin stated.

Viola could tell that the duke was enjoying himself, and she liked it when he looked happy. Because they were friends, she told herself hastily. Good friends. Just look how supportive Devin was being regarding her play cycle.

Mr. Marlowe had been far less confident that her idea had merit. Just now, the vicar was across the room, talking animatedly with Lady Caitlin while Miss Pettigrew sat silently, watching the pair of them.

Viola felt another stab of sympathy for the lady. This couldn't be a pleasant occasion for her.

The duke followed her gaze. "No going over there," he said in a low voice. "You are the one who instructed me not to appear desperate, don't you remember? He must come to you."

Joan and Otis had launched into a lively exchange with Aunt Knowe about the best plays currently being performed in London.

Viola wrinkled her nose at Devin. "You are the opposite of desperate since you appear to be completely uninterested in finding a bride! I count at least five eligible young ladies with whom you could be speaking, not including my sister."

"Joan is too excitable for me," Devin said, without a trace of apology in his voice. "She is very talkative. Have you noticed?"

"Her conversation is enthralling," Viola said firmly. "She's my best friend, and you mustn't be critical."

The duke waggled his eyebrows. "See how I'm moving both of them at the same time?"

She nodded.

"It's less lazy than moving just one," he informed her. "But you can take the emotion for granted."

"Irony? Sarcasm? Wit? Men of your sort use The Eyebrow for everything," Viola said. "I've been cataloguing the effect for years."

"Men 'of my sort'?" His voice shaded cool.

"Oh, dear, did you think that you were entirely original among men of wealth and consequence?"

He gave her a thoughtful look. "On the whole, yes."

"It's a masculine failing," Viola told him. "You all think that you're unique, when in fact you are remarkably similar."

He gave her a lopsided smile. "I assure you that I have virtually nothing in common with Otis, and we share a grandfather."

They both looked at Otis, who was arguing with Joan, hands waving, eyes bright with laughter.

"Your cousin is charming," Viola said.

"I am not." The duke stood, and for a moment Viola thought that she'd hurt his feelings, but he was looking down at her with his usual calm demeanor. "I shall separate Mr. Marlowe from his flock and bring him here, if you'll excuse me."

She nodded, and he strode across the room.

It was very kind of Devin to aid Viola in her courtship—if that was the appropriate word—of Mr. Marlowe.

Pursuit?

Pursuit was a most unattractive word.

Chapter Thirteen

$\mathcal{A}$ few minutes later, the Duke of Wynter returned with Mr. Marlowe, but without Miss Pettigrew, somewhat to Viola's relief. Mr. Marlowe greeted everyone and sat down beside Joan, giving Devin a questioning glance.

"My cousin wished to speak to you, Mr. Marlowe," Otis said, "because I've left the parish of St. Wilfrid's, where you were once a curate. In fact, I've left the priesthood altogether."

"I'm sorry to hear it," Mr. Marlowe said. Somehow his sympathetic eyes didn't make Viola's heart beat quite as rapidly as before.

"One can only truly be oneself," Otis said cheerfully. "And if oneself is better suited to a purple waistcoat, it is best to discover such a fact quickly."

"Otis and I agree that one area of life in which one must look for sincerity over performance is in the church," Devin said. "And *you*, Mr. Marlowe, are truly devout and an excellent vicar. I should like to offer you the parish of St. Wilfrid's."

Viola blinked. Devin was stealing *her* vicar! Taking him away to another vicarage.

Mr. Marlowe looked as surprised as she felt. "That is a remarkable honor, Your Grace. I'm not sure what to say."

"It's a pretty compliment," Aunt Knowe said, beaming. "You're very young to be in charge of such a large parish."

Viola threw her a jaundiced glance. She wouldn't be surprised if Aunt Knowe hadn't put Devin up to the offer, simply to get Mr. Marlowe out of the Lindow townhouse.

"I have made a commitment to the Duke of Lindow," Mr. Marlowe said, "an obligation to him for one year."

"I can speak for my brother," Aunt Knowe said promptly. "He would never stand in the way of a promotion of this magnitude. St. Wilfrid's is one of the wealthiest parishes in London and well situated too."

Viola was entirely unsurprised by her aunt's evident wish to toss Mr. Marlowe out the door.

"I do have some conditions," Devin said. "Otis has begun improvements to parish life that I support. The parish of St. Wilfrid's must be a true community. Attendance certainly increased in the last few months."

"My cousin refers to the reforms that I instituted to bring people to the church," Otis explained. "I offer sherry after services, for example, which creates a sense of camaraderie."

"A Sunday school run by Lady Caitlin Paget already exists, but Otis laid the ground for a parish school," the duke said. "I wish to encourage education of all kinds, including dramatic performances of biblical events. It is important that knowledge of the Bible is available to all."

Lady Knowe gave Viola a quick glance. One side of her mouth curled up.

For the first time, Mr. Marlowe looked less than enthusiastic. "I enjoyed the liveliness of Miss Astley's proposal," he said, "but I fear that the plays may prove divisive. My concern doesn't spring from the script, which I understand comes from Scripture. My fiancée, for example—"

"Miss Pettigrew's opinion is irrelevant to me," the duke said. His tone was very much "take it or leave it."

"Miss Pettigrew will be happy to learn that the two of you will live in London instead of the wilds of Cheshire," Aunt Knowe said. "Just imagine: Her mother will be only a short carriage ride away. They can join each other for a meal every day."

Mr. Marlowe didn't flinch, which Viola, for one, thought showed great strength of character.

"Miss Pettigrew was a few years ahead of us in school, so she likely read the cycle plays in literature class," Viola suggested.

"No, because she studied rhetoric instead of literature," Joan said, shaking her head.

"How on earth do you know?" Viola asked.

"She was famous for having argued the head-mistress to a standstill."

"What other improvements do you have in mind?" Mr. Marlowe asked hastily.

As the group began to discuss various parish activities—a harvest dinner was suggested by Otis, and given a nod by the duke—Viola lapsed into silence to think over Devin's offer of the parish.

She'd had a sudden realization.

Devin had done this *for her*.

He had realized the difficulty of having one's husband dependent on one's father. He was showing extraordinary thoughtfulness and kindness. In fact, she felt a little weak at the knees realizing just what a good friend he was.

"While I am honored by Your Grace's faith in me," Mr. Marlowe said, catching her attention. "I too have some conditions."

Devin's eyebrow swept into the air but with a glance at Viola, he replaced that expression with one of respectful interest. "I should be happy to consider them."

He overdid it a trifle, but Viola couldn't help whispering, "Bravo!"

"Hair powder is an affront to hungry people who cannot afford flour," Mr. Marlowe stated. "I shall never wear it, and I would hope that the patron of my living would support this decision." He didn't glance at the Duke of Wynter's snowy wig. "I have no expectations that he or other parishioners would follow my practice."

"Of course," the duke said. "I fully support your right not to powder your hair, nor wear a wig."

"I learned during my two years as curate that St. Wilfrid's is a very wealthy parish," Mr. Marlowe said.

"Mayfair is home to most of England's noblemen," Aunt Knowe contributed.

She was looking reluctantly impressed. Viola could have told her that Mr. Marlowe wasn't merely handsome; he was genuinely good. Genuinely concerned about the welfare of his parishioners.

"The parish can support an orphanage," Mr. Marlowe stated. "Were I to become its vicar, I would institute an orphanage to raise and educate abandoned children."

"I'm not sure there are many such children in Mayfair," Devin said, "but I will support it."

"Precisely," Mr. Marlowe said, with a touch of impatience. "The orphanage will not help only those unfortunates who happen to be born within the environs of Mayfair. We must look to the world outside our gilded gates. London is in desperate need of a foundling hospital, but we can start with an orphanage."

A moment of silence followed, during which Viola bit back a smile.

Devin cast her a glance that she couldn't read and said, "I understand, Mr. Marlowe, and I agree."

Viola realized that she'd never before heard the duke address the vicar as "Mr. Marlowe" rather than "Marlowe."

"As do I," Lady Knowe said. "My brother and I will support the orphanage. Moreover, if you put on a biblical play as my niece has suggested, we will guarantee an audience that will establish the building's charitable foundation."

Viola blinked. Had she just been given permission to marry a vicar?

If so, she knew why.

It was not because of Mr. Marlowe's virtue, per se, but because he had stood up to the Duke of Wynter. Because he had ethical standards and he stuck to them.

In short, the only thing standing in the way of her union with Mr. Marlowe was—

Well, Miss Pettigrew.

And Mr. Marlowe. She had to admit that he showed no signs of falling in love with her, even given his kindness in supporting her during her debut ball.

Her eyes went across the room to Miss Pettigrew, sitting extremely upright. Viola knew how difficult it was to sit among exquisite people feeling less attractive.

Perhaps it was immoral to pine for Mr. Marlowe, even if his marriage was likely to be unhappy.

An elbow gently bumped her in the side. "We are planning a visit to the vicarage tomorrow afternoon," Devin informed her. "Otis has been extolling the blue velvet upholstery in the drawing room."

"Of course," Viola said, pulling herself together.

"Lady Knowe would like to investigate whether it would be possible to build an orphanage on the church grounds, and Otis thinks that the cloister could house a temporary stage."

Viola nodded.

"Do you often lose track of conversations?" Devin asked, clearly amused.

She glanced up at him apologetically. "It's a failing of mine. I always seem to be thinking of three things at the same time."

"You truly aren't a candidate for a duchess," he observed.

"No, I'm not." Viola shook her head.

"Not for a vicar's wife either," he said in a low voice.

Her brows drew together.

"Parishioners? Endless meetings with the ladies who sew sheets for the poor, and the ladies who put flowers in the nave, and the ladies who do needlework renditions of Noah's ark? Even longer conversations with irritated ladies offended by the dramatic version of Noah's ark performed for the most virtuous of reasons?"

Sir Reginald's butler was at the door; they all rose. Mr. Marlowe hurried away to escort the Pettigrews.

Devin held out his arm and Viola took it. They led the way into dinner, as Devin had the highest rank in the room.

The very idea should have sent Viola's stomach into knots.

It didn't.

Chapter Fourteen

The following day

*O*tis, Devin, Mr. Marlowe, and the Pettigrews had been invited for tea before the visit to the vicarage, since St. Wilfrid's was a few blocks from the Lindow townhouse.

"Do you ever consider how odd it is that life revolves around *tea*?" Joan asked, as she and Viola walked into the drawing room. "Why not turnips?" She threw her hand dramatically in the air and announced, "The duchess will be receiving at three for a collation of cabbage."

"Polite society is organized around meals," Viola said. "I felt it acutely after I stopped being able to eat among strangers."

Joan paused and gave her a hug. "I'm proud of you."

"You were a tremendous help," Viola said, giving her a kiss on the cheek. "You and your silly *Wilde Child*."

"Did you keep it in mind yesterday while you were walking into dinner on the duke's arm?" Joan asked curiously. "You looked very calm. Ducal, even. Wilde, to be precise."

"Devin wishes to marry a woman from the nobility," Viola reminded her. "My mother married into the nobility, but my father was from the gentry."

Joan broke into laughter.

"What's so funny?" Aunt Knowe called from the settee.

"Silliness," Viola said, leaving Joan behind and walking over to her aunt.

"I adore that walking dress," her aunt exclaimed, looking at Viola from head to foot. "You look particularly delectable this afternoon."

Viola glanced down. It was the third gown she had tried on, if she were honest. She had chosen it because it made her feel important. More than merely a shy woman, a wallflower with a habit of hiding behind the drapes.

The lavender bodice was closely fitted with three large buttons, and the sleeves and neck were trimmed in silver braid. The slight military air made her look powerfully feminine. She wore her hair unpowdered, loose curls pinned around her head with the spangle-topped pins that Barty loved.

"Excellent choice," Aunt Knowe confirmed. She dipped her hand into the voluminous pocket of her *robe à la française* and pulled out a little tin. "I have a gift for you, Viola. I bought it in Soho yesterday."

"It's adorable," Viola said, taking the enameled tin. "Is it perfume?"

"Lip color," Aunt Knowe said, showing her how to flick open the top. Inside was a rosy pink salve. "Joan, do try it. If you like it, I'll send my maid to fetch another for you."

"Excellent!" Joan cried, rubbing her finger against the salve and darting over to the mirror over the fireplace.

Their headmistress's admonishments about the unladylike nature of face paint darted through Viola's mind.

"There's nothing worse than a prude," her aunt said firmly. "I haven't said anything to this date, darling, because I know that you prefer to be invisible. But tucking yourself into a neat little bundle isn't the way to escape who you are. You are a Wilde."

Viola nodded and rubbed a finger in the rosy-colored ointment.

"That dress is made to *stand out*," Aunt Knowe said. "Not blend into the wallpaper."

Viola took a deep breath and joined Joan at the mirror. Her stepsister was objectively one of the most lovely women Viola had ever seen. If Joan had been allowed to become an actress, she would be a star from the moment she sauntered from behind the curtains.

But that didn't mean Viola was nondescript.

Joan's lips had turned a deep rose that made her terrifyingly beautiful. As unattainable as Venus or Aphrodite.

Lip salve gave Viola an entirely different look.

"Oh, my goodness," Joan exclaimed, turning from the mirror to stare at Viola. "You look so—what's the word?"

"Desirable," Aunt Knowe said, coming up behind them. "You are beautiful, Joan, but if Viola were not so shy around men, she would have them all on their knees before her."

Viola saw what she meant. One might admire

Aphrodite, but one wouldn't necessarily want to marry her. Lavinia's design for her walking dress emphasized her curves, and the buttons drew attention to her bosom. The lip color did something too.

"Look at the two of us together," her stepsister said as she turned back to the glass. "I look overly bold; in fact, I think lip color probably isn't right for me."

"I agree," Aunt Knowe said. "That's why I didn't buy you a tin, Joan. You'd terrify anyone under thirty."

Joan pulled out a handkerchief and began rubbing off the color.

"But, Viola, you look enticing," Aunt Knowe said, meeting her eyes in the mirror and smiling. "Like a perfect lady—but one with hidden depths. And believe me, darling, gentlemen like hidden depths. They long for them, in fact."

"I don't believe I have any hidden depths," Viola said uncomfortably.

Aunt Knowe wrapped an arm around her shoulder. "The right man will take pleasure in helping you investigate the question."

"I spoke to the Duke of Wynter yesterday," Joan said, her face gleeful as she tucked away her handkerchief. "Did Devin ask me about myself? Did he?"

"No?" Viola asked.

"He was too busy inquiring why you were afraid of horses, and whether you had a mare of your own. I told him that cows were more to your liking, and he could buy you a nice Hereford if he wished to impress."

"Joan!"

Aunt Knowe was laughing so hard that they didn't hear the door open, and it wasn't until Prism cleared his throat and announced, "Lady Caitlin Paget," that they all turned.

"I didn't know Caitlin was joining us," Joan exclaimed.

"Miss Pettigrew is not a good choice for Mr. Marlowe," Aunt Knowe said quietly. "I assured Caitlin's father that I would chaperone her. I want to give the two of them a further chance to know each other, albeit in the presence of Miss Pettigrew, which is awkward. But necessary."

Viola frowned, but Aunt Knowe shook her head. "You merely want to rescue him," she said. "He's a good man, Viola, and he deserves better than that."

"I would have made a good vicar's wife," Viola said, feeling a little hurt.

"You would have tried with all your heart," Aunt Knowe said, neatly dodging the point as she walked toward the drawing room door.

They had barely finished bobbing curtsies when the door opened again. "Mrs. Pettigrew. Miss Pettigrew. Mr. Marlowe," Prism intoned.

"Such a pleasure," Aunt Knowe said, turning to Mrs. Pettigrew. "You'll have to forgive the duchess; she is suffering from an attack of the vapors."

In truth, on hearing that Mrs. Pettigrew was bid for tea, Ophelia had promptly been afflicted by a nervous headache that could be relieved only by retiring to the nursery and playing with Artemisia's new dollhouse.

Tea had been poured by the time Devin and Otis were announced.

"I offer deep apologies for our late arrival," Devin said, bowing before Aunt Knowe.

"My fault," Otis said cheerfully. "I couldn't seem to choose the proper upholstery for the day's journey."

"Upholstery?" Mrs. Pettigrew repeated, her brow pleating. "I understood from Mr. Marlowe that the vicarage has been refurbished with the finest furnishings."

"I was referring to myself," Otis told her. "I felt one shouldn't strike too bright a note, since I am returning, not to the scene of a crime, but to my former post."

They all looked, of course. Otis was wearing a green coat with matching pantaloons.

"His third trunk hadn't yet been unpacked," the duke said, moving to Viola's side.

Mrs. Pettigrew's expression was naturally sober; now it darkened.

"Lincoln green was a perfect choice," Caitlin said before Mrs. Pettigrew could share her opinion, "and the lace on your cravat is exquisite. Did you read the piece in the *Morning Chronicle* about how many men are newly employed by Sterling Lace? As I understand it, Mr. Sterling plans to open two more factories."

"Which means it would be positively virtuous to acquire another such cravat," Otis said. "I've been eyeing one embellished with lavender lace. Something like the color of your costume, Viola."

"This is Sterling lace," she said, touching her wrists, well aware that the Pettigrews did not seem to appreciate her daring gown.

"Do I understand that you are addressing Miss Astley by her first name?" Mrs. Pettigrew asked Otis. Her lips were pursed, and her eyebrows nearly met.

"I shall be the arbiter of my family's behavior," Lady Knowe stated.

Of course, that didn't stop Joan. "I much prefer birth names. It's quite the fashion these days, you know. Devin and Viola are on the very best of terms as well, are they not?"

"Certainly." Devin's expression didn't alter a whit, but for some reason Viola felt a delicious twinge anyway, as if he had looked at her and—

But he hadn't.

"More tea!" Aunt Knowe cried airily. "We have a most important errand this afternoon. A cucumber sandwich or two, and it's time to be on our way."

In the bustle of pouring fresh cups of tea and handing out the said sandwiches, Mr. Marlowe and the duke drew to the side of the room and began speaking quietly. Viola could only think that Mr. Marlowe must have decided to accept the post at St. Wilfrid's.

She stopped listening to the chatter about sandwiches and tried to think clearly. She had the distinct sense that Devin was no longer searching for the daughter of a duke.

Perhaps he had decided she, Viola, had sufficiently noble blood?

She felt a little short of breath at the thought.

"I was extremely fond of rhetoric," Miss Pettigrew announced, catching Viola's attention. "Rhetoric rewards the use of one's intelligence."

"I must be rotten at using my intelligence, or I don't have any, because I loathed it," Caitlin said. "I don't know if you are aware, Viola, but Miss Pettigrew was famous for her rhetorical abilities at Miss Stevenson's Seminary."

"I too found rhetoric difficult, as I am shy," Viola admitted.

"You appear to have outgrown the trait, Miss Astley." Mrs. Pettigrew's lips were drawn very tight and she directed a hard look toward Viola's mouth.

Viola promptly decided to wear lip salve every day.

"In a well-ordered mind, there is no room for shyness," Miss Pettigrew added, capping her mother's pronouncement.

"Do you have a well-ordered mind?" Joan inquired, less than politely, but no one could say that the conversation was precisely conventional.

"I do," Miss Pettigrew said, folding her hands in her lap. "My mother taught me that a well-ordered mind reflects a well-ordered soul. That, of course, is an objective toward which we should all strive."

"Miss Pettigrew, may I offer you another slice of lemon cake?" Aunt Knowe said, turning from her conversation with Otis to exhibit her unfailing instinct for the moment when the nursery was about to erupt into war.

"You must hear about Miss Pettigrew's well-ordered soul, Aunt Knowe," Joan chirped.

"I'd be honored," Aunt Knowe said. "Do share with us the secrets of achieving this desirable state?"

"One begins by knowing one's place in the world," Miss Pettigrew said.

"I have always insisted on that point," her mother agreed.

"I agree that lack of ambition is a partner to happiness," Aunt Knowe said, nodding.

"You misunderstand me," Miss Pettigrew said. "If one does not strive, life has no meaning. As Mr. Marlowe will regularly profess in his sermons, one must constantly practice a life of purity."

Caitlin's brows drew together. "It almost sounds as if you will be intimately acquainted with the content of Mr. Marlowe's sermons."

"My mother has always written my father's sermons," Miss Pettigrew said. "I will take the onerous task from Mr. Marlowe's hands. I have been trained by the best in the land. He can spend his time succoring the poor and ill, while I will tend to the moral garden, as it were, pruning weeds as they arise."

Viola watched as Caitlin glanced at Mr. Marlowe's back. He was still talking to the duke, but she had the idea that Caitlin agreed with her: Mr. Marlowe had no idea that he would be handing over responsibility for his sermons on his wedding day.

"Pruning weeds," Aunt Knowe said, with obvious fascination. "Mr. Marlowe will be in charge of discovering sins, and you will provide admonishments."

"I will be the scribe for his inmost thoughts," Miss Pettigrew said, dodging the question. "I will exert my powers to phrase the thoughts of his heart and mind, just as my mother has done for my father."

"Bishop Pettigrew has preached before the king himself," Mrs. Pettigrew said, a proud smile playing around her mouth.

"I must congratulate you," Aunt Knowe said, after a stark moment of silence. "If I understand your daughter correctly, in essence *you* preached before the king."

"One might take it so," Mrs. Pettigrew agreed, smoothing the black gloves that lay across her lap. "One mustn't congratulate oneself for such things. To be a cleric's wife, one needs a gift for rhetoric, such as my daughter possesses. But the only measure of any woman is whether she is a true lady."

A fleeting but grim stare left Viola in no doubt about Mrs. Pettigrew's opinion of lip salve.

Before she could formulate a response, Devin materialized at Viola's back, curled a strong, warm hand over her shoulder, and said, "If the ladies are agreeable, perhaps we could make our way to the vicarage?"

"Tick, tock, everyone!" Aunt Knowe cried, leaping to her feet in a way that suggested that the next time Mrs. Pettigrew visited, she too would have an attack of the vapors. "The weather is perfect for a short walk."

When they reached the entry, Devin took Viola's pelisse from the footman and helped her put it on. When his hands touched her shoulders, she felt a flash of heat that made her breath stop. Her heart sped up, which was absurd.

In short order, the group put on outer wear and traipsed down the front steps of the Lindow townhouse. Somehow, Viola didn't know quite how, it seemed there was no question but that Devin would be at her side.

He strode beside her silently, which she appreciated. Joan talked constantly, which gave her time to think. But Devin's companionable silence did as well.

The problem was that the only thing she could think about was him.

She'd grown up around handsome men, but she found it easy to dismiss the Wildes' sculpted features from her mind. And Mr. Marlowe with his finely knit cheekbones.

A sultry, angular face with a rough voice couldn't compare. Especially when you added the solitary pride that was almost visible around his shoulders.

Still.

Chapter Fifteen

$\mathcal{D}$evin walked slowly, until Lady Knowe, who was leading the group, disappeared around the corner ahead of him.

He came to a halt.

Viola glanced up at him inquiringly. She looked so enticing that he was having a hard time not kissing her in public.

He had glanced at her while talking to the vicar and instantly lost his train of thought. That old harridan must have said something unkind to her, and the expression on her face had lit an errant, fiercely protective fire in his chest.

"I didn't sleep very well last night," he said.

She looked startled. "I'm sorry to hear that."

"I found myself wondering whether the conversation between myself and my uncle at your debut ball might have convinced you that you are not well-suited to being a duchess."

"I already knew that," Viola said, her mouth turning up in a wry smile. "I detailed for you the list of my shortcomings, though the one you pointed to—an inability to keep my attention during a conversation—may be the most persuasive of all."

"That's your greatest failing?" He couldn't stop himself from smiling. Bloody hell, he *never* smiled.

"No," Viola said, cocking her head to look at him, and apparently taking his question seriously. "I have others, but they aren't related to being a duchess. If that is what is being discussed."

She ducked her head, and Devin had to take a breath because she was so damned sweet that he wanted nothing more than to snatch her into his arms and kiss her. Later, he told his instincts. Later.

"Perhaps not the normal sort of duchess," he said, keeping his voice steady. "Yet I am not a normal duke."

"Are you still trying to prove that you aren't like the rest of mankind? Or at least the species known as noble males?"

"I don't have to prove anything," Devin said flatly. "I'm a duke. I can do exactly as I wish. I spend days in my library working on mathematical problems. If I wished, I could do that in a cowshed."

A delightful smile trembled on her mouth. "A preposterous idea."

"I thought I needed a duchess able to attend social gatherings on her own. Now I realize that I may well accompany my wife if she asked me. In fact," he added thoughtfully, "it may be that I will be constitutionally prone to agreeing with virtually every request she might make."

"'Constitutionally prone'?" Viola smiled at him. "I think your wife will be happy to find that you are prepared to listen to her requests. Too many men think that their word and their ideas are the end of the matter."

Devin *had* thought that for years—not necessarily when it came to relations between men and women, but between dukes and the rest of humanity.

He hired good men to present all possibilities in any given situation, after which he made up his mind—and took responsibility for what followed, for good or ill.

"My father and mother could barely tolerate each other," he said abruptly.

Viola's eyes were warmly compassionate, and Devin realized that he didn't care if she married him out of pity. He would use every tool at his disposal. "My mother died when I was young."

Somewhat to his surprise, Viola didn't instantly melt into a puddle of sympathy. Instead her eyes searched his and she gave him a rueful smile. "Sometimes what one most misses is the idea of the person rather than the one who is lost."

Devin felt a jolt down his backbone. It was true that he had occasionally missed his mother, but never the mother whom he had known. Instead, he missed the mother whom he had imagined, the one who would have protected him from his father's blustery rages.

"My point is that a duchess can do and be whatever she wishes," he said, pushing the thought away. "My mother and father's marriage was arranged while they were in their cradles. It was eminently appropriate in every respect."

"I see," Viola said, nodding. "I'm sorry."

"No one would have arranged a marriage between us as babies, which I think is to our benefit. And I think you would be a marvelous duchess." Her eyes were shocked, so Devin added firmly, "I am going to woo you."

"I only agreed to be friends," Viola said.

But he could see in her eyes that she was protesting not his decision—which she had surely guessed—but her suitability.

Someone had convinced her that there was something wrong with her, probably the non-Wilde part of her. And yet Devin was absolutely sure that he would treasure every bit of her, the Wilde and non-Wilde parts.

"Otis tells me that I must woo you in order to win your hand, and I'm merely informing you of my intentions. I shall ask for a meeting with your father."

"My stepfather," Viola corrected him.

He took in her sweet face, earnest eyes, soft curls, and could imagine a small version of her with ease. "His Grace feels he is your father," he said with utter conviction. "He raised you."

A smile curled Viola's lips. "He does."

"I shall ask your father for permission to court you."

"Because your uncle told you to?" Viola asked. "I appreciate your fondness for Sir Reginald, but you shouldn't take his advice too seriously."

Devin took a moment to enjoy the fact that not only was Miss Viola Astley indifferent to his title, he was having to persuade her even to give him a chance.

"You are beautiful, kindhearted, and funny," he said evenly. "I would like you to be my wife."

"You—*really*?"

"As I said, my parents did not have a happy marriage," he said, threading his fingers through hers. "Yet since my uncle was merely a second son—a spare for the heir, as the saying goes—he was allowed to marry whom he wished. My uncle and aunt were very happy together. I know what such a marriage looks like. I had never imagined the possibility for myself, but now I can."

"You can?"

Viola looked down at their linked hands.

"Nay, don't be afraid," he said, his voice deep and sure. "Don't ever be afraid to look at me, Viola."

"It wasn't that," she said faintly, tightening her fingers on his.

He was watching her closely, determined to catch her reaction. Confidence was intrinsic to his very being, but for the first time in his life, he realized that if he saw fear or disgust in Viola's eyes, he would not pursue her. There was the vicar. Perhaps she still wanted to marry Mr. Marlowe.

The smile disappeared from his face, and he forced his features to be expressionless even as his heart thumped heavily in his chest.

He *knew* Viola now.

She didn't want to be a duchess, unlike every other young lady at the party. Even Lady Caitlin, if he bowed before her, would turn away from the vicar and accept his courtship.

But would Viola?

For the first time in a very long time, he felt uncertain. And yet . . .

He had seen shock in her eyes but not horror. Surprise, but not revulsion.

"You're going to woo me?" she asked.

"Yes."

"Even though I'm unsuited to be a duchess."

"I don't care. I want you, not a duchess."

"But you scarcely know me!"

"Not true. I do know you, and you are exactly the sort of woman with whom I want to spend the rest of my life. My uncle was right."

Her face fell. "Because I'm a mouse?"

"No!" His gut clenched at the expression in her eyes. "Because of this." The party had turned the corner ahead of them, and only Miss Pettigrew and Mr. Marlowe were still within view. He cupped her face and brushed her lips with his, and again.

"Oh," she breathed.

Her lips slowly slid open, and her eyes drifted shut.

Devin's breath hitched, and he took her invitation. She tasted like mint and honey as his tongue slid over hers. He who never stopped thinking found himself in the grip of temporary madness.

At least, he dimly hoped it was temporary. He definitely shouldn't be kissing Viola on a public street, where anyone might see them.

But he couldn't stop. Her tongue danced around his. Their kiss was deep and searching, as if they were speaking without words. He felt unsteady, aware of the street around them, but even more aware of her hand against his chest, fingers spread as if to feel his heart beating through his greatcoat.

She pulled back, and he let her go, of course. Her eyelashes swept open and in her eyes he saw the same startled recognition he felt in his heart.

"We shouldn't," she breathed, but as if she felt the madness the way he did, she tilted her head and her lips parted—

And they were kissing again, deep, searching kisses that weren't a language but music, he decided dimly, with the part of his mind that couldn't stop thinking.

The part of his mind that was expressing shock and noting that he hadn't the faintest inclination to surrender to an emotion like this.

He had watched his uncle and aunt turn to each other, once even kissing under the mistletoe, and decided that their vulnerability to each other equated with lack of self-respect.

But what was the use of being a duke if one didn't do exactly as one pleased?

Viola was on her tiptoes, one arm around his neck, kissing him back. Her other hand was pressed against his chest in a caress that he wished wasn't impeded by clothing.

What had begun as a simple press of lips was something else entirely now. He could taste jasmine tea, lemon tart, and under that something far better and sweeter: Viola.

Finally, even the still logical part of his brain fell silent and lost the ability to think, one hand holding her tightly to him, the other palm still cupping her cheek. Desire was like a torch burning in his gut, spiraling through his limbs.

It wasn't until Viola made an aching little sound in the back of her throat that he remembered that he was kissing her in broad daylight.

He pulled back and looked down at her. Her flawless skin was flushed pink and her breath was shaky.

"I didn't mean to woo you like this," Devin said, realizing with a queer jolt that his voice had deepened. He sounded like an old goat, rough and growly.

If goats were possessive, that is.

"Oh, my goodness," Viola whispered.

She shook her head. "Your kiss—your kiss was somewhat persuasive, Your Grace." Then she giggled.

Giggled!

He'd never liked giggles. They were childish, he'd thought. Naïve.

But now he realized that giggles were fragments of laughter. The way "joy" is shorter and sharper than the word "happiness." Giggles came when a woman was out of breath, and he loved the reason Viola was out of breath.

"We should catch up with everyone before we are missed," she said. "Is my hat straight?"

Such a simple question.

And yet his body flooded with emotion. This beautiful woman looking up at him, asking about her headgear . . . He might have her next to him, asking that question every morning.

"Yes," he said, clearing his throat. He took another look. "Actually, no." She was wearing a delightful little blue hat with a high crown, tied all around with striped ribbons and adorned with a bow and a sprig of flowers. "Should it be worn directly on top of your head?"

"Yes," she said. "Would you mind straightening it for me? It's hard to do without a mirror. I shouldn't want anyone to know that we were . . . canoodling in the street!"

He pulled her little hat to the top of her head. A few wisps of hair had fallen free, but he had no idea how to tuck them back into her coiffure. He held out his elbow. "My lady?"

"That kiss does not mean that I accept your—your courtship," Viola said. "My plan is to be an old maid."

He thought her plan had been to marry the vicar, but he didn't want to remind her.

"It would be more amusing to be a duchess," he said.

"Amusing?" She looked up at him with an impish smile, and he realized with a jolt that he adored her bonnet. It was precisely the blue that brought out the green in her eyes.

He couldn't kiss her in the street again. He planned to woo her, not make a scandal.

"Yes, amusing," he said firmly, banishing thoughts of just how much amusement a shared bedchamber would afford. "I have several estates. We can travel around the world, if you wish. Climb mountains. Explore the Nile." What else did Wildes do? "Explore that bog outside the castle. Bring home an elephant to put in the cowshed."

It was only because he was looking closely that he saw her face fall. "Is that what you wish to do?"

His mind boggled. He'd never had to consider what someone else wanted to do—and for the first time in his life, he actually wanted to consider her wishes. He wanted his wife to come first.

"I want to do whatever you want to do," he stated.

"I don't think you know me well enough to be kissing me in the street," Viola said, walking a little faster. "That is, we don't know each other well enough."

They rounded the corner and discovered Lady Knowe striding back in their direction. She gave Viola a shrewd look that took in her kissed lips, deftly separated the two of them, and linked her arms in both of theirs.

"Duke," she said, "you do realize that Viola and Joan are Wildes, don't you?"

"I am aware of that fact," Devin said.

"Kissing in public will result in prints being sent the length and breadth of the country," Lady Knowe stated.

Devin heard a soft intake of breath on the other side of Lady Knowe; Viola had apparently forgotten about the rapacious printmakers.

They were both silent as Lady Knowe walked them briskly down the block to the vicarage, talking of the weather.

Chapter Sixteen

$\mathcal{V}$iola was in shock.

She felt as if she were walking in a mass of cotton wool, even less able to pay attention than normally. When she was standing in Devin's arms, she had felt *safe*.

It was absurd. Ridiculous. And yet . . .

Some small part of her would always be a terrified two-year-old, walking into the noisy nursery filled with Wilde children. And some other part of her was still a fifteen-year-old, reeling from her first experience of male rage.

The whole of her had smelled Devin, felt his arms around her, kissed him, breathed with him, and relaxed, saying: *Yes. This.*

She felt as if her stomach would never clench with fear again, at least not while he was within earshot. She took a deep breath as they walked through the door of the vicarage and handed over their outer garments to a maid.

In the sitting room they found Otis trying to convince Mrs. Pettigrew that velvet was a durable upholstery fabric; she preferred a good, sturdy twill. Viola sat down beside Joan.

"Where were you?" her stepsister whispered.

"Walking slowly," Viola said, ignoring Joan's smirk.

"Your lip salve is noticeably absent," Joan said.

The vicarage sitting room was a pleasant room, with a bow window made from small triangles that sparkled with reflected light, casting violet shadows on the floor. Plump sofas and armchairs were strewn about the room, all of them upholstered in bright blue.

"I imagined dark blue," Viola said.

"I call this cherubic blue," Otis said from the other side of Joan. "Entirely appropriate for the building, as I'm sure you'll agree."

"You could call it celestial," Joan suggested with a laugh. She squeezed his arm. "Have I mentioned how pleased I am to have met you?"

"Leaving the inadvisable upholstery to the side, the room is cluttered," Mrs. Pettigrew announced shrilly. "There's a weapon where any ruffian might use it to assault the vicar." She pointed.

The walls were lined with shelves crowded with volumes of books, but all sorts of other things were stuck in among the volumes: a ceramic tub of mustard, for example, a dirty teacup, a crab made from clay, and a dagger thrust between two books of sonnets.

"The dagger is not mine," Otis said, "and nor is the crab. I always felt as if I were an actor playing a part, and this room made a decent stage set, in my opinion."

"The dagger must have belonged to my previous vicar," Devin said. "Of course, Mr. Marlowe may alter the room as he wishes."

"Not too much!" Caitlin said. "All the parishioners love coming here for tea and a cozy chat with the vicar. There's history here. That crab was made by little Joey Avon, for example, and now he's an apprentice in the silver trade."

"Joey's grown up," Mr. Marlowe exclaimed, leaning forward, blue eyes shining. "I can't imagine that, Lady Caitlin."

Caitlin dimpled and assured him it was true, and launched into tales of all the children whom he might remember from his years as a curate.

Looking about, Viola realized that Miss Pettigrew's afternoon was not proving a happy one. Clearly, Mr. Marlowe's fiancée wanted him to accept the appointment to St. Wilfrid's parish. She wanted to be near her mother. She wanted her husband to become a bishop, and a rich parish like this was an excellent means to that end.

But St. Wilfrid's included Caitlin, whose family was as important to the parish as Devin's—and Devin owned the living. Caitlin knew everything about the parish, and she was happily informing Mr. Marlowe of the health of all the parishioners whom he remembered.

In short, they had a friendship—or at least an acquaintanceship—that went back years.

Mrs. Pettigrew had been wandering the room, poking at books with a disapproving look, picking up a misshapen clay pig and putting it back with a click, running her finger along the shelves, pausing to squint at a pendulum clock that likely stopped ticking a century ago.

"This furniture will not do," she said now, returning to the group. "It is inappropriate: A lady prefers chairs with high backs and sturdy fabric."

Luckily Otis had taken himself off to consult with the housekeeper about touring the rest of the vicarage.

Caitlin smiled and admitted that her cats had destroyed several chairs in her home, sharpening their claws. "This velvet would be hanging in strips," she said cheerfully. "I believe Mrs. Pettigrew is right about the durability of the fabric."

"Although it *is* exquisite," Viola put in.

"I don't understand," Mrs. Pettigrew said frigidly. "Am I to believe that you allow felines to roam your home at will?"

"My cats are house pets," Caitlin explained. "They sleep in a basket in my room."

Miss Pettigrew's mouth drew in very tight. "Modern science indicates that cats carry diseases. Some say they do worse."

"Worse?" Caitlin said, straightening her shoulders, which Viola recognized as a danger sign from when they were in school together. Caitlin was endlessly sweet—but not when it came to defending her pets.

"Oh, no," Joan muttered. "If you'll excuse me, I'll make myself scarce." She stood up and sauntered away.

Caitlin had arrived in Miss Stevenson's Seminary a year after Viola and Joan, sent there by a father who had neither the time nor the inclination to cope with a newly motherless daughter. From his point of view, he had to marry again quickly in order to produce the heir needed to carry on his name and title.

Caitlin had been grieving for her mother and shaken by the loss of her home. She had distinguished herself on the first night at Miss Stevenson's by throwing an unprecedented tantrum when the maids tried to remove the kitten she had brought with her, hidden in a hatbox.

"I can assure you that cats are entirely harmless," Caitlin said now. "Unless you are a rodent, of course.

Cats are excellent at keeping down vermin. Indeed, I feel that any house without a cat is likely suffering from an invasion of mice, if not rats."

All those years ago, Joan and Viola had been parlor boarders, sharing a suite with two bedchambers and a parlor. When the battle over the kitten erupted, they invited Caitlin to take one of their bedchambers. "You and I can sleep together," Joan had told Viola. "I know you'll never allow that kitten to be banished to the stables."

"Scientists believe that a cat can steal breath from a sleeping person," Miss Pettigrew informed Caitlin.

"Miss Pettigrew, I assure you that is not the case," Viola said hastily. "When Joan and I were in school with Caitlin, her cat often slept on one or another of our beds."

"His name was Pitchy," Caitlin said, nodding. "If he stole our breath, apparently we had enough air to go around."

"My daughter attended the same seminary, a few years before you, and I clearly remember that animals were not tolerated," Mrs. Pettigrew said, with a look that suggested she meant to demand her tuition money back.

"Did you meet Mr. Marlowe while he was a curate here at St. Wilfrid's?" Viola asked Miss Pettigrew, trying to change the subject.

"No," Miss Pettigrew said shortly.

"We met last All Hallows' Eve," Mr. Marlowe said. He looked as eager as Viola to change the subject of conversation.

Viola blinked. *In the end of October?* She had met him in November. Could he and Miss Pettigrew have been betrothed upon their first meeting?

"We were introduced by my father," Miss Pettigrew added.

Viola felt another surge of sympathy. Instinctively, she glanced across the room at Devin. As if he felt her gaze, he looked up and their eyes met. The emotion in his was unmistakable. Joan was telling him a long story, her hands flying, and he was in need of rescue.

"Excuse me," Viola said, standing up and heading toward His Grace.

Otis appeared at the door. "Come along, everyone! Mr. Marlowe won't recognize the bedchambers after the changes I made."

Viola hadn't reached the duke, but he turned away from Joan and strode toward her as if her beautiful stepsister didn't exist.

Toward *her*.

Short, insignificant Miss Astley, who wasn't a Wilde, and wasn't a good candidate to become a duchess.

And yet . . .

Perhaps she was a good candidate to be the Duke of Wynter's wife.

Behind his back, Joan's face was alight with laughter.

"It's time to tour the vicarage, I believe," Viola said, feeling distinctly awkward.

Devin bent and said in her ear, "As long as you are not planning a future here." His voice rasped.

She gave him a saucy smile, certain on that point, if not on the question of being a duchess. "I'm certain that Mr. Marlowe would welcome my advice as regards renovation."

"No renovation necessary," he growled.

For the first time in Viola's life, she looked up at a man from under her lashes, the kind of look that Joan had given every male under the age of eighty since she was five.

Devin swallowed hard; she saw his throat move.

Viola let her smile widen before she turned and walked out of the room, following her aunt, aware that she was having one of the best days of her entire life.

"Have you thought about what I said?" Devin asked her as they climbed a set of narrow wooden stairs. He was behind her—every lady climbed alone as the steps were too narrow for fashionably wide gowns— and his voice tickled the back of her neck.

"Thought about what?"

"My decision to woo you?"

She reached the top of the steps and shook out her skirts as Devin stepped onto the landing. He wasn't handsome, the way Mr. Marlowe was. Her eyes moved to the vicar—

Devin grabbed her shoulders. "Look at *me*."

Was it wrong to feel thrilled by the intensity in his eyes? Yes, it probably was. Still, it felt that for the first time in her life, someone had chosen *her*. Her family loved her, but they hadn't chosen her. Barty, Cleo, and Daisy loved her, but she had saved their lives.

The duke was attracted to her, but he didn't love her.

How could he? They scarcely knew each other.

All the same, he had chosen her, even though she didn't fit any of his preconceptions about whom he wanted as his wife.

She pushed open the door of the room closest to her and walked inside. It was a small sitting room, likely designed for the mistress of the house.

Devin followed her. And pushed the door shut behind them, which was thoroughly improper.

"Are you trying to compromise me, so that I have to marry you?" she asked, not believing it for a moment.

He scowled. "I would never do that to anyone."

"You should open the door," she pointed out.

He wrenched open the door. The corridor was empty; she could hear Mrs. Pettigrew exclaiming from some other room about the presence of more celestial blue velvet.

Devin strode toward her, his eyes intent on hers. Viola leaned against the back of a high-backed sofa. "I'm not entirely certain what courtship entails," she said.

"Courtship is made up of stolen moments," he said. "In which we come to know each other better. For example, after our conversation yesterday, I am now fairly certain that you have no interest in bringing home an elephant to join Cleo and Daisy."

"You remembered their names!" Viola exclaimed and colored. "Why did you suggest an elephant?"

"One of my closest friends lives in India, and I'd like to visit him someday. He is a mathematician, and in one letter he described a herd of elephants wandering across the garden before his window."

"All I know is that they have long trunks," Viola confessed.

"They are loving," he said, moving closer. "They mate for life and never forgive an insult."

A sizzling feeling was coursing through Viola's veins. Instinctively, she knew that this feeling would lead a person to abandon the rules of polite society, no matter how firmly held. Devin's eyes looked at her so intently that he must be seeing all her cowardly bits and pieces, and yet he was still here, in this room.

Looking at a woman whom both of them agreed would not be a suitable duchess.

"What do *you* think courtship should be like?" he asked her.

Was it her imagination that his voice had taken on an even deeper note?

"Practice for marriage?" she said awkwardly. His eyes were stormy gray, yes, but it was a particular kind of storm. An invitation was being issued, silently. If emotion were a wire, it would be strung between them tightly. "One must learn to understand the other person. Why were you cross a few minutes ago?"

"I wasn't," he said.

"This is where you can imagine me raising one eyebrow," she told him. "You were practically growling."

One corner of his mouth crooked up. "You looked at that bloody vicar."

Just as she suspected. "Are those two words allowed to be in the same sentence? If you must know, I was comparing the two of you."

The storm clouds in his eyes darkened.

"He's very handsome," Viola said, feeling inarticulate and shy. She dropped her gaze and stared at his chest instead.

"I'm not." Devin crossed his arms, which meant that she noticed the breadth of his chest again. "But I'm the right one for you, Viola." There was utter confidence in his voice. In fact, she'd noticed that he was always confident.

It was probably a bone-deep part of him, in the same way that a little frisson of fear was commonplace to her.

"How can you possibly know that?" she asked. "You may be feeling something temporary. Your uncle suggested my name, and it was time for you to find a wife, and it was easier to choose me than find another."

"My uncle has nothing to do with it. Although I'll admit he was right."

Viola bit her lip. She couldn't help thinking that Devin would wake up one morning, take a look at her, and realize that he could have married a gorgeous, tall woman with flashing eyes and ducal cheekbones.

She darted a look at Devin. He wasn't watching her as if she were ordinary. At the moment, he was staring down at her with a sensual gaze that practically smoldered.

For *her*!

"May I lift you?" He patted the padded back of the sofa.

"Yes."

His outstretched hand wrapped around her waist, his fingers molding to her curves. Viola could feel the warmth of his hand and before she registered it, he put her on the back of the sofa and stepped away.

There was silence in the room as their eyes met.

"I like being able to see you across from me rather than from above," he said, a trace of a smile on his lips.

"You wouldn't like it if I were actually this tall," Viola said, scarcely knowing what she was saying.

"I don't care what height you are." Devin gathered her into his arms with an almost soundless groan. "When you are anxious, you bite your lip. If anyone is going to bite your lip, it's me," he whispered, nipping her bottom lip.

Viola found herself giggling, because how often does one see a duke with a hungry look? Dukes were given everything they wanted before they knew they wanted it. And they were never wild, because a duke—with his snowy wig, embroidered coat, and embroidered satin shoes—is the very epitome of civilization.

Yet Devin's eyes were both wild and hungry. They kissed until she gathered her courage and said, "What if you get tired of having a short, nonduchessy duchess?"

"I want a nonduchessy duchess. Which is nothing less than what I said from the moment I decided to find a wife."

"What?" she asked. She was trembling all over.

"I said I wanted a Wilde," he reminded her.

She stared into his eyes, trying to believe him. *Wilde Child* echoed in her head. If she was a Wilde . . . was she Wilde enough for him?

"I don't want just any Wilde. I want the most beautiful Wilde of all," Devin said, his voice rasping. "The woman with a wide mouth who laughs easily and taught me in the space of one day to love a giggle. Who knows about medieval plays and abandoned crows. The woman with a darling pointed chin and exquisite hazel eyes."

"Did you say that I have a 'darling' chin?"

He nodded.

"You've lost your mind," she said with conviction.

"I believe you're right." He gave her his rare, brilliant smile that transformed his features entirely.

Viola stared, thinking that Devin was not just ducal: He was magnificent. His rough-hewn features were manly in a way that she'd never noticed before. The opposite of her, who was always afraid.

Always a little afraid, she amended.

"I'm a coward," she said, blurting it out.

"As am I," he said, enfolding her in his arms.

"What are you afraid of?" she managed, before they sank into a kiss so fierce and passionate that she emerged shaking like a leaf, her knees weak.

"I'm afraid you'll say no and choose that bloody vicar over me," he growled. "I don't make impulsive decisions. You are my one impulse, and yet I know in my gut that it's the right one."

"Are you . . ." She cleared her throat and started again. "Are you sure you are not saying that you're in love with me?"

"No." The word was gentle but absolute. "I've known you less than a week, Viola."

She nodded hastily. And yet she couldn't help remembering that she fell in love with Mr. Marlowe at one glance.

Yet had she really been in love?

"Perhaps that's what courtship is for?" Devin asked. "Falling in love?"

His smile grew. "And kissing. Though if I can't find a handy settee like this one, I will get a crick in my neck."

"Because I'm short?" Viola felt a flash of humiliation. "I'm sorry."

He braced his arms on either side of her. "I like short." There wasn't anything complex in his eyes. He liked short.

Viola, having grown up in a family of giants, could scarcely believe it.

She kept her knees primly together, but she could feel the warmth of his body and the wintergreen smell that hung about him.

"Why do you smell like a pine tree?" she asked.

"My soap." He leaned closer. "You smell like flowers."

"Tobacco soap," she said, feeling as if she were babbling because there was something in his eyes that looked like tenderness. "Aunt Knowe has a few plants in the greenhouse that one of my stepbrothers brought back from the colonies."

"May I kiss you again?"

She drew in a quick breath. "Yes."

"May I put my hands on your back, to make certain that you don't topple over?"

She grinned at that. "You plan to kiss me dizzy, is that it?"

"You make *me* dizzy," he said. He leaned forward and licked her bottom lip. "Your mouth is absurdly sensual. When I first entered the drawing room for tea, I couldn't breathe for a moment. You shouldn't do that to a man without warning."

"Sensual? Me?" Her voice squeaked because, yes, there had been that moment when she stood in front of the mirror and Joan said she looked . . . and Aunt Knowe said . . .

But she had spent four years carefully looking at the feet of whichever man was bowing in front of her. The conviction that she was ordinary couldn't be abolished by a swipe of lip color.

"You're driving me mad, Viola," he said huskily. "I'm having a difficult time remembering that you're a proper young maiden and I can't shut the door. Yet courtship should include privacy."

The look in his eyes made her breath come in a little staccato gasp. "Perhaps I was wrong. Perhaps no one would mind if the door was closed briefly. Very briefly."

His eyes flared, which made her want to do something mad, part her legs and allow him to ease forward in order to—

Heat flooded up her bosom and into her throat. His eyes flickered. "I'm holding on to my gentlemanly credentials by a hair," he said, his voice gravelly. "Now I'm going to say something unforgivable."

Viola met his eyes and decided that nothing he could say would be unforgivable. "All right," she said.

"Your breasts, Viola, are meant for worshipping. How can you possibly have thought that you are ordinary?"

She squeaked with laughter. "That *is* unforgivable! You mentioned a part of my body that gentlemen are allowed to gawk at, but never name."

"I loathe that pretense," he said. "The idea that gentlemen aren't males, like the rest of the sex."

"Dukes? Are dukes men like anyone else?"

He was silent for a moment, thinking that over. "I gather you would say yes, grouping dukes with the rest of the eyebrow-raising male population?"

She nodded. Right now, perched on the back of a sofa, she felt such a strong wish to throw herself into his arms that she was having trouble concentrating.

Right.

Dukes versus men.

He bent just close enough that she took advantage and kissed him. It was all she could think about, to be truthful. The way Devin's mouth felt, firm and sleek. The rough sound he made in the back of his throat.

It couldn't be catalogued, that sound. But after only five kisses, she already knew it. It did something to her knees and stomach and all those parts that ladies aren't supposed to mention. They turned hot and tingling.

They—all those heated parts of her—made her head swim. When he pulled her closer, the only thing she wanted to do was yield, open her lips.

He pulled back when voices echoed in the corridor, and their eyes met, suddenly alert. His hands landed on her hips, ready to pull her to her feet.

But the voices receded, another door opening somewhere else.

"They surely have realized we are nowhere to be seen," Viola whispered.

"Quite likely." Devin cleared his throat but left his hands where they were. She didn't wear panniers under her walking costume, and his fingers were curling around her hips.

"What were we talking about?" she asked, dazed.

"We were discussing whether dukes are different from other men, and whether you are ordinary, and whether your breasts are the most beautiful thing that God put on this earth."

Viola gaped at him and then clapped her mouth shut.

Devin bent his head and nuzzled her cheek. "That can't be a surprise to you." His eyes were very clear, not stormy now. They were the color of twilight just before night falls.

Her smile was entirely unplanned; it flashed out of somewhere along with words that she couldn't believe she spoke aloud. "I like my breasts," she admitted. "I—I think they are very . . . nice."

"Nice!" Devin shook his head. "You truly have spent too much time with your siblings, who are all very fine, but since we're on this topic—and gentlemen really *do* make comparisons, Viola, it's part of the nature of the beast—your stepsisters are beautiful, lanky creatures. Thank God, you are not."

"I really don't think you should mention 'God' in a vicarage," she said, fighting a mortifying attack of shyness.

When he looked at her, she felt voluptuous. They were so close now that their breaths intermingled. Then he turned and reached the door in one large stride, shut it quietly, and returned to her side. "Just for a moment," he said.

A lifetime spent thinking that she wasn't as beautiful as the Wilde sisters, versus the utter conviction in Devin's eyes? She wrapped her arms around his neck and pulled him a tiny bit closer until their lips slid together and their tongues danced past each other in a dizzying caress that made her feel hazy.

His large hands were clamped on her hips again, making certain she was steady. Her stomach clenched, but for a very different reason than was customary. She nestled toward him, dropping one hand to his chest to feel his heart beating.

With a murmured word that she didn't understand, he deepened their kiss. Viola pushed away thought and clung to him, learning the music of kisses, the give-and-take of tongues, the way the thump of his heart sped up under her hand, the tension of his body, as taut as the strings of a violin.

His tongue invaded her mouth again and she had the sudden instinct to suck on it, so she did, and he let out a raw groan and all ten fingers tightened on her hips. She was busy learning, busy taking stock, and thinking about how it felt, and how his grip made her blood feel as if it was scorching—

When the door opened, she didn't even register the sound.

Chapter Seventeen

$\mathcal{W}$ ell, I *never!*" Miss Pettigrew squealed.

Devin raised his head reluctantly, looking down into Viola's flushed face and feeling a deep certainty that echoed in his bones. Her eyes were round with shock, and she looked utterly mortified.

His fault. He had shut the door. No matter that she'd bid him to do so, he was a gentleman, supposedly. Yet he had kissed her the way a man kisses a mistress, not a proper young lady. Theirs had been no docile peck on the lips: It was the forerunner to what he felt certain would be the best lovemaking of his life.

Raucous, sweaty, noisy lovemaking.

Viola looked as if she might explode with embarrassment. Her lips were swollen with his kisses, and he didn't want anyone in the world to see that, other than him. Anger at the invasion began to march up his backbone.

He straightened and turned his head. "Excuse me," he growled.

The vicar's fiancée stood in the doorway, hand on her heart, eyes hard. For a moment, he had a flash of sympathy for Marlowe, not that he had the faintest intention of allowing Viola to sacrifice herself at the marital altar.

Behind Miss Pettigrew's shoulder stood her mother and Lady Knowe, whose face was utterly composed. But she had a stern fury in her eyes all the same.

"Oh, no," Viola breathed.

"I believe our courtship has just been curtailed." Devin turned his shoulder to their audience and held her gaze, saying quietly, "You may jilt me later, if you wish."

He dropped a kiss on her lips, picked her up, and put her gently on her feet. "I'd like you all to be the first to know that Miss Viola Astley has agreed to become the next Duchess of Wynter. *My* duchess."

Miss Pettigrew still blocked the doorway, looking at him with seemingly genuine horror in her eyes, but Lady Knowe deftly nudged the lady to the side and strolled in.

"I told the duke after you asked for my niece's hand yesterday that Viola would never be able to resist you."

At his shoulder, Viola made a small sound, akin to a gasp. She knew Devin hadn't yet spoken to her stepfather. It stood to reason that she wasn't very good at deception; her eyes were too expressive. Luckily, it appeared that Lady Knowe was a master.

Devin wrapped his hand around Viola's. "Within five minutes of meeting Viola at the Lindow ball, I knew that she would be my duchess. It took me longer to convince her than I imagined."

"Your efforts to convince her were not worthy of a lady," Miss Pettigrew hissed, her lip curling. "The door was closed, you were unchaperoned, and we all saw where your hands were!"

Devin could feel rage rising in his chest, and he took a deep breath. He had promised himself as a boy that he would never behave like his father. But now fury boiled up inside him, as poisonous as stewed foxglove.

Words were lining up behind his teeth, but he forced himself to remain silent. He never spoke when he was angry. It was the habit of a lifetime, a desperate technique adopted to avoid turning into his father.

Miss Pettigrew's eyes were bright and sharp, and she seemed to have swelled above the waist like a bantam rooster scratching the dirt.

"Daughter," her mother said, "you forget yourself."

"*I* haven't forgotten myself," Miss Pettigrew spat, crossing her arms over her chest. "Earlier they kissed on the street, in the broad daylight, and His Grace just referred to her by her first name."

Lady Knowe fixed the Pettigrews with a stare that suggested they were night-grown mushrooms that had made an unwelcome appearance on the lawns of Lindow Castle.

"I address Devin by his first name, don't I, Devin?" Joan said brightly, popping into the room. "We already discussed that, and you'll remember, Mrs. Pettigrew, that I suggested your mores might be somewhat out of date."

"If you'll forgive me, Lady Joan, you have no need to engage in the sort of wiles displayed by Miss Astley," Miss Pettigrew said shrilly. Her hand moved jerkily, but no one in the room had any doubt about what she was gesturing toward. Apparently, she didn't care for Viola's bodice. Her mouth was a thin, disgusted line.

"You're quite awful," Joan said in a conversational tone. "You seem to have no understanding of dress"—her eyes made a scathing sweep of Miss Pettigrew's gown—"but I assure you that my stepsister's bodice is in the forefront of fashion."

"She—"

"*She*, as in my niece," Lady Knowe cut in, her voice sharp as a whip, "will soon be married to the Duke of Wynter, who holds the living of St. Wilfrid's, the very vicarage in which we now stand."

"Likely that marriage ought to happen soon, given the way his hands were—" That was the moment when the meaning of Lady Knowe's sentence sank into Miss Pettigrew's mind.

She began blinking rapidly.

"My daughter is very sensitive to sin, in all its forms and practices," Mrs. Pettigrew said, taking a step forward. She had turned somewhat pale. "In her enthusiasm, she misinterpreted what she saw."

"I expect," Miss Pettigrew said with a gulp.

"My brother will never countenance such impoliteness toward his daughter," Lady Knowe said flatly. At that moment she appeared to be a replica of her twin brother. "Mr. Marlowe is no longer welcome at Lindow."

Devin tightened his hand around Viola's small fingers. Miss Pettigrew had been genuinely disgusted by a simple kiss. She was not someone whom Devin wanted to have authority over the women of his parish.

Not to mention the fact that he still felt a burning wish to eviscerate her.

Viola spoke before he had a chance to extend Lady Knowe's judgment to St. Wilfrid's. "I'm certain that

Miss Pettigrew was merely startled by opening a door and encountering people whom she didn't expect to see. It can be shocking to find . . . to find a couple engaged in a private moment."

Devin frowned down at her. A moment ago she had seemed mortified, as if someone had stripped her naked in public. Wasn't she stricken by humiliation after having been caught in the act of kissing a man in a closed room?

Viola was looking at Miss Pettigrew, her eyes compassionate. "I'm certain that His Grace understands that a startled woman might say words she didn't intend. You didn't mean to imply that there was anything improper about a kiss shared by a betrothed couple, did you, Miss Pettigrew?"

"No," the lady managed to gasp.

"Nor that a betrothed gentleman and a lady cannot be trusted together without a chaperone." She smiled, she actually *smiled*, at Miss Pettigrew. "I'm sure that on occasion you and Mr. Marlowe have been alone together."

Devin's anger was drenched by a sense of wonder.

He had known Viola was kind and had an instinct to save everything from cows to crows. But he hadn't imagined that she would extend her mercy to the woman marrying the vicar whom she loved.

Hopefully, in the past tense: had loved.

Everything in him suggested that he should ban Mr. Marlowe from all premises that might contain his bride. No more soulful blue eyes around Viola. He could find a weathered, elderly vicar who would run an orphanage with calm deliberation rather than ethical fervor.

But he didn't want to disagree with his bride.

What's more, he had a suspicion that Viola was the kind of woman who would listen to advice and make her own decision, regardless of a husband's attempt to dictate. She grew up in Lady Knowe's nursery, after all.

"As a devoted mother, I trust my daughter implicitly," Mrs. Pettigrew said. "If she and Mr. Marlowe wished to talk in private, I would have to discuss it with Bishop Pettigrew, but we would likely allow a brief conversation."

"As I trust my niece," Lady Knowe said, turning her stony gaze onto Mrs. Pettigrew. "Which is why I am very disturbed at the implications of your daughter's statements."

"I apologize," Miss Pettigrew said with a gulp.

"There!" Viola said brightly. "I accept your apology, Miss Pettigrew. And now I'd like to see the rest of the vicarage."

Devin frowned. There was something deeply unpleasant about Miss Pettigrew. He truly didn't want her in the parish.

But Viola was looking at him, holding out her hand.

"Viola always gets her way," Lady Knowe told him, as they walked toward the hallway. She'd stopped looking like an avenging angel, sword in hand.

As Devin saw it, Viola could have her way, as long as she didn't keep thinking that Mr. Marlowe needed rescuing from his sour fiancée.

Viola had no interest in Devin's title or wealth, and he didn't have persuasive charm or pretty looks. Or virtue, for that matter.

But they had something between them, because that kiss had rocked him to his core.

The tour of the vicarage and grounds resulted in one triumph: A cowed Miss Pettigrew agreed that a play depicting the events of Noah's ark, put on in order to make money to support Mr. Marlowe's orphanage, would be acceptable.

"You'd better come home with us," Lady Knowe said to Devin when the tour of the cloister was over, Otis having established where the stage would be erected, the Pettigrews nodding with tight-lipped acceptance. "You need to speak to the duke."

"Yes," Devin said.

"You don't say much, do you?" Lady Knowe asked him.

"He can be very talkative on occasion," Viola said, tucking her hand into his elbow.

Lady Knowe snorted.

Devin didn't smile, but he came damned close.

"I don't know what your mother is going to think of this," Lady Knowe said to Viola, with a groan. "Ophelia will probably say I should have done a better job chaperoning you. But who would have thought Miss Pettigrew was such an inquisitive creature? She even opened the doors to the cupboards. I expected her to begin counting the linens."

Viola glanced around to make sure that the Pettigrews had returned to the vicarage and were nowhere in sight. "You don't have to worry, Aunt Knowe. I'll explain everything."

"Explain what?" Devin asked.

"Well, that it wasn't really . . . that it didn't . . ." She stopped, flustered.

Lady Knowe glanced at Devin, her eyes full of mischievous laughter. "I'll leave this to you, Your Grace."

He gave her a nod and waited until she strode away, leaving them alone.

Then he tipped up Viola's chin and said, "You're going to be my bride. My duchess."

Her eyes widened. "Not for such a silly reason!"

"No."

"Why?"

"Because of this."

It was a claiming kiss, a leisurely kiss, one that made him feel drunk. Her tongue met his and she made a sound in the back of her throat that sent him out of control. Not entirely. Just enough to shrink the world to their bodies arching together, gasping in union.

"That," he said huskily, a minute later. "I'd keep convincing you, Viola, but I don't want another lecture from Lady Knowe."

She was nestled against him, her cheeks flushed, eyes shining. "I don't know if our kisses are ordinary," she said shyly.

He cleared his throat, unwilling to let go of her. He hadn't had experience with kisses such as this. "They aren't."

"I've developed a fearful idea of what marriage might entail," she said. "Which is absurd because my mother and stepfather adore each other, and I've watched some of my siblings happily pair off."

He was having trouble concentrating because her lips had been kissed scarlet, and they were plump and soft. But they had to walk back to her house.

"I had a terrible experience at my first ball," she said in a rush.

Devin felt a cold pang in his gut. "Did someone— did anyone harm you?" He didn't recognize his own voice, likely because that wasn't his voice; it was his father's. There was the promise of murder in it.

"No, no," Viola said hastily. She had been holding on to his greatcoat, but she smoothed it, as if she were soothing a wild beast.

"You said you threw up," he prompted, remembering. "That must have been a harrowing experience."

"Humiliating," Viola said, glancing up at him and then looking back at his coat.

Devin was having trouble keeping his mind fixed on what she was saying because she hadn't been injured, and that meant his mind reverted to the languid way that she was stroking the rough frieze of his coat.

Which could be his chest. Her slim fingers touching him was the most erotic image he'd—

"I accidentally interrupted a private moment between a couple. The gentleman was furious. He was bellowing at . . . at his wife. He said horrible things." She swallowed hard. "I was *terrified*. I can't explain it; his words felt like blows, not directed at me, but still terrible."

Devin froze. It couldn't be. Of course, that scene years ago did happen in Lindow Castle.

No: Viola said *wife*. And the couple were arguing, not having sex.

Not him . . . but still terrible.

Perhaps he should question her more closely, but that might lead to a discussion of what he himself had done. Anyone might come across an arguing couple; his parents had likely shocked any number of people.

"It seems stupid now," she went on. "You must think me a perfect ninny. All I can say is that the rage in his voice did something to me. I was dreadfully nervous anyway, and on the verge of throwing up. After that . . . after that I couldn't imagine how I would ever trust a man not to erupt at me."

Devin was scarcely breathing. Her description spoke to an ancient, raw part of his soul, the part that had learned at the age of two not to visibly cower—which was his earliest memory of his father's bellow.

"My father was often enraged," he said. "I know exactly how you felt."

Viola came up on her toes and kissed his chin. "You gave Miss Pettigrew a furious look, but you didn't say anything."

"I do not speak when I'm angry," he said. "Because of that."

She blinked.

"What you described."

He had never been very good with words, perhaps because such a flood of words had bombarded the walls of his house: bouncing between his parents, flung with impunity at guests, servants, strangers. And always, in his father's voice, was the threat of violence and death.

"My father never challenged me to a duel," he said, stumbling into an explanation. "But he wanted to."

Viola looked astonished. "A man can't duel his own son!"

"The only reason why he never did it. I'm just saying that I understand what happened to you and I'm sorry that you experienced it."

"I never imagined this," Viola said. "I feel safe with you. I suppose that is the one promise that I would like before we marry: that you would never shout at me with such livid rage."

He cleared his throat. "As I said, I don't like to lose my temper."

"I don't either." She beamed at him.

"But I have lost my temper a few times in my life," he confessed. "On occasion, when pressed. Particularly, when surprised."

"As have I. I shouted at my stepfather once. No, twice."

Devin's eyebrow shot up, despite himself. "You shouted at the Duke of Lindow?"

She nodded cheerfully. "Completely lost my head. He said that Barty had to go back into the forest, that he should grow up and be a wild bird."

"Barty is your crow?"

"Yes, I have to introduce you. Barty is a very good judge of character. He'll like you immediately."

Devin wasn't sure of that. He hadn't had a dog when he was a boy, because future dukes didn't have *pets*, according to his father. But also, Devin had decided on observation, because dogs tended to growl and back away, even when his father was in a good mood.

"At any rate, I lost my temper and shouted at the duke about Barty's wings and swore that I would go live in the forest before I would allow Barty to be exiled there alone."

"And?"

Viola grinned. "He burst out laughing, because I am afraid of the dark, and I dislike being in the woods by myself, and I don't even go to the stables because I'm wary of horses—but here I was, announcing that I was moving to a forest to take care of a baby crow?"

Devin knew what "wonder" was. It was what you felt when you saw a rainbow, or a huge waterfall, or the Thames frozen over.

Or Viola.

"Barty's wings don't work properly," she said, obviously having no idea that he was in the grip of . . . something. "My stepfather didn't understand that, but I managed to explain it and ever since, Barty has lived with us, of course."

Who knew that wonder could flood one's body the way rage did? Or desire, for that matter?

But now, looking at a woman to whom he'd somehow managed to get himself betrothed, who was willing to live in a dark forest to nurture a small, defenseless creature?

This—*this* was the luckiest thing that ever happened to him in his life, including the moment he was born into a world that considered him a duke.

Chapter Eighteen

$\mathcal{W}$hen they reached the Lindow townhouse, Viola was startled to hear from the butler that the Duke of Lindow was waiting for them in his study. Prism had a serious look, even as he murmured congratulations to Devin.

Viola was only just beginning to get her head around what had happened.

Thanks to Miss Pettigrew, she would be a duchess? Inconceivable.

She had thought her stepfather would want to talk to Devin alone. She had thought . . . What had she thought? This situation—marriage—had blown up in her face. It wasn't unlike the moment when Barty fell from a pine tree, landed on her shoulder, bounced off, and lay on the ground at her feet, dazed and blinking at her.

One minute you were alone—and the next you weren't.

When they walked into the room, Devin's hand was warm in the middle of her back. Her stepfather was at his desk and, unusually for him, he was scowling down at his papers.

Not just "papers," it turned out after they got through greetings, because her stepfather reached down and grabbed a broadside.

All the Wildes knew exactly what a print looked like. This one was larger than most, Viola registered with a thump of her heart.

"You opened my daughter to invidious commentary," the duke said to Devin, in the clipped voice that was the closest he ever came to sounding enraged. "The stationer apparently received this sketch and rushed it into print an hour later. Tell me why I should trust you with my daughter!"

Devin was staring down at the sheet, his jaw clenched. Viola tucked her hand into his and gave him a squeeze.

"Which stationer?" Devin said, the words sounding like quiet gunshots.

Her father waved his hand. "It doesn't matter who printed it. *You* made an exhibition of my daughter in a public street, and this is the result!"

"I was there too," Viola said, deciding that she had to see it herself, even though her stomach was clenching. It must be terrible, or her stepfather wouldn't be furious.

It was terrible.

The print showed Viola hitched up against Devin with her legs around his waist, in exactly the position that the lady had been all those years ago, at the ball. Viola was kissing Devin, her bonnet askew.

She looked . . . dissolute. That was a polite word for it. Her lips were pursed and she seemed to be attacking the duke.

She was still staring when Devin took the print, crumpled it, and dropped it. "I would be grateful for the name of the stationer."

"What does it say at the bottom?" Viola asked. Her stomach was churning. She'd been stupid, so stupid. She knew that reporters didn't respect her the way they did the Wildes.

They wouldn't have dared make this sketch of Betsy.

She turned to Devin. "I'm sorry," she whispered.

"You're sorry?" Her stepfather's tone was even more clipped. "Wynter is the gentleman here. Or supposedly so."

"Our kiss had no resemblance to this abomination," Devin said, the rumble in his voice matching her father's.

Viola grabbed the sketch from the floor and pulled it open just enough to read the title at the bottom. *Viola Follows Family Tradition & Lands a Duke the Old-Fashioned Way!*

"That doesn't make any sense," she said, reading it again. And again.

"It's rubbish," her stepfather snapped. "It's a veiled reference to your mother. The point is that I would have thought you, Wynter, being a duke, would show better judgment. Of all my children, Viola has avoided invidious attention, and yet you engaged in public intimacies that would shock even Betsy!"

"I assure you that our first kiss was only akin to this because it happened on the street," Devin said evenly. "It was merely a kiss."

It wasn't an apology, but an explanation.

The duke folded his arms over his chest. "I've sent my solicitor to Doctors' Commons for a special license."

Devin nodded.

"What?" Viola asked. "No!"

"I'm sorry, dearest," her stepfather said. "I gather from my sister that a similar incident at the vicarage was seen by one of the Pettigrews. They will almost certainly share their experience."

"Not if I have anything to do with it," Devin growled.

Viola had a flash of pride. He might not like to talk when he was angry, but at the moment he was both communicative and in control of his temper.

"The women just spent the afternoon poking their noses into every cupboard in the vicarage," Devin continued grimly. "*My* vicarage."

"Miss Pettigrew won't say anything," Viola said hastily, squeezing his hand tighter. "It was merely a kiss," she told her father. "Another kiss."

"It won't be Miss Pettigrew," the Duke of Lindow said, a deep weariness in his voice. "The story will be sold by her maid, or even a scullery maid, or no one will know how it got out of the household. Your aunt tells me that the two of you were in a closed room, alone, and you were interrupted at an inopportune moment."

He stopped talking and took a deep breath. It seemed that her stepfather—who never lost his temper—was on the verge of doing so.

"I apologize," Devin said. He looked down at Viola. "I take full responsibility for closing the door."

Viola dropped his hand and put her hands on her hips. "I *told* you to close the door!"

"No gentleman would have listened to you," the Duke of Lindow stated.

"Oh, for goodness' sake," she cried. "We were kissing each other. We both wanted that door shut—not for the reasons you may be thinking," she told her stepfather, "but because the Pettigrews were nosy."

"I wanted the door shut in order to kiss you properly," Devin said stubbornly.

Viola scowled at him, but she saw the look in his eyes. She didn't know desire very well, but she recognized it. She smiled back.

The Duke of Lindow groaned.

The door sprang open, and her mother hurdled into the room. "Viola, dearest!" Ophelia cried, holding out her arms.

Viola flew into her embrace.

Her mother gave her a squeeze, pulled back, and cupped her face with her hands. "Do you want him? I don't give a rat's ass if he's a duke or not. Nor how many prints are circulating either." She gave her husband an exasperated look. "None of that matters."

Viola blinked. "You never swear."

"Profanity is a natural response to one's children being threatened," her mother said. She put Viola to the side and looked at Devin.

Viola looked too.

The two dukes were wide-shouldered, muscled, and glowering at each other.

"My goodness," her mother said quietly, her breath brushing Viola's ear.

"They're both large," Viola said. "And we're small." Her mother was the only woman in the family who didn't make her feel like a tree stump next to willows.

She glanced at Ophelia and saw her mother's eyes were on her husband with a slightly dreamy emotion in them.

"Mother," she said, nudging her.

Ophelia shed her bemused air. "Do you want Wynter, poppet? Because if you don't, your father will send him off with a flea in his ear."

Viola didn't think it would be quite that easy to get rid of Devin, but more importantly . . . she didn't want to.

"Devin makes me feel safe," she said. "I can eat around him."

Her mother's mouth eased into a smile. "One wants to eat."

"You know what I mean."

Ophelia's arms closed around her again in a tight squeeze. "Dearest, if I could have made the last few years easier for you somehow, I would have. But you solved it by yourself!"

"With some help," Viola said.

Her mother's brows drew together. "Ah, yes, Mr. Marlowe."

"I was thinking of Joan," Viola said.

"Excellent!"

Devin advanced and made an elegant bow. "Good afternoon, Your Grace. I apologize for the occasion that spurred the wretched print. But I will never regret my first kiss with Viola."

Viola felt a little smile curling her lips. Her heart was beating quickly, and she could hear it in her ears. Was she really going to do this? Become a *duchess*?

"I request the honor of your daughter's hand in marriage."

Ophelia looked back at him with her direct gaze. "My husband and I do not consider ourselves the most important people in that regard. Have you asked my daughter the same question?"

"There has been little time," Devin said. He walked to Viola and caught up her hands. He looked down at her, and his expression made a rush of blood rise in her cheeks.

He wasn't beautiful, and he wasn't particularly interested in orphans, or animals—she had the sense that he wouldn't know what to do with a pet cat or dog—but he was . . . *dear*. What's more, she only had to meet his eyes to feel a surge of sensual longing coursing through her whole body.

"Will you marry me?" Devin asked. "Will you be mine, Viola, for better and worse, in sickness and in health? I know you aren't in love with me, but I believe that we will be happy together."

Viola forgot that her parents were in the room. She turned her hands until she was holding his as well. "I may not be a very good duchess." She had to say it. She had to give him one more chance to come to his senses and realize that he could have a diamond of the first water, a paragon, the most ladylike lady in polite society.

"I don't want a good duchess," Devin said, his voice deepening. "You'll be a wonderful Duchess of Wynter. *My* duchess."

Behind them, the sound of a door quietly closing startled Viola. She looked around and discovered that her parents had left the room.

"Your father nodded to me," Devin said. He gave her a gentle tug and led her to a sofa. "I believe that constitutes consent."

As they sat down, he kept one of her hands, running his fingers over her knuckles before bringing it to his mouth for a kiss. "We needn't use the special license. I will tear apart the printmaker who created that abomination. I'll do the same for any printer who issues a depiction of our kiss in the vicarage."

Viola looked into his eyes and saw certainty there. More than certainty: ferocity.

"I will always protect my family," he said, a growl in his voice.

She gathered all her courage. "Yes," she said, her voice coming out in a rasp. She cleared her throat: "Yes, I will marry you, Devin."

He didn't say anything for a moment. Then they moved together, their bodies leaning toward each other in perfect unison. One of Viola's arms curved around his neck just as their lips met.

They kissed slowly, their lips moving gently, until desire built up between them and turned to greed, and Viola's tongue slipped between his lips. She felt Devin shudder, as his tongue twined about hers, sending streaks of heat through her body.

His hand flattened on her back, pulling her closer. "May I hold you more closely?"

"Mmmm," she said, putting her other arm around his neck.

With a smooth motion, he drew her into his lap until her back rested against one of his strong arms. He bent his head and she eagerly opened her mouth, reveling in a kiss that felt *right*.

"My heart is thumping," she whispered sometime later. She could feel the flex of strong legs beneath her, and the warmth of his arm, strong as a curving steel bar, at her back.

She took an arm down from his neck, flattened her hand on his chest, and smiled because his heart thundered under her fingers. It made her breathless, as if she'd caught a wild beast.

He made a husky sound—amusement or agreement, she didn't know—and sealed his mouth to hers again. He kissed her fiercely, nipping her lip, returning to her mouth, until they were both gasping.

"You can have all the time you want before we marry," he said throatily, "but bloody hell, Viola, I hope you don't take months. I want you more than I've ever wanted a woman, though I feel guilty saying it."

She drew back and whispered, "Why?"

"I'm a cold bastard, and you're so—I have the idea that you're the kindest person I've ever met." His hands tightened on her. "I don't want to be married out of pity, Viola. I'm not one of your rescues. You're ideal, an idealist—and I'm not."

Her eyes met his fierce gaze and she understood that although he would never say it, and probably didn't even know it, she wasn't the only one who was afraid. Which meant he wasn't the only one who had power in their relationship. He didn't wish to be found wanting either.

Yet she couldn't imagine that the day would come when she would want to be anywhere but at his side. This wasn't like falling in love with an unfamiliar vicar who happened by for tea.

She didn't revere Devin's eyes or his chin—though now she realized that a square chin was far better than a gently sloped one. She didn't want to help him in his life's work, because she didn't understand mathematics.

But she wanted to talk to him and get to know him. Find out more about his terrible father. What about his mother? Why was he so protective?

And the relentless sensual urge that made her knees tremble told her something else: She wanted him profoundly, to the very center of her being. That, more than anything, meant she should marry him.

"Do you think desire is enough?" she asked.

Somewhat to her surprise, he took a moment to think about it.

"I desire you. But I also admire you, Viola. The idea of marrying you is exhilarating, as if I'd solved Fermat's Conjecture, the most complicated mathematical theorem that exists."

"Oh," Viola breathed.

"Otis says that I'm cold-blooded, and I expect he's right. But I will try. I will try to be a good father to our children."

"You'll be a wonderful father," she said.

"I don't know how to do it, other than not to shout at them."

"I'll teach our daughters how to fence, in case you challenge them to a duel," Viola said, laughter gurgling in her throat.

But he shook his head, eyes dark. "I'm serious, Viola. You were terrified by seeing a husband and wife argue, do you remember?"

She blinked, and remembered in a fit of embarrassment that she'd told him the copulating pair at the ball were married. She nodded.

"That was my childhood," Devin said. "My father didn't want me to attend Eton, so I was kept at home. He liked having an audience, and I was often summoned from the nursery to learn an important lesson about being a duke—which generally consisted of watching my father howl with rage."

"He didn't hurt you, did he?" Viola whispered, seeing that Devin's eyes were tight and his jaw firm.

"No. He sometimes threw vases and shoes, but even as a young boy, I was nimble."

Viola wound her arms around him and put her cheek against his chest. "I am sorry."

"I don't want you to marry me out of sympathy or pity, Viola. I'm not Barty. Or Mr. Marlowe."

She wrinkled her nose at him. "You are very emotional. Luckily for you, I'm used to drama from growing up with the Wildes."

He physically recoiled. "I am *not* dramatic. Or emotional."

Viola smiled. "As for treating you like a wounded bird, why would I? You're a duke. You're the highest in the land, exquisitely dressed, wealthy, powerful, and self-sufficient. I don't feel sorry for you in the slightest. After all, your father *didn't* challenge you to a duel, and Sir Reginald obviously loves you, as do Otis and Hazel."

There was an arrested look on Devin's face that Viola tucked away in her mind to think about later.

He smiled, not the vivid smile that changed his features, but a sleek, satisfied smile, like a predator who had rounded up just the right supper. "You're right," he said, his voice purring. "Let's go back to where we were before. You're marrying me because of *this*." He caught her against him.

Viola gasped with surprise and instantly succumbed, her thoughts blurred by a kiss that was carnal—and possessive.

"You are worried," he said sometime later, his

voice a throaty growl, "that we're marrying for the wrong reasons. But this is the best reason I can think of, Viola. I don't care that you're a duke's daughter, or that you're incredibly beautiful, or that you make me laugh."

He stopped.

"You don't want to marry me for those reasons," Viola said, treasuring the fact he thought she was beautiful. "But?"

"I care about kissing you," he said. "I'd like to do it again. Often."

Her heart bounded and she smiled at him. "I'd like to kiss you often too."

"And more," he said, watching her closely. "I want to make love to you, Viola. Every night and probably mornings as well. I want to see you over the breakfast table, sweep off the dishes, and make love to you there. And in the dining room," he added. "On every table in the house."

There was a brisk knock on the door.

Devin held Viola's gaze for a long second, turned his head, and said, "Enter."

Ophelia bustled in. "That is the extent of time that your father will allow the two of you to be alone," she announced. "And here you are, standing at a proper distance from each other."

Viola managed a wobbly smile at that patent fib, got to her feet, and walked toward her mother. "Of course we are."

Her mother's eyes swept over Devin, undoubtedly registering the smoldering look in his eyes, even though he stood easily, like a man whose conduct is never questioned.

"Your hair," she said to Viola, nodding toward the mirror on one wall. "Your father will be here in three minutes."

Viola ran to the glass.

"If you don't mind, Duke, I'll straighten your cravat. Viola is the most tenderhearted of my children, and if you hurt her, I'll eviscerate you," her mother told him, all in precisely the same charming tone.

Viola tucked an errant curl back into her coiffure, listening as hard as she could.

"I will do my best," Devin said. "No one can promise another person a happy life. But I will do everything in my power to make certain that Viola is safe and joyful."

"Good enough," the duchess said.

Viola turned and started back toward them.

This was happening. It was truly happening.

She walked to Devin's side, swallowing back her smile. She said, "Mother, I've decided to marry the Duke of Wynter by special license."

Next to her, she felt the faint tremor that went through Devin's body, even though his expression didn't change.

Chapter Nineteen

$\mathcal{V}$iola watched as her stepfather entered the room, went straight to his desk, and plucked up another copy of the offensive print.

For a man who'd sired ten children and raised twelve, he didn't look old. He was tall and broad-shouldered, and he stood as tall as he must have forty years ago.

"I spend money and time destroying prints that I find offensive," the Duke of Lindow said, by way of greeting.

"This will be your task now," Ophelia said. Viola's mother was watching Devin closely; he might not have realized it, but the comment was a test.

Devin wasn't a conventionally handsome man. He didn't have celestial blue eyes or a slim figure or a graceful gait. He didn't carry a cane. He danced with abrupt finesse, going through the figures of a dance with precision. You could trust him to turn in precisely the right direction, at precisely the right moment.

You could not trust him to look like a graceful willow, which was how the Wilde dancing master had described gentlemen on the dance floor.

That suggestion had never worked with her stepbrothers either.

But if Devin didn't have the tools that marked a gentleman as not merely civilized, but intrinsically aristocratic . . .

He did have one asset, one that he used rarely.

He gave Ophelia his blinding smile, the one that transformed a rough-hewn set of features to a gloriously beautiful face.

At least as she saw it.

Her mother drew in a swift breath, and Viola had to choke back a giggle.

"I meant to ask for Viola's hand in marriage as soon as I could speak to the duke. From the moment I met her at the Wilde ball, as a matter of fact."

"I don't know when you met Viola at the ball," the duchess said, her tone still guarded. He hadn't quite won her over. "What I remember is that you asked for an introduction to my daughter Joan, but inexplicably didn't mention Viola."

"I had thought to marry Joan," Devin said. "We would not have suited."

A snort from her stepfather seconded that assessment.

"I met Viola, and realized that I didn't want to marry a duke's daughter—which my father on his deathbed had instructed me to do."

Her father rocked forward on his toes, his jaw set. "Viola *is* a duke's daughter."

"Oh, I know." This smile was a wry one, a small

version of Devin's most potent weapon. "But I don't want to marry a duke's daughter. I want to marry the young lady I found hiding behind the curtains, who proceeded to chastise me for arrogance and lack of consideration, and all the time looked at me with those eyes—"

He stopped. "Viola is beautiful, of course, but that isn't it. That wasn't why I meant to ask you for her hand in marriage. It wasn't her beauty, nor her parentage. It was simply *her*."

Viola could feel happiness filling her like a cup under running water. Devin wasn't trying to convince her parents. He was just telling the truth as it was self-evident to him.

Her stepfather liked it too. His jaw eased.

Ophelia was still looking at him closely. "My daughter is the most tenderhearted of our children," she repeated.

"I am ready to build any number of cowsheds," the duke said promptly. His eyes gleamed with amusement and perhaps even a hint of pride. "I have committed to building an orphanage attached to St. Wilfrid's."

"I wasn't speaking merely of Viola's compassion," her mother said. "I meant that she is tender spirited. She will not thrive if you are peremptory with her."

"I'm in the room," Viola said, feeling indignant.

"Viola is a strong woman," Devin said, his hand curling around hers. "But I do not plan to be peremptory with my wife."

Her mother didn't look entirely convinced.

"I wouldn't thrive in a garret on bread and water," Viola said impatiently, "but I will be fine in other circumstances."

Devin looked taken aback. "I assure you that I would never imprison anyone, especially my wife." There was a touch of offense in his voice.

"That was just an example," Viola said.

"If any of my daughters are mistreated by a husband, I have instructed them to return to our house," Ophelia said, fixing her eyes on Devin.

"I cannot imagine why—" Devin was beginning to look truly affronted.

"Because of your father," Viola's stepfather said, intervening. "I'm afraid there are few people in polite society who didn't witness scathing battles between your father and mother."

"I have a different constitution from my father," Devin said. "In his defense, he regularly shouted but was never truly threatening; my parents would trade heated words until my mother lost patience and moved away, for months at a time."

Viola shifted their hands to squeeze Devin's hand. His face was inscrutable, but his profile looked even harsher than usual.

"Stop it, both of you," she ordered, giving her parents a direct look. "I have chosen to accept Devin's hand in marriage. He is not like his parents *at all*. He never raises his voice. But more to the point, this is my decision, not yours." She looked pointedly at the duke. "You have always told us that we could choose our own spouses."

"This isn't a customary betrothal," His Grace said. "There hasn't been time to come to know him. We haven't shared more than a meal or two. Have you discussed practicalities, such as where you'll spend most of your time?"

"I don't care," Viola said, looking up at Devin. Her

head scarcely reached his shoulder, so it was a long way up. "We'll probably live quietly, perhaps in the country." She paused. "If you wish?"

Devin looked down at her and suddenly she knew exactly what that expression was: *hunger.*

"I will live wherever you are," he said. The truth in his voice rang in the room, and she saw her mother relax.

"To return to your original point," Devin said to the duchess, "no one is going to print execrable trash about my wife and be open the next day to print even a Psalm. I shall make certain the printers understand that Viola is not to feature in any print, as it might result in damage to a printing press."

"I'll admit that never in these years of battling prints did I consider violence," the duke said thoughtfully.

"You had no need," his wife pointed out. "The boys shrugged off the broadsides. Alaric actually considered framing the one pairing him with Empress Catherine until Willa objected. Alaric is the duke's oldest living son and Willa is his wife," she explained to Devin.

"I don't think of it as violence," Devin said. "I will protect my family by any means possible, and the printers might as well learn that now. But in the end, it's up to Viola."

Viola looked in surprise as all three of them looked to her. "Me?"

"You," Devin said. "I would like to avenge this insult, but I watched my father make decisions for his wife too many times, and you are the one insulted."

Viola's mouth shaped the word "oh," but no sound emerged. Her mother was chuckling and even the duke had stopped looking surly.

"I vote for a warning," Viola said.

"*One* warning," Devin said.

She nodded.

"Can't believe I didn't think of destroying the printing press," her stepfather mumbled, coming over and wrapping an arm around his wife. "All those prints about North."

"North didn't care," Ophelia said, "even when they were comparing him to a Shakespearean villain."

"North didn't mind," Viola agreed. She swallowed. "I do. I don't want any prints of me sold, even if they're nicer than . . . than that. I just don't like the idea of it."

Devin nodded. She had a feeling that the printing press—perhaps all the printing presses of London—were shortly to find themselves being given a ferocious warning, but she decided not to worry about it.

"Wynter, you and I need to talk about how to present your betrothal to polite society," the duke said. "Or rather, your marriage, if you use the special license."

Viola's stomach was clenching again. She literally could not imagine walking into a ballroom. "The Season is over for me," she stated.

Silence.

She looked at her mother apologetically. "I can't do it. Knowing what they all will be saying about me, how fascinating everyone will find Devin's choice . . . I just can't."

Devin took her hand. "If you will excuse us, Your Grace, I'd like to speak to Viola in private again. We won't be long." He had that trick of asking a question but assuming the answer.

Viola was unsurprised when her father nodded.

The Duke of Lindow was a man who generally got his way, but he wasn't a fool either. He'd met his match in the Duke of Wynter, and never mind the fact that his future son-in-law was much younger than he.

Viola found herself grinning from ear to ear.

Her mother caught her in a hug. "You were my shy baby, so I always imagined you married to someone sweet and retiring."

Viola looked over her shoulder and knew that Devin was listening. His eyes had a distinctly wild glint. He was *not* sweet.

She had a strange feeling that she knew who was in his thoughts: Mr. Marlowe. The vicar was sweet.

"Viola needs someone to protect her," the Duke of Lindow said. "You might as well suggest that she marry Marlowe!"

Viola held back a smile.

Thank goodness, she hadn't truly been in love with the vicar. Of course, she would have had her way eventually—*if* Mr. Marlowe had wanted to marry her and *if* Miss Pettigrew weren't standing in the way—but it would have been a battle royal.

The duke was now giving Devin the sort of look that he gave his sons: one of pride and respect.

"I'll walk into that ballroom next to you, Viola, and believe me, no one will say a word about my choice of duchess," Devin said.

Viola did believe him, or rather, she believed that he meant it. You couldn't say he was arrogant: It was more that he was a force of nature. A rock or a mountain.

A rock who didn't understand the nature of gossip.

"You may have ten minutes alone," Ophelia announced.

Viola glanced at her mother and discovered that she was smiling. Apparently she too recognized that Viola would be better off with a mountain than a gentle vicar.

Chapter Twenty

As her parents left, Viola allowed Devin to draw her down to sit beside him.

"I want to make certain that you don't have dreams of a wedding like your stepsister Betsy's," Devin said. "I don't want you to feel forced. I will wait if you would prefer. I will court you, and be damned with gossip."

People had lined the streets to see Betsy and shout congratulations to the bride. The very idea made Viola shudder.

"I don't have any wish for a big wedding, but I never imagined that my husband would be forced to marry me either," she said.

"If you wish to wait, we'll wait. I am a duke and no one under the monarch can make me do something if I don't wish it." His eyes were intent on hers. "I know we don't know each other very well, but—"

She put a hand on his arm, and he stopped. "I do know you, Devin. You're kind and considerate. While you were angry with Miss Pettigrew, you didn't dismiss Mr. Marlowe because I asked you not to. When you considered destroying the printing press, you asked me for my opinion first. You are everything I like in a man."

"I'm not as kind as the vicar. To be completely honest, I'm not really interested in orphanages, though I have no objection to building one and supporting it."

"We don't have to be interested in the same things," she said, a smile growing in her heart. "I don't expect you to spend time with me in the cowshed."

He leaned toward her, eyes hungry. "Actually . . ."

Viola was suddenly breathless.

"I like the sound of a cowshed," he said, his lips close to hers. "Fresh hay . . ." The sentence drifted off because she opened her lips, greedy to see if kissing him was as powerful every time.

It was.

Viola stroked his tongue with hers, and unable to stop herself, reached out to clutch his coat and pull him closer.

"You're little but fierce," Devin murmured.

"Not a mouse?" Viola asked.

He didn't answer, but only because his arms were around her and somehow he'd managed to pull her into his lap. Surrounded by his strength and warmth, she could feel desperation coursing through him. *For her!*

She started kissing him as fiercely as she knew how, letting her body tell him all the incoherent things she felt, things that had nothing to do with the virtuous Mr. Marlowe or, indeed, virtue at all. She felt overheated and wild, every bit of her attuned to his body: to the catch in his throat, the hoarse, helpless sound when she rocked against him, the way his hands were trembling.

She didn't even notice Joan was in the room until Devin pulled back. Viola was staring at him, trying to reconcile her normally demure self with a new version of herself that saw nothing wrong with ripping off her fiancé's neck cloth and licking his neck.

Not that she had, of course, but she had imagined it.

Joan was standing not far away, an arm melodramatically cast over her eyes. "Mother sent me to fetch you, Viola. Your Grace, my father is waiting for you in the library and I wouldn't be tardy, were I you."

"Devin," Viola breathed. "I . . ."

"I as well," he said, his penetrating gaze hungry. The roughness in his voice made her squirm in his lap. His eyelids drooped and he stood, bringing Viola to her feet. "All right?"

Viola was turning pink. She almost—*almost*—blurted out that she "needed" him. The only explanation was that she had temporarily lost her mind.

Devin took a deep breath and shook his head. "Whatever just came into your head, don't say it until we're in private, Viola."

"I don't want to know what's in either of your heads," Joan remarked.

Viola pressed a hand to her chest, willing her heart to stop thumping.

"Lady Joan, I will be honored to call you sister-in-law," Devin said.

"I don't know that it's such an honor," Joan said, laughing. "You picked the better Wilde sister by far. Now come along!" She turned and marched toward the door.

Viola caught Devin's arm as he turned to follow Joan.

"That was—" The right words didn't come to mind. Improper? Marvelous? Terrible? Bad? Good? *Wrong?* Words tumbled through her mind like dried weeds.

He took a deep breath. "Special license, so we needn't call the banns?" His eyes bored into hers, and for once, they were *not* unreadable. They were hungry, and possessive, and believable.

That little part of Viola that always felt anxious about not belonging, calmed.

"We belong together," she whispered.

He glanced at Joan, waiting by the door, and bent his head closer to her. "I can't wait to see your cowshed."

They walked to the door together, hand in hand.

Chapter Twenty-one

Three Days Later
St. Margaret's Church

$\mathcal{M}$iss Viola Astley married the Duke of Wynter in a ceremony that, had the bride bothered to envision her own wedding, she would have considered perfect.

St. Margaret's Church, next to Westminster Abbey, was closed to all visitors, and only her dearest family thronged in the front pews. The Murgatroyds were practically Wildes at this point: Sir Reginald sat beside Aunt Knowe; Hazel had claimed Diana and North's baby Peter and cuddled him the entire time; and Joan and Otis sat together, wearing equally naughty expressions. Even Willa came, leaning on Alaric's arm, and risking—as Aunt Knowe said—a baby born in the pew.

Devin was magnificent in a suit fitted to such perfection that Lavinia had reached out and touched his coat. "I adore the cut of this lapel," she had said dreamily. Parth had swooped in and advised Devin to ignore his wife. "I know she looks as if she wants to rip the coat off your body," he had advised, "but she just wants to inspect the lining."

Viola forced her attention back to the words of the marriage ceremony. "Will you, Viola Astley . . ." The Dean of Westminster Abbey, the Very Reverend Henry Damson, went on and on, listing a frighteningly precise inventory of all the things that she and Devin might have to weather together.

"Yes," she said, looking at Devin, not at the ground, "I will."

When he slid a ring on her finger, Viola smiled down at the exquisite circlet. "Not my mother's," Devin had told her the night before. "We will begin our own tradition." The ring was silver, with a pattern of leaves adorned with small diamonds and a very large diamond for good measure.

"You may kiss the bride," the dean remarked, scarcely making himself heard over the joyous shouting of the Wildes, who had taken the lack of fellow guests as a sign that they could be themselves.

There it was.

They were married, not just *in sickness and in health*, but *till death do us part*.

Devin's mouth quirked as he looked down at her. "My duchess."

"My duke," Viola returned.

He bent his head and kissed her until the dean coughed. Devin lifted his head and caught her against him when she lost her balance and teetered on her heels.

They walked back down the long aisle of St. Margaret's like that, Devin's arm wrapped around Viola's waist, her body tucked against his.

Ophelia was crying; the Duke of Lindow was

laughing. Aunt Knowe seemed to be having an amiable argument with Sir Reginald. Otis was elbowing Joan; Erik was smirking; Parth had forgotten all rules about public decency and was kissing Lavinia passionately. In fact, when the Wildes and Murgatroyds filed out of the pews and followed the bride and groom, the families left those two behind, everyone crowding about to watch Devin and Viola sign the register of the parish.

The wedding breakfast passed in a blur of champagne and joyous toasts, along with all matter of delicacies created by the Duke of Lindow's French cook.

Until it was time to leave.

Feeling dazed but happy, Viola climbed into the Wynter carriage, clutching handfuls of silken gauze from the beautiful gown that Lavinia had appropriated from one of the *modistes* who enjoyed her patronage. Behind her, the duke—her husband!—said a last word to Sir Reginald, nodded to the duchess, and swung himself into the carriage to sit opposite her.

As the vehicle lurched into motion, Viola forced herself to look straight at Devin. No more sideways glances just to make sure that he was still in the church, and hadn't changed his mind.

His eyes were possessive . . . desirous . . . cautious.

"I think that went well," she said. "Don't you agree?"

"The breakfast or the ceremony? I liked the moment when Barty responded to the dean's question," Devin said.

"If any of you can show just cause why they may not lawfully be married, speak now, or else forever hold your peace," Viola said ruefully. "He was silent until that moment!"

"He squawked loudly enough that everyone knew his opinion on the matter," Devin said, grinning.

"He's not usually noisy," Viola said, trying to get her mind around the idea that she was going to be living with a stranger. A virtual stranger. Not a complete stranger. Anxiety began to press on the back of her throat. "He won't bother you," she said. "Usually he sleeps in my room, but of course that needn't happen. I mean . . ."

She stopped, realizing that she had absolutely no idea if they would share a room. Her parents did, but that was unusual. Scarlet heat swept up her chest into her cheeks.

Devin leaned forward. "Our marriage happened quite quickly," he said. "My butler, Binsey, has prepared the duchess's suite for you, naturally."

Viola nodded.

"It's on a different floor from my chambers," he added.

Her eyes widened.

"My mother preferred to be out of earshot."

Viola didn't know what to say. "I'm sorry."

"Luckily, the townhouse is large enough that she didn't have to move to the servants' quarters," Devin said, looking completely unmoved by the memory.

"You won't hear Barty squawking!" she exclaimed, realizing why he had told her about the duchess's suite. Even more embarrassing thoughts crowded her mind. Did that mean that they wouldn't be consummating the marriage?

Her mother's instructions regarding marital intimacy had been profoundly different from her headmistress's. Ophelia seemed to think that bedding one's husband was one of the most pleasant things in the world.

"I won't hear Barty squawking," Devin confirmed. "Unless I tempt you into sleeping in my chambers, of course."

The carriage jolted, and Viola reached out to grab the hanging strap.

"Perhaps you should join me on this seat," Devin said. "The front seat in a carriage is safer."

She eyed him. "The carriage merely swayed because it rounded a corner," she said, wishing that the flush in her cheeks would go away.

Devin gave her a smile. A small one that didn't involve curling the corners of his mouth as much as a look in his eyes. It made sensation race through her, giving her the breathless feeling one has on a summer night when a star flashes across the sky like a beacon from some other world.

His smile deepened until it actually involved his mouth. He had a beautiful mouth. His bottom lip was deep and perfectly curved. She'd like to . . .

She wrenched her eyes away.

"Since you won't come to my seat," Devin said, "perhaps I should move to yours." His voice was shaded with amusement, but underneath was an emotion that she recognized: carnal desire. "Emotion" didn't seem a strong enough word for whatever it was that hovered in the air between them.

It was more elemental, like those shooting stars that demanded to be noticed.

Had she really wondered whether they would consummate their marriage?

He waited, eyes patient. "All right," she said, moving to the side. "I have to warn you that my panniers are wide. The dress was designed for a lady with more generous proportions than I, and Lavinia's seamstresses were up all night reshaping the skirts."

"I would guess that the lady's generous proportions didn't include her bosom," Devin said, his eyes drifting from her face to her bosom. "I love that gown."

Viola glanced down and just stopped herself from tugging at the bodice.

"The light coming through the stained glass made you look as if you were dusted with gilt from head to foot," Devin said.

Viola swallowed hard but didn't trust herself to speak. She felt as if she were breathless from running, though she was doing nothing more arduous than meeting Devin's eyes.

"Why on earth do women bother with so much fabric?" Devin asked, rising with perfect balance in the swaying carriage, picking up her skirts, and sitting down with a lapful of silk.

"I don't like a large pannier," Viola said. "But on occasion it feels magnificent, as if one were a ship in full sail."

"I can't say I have any interest in experiencing it."

Viola tried to think of something clever to say, and failed. She was used to feeling shy, but not around Devin, and this current bout of shyness was particularly inconvenient.

If she were more courageous, she could lean against his shoulder.

Or put a hand on his arm, turn her head, and indicate that she'd like to be kissed. But how does one *do* that?

Wilde Child, she thought, and shook the thought off.

She wasn't a child, and she was no longer a Wilde. Now she was . . .

"What is my last name?" she asked Devin. "I'm used to thinking of you as the Duke of Wynter. I didn't notice when we signed the register."

That startled a crack of laughter from him. "My name is Devin Lucas Augustus Elstan, Duke of Wynter, along with some secondary titles that I don't bother about."

"Elstan," Viola said thoughtfully.

"You are Viola Annabel Elstan, Duchess of Wynter."

The words hung in the carriage, the only other sound the rattle of wheels along the street. Viola was trying to decide why Devin's voice sounded tender when he said her name. Her new name.

Because he chose her, she thought.

Happiness swirled in her chest. Devin had chosen *her* to be his duchess. Even before the threat of scandal, Devin had made it clear that he had meant to woo her.

Her husband pulled off his gloves and tossed them on the seat opposite. "I imagined you as my duchess only a few minutes after meeting you." He gave her that smile. The joyful one that awakened every limb of her body and made her want to melt toward him.

She busied herself by removing her gloves as well.

"When I imagined a Duchess of Wynter, it didn't occur to me that she would reside anywhere other than the floor above me. Had I bothered to consider the matter, I would have assumed that we would come to a mutually agreeable arrangement as regards intimacies."

She darted a look at him.

"Once a week? Twice a week? Once a month? Whatever Her Grace desired."

The look in his eyes should be outlawed.

Whatever Her Grace desired?

"Ah," Viola said, making herself sound like a hopeless ninny. She had her gloves off. What should she do with them? He had tossed his on the seat with a careless bravado, as if he meant to do something important with his bare hands.

She couldn't imply that. Instead, she stared down at the silk. *Whatever Her Grace desired?*

"Of course," Devin said, that gleam of amusement as clear to her ears as if he rang a bell, "if the duchess is not quite certain what she desires . . ."

Viola gulped. *Wilde Child*. Not child. Duchess. She straightened her head and met his eyes. "I am not experienced in these matters."

"It's my first marriage as well," Devin said.

"That's not what I meant. I meant—" Her mind boggled.

"Country matters?" he suggested.

"What?"

"As Shakespeare had it."

"I am not very literary. In fact, I loathe long poems." She straightened again. "I'm sorry if I disappoint you in that respect."

"I never read poetry," Devin said. "One of my tutors was supposed to teach me Shakespeare, but he was dismissed before we finished the comedies. I've never read *Hamlet* or *Lear*, for that matter."

"You haven't missed anything!" Viola exclaimed. "Joan adores the theater. She made me read *King Lear* aloud to her three times while she acted all the female parts. It's a nasty play about unpleasant people."

"I shan't bother reading it, in that case. I already see how useful marriage will be."

That made Viola look at him again. "I'm actually not a very useful person."

Another smile. "You needn't be. I hope you will be a happy person."

"No one can be happy all the time," Viola observed. She took courage from the taut intensity in his expression. Devin *wanted* her. He was presumably feeling the same thing she was: a deep awareness of his every move. From the corner of her eye, she could see his unbearably erotic, ungloved hands. Those hands had caressed her in the vicarage.

Tonight, she was certain, they would caress her in other places.

The thought made her feel hungry. Unladylike. She cleared her throat. "What shall we do this afternoon?" she asked brightly. Just in time she closed her mouth, before she clarified *before bed*.

"My household is eager to meet you," Devin said.

"Oh, yes," Viola said without enthusiasm. She knew how to run a great house, of course. She had been raised to manage a household, talk to butlers, keep the house accounts. Every year Ophelia gave her daughters an imaginary household and had them plan all the servants, down to the bootblack.

Two days later, they would meet and compare budgets. Viola always hired too many outdoor staff and hardly any upstairs maids, because she hated being watched.

"*Our* household," Devin amended.

Viola nodded and summoned a smile. Was she supposed to say that she was eager to meet them? Many young ladies longed to run a ducal household. None of the Wildes did.

They all knew how much work it was.

Devin moved slightly closer and Viola's skin prickled to life. "What do you want from me?" he asked, his eyes serious.

"In what respect?"

"As a husband. Other than the given: respect, affection, duty. And fidelity."

Viola had seen plenty of marriages in which those attributes didn't seem to be a given, but she was happy to hear they would be in hers. Her bout of shyness eased. "I feel safe with you."

"Good," he said, his voice a low growl. "I will always protect you, Viola. I will give my life for yours."

"I hope there's no need for that. I would like a kiss," she said.

His face eased. "What sort of kiss? Here?" He kissed her forehead.

"No."

"Here?" He kissed her cheek, the way one kisses a child.

Viola turned and caught his neck cloth. "I have some rules for marriage. No shouting."

He nodded.

"No treating me like a child. I am younger than you, but I am an adult." She was quite certain of that. There was nothing like experiencing profound humiliation to drive one to maturity. She often felt three or four years older than Joan, even though their birthdays were not far apart.

"You are my partner," Devin promised.

"I do not want to spend the afternoon touring the house and meeting the members of your household."

"No?" He looked startled but nodded. "We can do whatever you wish."

She tugged on his neck cloth, ruining its perfectly starched edges. "I want to consummate our marriage, Devin. If I have to wait until this evening, I will be twice the nervous wreck that I am already. I may look calm, but I am not."

His hands came up over hers and then fell away. "We won't do *anything* that frightens you." There was something fierce in his voice. "I have no interest in that."

"Kiss me," Viola said, tugging again.

He bent his head and brushed his lips over hers.

Annoyed, she nipped his lower lip and licked the reddened mark.

His eyes kindled and his lips opened against hers. "The duchess commands?"

"You said that I could have anything I desire," she reminded him.

"I don't want to frighten you."

"I'm not frightened of kisses," she said impatiently. "I'm nervous because I don't know what's to come. I don't want to spend the entire day with my stomach in knots."

His voice dropped to a velvety purr. "I completely understand, and I sympathize."

"I can assure you that if I spend the day walking about the house making small talk with your housekeeper, introducing my maid to the butler, finding out what the accounts and the house book look like . . . by the time supper comes about I will be a babbling idiot."

Devin stared down at his wife—his wife!

The word echoed around his mind.

Viola was the most complicated mathematical theorem he'd encountered in his entire life. She looked and sounded like a young lady, but she didn't act like one.

Above all, above even her training as a lady, she was honest.

She was gazing up at him now, her eyes a mix of bravado and fear.

"We could wait to consummate our marriage," he said, although his body was thrumming with a deep pulse of desire. "We could wait days, weeks, even."

He'd probably spontaneously combust. He laid one finger on the flawless skin of her cheek. It was as delicately tinted as the first blush on a peach, long before it should be taken from the branch.

And yet, here she was: demanding to be plucked.

He had an unnerving sensation that he would never entirely understand Viola. No. That was unacceptable. Of course, he would come to understand her.

She shook her head. "I do not wish to wait."

"Why not?"

She blinked and her brows drew together. "Do you not wish to make love tonight, Devin? Because I didn't want *you* to feel uncomfortable."

He managed not to laugh. "I have a suggestion. I shall carry you inside the house, nod to my butler, and climb the stairs."

Her eyes rounded. "You'll carry me up the stairs?"

"To *my* bedchamber, not yours. I'll play your lady's maid and remove your gown myself."

"Oh." She said it softly and he couldn't tell what she thought. "Oh" wasn't "no." "Won't your household think—"

"Ours is not the usual wedding, planned for eight months and celebrated with four priests and a hundred guests. My household knows—nay, all of London knows—that I want you for my wife so much that I cannot wait. I *will* not wait."

He could see a smile in her eyes. "As far as London and polite society is concerned, ours is a story of irresistible love."

Viola took a deep breath. "All right."

Just as well, because they were about to round the corner to Devin's townhouse. "My butler is idiosyncratic, but excellent in many respects. He has a room prepared for your maid, and after consultation with your father's butler, a birdcage has been placed in the corner of every room in the house, positioned on the floor, door open."

"Barty can't fly well, you see," Viola said apologetically. "He is very good about retiring to a birdcage."

"My father and his friends used to duck behind a screen, and we would continue talking to the sound of urine hitting a chamber pot," Devin said.

"My mother had all the chamber pots removed from the dining areas of the castle, but my understanding is that the practice used to be widespread."

"You're not offended by mention of chamber pots, are you?"

Viola smiled. "My mother considers bodily functions to be private, but not shameful."

"I see," Devin said, guessing that unlike most ladies, Viola would have a thorough understanding of what was entailed by the wedding night.

Her eyes met his, clear and untroubled. "We haven't known each other long, but I have learned some things about you, Devin."

"The fact I am very possessive?"

That wasn't polite, as it carried the implication that his wife might be unfaithful, but Viola didn't seem to mind. She reached out and clasped one of his hands. "You solve problems."

"I what?"

"You solve problems. When Otis felt trapped in the priesthood, he came to you. When Sir Reginald was afraid that Otis would move to Spain, he came to you. I haven't found out what else you've done, but I'm absolutely certain that you are the pivotal person in the Murgatroyd family."

"Only due to birth," Devin said.

She shook her head. "Your father was born to the same role, and he was your opposite."

The carriage was drawing to a stop, and he truly didn't want to discuss his father.

"I can't solve every problem," he said. "I'm not certain that I can stop all the printing presses in London from creating images of you."

It had been nagging at him, the memory of that print with its rompish, dissolute view of one of the most treasured moments of his life.

In an odd way, the pure vulgarity of it reminded him of his former mistress, Annabel.

His *affaire* with the widow had begun well enough, until she'd confessed to a wish to make love in public, which turned out to be a plot to lure him into marriage. She apparently intended to threaten him with her ruination if he didn't marry her.

It was ironic that a vulgar print had led to his marriage, since the earlier incident had hardened his heart against any sort of breach of privacy. He had turned on his heel, left her, and never saw her again—not difficult since he rarely went to society events.

"I understand," Viola said. "I grew up with the knowledge that most of England was interested in the Wildes, remember? If prints are made, it will not be your fault."

A footman swung open the door and Devin stepped down, noting that Binsey was ushering the household into ranks before the house. Clearly, they had been waiting.

He turned to give his hand to his bride, feeling a surge of pride. He had no doubt but that he had won a treasure. Viola would be the best Duchess of Wynter in the history of the title.

She took his hand and put one delicate, silk-clad foot onto the box his footman had placed before the door and smiled brilliantly at all those clustered on the steps and sidewalk. "Good morning!" she called. She began to gather her skirts, but Devin stepped forward and picked her up in his arms.

Viola laughed, startled, even though they had just discussed it.

Looking down at her face, he felt a swell of emotion that made him uncomfortable. He lifted his head and announced, "I am honored to present my wife."

The household responded with applause, which surprised him. He considered himself a fair employer, and he paid well because it made economic sense to retain excellent servants instead of hiring and training new ones. But he didn't have any illusions that he was a beloved master.

Viola's smile strengthened and she waved.

He strode forward and the servants fell to the sides.

Chapter Twenty-two

$\mathcal{V}$iola kept a bright smile on her face. It was her *brave* mask, donned for public occasions. Devin had a large household, of course. His townhouse was a mansion, set back from the street, fronted by a sweeping circle for carriages. Made of white stone, it shone in the sun with the palatial gleam of a well-maintained ducal residence.

He climbed steadily up wide marble steps that led to a fan-vaulted entry door with Corinthian pillars on either side, like stolid guards.

At the door he turned back to face all those gathered, Viola's skirts sweeping around his feet. "The Duchess of Wynter. My duchess, and yours." He gave the group his rare smile, and Viola listened to their applause grow to cheers.

Devin held himself with the air of a man who had no interest or need in others. He acted as if he were unloved.

But she'd seen how much his cousins adored him, and now, looking around at the open, happy faces of his servants, she had the sudden idea that he simply didn't know what love looked like. Or what friendship and admiration looked like. Loyalty.

His butler waited for them in the entry, garbed in impeccable livery that looked more like a gentleman's coat than butler's attire. He swept into a bow.

"Binsey, my duchess," Devin said, but by the time the butler straightened, Devin had strode past him.

"It's a pleasure to meet you, Binsey," Viola cried over Devin's shoulder.

"Good afternoon, Your Graces," the butler said, trotting after them.

"Everything prepared, Binsey?" Devin said.

"A light luncheon has been prepared. If Her Grace desires anything in particular, I can have a different meal prepared immediately."

Viola felt pinpricks of embarrassment at the idea that Binsey was watching Devin head toward his bedchamber. Her cheeks were burning. Everyone knew where they were going and for what reason.

But that was true of every newly married couple, she told herself. No need to whisper *Wilde Child*, because being a Wilde couldn't help her in this situation.

Besides, under the embarrassment, desire was rioting through her veins. Devin's arms surrounded her, and she had a sense of the fluid strength behind the elegant muscles she'd only seen clad in wools and silks. There was an intensity to his face and walk that made her tremble.

"Viola is not persnickety," Devin said to Binsey, not turning his head.

He began climbing the stairs, leaving the butler behind. Viola's silk gown swept the marble with a soft whoosh. She leaned her head against his arm and gave him a little poke in the chest. "What if I *am* persnickety?"

"Are you?"

"My point is that you don't know. Perhaps I desire tomatoes plucked under a full moon, or cabbage only on Tuesdays."

"Is that a possibility?"

"One of my mother's cousins won't eat a nightshade vegetable unless it was picked under a full moon."

Devin reached the next floor without showing the faintest sign of being out of breath, and turned left. "You regularly sit around in a cowshed. You have a pet crow who toilets in the corner of your bedroom, albeit in a cage. You are not persnickety." He paused in front of double mahogany doors presumably leading to his bedchamber. "Do you remember my father's collections?"

Viola was enjoying the sensation of leaning against his chest. "Yes," she said, a little dreamily.

"There is a collection in this room," he said apologetically. "Hell, there's a collection in most every room. If there had been time before our wedding, I would have had the house completely refurbished."

"Butterflies?" She wriggled. "Let me down if there are pinned butterflies in the room, Devin. We'll have to go somewhere else. The duchess's chambers will do."

"No, the butterflies are in the country." He tightened his arms, turned his shoulder, and bumped open the door. He pivoted to face the room and set Viola on her feet.

His bedchamber was large and well-proportioned, with light pouring from two mullioned windows hung with gauzy curtains. The bed commanded most of the space. It was surprisingly feminine, with flowers inlaid in ebony twining about the headboard and wreathing the bedposts.

"I was born in this bed," Devin commented.

Something in his dry tone made her twist to look up at him. "And?"

"This was my mother's bed, but she had it moved here in recognition of the fact that she had done her duty by producing an heir. The duke was not welcome to knock on her door again. There was no question of a spare."

Viola would have said something about the fractious nature of his parents' relationship—though what there was to say, she didn't know—but her eyes had landed on the opposite wall and before she could stop herself, her mouth fell open.

"Chamber pots!"

"Indeed," Devin said, his voice completely emotionless.

Row upon row of chamber pots adorned the far wall, mounted on walnut shelves. They ranged from a blue ceramic pot, trimmed in gilt and adorned with delicate paintings of ladies, to a simple tin pot, to—

"Is this made of gold?" Viola asked, rounding the bed. A gleaming pot reflected back the muted glow of sunshine.

"Gilded bronze," Devin said, remaining where he was, arms crossed over his chest. "Supposedly once used by King Henry VIII."

"There must be fifty pots here," Viola said, astonished. Some had tops and others small legs. Now that she'd rounded the bed, she saw that another row of pots was arranged along the floor.

"Seventy-two in all. Would you like me to have them removed immediately? I could call Binsey. I didn't think of it; I apologize."

Viola turned around. Because his arms were crossed over his chest, Devin's blue frock coat strained over his shoulders. His eyes were dark and intent, watching her without a smile. Somehow the room shrank to the intimate shape of the bed between them.

She felt as if she was breathing honeyed air, as if carnal possibilities danced in the sunshine like the best wine. She let the corners of her mouth curl into an invitation that sang in her heart. "I don't need to use a chamber pot. They needn't be removed."

"I didn't ask if you would like to refresh yourself in the duchess's chambers." He looked unapologetic, and she had the sense that his graceful strength was taut, waiting for her to move first.

"Chamber pots are only useless as a collection. We could use them for other purposes," she said. "The gold one, for example. You could put it on your desk and use it for . . . for quills."

"It's too large for quills," her husband said, amusement running through his voice. "I'll have it sent to your chamber."

"I'm sure I can find some use, besides the obvious," Viola said, coloring again. "I'll put letters in it, or embroidery yarns."

They stood across from each other, the bed between them. How could she possibly have considered marrying a slender man of God? What she wanted was a medieval warrior, sturdy and principled, ready to put on a suit of armor to protect his wife and family.

Viola put her hands on her stomach, realizing that her untidy breathing was mirrored in her trembling knees. "I would prefer to get this over with," she said, the words tumbling from her mouth. "I am telling myself—I am trying to be—" She couldn't say it. *I'm afraid that you'll be bored. That I will fail as a lover. That you'll regret this impulsive marriage.*

Devin made his way around the bed to her, unhurried, his eyes focused on her face. "You needn't try to be anyone other than yourself, Viola."

"I may be inadequate," she said, putting her cards on the table, as Aunt Knowe would say.

His smile began in his eyes, a sensual amusement that warmed her cheeks to another blush as it spread across his face, his expression changing from taut observation to lazy erotic happiness.

He put a finger on her cheek and ran it downward. "I thought that my wedding night would be a matter of formalities in a dark room. A question of carefully oiled body parts meeting with polite disinterest."

Viola managed a smile. His finger wandered lower, drawing a sleek line down her throat, softly caressing the line of her collarbone.

"Instead, I have been given a bedchamber smelling of strawberries and a bride more beautiful than I could have imagined. Did you notice that Binsey has set the table over there with champagne and more?"

Deep inside, Viola's body was still quaking, but perhaps it was from desire rather than fear. "Your butler knows you," she managed.

"My heart is pounding," Devin said. He pulled off his coat and tossed it toward the end of the bed. "Feel." He picked up her hand and placed it on his chest.

Under her fingers an urgent rhythm thumped. Viola swallowed hard. He watched her, eyes gleaming under heavy lids.

"The last thing I want to do is claim conjugal rights before you are ready, Viola. We can eat our lunch and nap together like the octogenarians I hope we will be someday."

A stifled giggle escaped her. "The whole house thinks we are . . . are doing otherwise."

"We can surprise them." A smile lurked in his slumberous eyes. "We have a lifetime to make love to one another."

She stared at him in fascination, feeling the thumps of her heart. "That is true, isn't it?"

"Yes. Would it be acceptable to you, my lady, if I removed my shoes?"

"Yes, of course." She fluttered her hands. "Of course!"

He took them off. "My wig and my neck cloth?"

"Certainly."

She watched as his corded neck emerged from the high-necked wrap of starched linen that had been shaped into the flounces that signaled a gentleman. Devin's neck cloth was far simpler than those of men with lesser titles. Dark curls emerged from his wig flattened, and he ran his fingers through them with unmistakable relief.

"You don't like wearing wigs?" she asked.

"Loathe them," Devin said. "I give you fair warning, Duchess, that I don't wear them in the house, and outside only when I must. I gather a wig would be more comfortable if I shaved my head."

"Don't do that!" she cried involuntarily.

His smile ravished her, making her legs liquid. "I won't. May I remove my stockings?"

He was wearing a shirt of thin lawn that ended in graceful cuffs covering his hands to the knuckles. Narrow pleats sewn on the shoulders did nothing to hide their breadth and made her long to see what he looked like naked.

Not graceful, not slender, not porcelain white.

"Shirt?" she suggested daringly, after his white silk stockings had landed on a chair.

His eyes were shining. "If you insist."

"I do insist," she said, coloring again.

"I shall attempt to obey my lady's every command," Devin responded, his voice oddly serious.

"Even if I instructed you to do something absurd?" she asked.

"Such as?" He was nimbly undoing the simple tie that closed his shirt in front.

"Use all those chamber pots."

His laughter rang out from under the shirt. "In one night? 'Tis beyond my power, even if my duchess commands."

The shirt came up and flew to the side, but Viola was too distracted to track its flight. Fascinated by golden skin and a taut shape that made her stomach curl, she took a step toward Devin.

And stopped, finding that her hands were hovering. She tipped back her head and looked up. "May I?"

"As you wish," Devin said, his voice thick with desire.

Anxiety and desire clenched her throat, so she just nodded and put her palms on his warm skin. Beneath her hands was potent masculine strength, her fingertips teased by short golden hairs, hardly visible except where the sun struck them.

"Why is your body hair golden and the hair on your

head dark?" she asked, trying to steady her voice because her knees were shaking.

He shrugged, which moved the finely chiseled muscles marching down to his waistband. She slid her hands down, loving the way the muscles bunched to meet her palms. He made a sound in the back of his throat, like a small growl.

"I didn't know that men have nipples," Viola said, looking back up at his eyes. "Unnecessary, don't you think?"

"They can be a source of pleasure," Devin said, his voice velvety with desire.

She felt herself coloring again. She took her hands down and fell back a step. "This is embarrassing."

Devin turned and she watched him walk toward the small table on the other side of the room, set with a blue cloth and matching dishes. He poured glasses of champagne and returned, seeming not to notice that she was frozen in place, like a silly rabbit in the snow.

"Let's drink to our marriage, shall we? Are you hungry?"

"No." She took the glass. Her fingers brushed his and she felt the shock of it down her legs. Instinctively she met his eyes and knew that he felt the same.

He raised his glass with a lopsided smile. "Do you know how lucky we are? Many couples feel nothing but trepidation, whereas I feel the opposite." He took a swallow. "Would you like me—or a maid—to help you out of your gown, Viola?"

"Yes," Viola said, firming her mouth. "You, please."

He didn't say anything, but she saw his eyes lighten with naked desire. That, more than anything, steadied her nerves. *He* wasn't entirely composed either.

She lifted her arms and started pulling out hairpins. She had worn her hair in loops and curls, and her mother had dictated no powder . . . a choice she now understood.

"I'll help." A long stride put him at her side. He pulled out a hairpin. "There are tiny silk roses on each pin. I didn't see that."

"Lavinia," Viola said. "She takes great delight in dressing all of us. She adored this sudden wedding." She tipped back her head to see his face. "I must warn you that I will be a frightfully expensive duchess since she will want to dress me, but if I ever spend too much, you must tell me. I can rein her in."

He shook his head. "Lavinia—if I may refer to her as such—is a genius."

His hands skimmed her head as if butterflies were gently touching her. With a silky swoosh, her hair unwrapped and fell down her back. He made an inarticulate sound that made her smile.

Devin pulled the last few hairpins while she gathered chestnut locks and pushed them behind her shoulders.

"The gown itself comes off first. It's pinned to the sides of my bodice."

He stilled for a moment, and his nimble fingers brushed her collarbone. "I like this gown."

"I thought it was slate blue," she said, starting to pull out the pins that held it to her stomacher, "but Lavinia says it's robin's egg blue." Viola made herself stop, because she was prone to chattering from nerves.

"I think it's the color of juniper berries," Devin said, somewhat surprisingly. A moment later he carefully drew the gown away and draped it over a chair. "The stomacher next?"

"No, the gown petticoat," Viola said, putting her fichu to the side and untying the bows that held on her petticoat. There was a swish as folds of blue silk relaxed to the floor. She stepped forward, out of the puddled cloth, and turned to face Devin, chin high.

"Now the stomacher." She began pulling pins from the stiffened triangle of embroidered fabric. "And then the panniers."

Devin gave her a fascinated smile. "I feel as if I am unwrapping a present," he said, once the panniers were off. He began working on the back lacing of her stays.

It had taken two maids a good hour to dress her this morning; Devin was much faster, perhaps because he had more ambition.

Finally Viola wore a chemise, along with high heels and clocked silk stockings that tied with a bow. Her chemise was nearly transparent, with a very low neck to make certain that no hint of white peeked from under her gown.

Devin's eyes caught on her breasts. "I can't think what I did to deserve this," he said, in a stupefied, wry voice that made her laugh.

"*I* am the mere miss who became a duchess!" she pointed out. Her eyes traveled from his head to his legs, and desire flared in her veins again like heady wine. *He* was much more than a duchy, but she couldn't find the words without sounding silly, like an awed child.

Devin stepped forward and took her hands. "I always knew that I could buy a beautiful duchess. You didn't want to be a duchess, and you married me anyway. You didn't want to be a spectacle, and yet you kissed me on the street. You wanted a vicar, not a duke."

"I wanted to marry you," Viola said. "It was absurd of me to even look at a betrothed man."

A look crossed his eyes too quickly to interpret.

"I didn't really want to marry Mr. Marlowe," she said, trying to be clear. "He was safe, perhaps more so because he was betrothed." She cleared her throat. "Are you . . . are you going to remove your breeches?"

"If you will allow." He dropped her hands and unbuttoned the fall on his silk breeches.

"I know what is to come, though my mother might have forgotten some important details. Such as the fact that you—that men—have nipples. Do you . . . is there anything else I should know about?"

Chapter Twenty-three

A smile began somewhere in the region that Devin vaguely considered to contain his heart and spread through his whole body, searing desire replaced by amusement. "You do know about this?"

He ran one of his hands down the front of his silk breeches, where his tool strained toward her, desperate need making him harder than he'd been in his entire life.

Viola's cheeks were stained berry-colored, but she followed the path of his hands, her lashes fluttering. If she had no idea that men had nipples, then she had never seen a naked man.

Of course she hadn't. She was a lady.

"I am not quite an idiot," she said with dignity, a smile playing at the corners of her mouth. "I've seen my baby brothers when their nappies were being changed. But they were always wearing chemises." She paused. "You do not look like what I remember."

Devin didn't let himself roar with laughter because her comment was dignified, but inside joy bubbled up like lava. He slid his breeches down and stepped away.

"Definitely not the same size," Viola said faintly.

"It grows as a man grows," he said, curling his hand around himself, a rough movement meant to remind himself that the whole day stretched ahead. Viola might change her mind about consummating their marriage today.

What happened next was up to her, not him.

Viola might be shy—but she was brave. He saw that courage now, the steel backbone of a woman who is unflinching in the face of the unknown—because she raised dazed eyes to his face, caught hold of her chemise, and pulled it over her head.

Her body was revealed to him slowly: slender legs, plump thighs, a downy nest of chestnut hair between her legs, a gorgeous curve to her hips, breasts . . .

His breath caught in his throat and his tool spasmed in his hand.

The chemise fluttered to the ground and she stood before him, cheeks red, wearing only stockings and exquisite blue shoes. Acting from instinct, he knelt at her feet and said, "My lady, may I remove your shoes?"

She nodded and placed an impossibly small foot in the palm of his hand. He removed both of her shoes, set them carefully to the side, and reached to untie the bows that held up her stockings. They fell down her legs, light as gossamer on the wind.

He stayed where he was, looking up at her, bringing her hands to his lips. "I would have gone on my knees to ask you to marry me, Viola. I want you to know that."

"You made your intentions very clear." She smiled and sank to her knees in front of him. "You like the fact that I didn't want to be a duchess. I like the fact that you chose me, even though I wasn't the woman you intended to marry. I'm not a duke's daughter by blood. I don't have golden hair. I'm not important, or exquisitely beautiful, or wildly admired. I'm notorious only for having thrown up in a lemon tree."

"You are everything I want," Devin stated.

Viola took a deep breath and his eyes flew to her magnificent bosom. Her breasts were full, shaped with the delicate precision of a deep-belled flower, topped with furled nipples.

"Your nipples and mine don't deserve the same name," Devin said, realizing his voice had dropped into a deep register he scarcely recognized. "Yours are exquisite, and mine are no more than flat coins."

"I like yours," Viola breathed.

He waited and she leaned toward him, erasing the empty air between them. Her lips rested on his for a moment before his arms swept around her and he licked her lower lip. She opened instantly, arms winding around his neck.

With a murmur, he rocked back on his heels, bringing her with him, their mouths fused in erotic discovery. Devin rose with Viola in his arms and turned to the bed, still kissing.

He laid his duchess gently on the bed but she clung to him so he followed, enfolding her in his arms, aligning their bodies—his hard planes and her ripe curves.

Still they kissed, every stroke of a tongue enflaming erotic desire that already rioted in their veins.

"Jesus," he gasped sometime later. He was half on top of Viola, elbows on either side of her head, kissing in a way he'd never experienced before. It was overwhelming. The first kiss they shared—a sweet meeting of mouths, albeit meltingly erotic—was a distant memory. These kisses were feverish, their hearts thudding through skin that had never felt thin until this moment.

Viola's eyelashes fluttered and opened. She looked dazed and exuberant, lustful and curious . . . all emotions expressed without words. Her hair tumbled in wanton curls around her head.

"I don't know why people don't kiss all day long," she said in a stunned voice.

A choked laugh burst from his chest, but her hand was running down his body, leaving fire in its wake. He shifted to his side and curled his hand under her right breast. Her nipple was coral red, like a holly berry on a snowbank.

"There are other kinds of kisses," he growled, his mind clocking how inarticulate he was.

Viola's eyes widened and she nodded.

After that, the world splintered into gasping moments: her body twisting under his, the first moan that broke from her lips, the first time he allowed his hand to slip between her soft thighs, allowed a finger to dip into her heat, stroked until she arched off the bed, the ivory curve of her body giving him a fierce wish to pull her beneath him—but no.

He waited, clenching his teeth, showering her with kisses, coaxing her desire higher and higher until with one startled cry she broke, shaking in his arms, burying her face in his shoulder.

Devin caressed her throughout her deep pleasure, memorizing the rosy hue in her cheeks, her gasps, the way her eyes changed from feverish to slumberous.

"That was better than alone," she gasped, as he waited, cradling her, wanting her to speak first.

He rarely laughed. Was marriage to Viola going to change him into a chortling type of fellow, one whose mouth was constantly curved?

"Hmm," he said, choking back laughter, bending over to kiss her again.

"I like your hair," she said drowsily.

"No going to sleep," he said with sudden urgency, adding, "Unless you'd like to stop there, Viola, because we can. Stop. There's tomorrow."

"I was thinking how many tomorrows we have," Viola said softly, turning toward him. Her breasts swayed, making his tool pulse against his stomach. "I'm glad we didn't waste time with courting, Devin. That would have taken weeks or months, and all those days would have been lost, when we could have been spending them in bed."

Devin had a feeling of vertigo, as if he were standing at the precipice of a mountain, not sure how he got there, staring down into the depths.

His wife was watching him, bright eyes shining, talking of tomorrows spent in bed. It felt impossible, on some primitive level. And yet here she was.

He ran a hand down Viola's curves, over the sweet

round of thigh, dragging a flat thumb over her most intimate part. She shuddered all over.

"Wait!" she cried, grabbing his wrist.

He pulled his hand away as if it had been burned. "Of course."

"It's *my* turn," she said huskily.

Chapter Twenty-four

$\mathcal{T}$he one thing that her mother had impressed upon her was that Viola should not play the role of a fainting maiden. "You have the chance to be much more," Ophelia said firmly, the night before. "I see it in Devin's eyes. He doesn't *expect* you to do more than lie back and accept whatever happens—what gentleman does?—but he will celebrate it if you take initiative."

"What does that mean?" Viola had asked.

"Follow your whimsy," her mother had said, smiling. "And remember that Rome wasn't built in one day."

To Viola's mind, if Rome had been filled with men like Devin, it might well have gone up in a day. She rolled on her side, allowing her eyes to savor all parts of him. After a woman has shrieked in a man's ear, she can stop worrying about whether she looks like a lady.

A lady doesn't ogle.

Viola ogled.

Devin had large, shapely, broad shoulders, and strong legs. Golden hairs glinted on his chest and on his legs, and even in a slender line down his stomach.

"It's as if you've been gilded," she said, reaching out to trace that tantalizing line with her finger. Under her touch, his stomach clenched.

He made a rough sound and reached forward, wrapping a hand around himself.

"May I do that?"

He cleared his throat. "Certainly." His hand fell away.

Viola reached out and wrapped her hand around him, just as he had. She tried tugging, as he had, and a wild sound broke in his throat. A pulse of triumph went through her. She wasn't lying around like a wilting violet! She was—she was—

"What *am* I doing?" she asked, perplexed.

"There are many terms that apply," Devin said, his voice strangled.

A primitive instinct took over and Viola's hand tightened on the silky skin. All her senses were alive, delighting in Devin's groan, in the way his body arched toward her hand, the way his hand tightened on her thigh as if barely controlling himself.

"Enough," he said a moment later, wrenching his heavy-lidded, intense gaze away from her hand. She let go reluctantly.

He reached for her breasts, and while she was still startled by the erotic ache that followed the brush of his fingers, his mouth followed. After that, moments passed in a blur of pounding heartbeats, shattered moans, and aching limbs.

Every time Viola felt a flash of embarrassment, she would feed her courage not with a muttered phrase but with the look in her husband's eyes. With the thud of his heart, the tremble in his fingers as he touched her, the way his thick shaft seemed to grow harder every time she caressed it.

His desire was in every growled word, in his hard kisses, in the longing she saw in his eyes. Culminating in the moment when he braced himself above her and said, "May I?"

It was like their marriage vows but more intimate, more quiet, perhaps more heartfelt.

"Please," Viola breathed, having shed her embarrassment.

His fingers slid once more between her legs, and she said, "*Yes.*"

Devin gave a choked laugh that might have been a groan, tucked her under his body, and slid slowly into her warmth.

Her eyes widened as he slid home, and he asked, "Too painful? Shall I withdraw?"

"No," she said with a gasp. "Well, not much. I hadn't imagined . . ."

But she didn't finish the thought. It pinched when he moved, but she couldn't pay attention because an erotic storm was gathering in her veins, slowly, like huge storm clouds building in her body, forerunners of an all-encompassing tempest.

Devin lavished kisses on her face and eyes, coaxing her into kissing him even though she couldn't pay attention to more than his slow movements, each one sinking deeper into her, as if she were unlocking a door that he longed to enter.

All the time the storm built until Viola couldn't think, as fierce need dictated that she not lie quietly any longer. She just couldn't. Following instinct, she bent her knees and thrust up awkwardly, meeting his stroke, a pant breaking from her mouth.

"Am I allowed to do this?" she gasped.

One look at his expression and she felt no shame. Every feature was lit by ferocious desire and the oath that broke from his lips built the storm higher until she was panting, reaching for it, her fingers biting into his arms as she tried to match his strokes, arching to meet him.

He reached down between them, brushed his fingers against her—and the storm broke and she cried aloud, shaking, her body losing the rhythm they had established.

Devin looked down at his tousled, beautiful, erotic wife and lost control in the act of love, for the first time in his life.

He dropped his head and thrust forward, blind to everything but the feel of her, the perfume of her skin, the tight grip of her body.

He lost himself, and only hours later realized that perhaps he had also found himself.

Chapter Twenty-five

*V*iola woke as twilight was darkening the room. Purple shadows gathered in the corners of the huge bedchamber; she blinked, wondering where she was. The shelves lining the wall came into focus. Chamber pots. She was in the duke's bedchamber.

Her duke's bedchamber.

One could even say that those were her chamber pots. Her mind boggled, thinking of where such a collection could find a home, but the sound of deep breathing jolted her from that housewifely thought.

She turned stealthily, remembered pleasure echoing in small aches and twinges.

Devin was lying on his stomach, head resting on his arms, face turned away from her. His shoulders bunched with muscle, covered with smooth skin that still appeared gilded, even in the waning light. It was curious to her: She would have assumed that his skin would be as creamy as hers, untouched by sun.

She had heard that her stepbrothers threw off their shirts when they were breaking horses, but since she shunned the stables, she had never seen it herself.

Another embarrassment to chalk up to her shyness: Had she visited the stables more often, she might have realized that men were adorned with useless nipples.

Last rays of sun were slanting low, gleaming on his round arse. She'd never given the faintest thought to men's posteriors. And yet . . .

And yet.

Devin's was surely the finest of its kind. In fact, she decided in a rush, his entire body was the finest of its kind.

Without a word, he opened his eyes, rolled to the side, and ran a hand over her shoulder. And over her breast. His hand curled and he let out a low male sound of appreciation.

"You sound like me drinking hot chocolate!"

His thumb gave her nipple a lazy caress, making Viola shiver. "Are you hungry?"

"Yes. How can your hair look elegant after a nap and . . . everything else?" she said, almost crossly. He appeared to have just emerged from the hands of his valet, whereas she didn't need a mirror to know that her hair had erupted around her head in wild curls.

"You look well ravished," Devin said, a smile curling his mouth.

Viola pushed up to sit and began patting her hair. "Embarrassing," she muttered.

In one swift movement Devin pounced on her. "Unless you're ravenous, I suggest—" Whatever he meant to suggest was lost because his lips closed on hers and he pulled her under him.

It wasn't until the room was truly dark and Devin had lit the fire in the fireplace, then the lamps, that they finally made their way to the table in the corner,

Devin clad in a dressing gown, and Viola in one of his exquisitely pressed shirts, the wrist bands turned over many times until she had thick wads of fabric at each elbow.

Binsey had left them a light meal covered with silver domes.

"I'll ring for fresh food," Devin said, lifting a dome to reveal plated chicken.

"Nonsense, let's eat it," Viola said. "That chicken looks excellent. Do you have a good cook?"

"I think so," Devin replied. "I don't pay much attention to food."

"I do," Viola said cheerfully.

"I have a French cook at the Northamptonshire estate," Devin said, uncovering cooked vegetables.

Suddenly Viola thought—for the first time in quite a while—of that awful ball years ago and the gentleman's threat that his wife would have to live in the country. Despite herself, a shiver went through her.

"What are you thinking about?" her husband asked instantly. She didn't know why she ever thought Devin's eyes were cold. Now he looked at her with the same warmth with which he regarded Otis.

Which was sensible, she reminded herself. For all Devin claimed to have no friends, Otis was clearly as dear to him as Joan was to her.

"I was thinking about a bad man whom I met," she said lightly.

His eyes darkened. "I hope he didn't hurt you."

"Not in a physical way," she said, struggling to explain. "I told you about the angry man."

Devin made a low noise that sounded like a growl. "Who was it? I'll teach him to terrify young women."

"He didn't threaten me," Viola said. "He was angry, that's all, and I had never seen a truly angry man. My stepfather is angry sometimes, but he is always in control. My mother is calm by nature. Aunt Knowe gets vexed, but she's never enraged."

"Ah." He didn't say anything for a moment. "As I've told you, my father was angry a great deal of the time. If you added up the hours, I suspect he was angry for most of his life."

Viola tentatively reached out a hand to touch his.

"It leaves its tracks," Devin said slowly. "You chide me for not showing emotion, but I know better than most that some emotion is better kept silent. An angry man can damage those around him if he can't control himself."

"What frightened me," Viola said, "was the idea that all that rage brewed behind a gentleman's attire and fine manners. I will never forget the way rage boiled out of him."

"This was the married couple whose argument you interrupted?"

"I wasn't precisely accurate before," Viola said. She felt herself turning pink. "You see he was engaged in . . . in an activity."

Devin looked up sharply. "At a ball?"

She nodded. "A ball at Lindow Castle. It was my first such public event. I wasn't enjoying it, and I decided to escape through the servants' entrance."

"A gentleman was tupping a woman in the hallway, where any young lady might happen on them and be horrified," Devin said harshly.

There was something ferociously judgmental in his voice. "That wasn't the part that bothered me," Viola said. "It was a shock, but I once rounded a corner and came on one of my brothers and his wife look-ing quite disheveled. I wasn't a complete idiot, even as a girl."

"*You* were not the idiot; he was," Devin said. He put down his fork.

"That did bother me," Viola said, trying to explain. "In retrospect, it was almost funny because she wore yellow shoes and it looked absurd. But I was in a state of highly strung nerves—" She broke off. "It all sounds stupid now. I can't believe it had such a power-ful effect on me."

"But it did." Devin's voice was grim, and Viola had a sudden image of him hunting down the man, all these years later, and exacting a punishment.

"Only because I was already on the verge of throw-ing up in public," she said hastily. "You see, the woman in question was trying to trap the gentleman into matrimony. He mistook me for a witness who would force the question, I gather."

"A mistake."

She waved her hand. "He lost his temper and shouted because he thought I was part of a nefarious scheme, you see. He told her that if they married he would force her to live in the country. It was—"

She broke off. "What's the matter?"

Chapter Twenty-six

$\mathcal{D}$evin stared silently across the table, unable to answer.

Viola reached out and her warm hand curled over his. "It wasn't such a terrible experience, Devin. I never told my father because I knew he would be most displeased."

"For good reason," he said hollowly.

Fear was curling in his stomach in a way he hadn't felt since childhood.

He hadn't given much thought to his marriage: From the moment he met Viola, he knew he had a fierce need to win her, and that was that. It felt *right*.

Now he realized that feeling "right" was just an inarticulate way of saying "love." He was in love with his wife, desperately, wildly in love with his wife, and she was telling him that he was the reason for the greatest anguish she'd ever experienced.

His rage had thrown her into such fear that she experienced crippling shyness for years afterward.

A dark feeling swept through him, blurring her concerned expression.

"Devin," she said, her fingers tightening. "You *must not* find and punish the gentleman in question. I never told anyone of the episode for that reason: It wouldn't be fair to him. He didn't want to marry that woman."

With a hollow pang, Devin realized that he had wronged his former mistress as well: In his fury, he assumed that Viola was a witness, but in fact, Annabel's claims of innocence were just. He had launched his fury at two innocent women, one whose only crime was to make love with him in a quiet corridor.

But Viola was looking at him, so he summoned up words, though not the right words. "My father used to threaten my mother with life in the country regularly," he said numbly.

That wasn't it, of course.

The threat had come out of *his* mouth. He had no memory of saying it at all. He searched his memory, and what came back to him was blinding fury at being betrayed.

Not the actual threat, spoken by him.

The very same threat that echoed through the halls of this house and made his childhood hellish and sent his mother fleeing to live far away.

No memory of Viola either, a very young Viola, terrorized by his violence.

"I'm sorry," Viola said now. "It's a terrible thing for a spouse to say and for a young boy to hear."

"The late duke used to hurl insults and threats but for the most part—unless you were foolish enough to take up his offer of a duel—he limited himself to dismissing servants and throwing the odd vase." It was no justification.

None.

"Is that why your mother would flee the house?"

That dark coiling fear had its talons in him now. Viola would leave him, if she knew. She would be right to leave. He nodded, struggling to shape words, and finally forced himself to speak. "She came and went throughout my childhood. For the most part, she lived elsewhere. She would come home for a time, until there was another battle, at which point her trunks would be packed and she'd be gone again."

"She must have hated leaving you behind," Viola said, her eyes a warm hazel.

"No," he said, before he thought better. "I don't believe she cared either way. She certainly never considered taking me with her."

Viola got up and came around the table. He looked up at her. "Push back," she said, in a tone that implied he was dreadfully slow. She settled onto his lap, tucking her head against his chest, catching up one of his hands and bringing it to her lips.

He looked down at the lush sweep of her lashes, her lips, cherry-colored and swollen from kisses, her pointed chin, and felt another wave of inexplicable emotion.

Love—and *fear*.

With a sudden deep pang, he realized that no matter how indifferent he pretended to be to his mother's departures, the memory of an entryway full of trunks and a brittle, furious duchess poised to slam out the door was deeply ingrained in his memory.

He could see down the gaping neckline of his linen shirt to the swell of Viola's breasts, creamy curves just visible through the fine fabric. With the arm that wasn't cradling her, he reached out for his glass of wine. "Drink," he said, touching her bottom lip with the rim of the glass.

Viola tilted her head back, and bronzy-brown silken hair fell over his arm in disarray. Smiling at him, she opened her mouth. He tipped the glass, watching the ruby liquid meet her tongue, and the sensuous ripple of her throat as she swallowed.

"Now you."

Obediently he lifted the glass and took a swallow.

"What do you taste?"

"Wine."

She poked him. "My mother trained us to know ales and wines. I taste currants and plum, and a very fine plum at that."

Devin glanced at the wine bottle. "French." He brought the glass to her lips again and then adjusted her carefully to kiss her afterward. "It tastes like red wine, which is not as sweet as you."

"This may be the best wine I've ever tasted," she said sometime later, with that beguiling giggle.

"I think you've enchanted me," he said, giving her another sip.

"Imagine me raising an eyebrow. You don't appear enchanted." Her eyes ranged over his shoulders. "Perhaps enchant*ing.*"

"Would you ever leave me?" he asked, the words leaping from his mouth without permission. An ache in the pit of his stomach told him that he should tell her the truth. He should confess.

But on their wedding day? To confess to such a degenerate encounter—copulation in a corridor, loss of his temper, shouting words that he couldn't even remember . . . It would ruin everything.

He couldn't.

"No, I will not," Viola said, her eyes on his.

Tomorrow, Devin promised himself, and dipped a finger into the wine and painted her lips.

She licked them and tugged at his neck. "Kiss me again."

"Are you inebriated, Duchess?"

"No," she said, shaking her head. "No Wilde is inebriated unless she wants to be." But she giggled.

"What does a Wilde do if she wants to be inebriated?"

Viola leaned farther back against his arm and took up the wineglass herself. She watched him over the rim with an impish expression before she tipped her head and drank. "She might forget her ladylike deportment."

"I would like to see that," Devin said, heartfelt.

"I do feel a trifle boozy, as it happens," she said, giving him a smile that nestled in his heart. She inched her legs apart. His shirt was rucked up, barely covering her thighs. A rough, needy sound broke from his throat.

And turned into a growl when Viola grinned at him with an expression that he'd never seen before but hoped to the depths of his being that he would see often. Every day. Twice a day.

She dipped her fingers into the wine and slid her dripping fingers under the hem of his shirt.

He stared at the sprinkle of red wine leading to the hem, and at the way her hand obviously slipped between her legs, and the way her head fell back against his arm and she smiled at him with wicked, laughing mischief.

"By God," he said, dumbfounded, "I married a Wilde."

Her smile was slow, voluptuous . . . welcoming.

Confession could wait.

She was here, with him. It could wait.

Viola wiggled her fingers, sighed, and laughed when he snatched up the hem of his shirt.

Chapter Twenty-seven

$\mathcal{T}$he morning after her wedding, Viola woke up early. Never mind the fact that they were in the elegant precepts of Mayfair; somewhere a cockerel was crowing.

She raised her head looking for Barty before remembering that she'd arranged for her crow to spend his first night in the kitchens. She hadn't wanted him to be lonely in the duchess's bedchamber, in case she spent the night with her new husband.

Which she had.

She put her head back on the pillow, silently taking stock of the fact that she had slept with a man. She and Joan had shared many a bed, from the nursery to the night before her wedding, when Joan got teary and declared that she didn't want to let her go . . .

This was different.

Her husband slept on his stomach, sprawled in the bed, head on his arms, his biceps a seductive curve. His body was long and elegant, the sheet caught around his hips as if he were one of the Greek statues that apparently thronged in his study.

Male fingers were unlike female fingers, she discovered by picking up his hand and examining their tensile strength, the span of his palm, the azure vein that ran down his wrist.

Devin stirred, lazy eyes opening, shifting to his side. She abandoned his hand and nestled against him, reveling in the fact that he was warm and alive, unlike the cold marble of Greek statues. When she had first joined the Wilde nursery, as a small child, she felt as if she'd fallen into a hurricane of activity that swirled around her.

Life with Devin was the stillness in the eye of the storm: a quiet, absorbed, intense space for the two of them, the tall walls of the ducal manor sheltering them from the world.

He leaned over and kissed her, his lips lingering on hers, a hand curling around the curve of her cheek.

"Sore?" he murmured.

Viola felt herself turning pink. She nodded.

He tipped her chin up and kissed her. "This is my first day as a married man." His hand slid down her spine and over the curve of her bottom, tightening.

Viola stopped feeling embarrassed and pressed closer to him, her plump breasts flattening against his chest.

Long minutes later he raised his head from her lips and asked hoarsely, "Do you think you might feel better after a bath?"

Viola had a hand wrapped around his erection. She'd thrown back the sheets and she was exploring how this unfamiliar body part worked. When she tightened her grip, Devin's breath caught in his throat. When she twisted her wrist, he groaned aloud.

"I like this," she said, grinning at him. "It's fun."

"'Fun'," he repeated, sounding dazed. "I have to—"

Viola stroked him again, adding a little twist at the top. "You resemble a mushroom."

Devin caught her wrist with his long fingers. "You're ravishing me, Viola. If you keep going . . ."

"You'll spend?" she asked. Ignoring his grasp, she slid her hand up and down again, loving the burning heat of his . . . "What do you call this?"

"My cock," Devin said.

She tried the shape of the word without giving it sound. It was too improper to say aloud.

"Last night I couldn't see what was happening." A giggled escaped her. "This is so immodest, first thing in the morning." She paused, her eyes widening. "Is this why married women have breakfast in bed?"

"Modesty has no place between husband and wife," Devin said hoarsely. He took her mouth, his tongue tangling with hers, sending shivering bolts of heat through her limbs.

"Am I doing this correctly?" Viola whispered. His response wasn't intelligible.

Her mind blurred when his fingers wrapped about hers and tightened. When Devin's breath roughened and his body went rigid, one hand tightening around her arse, she pulled back just enough to watch—but as his breath came faster, she forgot to look down. Instead her gaze caught on her husband's face.

In the grip of desire, Devin looked younger, his face filled with an uncomplicated pleasure. *That's it*, she thought. That's what she wanted for her marriage. Oh, not marital intercourse alone, but that look on Devin's face. He didn't look austere or ducal. His eyes stayed with hers the whole time, as their hands moved in unison.

He came with a deep, broken groan, and Viola watched with fascination. A minute later he drew in a long breath and pulled the sheet over himself, wiping his chest. "Curiosity satisfied?" Devin asked, his voice a lazy growl.

"Yes," Viola said. She had a lifetime to learn how to give her husband pleasure. She wanted more: She wanted to be a *pair*, the way her mother and stepfather were. She wanted a union in which she . . .

"You're gone again," Devin said, laughter in his voice.

She shook her head. "I'm here!"

She had to break through his solitary nature somehow. Not by pushing him, or forcing him to act. But somehow opening a door that he would walk through and realize how much he was loved by Otis and Hazel. By Sir Reginald.

The idea fluttered in her chest.

She realized suddenly that she hadn't cared a jot for Mr. Marlowe; it had been vain of her to think to rescue a man the way one might save a baby crow or a calf.

Devin finished rubbing his chest, flung the sheet to the side, disentangled her limbs from his, and helped her put his shirt back on. He rang for her maid and escorted Viola to the bathing room. She accompanied him silently, thinking hard.

Her husband was himself again, his jaw firm, eyes cool, face ducal.

Yet his eyes softened when she gasped at the magnificence of the ducal bathing chamber, which featured a copper bathtub, softly glowing in the light streaming in the window. "I've never seen such a large bathtub," she gasped.

Devin smiled. "Large enough for two." He tipped up her head and brushed a kiss on her lips. "Done thinking?"

"Is anyone ever done thinking?"

"No. But you think more deeply than anyone I know."

Viola hesitated. "Does it annoy you? Joan finds my absentmindedness frightfully irritating." She hurried to add, "I can try very hard not to think, that is, not to think of other things when I ought to be participating in a conversation. Even my mother says that I test her patience."

He shook his head.

"Tell me more about the bathtub?" she asked brightly, resolving to keep her mind on domestic matters. "Did your father acquire it in Italy?"

With that, Devin burst out laughing and kissed her again. "You don't care about the bathtub, Viola."

"I could care about the bathtub," she argued. "You needn't worry that I can't manage the household, because my mother has made certain that I can."

"You are my absentminded duchess," he said, cupping her face in his hands. "I have a housekeeper already."

"And you are my duke," she countered.

She couldn't read the expression on his face, but she had the feeling that Devin didn't care to be anyone's possession. Never mind. He was *hers* now. It was up to her—not to rescue him, but to . . .

To love him?

That was it.

She had to love him. And be an excellent duchess.

An indispensable duchess, so that if he grew irritated with her shyness and tendency to become distracted, it would be too late for him not to value her.

She had conquered her shyness and she could focus her attention as well. Three hours later, she was reviewing the linen closet with the housekeeper. Every time she started to think about something other than sheets or quilts or guest chambers, she pulled her attention back to the task at hand.

When Devin walked into the housekeeper's parlor, the lady leapt backward and dropped into a curtsy. "Your Grace!" she cried. "I never—welcome—may I be of service?"

"I came to say hello to my wife," Devin said. He was entirely the duke once again, Viola noticed with disappointment. His costume was black and scarcely relieved by the simple knot of his neck cloth. His eyes were cool.

"Good afternoon!" Viola said cheerfully.

His expression darkened. "I don't want to be greeted that way."

"Oh, crickets!" Viola said, but she managed to keep the words from being audible. She dropped into a deep curtsy. Of course, he would adhere to the trappings of dukedom. Her family's informality was most unusual among the peerage.

The housekeeper had apparently decided that Devin didn't need her, because she edged past the cupboard and fled out the door.

"Good afternoon," Viola said, straightening.

Strong hands caught her shoulders. "Not that either. This." Devin took her mouth in a hot, hungry kiss.

"Oh, goodness," Viola said, sometime later. "I can't greet you with kisses!"

"Yes, you can," he told her. Then he added, "In our house, at least." He had lifted her to the back of a sturdy armchair, so her eyes were level with his. "I came to invite you to my study, to introduce you to all the statues before I have them hauled away. The keeper of the Ashmolean Museum has agreed to take them off my hands."

"Mrs. Ulrich hasn't finished showing me the household," Viola said. Even she could hear the longing in her voice. "Perhaps you could take me back to the bedchamber and we could . . . count the chamber pots, Devin," she said, the words coming out in a hurried whisper. Her cheeks were burning at the immodesty of that question.

He shook his head. "You're sore." His hand ran down her curves, and even through her corset she could feel his hunger. "For the first few days, you'll sleep in the duchess's bedchamber."

Viola decided she didn't have to voice her opposition at the moment; he'd find out soon enough.

"Did Mrs. Ulrich show you your bedchamber?" Devin asked.

Viola nodded. "I've seen everything except for the duchess's sitting room. She did tell me most of the collections are going to that museum in Oxford, even the chamber pots, though I told her I might keep one or two."

"You haven't seen my mother's sitting room yet?" Devin asked.

Viola shook her head.

"It's next to the duchess's bedchamber," Devin said, taking her hand and drawing her out the door and toward the stairs.

"I thought you were hard at work on a mathematical theorem," she said.

"I found myself thinking of other things," her husband replied, a thread of amusement running through his voice.

On the third floor, he pushed open a door to a large chamber, wallpapered with tangled vines that curled from the floor to ceiling in pleasant abandon. A small desk stood before the window, and one comfortable armchair had been placed before a fireplace tiled in blue ceramic.

"How charming," Viola said, walking in.

"I think it's sad," Devin responded.

She looked at him inquiringly.

"My mother used to retire here, gustily weeping. If that sounds unkind, I don't mean it to be. My father was impossible to live with, and she did her best."

"I can imagine it must have been very difficult," Viola said. "What did you do when your mother was in such distress?"

"I hid in my nursery or my bedchamber," he said. "Depending on my age, of course. To comfort her would be to draw my father's wrath. They would scream at each other until her nerves broke and she started weeping; he would be ashamed, and the tumult would pass." There was a harsh inflection in his voice, a weary acceptance.

Viola tucked herself under his arm. She didn't say anything and neither did he, for a moment.

"Shall we have this wallpaper changed?" Devin asked.

She actually liked the vines, but one could be a novice at marriage and still realize the wallpaper had to go. She wrapped her arms around his waist and began walking backward, drawing him with her.

"Let's sit down."

He raised an eyebrow but followed and sat when Viola gestured toward the chair.

"I would be very happy to become accustomed to this," he said, sometime later.

His arms were around her, and his chin was resting on her hair. Viola smiled to herself. Devin might think that marriage was nothing more than a social contract—or however he'd put that nonsense—but he liked touching her. And being touched by her.

Chapter Twenty-eight

Three weeks into his marriage, Devin found himself awake in the middle of the night; not being one to lie to himself, he realized he was happy.

"Happy" wasn't a strong enough word.

Viola was in and out of his study all day. In years past, the slightest interruption would have irritated him, but now he didn't mind at all. Viola always slipped over to him and gave him a kiss before she shared whatever thought she'd had, whether it was to do with the house or the church or—increasingly—*The Play of Noah*.

Devin found he didn't even mind hearing about Mr. Marlowe, as long as the mention of the vicar's name was preceded by a hungry kiss.

He was almost certain that he'd managed to supplant Mr. Marlowe in Viola's affections. She talked about the vicar in a matter-of-fact manner and showed no signs of pining for blue eyes.

All the same, Devin realized something had bothered him enough to wake him in the deep of night. Plans for *Noah* were in full swing, and from the sound of it, Otis was there every day. Tradesmen had been selected to play the parts, and they were already rehearsing, even though the stage wasn't finished.

He narrowed his eyes, staring into the dark. Viola hadn't said anything about Miss Pettigrew lately. In fact, searching his memory, he couldn't remember a single mention of her in a week. Yet Viola had just told him again that she had to consult with the vicar about some aspect of the play.

He'd be damned if Mr. Marlowe had a chance to charm his wife. Not that he thought the man would ever be adulterous—Marlowe was a man of God, if there ever was one—but because of Viola.

Because of Viola's infatuation with Marlowe.

Devin rolled on his side and looked at his sleeping wife. She was everything he wanted in life. Even if she never felt the same way about him as she had about Mr. Marlowe, he would take what he could get.

Chestnut hair tangled around Viola's face as she slept, her hands tucked under one cheek. He could see the slope of one rosy cheek, long eyelashes, a glimpse of her chin. He took a long, slow breath, pushing down emotion that threatened to erupt in an uncomfortable way.

He was being absurd.

Correction: He was *feeling* absurd things. It was likely only because she was his wife, and he'd never had such a possession before.

Not that a wife was a possession.

No person could be possessed . . .

But at that point his thoughts tangled again, because of the mere idea of Mr. Marlowe, for example, thinking that he could give Viola counsel. If she wanted counsel, *he*, Devin could counsel her.

Though not if he was buried in his study.

He needed to be on the spot, watching the stage go up, helping with the rehearsals. Every day these inconvenient feelings grew stronger, even as he assured himself that they were inconsequential.

Viola would leave for the vicarage in the morning, and he would find himself unable to work on his theorem, even—shockingly—slightly bored by it. Yesterday he had given his secretary more time than normal and found himself listening to a lengthy report about an ongoing trial, set in motion by the government to vanquish radical movements. It had already resulted in one acquittal by a British jury, with a few more hopefully to come.

"I could give you some writing about the philosophy of human rights," his secretary had said earnestly.

Consequently, Devin's bedside table was stacked with books that he thought were probably radical tracts; nothing called *Justice for the People* was likely to be cheerful reading for a duke.

Moreover, Viola was challenging many of his beliefs. He had thought that a duke *must* marry a woman of noble blood.

Now he knew that was absurd.

As he watched her sleep, she gave a sudden start and rolled onto her back. She frowned and said, quite clearly, "No, Barty, no!"

Devin choked back a laugh. Barty had proved to be a naughty houseguest, though a very affectionate one. The Wynter livery was adorned with gilt buttons, and slowly but surely the footmen were losing their buttons. Barty was an expert at waiting, hidden, and then darting out or taking a short flight, prying off a button with his sharp beak, and absconding with it.

With a sigh, Viola turned again, reaching in his direction. Eyes still closed, she curled against him, flinging a slender leg over his.

Devin's cock was already stiff but impossibly it swelled even more. He held his breath. He wouldn't wake her. They'd already made love three times. He wouldn't . . .

Viola made a sleepy noise and opened her eyes. "There you are," she whispered.

"I am." His voice was hoarse with longing.

"I was dreaming something about Barty, and you came into the breakfast room . . ." Even in the dim light, he could see her face reddening.

"What happened?" he asked, putting a hand on her hip.

"You once told me that—" She stopped again.

"I'd sweep all the dishes off the table and put you on it," Devin said. His hand slid down her hip and under her nightdress.

"In my dream, you didn't ask me," she whispered. "You just ravished me."

"As you wish," Devin said, not even bothering to hold back a grin.

Chapter Twenty-nine

$\mathcal{A}$ few weeks later, Viola and Devin were having luncheon before Viola left for the vicarage.

"How is the play?" Devin asked, managing to look truly interested, even though she suspected he was thoroughly bored by the topic.

Viola hesitated, and decided to tell him the truth. "The play itself is well in motion, but there is tension in the vicarage."

He raised an eyebrow and she didn't even bother to correct it. "Otis and Joan keep coming up with impossible schemes; the latest was that they wanted to borrow a lion from the Royal Menagerie. Miss Pettigrew never cares for anything they suggest," she said, with a sigh. "Joan doesn't like Mr. Marlowe. Caitlin doesn't like Miss Pettigrew."

"You are not to go anywhere near a lion."

"In a cage," she added.

Devin wore his most ducal expression, the one he reserved for public moments. "Cage or not, I forbid it."

Viola had argued against the lion, but she didn't care to be ordered about either. "You must not forbid me to approach a lion," she stated.

Her husband gave her an astonished look. "Viola, you're afraid of horses. Why would you want to become acquainted with a lion?"

"I don't, but that's not the point. You could *ask* me to stay away from lions, but you can't *order* me to do so. I'm your wife, but I'm not chattel, nor a child who can be told what to do."

Devin sighed. "Viola, have I ordered you to stay away from the vicarage?"

"No."

"In that case, you can assume that I understand the limitations of my authority."

She frowned at him. "What do you mean?"

"I mean that if I had my way, you'd have nothing to do with Mr. Marlowe."

"Why not?" She put down her fork. "You can't think that I . . . that I would be unfaithful to you with Mr. Marlowe!"

He gave her a haughty look. "No duchess would do such a thing."

"Poppycock!" Viola said, starting to get irritated. "You forget that I know perfectly well that duchesses are as liable to commit adultery as any other person in the world. I grew up knowing that Joan's yellow hair was the result of her mother's infidelity. Even if we had wanted to avoid the unpleasant truth as children—and we did!—someone was always informing her."

"Are you informing me that you would be unfaithful, given the inclination?" Devin's voice was frigid now.

"No," Viola snapped. "But I wouldn't ask your permission either. You could *ask* me, rather than ordering it."

Devin stared at her and shook his head. "Please don't be unfaithful to me, Viola."

"I would never be unfaithful to you, Devin."

"Why not?"

Because I love you, she thought.

"Because it would be unethical and immoral," she said instead. "I said vows in the church in front of man and God, and I will keep them."

Something eased in his face.

"You really thought that I would do such an awful thing?" Viola asked, her throat burning.

He leaned across the table. "I did not." He hesitated. "I don't like hearing about Mr. Marlowe and his unfortunate betrothal."

"Miss Pettigrew's father arranged the match."

"Such arrangements are not uncommon," Devin pointed out.

Something about his expression made Viola feel nervous, which was absurd. Her husband was as gentle as a lamb. No, that wasn't quite right. But he was always in control of his temper. Even when a housemaid dropped one of the antique chamber pots when they were being packed for transfer to the museum, he hadn't become in the least riled.

In fact, she didn't know what *would* provoke his temper.

"That is true," Viola admitted. She could feel heat creeping into her cheeks. "But some ladies seem to feel that Mr. Marlowe would be happier with a different wife. Or fiancée."

Devin put down his toast and didn't speak for a moment.

"I am not one of them!" she said hurriedly.

"You feel that Mr. Marlowe will be happy with Miss Pettigrew?"

"No!" Now she was really turning red. "Well, no one could truly think that," she said awkwardly.

Devin glanced at the footman who stood against the wall, and the man scurried out of the room, closing the door behind him.

"Not long ago, you wanted to marry him yourself."

"Not really," Viola said, floundering.

"Do you remember that I met you in the library, waiting for Mr. Marlowe? No young lady would secretly meet in a room where she was very likely to be caught, unless she wished to be compromised." His voice was matter-of-fact.

Viola swallowed hard.

"We married not long after that incident, and under similar circumstances," Devin said. "I do not expect more than marital affection, Viola, but I would be very displeased to think that you were pining after another man."

"I'm not pining!"

He leveled a glance at her. "I hope not."

"My feelings for the vicar were inconsequential," she added. What she felt for Mr. Marlowe was nothing compared to what she now felt for Devin.

"We both know that," Devin said flatly. "No one falls in love based on such a brief acquaintance." His expression suggested that no one loved at all.

"I suppose that's the problem with Mr. Marlowe and Miss Pettigrew," Viola said, pushing away the feeling that she was withering inside. Of course he didn't love her.

"I shall accompany you to the vicarage today," Devin said.

Viola was surprised. "You will?"

Her husband looked at her calmly across the luncheon table. "Of course."

"But I thought you were—your theorem?"

"I finished my current letter and sent it off." He put down his soup spoon. "It may be that I have done everything possible with the number 27."

Viola couldn't pretend to know what he was talking about. "So . . . number 28?"

"No."

When she frowned, he added, "Mathematics doesn't work like that."

"I'm so glad that you're coming to see the progress on the play!" Viola said, abandoning the question of mathematics.

Devin got up deliberately and walked around the table. "We just had our first marital disagreement."

Viola smiled up at him. She felt slightly bruised, but it wasn't important. He didn't mean to imply that she might be adulterous. He was just—

Before she could finish that thought, he drew her to her feet. "We must celebrate."

Her mouth fell open. "Celebrate?"

He nodded. "We didn't shout at each other."

"Of course not!"

His kiss might have begun as a celebration, but before long it turned to a devouring kiss, a possessive, wicked kiss. Sometime after that, Devin turned the latch on the door. And pushed the dishes to the side.

Viola was shaking with desire, her eyes shining, her hands roaming over his shoulders.

He bent over her, hands running up her bare thighs, pushing her voluminous skirts out of the way. "I'm not asking you," he stated, his eyelids drooping.

"Oh," she breathed, realizing he was quoting her, from her dream. She wound her arms around his neck. "I like this way of arguing."

An hour later, Viola realized she had come to an important conclusion. Devin loved her. He did. But he probably would never say so. In fact, she had the distinct idea that he himself had no idea that he loved her.

It wasn't in his vocabulary. His wretched parents had abhorred each other. Viola spared a sympathetic pang for his mother—but she left her little boy behind every time she left. And when she drank stewed foxglove, she abandoned him for good.

No, Devin had no idea what love was, and he didn't know he was experiencing it now. All the same, she felt desperate to hear the words from him. To hear him acknowledge that the emotion existed, and that they shared it, and that she loved him.

To say it aloud.

Yet she was desperately in love with him, and she didn't have the courage to say so. The memory of his face talking of love, dismissive and even a trifle scornful?

It was enough to stop any woman from blurting out her feelings.

THE DUKE AND Duchess of Wynter didn't arrive at the vicarage until nearly four o'clock, and an observant person might have noticed that the duchess's lips were swollen, and she had a slightly dazed look about her.

The duke was as austere as ever, but a very, very observant person might have noticed that he kept glancing at his wife, and his gaze would catch and trail across her cheeks, or even her low-cut bodice before he would look away again.

Had that observer known His Grace very well, she would have seen an intentness in his gaze that generally he bestowed only on mathematical theorems.

The grounds of St. Wilfrid's were bustling with people running to and from the cloisters, where the stage had been erected.

Devin put a hand on his wife's back as he escorted her into the vicarage. It was stupid, but he wanted that sign of ownership. Viola was his to seduce, his to touch, his to . . .

To care for.

No matter what she said.

As they entered the front door, Mrs. Pettigrew emerged from the sitting room door with all the force of a stone flung from a boy's slingshot. "Your Grace!" she cried. "I mean, Your Graces!"

Devin took Viola's pelisse and handed it to his groom, who had accompanied them. "Mrs. Pettigrew," he acknowledged.

Viola inclined her head. "Good afternoon, Mrs. Pettigrew."

The lady paused just long enough to drop a curtsy in their direction and said, "Mr. Marlowe is in the sitting room, if you're looking for him. As is my daughter. I shall . . . I shall request tea."

"That was odd," Devin said, handing his greatcoat to the groom.

Viola looked up at him. "I believe that she is worried about the success of her daughter's marriage."

They were almost to the door of the sitting room.

"It is my firm belief that His Grace is squandering money by supporting this performance," Miss

Pettigrew declared from within. "As you know, Mr. Marlowe, I have no patience with people of quality wasting their money on trifles. It sets an unfortunate precedent for their inferiors. Do you not agree?"

Devin couldn't hear any reply from Marlowe. Viola came up on her toes and whispered, "He rarely answers, but she doesn't notice."

Miss Pettigrew certainly seemed unperturbed by her husband-to-be's silence. "I assure you, Mr. Marlowe, that I shall encourage no such vanities when I am the mistress of this vicarage. As your wife, I will promote virtue above sin."

"Well, that's good to know," Devin said to Viola. "One wouldn't want a vicar's wife who was actively promoting sin."

Viola looked up at him, her eyes filled with laughter, and desire ran through his veins like summer lightning. The corridor was dimly lit and yet his wife glowed like a jewel. "You're damned beautiful," he said, leaning over until the words dusted her lips.

She giggled. "I'm not beautiful, Devin!"

"Yes, you are."

Miss Pettigrew had apparently given up waiting for a response. "Next year, when we are married, I shall simply point out—kindly, mind you—that people are better preached out of their follies than entertained by more follies. No more plays. Do you not agree, Mr. Marlowe?"

Devin wasn't listening because he had decided to kiss his wife into agreeing with his assessment of her beauty. Her hand was curled behind his neck and he had an arm under her bottom, supporting her against the wall.

"Your opinion is very clear," came Mr. Marlowe's voice.

Beneath his caressing hands, Viola shivered. "We shouldn't kiss here," she whispered.

He loved the husky catch in her voice. The way she transformed from a prim duchess to a lover, her nipples hard against his chest.

"What on earth are you finding interesting at the window?" said the strident voice from within the sitting room.

"Mrs. Pettigrew will return at any moment," Viola murmured.

"We could go upstairs," Devin replied, his voice no more than a thread of sound. "I'm quite fond of the small sitting room at the top of the stairs."

"You don't smile enough," his wife said, and kissed him again.

"There's naught out that window but a clutch of tombstones," Miss Pettigrew said. "Falling over, all of them. I assure you, Mr. Marlowe, when I am mistress of this vicarage, the sexton will have to do better than that. Each of those stones will face straight ahead in an organized fashion."

Devin leaned his forehead against Viola's. "Could we please go home? We could visit the stage tomorrow."

"Go home and go straight to our bedchamber, I take it?" His wife's eyes had a languid invitation in them. They had come to a silent agreement that they slept together in the ducal bedchamber, and the duchess's chamber was merely for dressing.

He nodded.

"My goodness, how very *peculiar*," Miss Pettigrew exclaimed from inside. "That is Lady Caitlin, is it not? What on earth is she doing?"

"Oh, no," Viola whispered, pulling away from Devin's kiss. Her head bumped softly against the wall.

"Teaching the children, I believe," Mr. Marlowe replied.

"She—she's sitting on a tombstone!"

"Who is sitting on a tombstone?" Devin asked, his lips skating over Viola's cheekbones. "Let's go home. I want to kiss you privately."

"It appears so," Mr. Marlowe said.

"She ought to know better! The daughter of a lord!" Miss Pettigrew spat out the words.

"Caitlin must be sitting on a tombstone," Viola said. "Let me down, Devin. Miss Pettigrew will come bursting out in a moment, on the way to shouting at Caitlin that she's not allowed to be in the churchyard or some such thing."

"She will?" Devin carefully put his wife back on her feet and straightened the frivolous scrap of silk and lace that topped her curls. "Perhaps we should return to our house before we find ourselves embroiled in an embarrassing scene?" he asked, knowing she'd refuse.

"Certainly not," Viola said. "She's *horrid* to Caitlin, which is unfair, because Caitlin is genuinely good."

"I can think of nothing more insalubrious than dragging those young innocents into a graveyard," Miss Pettigrew said, her voice rising. "I shall speak to her at once."

A black figure swept through the door into the corridor. Miss Pettigrew's hand fluttered to her heart. "Bless me!"

"Good afternoon, Miss Pettigrew," Viola said. "I'm sorry to startle you. The duke and I just arrived and were hoping to know how preparations for the play are proceeding."

Miss Pettigrew curtsied, her mouth a tight line, and then opened her lips just enough to say, "If you'll forgive me, I shall return in a moment."

Viola sighed as the lady slammed out the front door. "Miss Pettigrew has a frightful time controlling her temper, and no one seems to make her more incensed than Caitlin."

Devin tucked his hand into Viola's. They walked into the sitting room to find Mr. Marlowe leaning against the window frame, looking outside intently. He didn't hear them enter.

They paused just behind him and glanced past his shoulder out the window.

Lady Caitlin was indeed sitting on a tombstone. She was wearing a charming gown, hand-painted with sprigs of spring flowers. She and the children had spread out some bread, apparently hoping that a bird would snatch a crumb or two.

At the moment she was leaning forward, holding out her palm to a sparrow recklessly considering a free lunch. Pale sunlight streaked her hair with shining threads, as if gold were woven into the strands. She looked extraordinarily pretty, perched on a mossy tombstone.

Viola's mouth opened to greet the vicar, but Devin's grip on her hand tightened.

Miss Pettigrew was advancing through the graveyard like an avenging angel in serviceable cambric. The sparrow cocked its head and flew straight into a tree; Caitlin gave a chuckling, infectious laugh and said something to the children.

"Good afternoon, Your Graces," Mr. Marlowe said, turning to them.

"Perhaps you ought to join the graveyard set," Devin said, nodding at the scene outside.

Those were Mr. Marlowe's parishioners, small though they were, who had hastily scrambled up from the ground and were milling about as Miss Pettigrew laid down the law. Devin cleared his throat. "Your fiancée appears to be annoyed."

The children had caught the giggles from Caitlin. Miss Pettigrew's back grew straighter and more outraged, even though Caitlin was now listening soberly, without a sign of amusement.

"The matron will be waiting for them with bread and milk," Mr. Marlowe said. Sure enough, the group began trailing out of the graveyard.

Devin didn't know much about women's apparel. But it didn't take a *modiste* to compare Lady Caitlin's flowery gown, albeit with a modest neckline, to Miss Pettigrew's sturdy gown, cut high to the throat.

He glanced at Marlowe and saw stark longing in his eyes. The poor sod.

Caitlin was at the tail end of the procession, holding one small urchin by the hand while solemnly agreeing with whatever Miss Pettigrew was preaching about.

Mr. Marlowe cleared his throat and moved away from the window. The door burst open two seconds later and Miss Pettigrew reentered.

"I was correct," she said triumphantly. "Lady Caitlin was actually leading a Bible class! She is now saying farewell to those poor children—we must hope that they live to take another lesson, given the insalubrious air in the graveyard—and she will be here shortly. You must point out the error of her ways, sir. The error of her ways."

"I didn't see any error," Viola said.

"Neither did I," Devin said.

Mr. Marlowe walked toward his fiancée. "I'm certain that Lady Caitlin did not intend to endanger the health of her students."

"I do wish you would wear proper clerical garb during the week," Miss Pettigrew said irritably. "My father always wears his bishop's robes, I assure you. Clerical garb lends a touch of authority."

Mr. Marlowe glanced at Devin with discomfort. "Miss Pettigrew, this is not—" he began in a soothing voice.

But his fiancée was clearly unrestrained by any notion that she should curb her thought or speech in front of guests, whether noble or not. "Lady Caitlin has something of an impudent air about her," she said, cutting him off. "She does not show you the respect that you are due, as the vicar of one of the largest and most wealthy parishes in London."

"I have noticed nothing out of the way," Mr. Marlowe said flatly.

"Well, I have," Miss Pettigrew said. But she seemed unable to continue, and the room lapsed into silence.

Viola squeezed Devin's hand. "How is construction of the stage coming along?"

Miss Pettigrew swung her head about with all the grace of an enraged bull. Devin managed to catch her eye just in time to silently remind the woman that no one, under any circumstances, was allowed to be rude to his duchess.

She snapped her mouth shut.

"The men have been remarkably efficient, Your Grace," Mr. Marlowe said. "I have no doubt but that the stage will be erected in time for the performance next week."

"Shall we be seated?" Devin asked Viola, deciding that Miss Pettigrew had no intention of playing the role of hostess.

Caitlin entered the door and Devin turned his hand to squeeze Viola's. Not that he was entirely sure what the language of squeezes meant.

"Good afternoon, Your Graces, Miss Pettigrew, Mr. Marlowe," Caitlin said, dropping into a faultless curtsy.

Viola dropped Devin's hand and walked across the room to embrace her friend.

The vicar bowed. "Lady Caitlin."

Miss Pettigrew apparently felt that the greeting they had exchanged in the graveyard was serviceable enough for the moment. She glared at her fiancé and nodded in a commanding fashion.

Mr. Marlowe cleared his throat. "Lady Caitlin, Miss Pettigrew fears that the graveyard is not a healthy place for children."

"I was teaching them about St. Francis of Assisi," Caitlin explained.

"What an excellent notion!" Viola said.

The battle lines were clearly drawn, and poor Marlowe was stuck in the middle.

Devin gave Caitlin a wry smile. "You were hoping that a London sparrow would mistake you for a saint and eat from your hand?"

"Assisi?" Miss Pettigrew demanded. "Who is that? A Roman Catholic of some sort?"

"As it happens, yes," Caitlin replied, turning to her. "A saint, and the founder of the Franciscan order."

"We shall have no talk of Papists in this parish," Miss Pettigrew stated. "You'll frighten the children, Lady Caitlin. Perhaps talk of boiling oil does not affect you. But I was raised to have the kind of sensibility that abhors such details."

Devin settled back in the sofa, drawing Viola more snugly against him. Then he said, in her ear, "This is better than a play about Noah."

Viola was biting her lip and likely thinking that the pinched and unpleasant Miss Pettigrew would make her favorite vicar a terrible wife.

"Francis of Assisi had nothing to do with boiling oil," Caitlin pointed out. "He greatly loved animals, and birds ate from his hand."

Miss Pettigrew indicated with one twitch of her lip what she thought of saints who frolicked in the barnyard. "Birds—nay, all animals—have no place in the life of children. Your task, Lady Caitlin, is to teach the orphans to behave in a manner that reflects their station. They must learn to be neat and clean, and sit quietly at all times."

"Only two weeks ago, many of these children were living on the streets of London," Caitlin protested.

The orphanage building had not yet been erected, but Mr. Marlowe had launched into the project without delay, hiring women from the area to care for the children.

Miss Pettigrew shuddered. "The less said about that the better. And certainly not in the presence of a duchess!"

"Why not?" Caitlin asked, turning to Viola. "Are you horrified? I do not consider my task to be teaching children to sit quietly. I was teaching a Bible class, not a lesson on deportment."

"I am not horrified," Viola promised.

"I am," Devin said, but he muttered it in Viola's ear.

"Nowhere in the King James Bible does it advocate touching filthy animals," Miss Pettigrew announced.

"God created the great whales and birds, and saw that they were good," Caitlin protested, in a brisk summary of Genesis.

"Behold the fowls of the air: for they sow not, neither do they reap, nor gather into barns; yet your heavenly Father feedeth them. Are ye not much better than they?" Mr. Marlowe said. He was standing before the mantelpiece, curls tumbling over his eyes.

Blue eyes, fixed on Caitlin's face.

It occurred to Devin that no one could consider Mr. Marlowe an object of pity if he married a daughter of the peerage, who was both remarkably pretty and truly pious.

"Yet I believe Miss Pettigrew has a point," Mr. Marlowe continued, demonstrating nimble peacemaking abilities. "The children will hardly learn to summon birds in a mere half hour."

"He's working on growing a backbone," Devin murmured in Viola's ear.

"Hush!" she told him, but he saw his wife's lips curl in a smile.

"I was hoping to make Francis seem alive to them," Caitlin explained.

"St. Francis is *not* alive," Miss Pettigrew said, clearly aiming to end the discussion.

"Incontrovertibly true," Devin said.

Miss Pettigrew glared at him, but he noticed that

Caitlin was looking back at the vicar, eyes full of suppressed emotion.

"Tea!" Mrs. Pettigrew announced, bustling in the door, followed by a young maid.

"Look at Caitlin," Devin murmured in Viola's ear. "Desiring the vicar has to be a sin." Suddenly he remembered that his wife was guilty of the same fault.

Thankfully, she gurgled with laughter.

Chapter Thirty

In the last days before the play of Noah's ark was performed, the Wilde family was constantly running in and out of the vicarage. Ophelia had flatly refused to give anyone, especially Joan, permission to act on the stage, but Erik had put himself in charge of prompting the cast if they forgot their lines.

Lavinia's love of costume meant that she was forever running over to measure one of the children playing the role of an elephant or a squirrel. They were allowed to pick the animal of their choice, not necessarily biblical, and she was doing her best to create trunks and fluffy tails.

Viola walked in the last day before the performance on Devin's arm, hardly able to stop smiling. That morning . . .

Well.

Suffice it to say that when she looked up from breakfast and found her husband regarding her lazily, her flush began somewhere around her toes and kept climbing. When they reemerged from the bedchamber a couple of hours later, Devin said that he thought he'd accompany her to the vicarage.

"Are the battle lines still drawn?" he inquired as they walked down the street.

"They grow more firm by the hour," Viola said worriedly. "Miss Pettigrew has an unnerving way of saying precisely what she thinks, no matter how rude it might seem to the people who hear it."

"I would imagine that a vicar's wife should be extraordinarily tactful," Devin said.

"That would be helpful," Viola said. She slipped her hand through Devin's arm. "Sometimes I see a desperate look on Mr. Marlowe's face."

Devin glanced down but decided not to answer. His vicar's desperation was unfortunate, but as long as Viola didn't sound overly agonized, he didn't care.

The moment he and Viola entered the vicarage, it was clear that things had gone from bad to worse.

"Alive!" Miss Pettigrew bellowed from the sitting room. "I suppose that is the argument that you used to convince the duke to provide support for this—for this monstrosity. The very idea of making Noah seem alive is grotesque."

"Amazing," Devin said. "I feel as if time has stood still, although I was here over a week ago. Shall I scoop you up and kiss you against the wall?"

"Oh, dear," Viola said, paying no attention. "Perhaps Miss Pettigrew saw a dress rehearsal. Caitlin told me yesterday that she had refused to read the script."

"Too late to change direction now," Devin replied. "It's astonishing how one can hear her voice all over the building."

On entering the sitting room, they found Miss Pettigrew and Mr. Marlowe on one side of the room, and Caitlin on the other. They all got through a round of greetings, but anyone could see that Miss Pettigrew had more to say.

"She's swelling up like a frog on the riverbank about to sing," Devin murmured to his wife, as they seated themselves.

"I love being married," she whispered back. "I was thinking the same thing but far less poetically."

Devin didn't answer for a moment, consumed by a wash of unusual emotion. Viola liked being married. That was good. Excellent, in fact. That was excellent. One wanted one's wife to be agreeably inclined.

"Are you all right?" Viola asked.

He blinked and looked down at her. "Of course."

"We have been discussing the heathenish play that will scar the souls of children watching the performance!" Miss Pettigrew said shrilly. She turned to Viola and Devin. "On hearing the details, my mother had to retire in order to calm herself. I assured her that I would inform Mr. Marlowe that the play cannot go on."

"Mr. Marlowe will undoubtedly note that I, rather than you, am responsible for that decision," Devin told her.

Viola elbowed him, which he took to indicate delight in the fact that Miss Pettigrew was once again swelling like a frog on the edge of song.

"Lady Caitlin's idea of a performance that includes animals is ill judged and ill conceived."

Caitlin was seated on the opposite side of the room, her eyes downcast.

Since the lady showed no inclination to defend herself, Devin took it on. "Lady Caitlin had nothing to do with the cycle plays," he said. "My duchess proposed the idea, and I agreed. Everyone has known for weeks that the play was to be performed. I fail to see what could have led your mother to experience a bout of hysteria at this late date."

"It includes *animals*, live *animals*, inside the cloister," the lady spat. "I was told that children would be dressed as squirrels and other small animals."

"The live animals were my idea," Viola said. "You do remember my pet crow, don't you, Miss Pettigrew?"

She pulled herself upright. "Not on the stage!"

"You'll be happy to know that Barty will not be able to voyage on Noah's ark," Viola said. "He might be discombobulated by the crowd. My pet cows will not be there either."

Caitlin finally raised her head and looked at Devin and Viola. "Mrs. Pettigrew was quite upset to learn that animals will join Noah on the stage."

"Disgraceful!" Miss Pettigrew interjected. "Tell them it is unacceptable, Mr. Marlowe!"

All heads turned in unison to the vicar.

He looked deeply discomfited. Devin felt a flash of sympathy. Mr. Marlowe was in over his head.

"*Rats,*" Miss Pettigrew cried with a gasp. "Lady Caitlin didn't tell the truth because she wouldn't dare. She is bringing rats into the church!"

Caitlin gave Devin a rueful glance. "I asked the children to bring their pets. Johnny Pratchett has a pet rat named Sam. As I explained to Miss Pettigrew, I can't inform Johnny that Sam is not welcome—"

Miss Pettigrew cut her off. "It's not just the rat. That boy has been carrying the vermin in his pocket. Next to his skin. He will no longer attend the Sunday school, as I told his mother. While we are on the subject, I have a feeling that this play is not all it should be. Mr. Bristow told me that it was quite humorous. 'Humorous' is not an appropriate adjective for a biblical performance!"

She surged to her feet. "Mr. Marlowe, I believe that we should discuss the advisability of the play with my father, Bishop Pettigrew. It is my decided opinion that this play will be the ruin of your reputation."

Caitlin, Viola, and Devin stood as well.

"Come," Miss Pettigrew said to her fiancé. She turned on her heel and left the room. Caitlin was obviously on the verge of tears. She dropped a curtsy and left without a word.

"Oh, dear," Viola murmured.

"Mr. Marlowe, if you'll forgive us, I shall have a private conversation with my duchess, after which I shall make a ruling about pet rats in the cloister," Devin said briskly. He slipped his hand into Viola's elbow, drew her out of the door, and directly up the stairs and into the small chamber. "My favorite room!" He closed the door behind them.

The sound of Viola's giggle was smothered by his kiss.

For a few moments there was nothing in Viola's world other than her husband's hard arms and the way his mouth ravished hers, gentling to something near tenderness.

His hand was just sliding down her back when Viola heard voices and pulled away. Miss Pettigrew and Mr. Marlowe were apparently coming up the stairs.

"We can't be discovered again," Viola whispered. "It would be too embarrassing."

Devin's voice was hoarse. "I want you, Viola."

She smiled at him. "Shall we return home?"

His eyes focused behind her shoulder. "No."

"What?"

Devin took a long step, pulled open a door, and revealed a small room lined with shelves from top to bottom, on which were haphazardly stacked plates, saucers, and soup bowls. There were at least three or four soup tureens and what looked to be twenty or more teapots, all crowded together.

"My goodness," Viola said, stupefied by the sheer volume of china.

"My father went through a relatively brief stage during which he was collecting Staffordshire pottery," Devin said. "After he died, Binsey suggested that we donate it to the church. There was no space in the vicarage kitchen, so we had shelves built here."

"You want to kiss me inside a china closet?"

By way of answer, he bent his head to kiss her and simultaneously backed her into the closet.

The wild beating of Viola's heart was the only thing she could hear after the click of the door shutting. The darkness was velvety and complete; if Devin's body hadn't been in front of her, she wouldn't have known he was there.

"Are you all right?" Devin asked. "Some people would be terrified." He pushed open the door until a wide crack of light fell between them.

"That's better. This is absurd!" Viola said, giggling. "What are we doing in here?"

"Kissing," her husband said, a wicked, laughing lilt in his voice.

She shook her head. "Are you still the Duke of Wynter? When I first met you, I thought that you were dignified."

"I believe so." His hands slid around her waist. "All the crucial parts of me still seem to be here." He brought his body smartly against hers and even through her skirts she knew what he was referring to.

Just as she leaned forward to kiss him, the door to the outer room opened.

Viola startled, and Devin's mouth covered hers before she could gasp. Through a sensual haze, she heard Miss Pettigrew say, "I am certain that my mother would excuse the impropriety of a private meeting, Mr. Marlowe, though you should leave the door open."

That was followed by the sound of a door shutting. "I think it would be best to be truly private," Mr. Marlowe stated. "Miss Pettigrew, in the future, I would prefer not to discuss parish matters before the duke, duchess, or Lady Caitlin."

"I have nothing to hide," his fiancée snapped. "It's quite chilly in this room. The chimneys are inadequate."

"Please be seated, Miss Pettigrew. I shall build up the fire," Mr. Marlowe said.

"The settee has its back to this closet," Devin whispered.

Mr. Marlowe apparently added a log, because a crackling sound filled the tense silence between the betrothed couple.

"It would be frightfully embarrassing if we're caught here," Viola whispered.

The duke shrugged, and sank downward, his hands caressing her legs on the way down.

"What are you doing?" she whispered, bending over.

"Seating myself." With a quick movement, Devin pulled her into his lap. "We might as well be comfortable." The shaft of light now fell across their faces, illuminating an expression that Viola had never seen on her husband's face. He looked . . . naughty.

In fact, she had the sudden impression that had his childhood been different, Devin might have been a very naughty boy, the kind who gives his parents no end of grief. Not unlike her younger brother, the architect of a practical joke that had him temporarily expelled from Eton.

"You want Marlowe to be happy," Devin said softly, his eyes probing her face.

"Yes, but *not* because I have a lingering affection for him," Viola said, brushing her mouth with his.

"Would your friend Caitlin marry him, were he free?" Devin asked, a ghost of a smile in his eyes.

Viola nodded. "I believe she would. She would be a marvelous vicar's wife. She's far more sensible than I am."

"I like you just as you are," Devin said.

Viola had to thank him, which led to a kiss that made her tremble all over.

Rather surprisingly, on the other side of the door, Mr. Marlowe had begun arguing with his fiancée about the play. "Biblical cycle plays have been an old and honored part of church ceremonies for over two hundred years. More to the point, *The Play of Noah* is a matter of two nights. I see no cause for alarm, Miss Pettigrew, even if the play is somewhat humorous."

Miss Pettigrew snapped back, "Medieval or not, the play is being performed in your parish. Nay, the performance is in your own cloister. *My* father would never allow a play to be produced in his own church!"

"I explained to your father that the play was a direct request from the Duke of Wynter, who owns the living of St. Wilfrid's. It was not in my purview to refuse him."

"Deflecting, poor fellow," Devin murmured.

"Naturally, I must agree with everything you say, Mr. Marlowe. However, please note that the play will damage *your* reputation, should there be anything the least indelicate about it," Miss Pettigrew pronounced. "Many people of quality, including Bishop Pettigrew, shall attend."

"The tickets are all sold," Viola whispered happily. "We shall make enough money to support the orphans for the entire coming year."

"I am pleased to know that excellent attendance is expected tomorrow," Mr. Marlowe said.

"We may be trapped in this closet all morning," Devin said. "They're arguing like a married couple." His face looked even more angular because of the slash of light cutting across it.

"Thank goodness, we don't fight like that," Viola said, her hands running through his thick hair. "I love it when you don't wear a wig or powder."

"We can only hope that the audience will not be so offended that they leave in high dudgeon," Miss Pettigrew said.

Devin eased Viola back against his right arm.

"Did you hear something?" Miss Pettigrew asked, her voice rising. "I think I heard a rustling. If this vicarage is infested with vermin, I will *not* move here, Mr. Marlowe. Married or no, I will not expose myself to disease."

Devin was amusing himself by running his hands under Viola's skirts.

"My wife must live where I live," the vicar said evenly. "Many church buildings are infested with mice. I may choose at some point to take a living in one of the poor areas by the docks, for example. A vicar cannot live apart from his parish."

Devin nipped Viola's earlobe. "The man is truly developing a backbone."

"All the more reason to ensure that the play is not scandalous," Miss Pettigrew said after a small pause. "Bishop Pettigrew is paying a visit tomorrow precisely to further his acquaintance with you." Her voice had a desperate tone. "You may well be the person to succeed him, someday."

"I do not wish to become a bishop," Mr. Marlowe stated.

"Cat is among the pigeons now," Devin murmured, but he tilted Viola farther back against his arm and took her mouth.

She missed Miss Pettigrew's response. In fact, by the time she surfaced from a long, intoxicating kiss, the drawing room was silent.

"Thank goodness, they're gone," Viola whispered breathlessly.

"No." Her husband's hand circled her wrist. "He's still in there. She stormed out. The poor sod is contemplating his fate. We may have to remain here all day, Viola. What in the world will we do to amuse ourselves?"

Viola felt her heart swell as she met Devin's laughing eyes. She hadn't known it was possible to adore someone this much.

"I love you," she whispered, the words flying from her mouth. "I'm in love with you."

He frowned.

"I know you don't feel the same," Viola said. "I understand. I just want you to know." But she held her breath anyway.

He put a finger to her lips.

The door opened in the outer room, and a woman's voice said, "Mr. Marlowe? Am I interrupting you?"

"This truly is as good as a play," Devin rumbled in Viola's ear. "Who cares about Noah? We have a comedy of manners right here in the vicarage, and for free too."

She was trying to catch her breath. His hand had crept higher under her skirts and he was drawing tender circles on her inner thigh. "Who . . ."

"Your friend, the third participant in this drawing room comedy, of course," her husband said.

"Cat," Viola breathed.

Sure enough, Caitlin said, "I wish to apologize for provoking your betrothed. It is the fault of my particular deadly sin."

After a silence, Mr. Marlowe said, "I find it hard to believe that you sin."

"I'd say we're at the opening of the fourth act," Devin said.

"Envy," Caitlin said, her voice clear. "Miss Pettigrew is very sure of herself, whereas I am always uncertain. In fact, I am only confident of my own wrongdoing. Quite through no fault of her own, Miss Pettigrew's self-command makes me envious."

Viola gasped softly. "She's declaring herself!"

"She has to," Devin said. "The fellow would be giving up a future bishopric for her, and he's not going to declare himself, as it would be unethical."

"He doesn't want to be a bishop," Viola said. "You heard him."

"Lady Caitlin," Mr. Marlowe said, his voice rumbling in his chest.

"If he tells her to trust in Providence, I'll . . . I'll kick him," Viola muttered to Devin.

"Are you worried about the Noah play, Mr. Marlowe?" Caitlin interrupted. "Because it is a lively play. Miss Pettigrew might—well, she might have a point."

"Bloody hell," Devin muttered. Meanwhile, though, his fingers slid even higher on Viola's thigh. She was having trouble thinking. Her veins were slowly heating, desire sliding through her like hot tea on a chilly morning.

Devin's breathing had become deeper. Suddenly, in a welter of desire, she had a clear thought: If her husband would have been *naughty*, if his natural bent was disobedience, she was the perfect wife for him, because she grew up surrounded by naughty children.

Devin would have risked his life had he flouted his father's rules as a child.

Not any longer.

"What could possibly be indelicate about Noah and his ark?" Mr. Marlowe asked.

The Wildes practically defined the term "naughty"— from Ophelia's youngest daughter, Artie, to the older boys she grew up with. A smile growing in her heart, Viola moved from the shelter of Devin's arm and braced herself to stand.

"No," her husband growled, his voice just soft enough not to be heard.

"The play is medieval," Caitlin explained. "They had more exuberant attitudes toward Scripture at the time."

"Such as?" Mr. Marlowe's tone was distinctly skeptical.

"Genesis 9:21," Caitlin said unhappily. *"And Noah drank of the wine and was drunken."*

"And uncovered himself?" Mr. Marlowe asked, obviously horrified.

"No!" Caitlin cried. "No, no, but the play does include the part when Noah curses his son Canaan. Naturally, the text plays up drunkenness. I gather the part of Noah would have been played by a tapster."

"Bloody hell," Devin muttered.

Putting a hand on his cheek, Viola whispered, "Don't move." Moving as slowly as she could so that her skirts didn't rustle, she made her way to her feet, turned, pulled up her skirts until she was holding huge wads of cloth in each hand, and sank back down, her knees on either side of Devin's hips.

"I've died and gone to heaven," her husband said in her ear.

Viola wound her arms around his neck and leaned forward until her breasts were brushing against his coat. "We're making love in a vicarage, with the vicar just through the door," she whispered. "This is very scandalous."

Devin reached out and very slowly eased the door shut until just a line of light entered the closet. "We are?"

Viola didn't answer because Devin was kissing her with a searing need that answered his question. In the room, Caitlin had launched into a tangled explanation of why the Noah play, or any medieval biblical play, was important. "I wanted the children to—to—"

"See Noah as a living person?" Mr. Marlowe asked incredulously. "By showing a saint cursing a family member while drunk, performed by actors accompanied by rodents?"

"It sounds terrible put that way," Caitlin said. "Those details are in the Bible. Well, not the rat."

Now that only a thread of light was coming through the door, Viola felt as if all her senses other than sight had flared into being. Her stockings tied just above her knees, and her naked thighs rested against the fine wool of Devin's breeches. It was unbearably erotic.

His fingers dipped between her legs.

She took in a silent gulp of air.

"I want you," Devin whispered roughly in her ear. "May I take you?"

"Oh," she breathed, her blood singing with desire. His fingers caressed her skillfully until she bit back a sob and buried her face in the crook of his neck.

"I'll take that as a yes," he said.

"Noah just becomes a trifle inebriated," Caitlin said, desperately. "As it describes in the Bible, when Noah drank the wine that he had made. This particular play was performed by ale makers, in the Middle Ages, that is."

There was a moment of silence.

"So Noah is a drunkard," Mr. Marlowe said. His voice was hard to read.

"Shouldn't he be more horrified?" Viola whispered. Her heart was thumping.

"He merely drinks a bit too much. It's funny," Caitlin said. "Mr. Higgins is interpreting his part liberally."

"I should have paid more attention," Mr. Marlowe said. "I've been too busy with the parish and the orphanage."

"He almost sounds amused," Viola whispered. She was having trouble listening, because her husband knew exactly how to touch her in such a way that she could scarcely shape a sentence.

"I don't give a damn," Devin whispered back, his voice ragged. "I'm as drunk as Noah. Drunk on your hair, and your eyes, and the rest of you, or I wouldn't be in this bloody closet."

He thrust one thick finger inside her warm heat, then two, barely catching Viola's gasp with his mouth. At his urging, she found herself riding his hand, her palms cupped around his cheeks, her mouth sealed tight to his.

"Tell me, Lady Caitlin, what are you doing here?" Mr. Marlowe asked.

"Doing here?"

"You don't belong in the vicarage," he said bluntly. "Young ladies of fashion appear in church only on Sunday, wearing their very best new gowns. Yet you are teaching a class to the orphans, you are a member of the sewing circle, and you have entered into the parish's fundraising efforts, to the extent of staging a drunken biblical character."

Fire was spreading through Viola's limbs, and keeping silent was torture.

Devin was fumbling at the fall of his breeches and at last, to her exquisite relief, he eased her down onto something broad, hot, thick . . . His cock.

She kissed him fiercely as she slowly, slowly, took him in. All of him, from the peppermint on his breath, to the fierce heat as they came together, to the embarrassment of actually hearing how aroused she was.

"When I was growing up, we took an active part in our parish," Caitlin said. "My mother taught the local

Bible class. A week after my mother died, my father sent me away to school. I felt like an orphan. I have a special affection for those children."

"Bloody hell," Devin said in a near-soundless growl. "I can't . . ." He tilted his hips and pushed home the last inch.

"You feel marvelous," Viola whispered. She was kissing him frantically, letting her lips do what her eyes would, had she been able to clearly see the angles of his face. Caress him, love him. She rose up on her knees and then pushed back down.

"It is commendable that your mother was active in her parish," Mr. Marlowe said.

"I find it hard to believe that you would dissuade ladies from participating in parish affairs, Mr. Marlowe," Caitlin said. "Are only bakers' wives allowed to teach Bible classes?"

"No!"

"He's making a mess of it," Devin muttered. His voice was raw with desire. His hands had slid around her hips and his fingers bit into her flesh, pulling her sharply down.

"I'm in charge," Viola whispered, wiggling.

Lightning was darting through her limbs; her toes were curling in her slippers. A few more rough strokes and she'd be lost.

"We can't," she whispered in his ear.

"We already are." Devin braced himself against the ground, moving his hips in short, sharp thrusts.

"Wait," Viola breathed.

"You know that there are many married women active in this parish," Mr. Marlowe was saying. "I am grateful for them. Young ladies are supposed to be busy with other things."

"I should be sitting at home embroidering a sampler, is that it?" Caitlin's voice was controlled, but even a child could hear her rage.

Devin wrapped his arms around Viola and kissed her ear. She could feel him throbbing inside her, and even without either of them moving a muscle, tension surged in her body. Her legs shook.

"Wait," Devin ordered in a low, rough voice, echoing her.

"I can't," Viola squeaked. "I have to move, Devin."

"No."

It felt delicious, as if her body had become only sensation, only need.

"No," her husband commanded again. His lips skimmed her cheekbone and he bit her earlobe.

Viola's interior muscles were clenched around him, trying to find the last friction that—

"Stop that," Devin said in her ear. She could hear lust and laughter in his voice.

"I think I might die," she told him, very seriously, very quietly. She flexed her interior muscles again. "Can you feel that?"

"Hell, yes. Lovely bride, beautiful bride," he said, crooning in her ear. "Just stay still, all of you, still. You can come after they leave the room. Not before."

"Attending a champagne breakfast," Mr. Marlowe said lamely. "Later, when you are married and have children of your own, you will undoubtedly be—" He broke off.

Viola tipped her head back and looked up at the velvet darkness. Her entire body was focused around one point. If she rose even the smallest amount and slammed back down, that would do it, propel her into a wash of pleasure.

"Don't even think about it," the devil said softly.

"How can I not think about it?" Somehow she managed to keep that cry to a whimper.

Devin grinned at her, his eyes glinting in the dusky light, and flexed his hips. Viola felt her lips shape into a circle, struggling to bite back sound.

"Good girl," he breathed. "Let's do that again."

"You are by far the youngest woman in the sewing circle," Mr. Marlowe said, digging his own grave. "You don't look the same as the other women."

Viola's senses had narrowed to the hard feeling of Devin inside her, the uncontrollable shaking of her limbs, the moans silenced by his mouth. He settled into a steady rocking. Disconcertingly, Viola felt a drop of sweat on her neck but still she clenched her teeth and fought back against the pressure to explode.

Mr. Marlowe and Caitlin had fallen silent. "Perhaps they left?" she whispered.

Devin shook his head. "Silent glares, I think."

Each time the pressure built up like a kettle on the boil, her fiendish husband would stop moving altogether, leaving her trembling as his mouth lingered against hers.

Suddenly Caitlin burst back into speech. "I do not wish to spend the morning embroidering the alphabet on a sampler to hang in the nursery. I do not wish to attend champagne breakfasts. I don't care for wine in the morning."

"Think about something else," Devin instructed Viola, a wicked, enticing voice full of laughter. "For example, your vicar is going to end up a miserable bishop with a shrew for a wife."

"You want to *talk*?" Viola leaned forward and nipped his earlobe; she could feel his responding shudder through her entire body. It occurred to her that she was giving him altogether too much power over the situation.

"Yes, let's talk," she whispered, caressing his cheekbone with her lips. "Could you help Mr. Marlowe?"

"Me?" Devin's sleepy eyes didn't fool her. He was as consumed with desire as she was. She could hear it under all that amusement, a taut wire of dark lust as intent and uncontrolled as her own.

"You solve problems," she reminded him. "People bring you problems, and you fix them."

"You want me to help my rival?"

Viola knew she probably looked feverish; she could feel her eyes were glittering. She eased her knees apart and sank lower, just a hair. "He is no rival of yours," she breathed. "Please help him."

Devin chuckled into her hair, the sound so low that hardly a strand trembled.

"Obviously, Marlowe should marry Caitlin," Viola whispered. "Can you please make it happen, for me?"

"He's too stupid to save," Devin muttered.

"Still . . . please?"

"Damn it," Devin said. "I can't believe I'm considering this."

He licked Viola's lips and she opened to him, pulling his head closer to hers. It felt as if she had become part of him, or he part of her.

"I don't wish to go to a dance in the afternoon either," Caitlin said, raising her voice far above a ladylike cadence. "I like dancing, occasionally. I do like wearing beautiful dresses. But I have no interest in changing my gown ten times a day!"

"Why would you?" Mr. Marlowe asked, sounding genuinely mystified.

"Fool," Devin muttered against Viola's lips.

"Don't you have any idea what the life of a lady is like?" Caitlin demanded.

"You . . . you go visiting. Dress elegantly, go shopping, and dancing, perform music and, and—"

"And find a husband!" Caitlin completed his sentence.

Viola shook her head. She lifted her hips just a touch and pushed down again.

Devin made a sound in the back of his throat.

Thankfully, Caitlin spoke at the same moment. "I am sorry that you find I am an inappropriate addition to your parish, Mr. Marlowe. I certainly did not mean to inconvenience you." Her tone was as arctic as the north wind.

"Lady Caitlin, I never meant to make you feel unwelcome."

"All right," Devin whispered. "I'll do it. For you, if not for the good of my fellow man."

"I shall not bother you in the future," Caitlin said icily. "I had no idea that church activities in St. Wilfrid's were reserved for those over the age of thirty."

"I didn't mean—"

"Too little, too late," Devin muttered. "I'm getting sick of this closet." His fingers were floating over the curve of Viola's upper thighs. She grinned at him, dizzy with power, and repeated the movement that she knew would set him on fire, catching his groan with her lips.

"I know what you meant," Caitlin said, shakily. There were tears in her voice. "I shall not vex you any further. Miss Pettigrew will be happy to see the last of me."

"No!"

"Getting his balls back," Devin murmured.

"Caitlin," Mr. Marlowe said, voice husky. "Oh, God, Caitlin."

"He swore," Viola whispered. "He used her first name!"

Devin was clearly weary of being an audience. He pulled her body firmly down to his and crushed her mouth under his. Viola melted against him and his hips tilted up, pressing his shaft even deeper.

Her eyes closed, she was fighting a battle to stay silent as her limbs turned to fire and she began to shake. The next moments passed in a silent conversation, spoken in a language of tongues, pressing bodies, and small inarticulate noises.

Viola's lips danced over Devin's cheekbones and pressed shut the thick fringe of his eyelashes . . . and let go only because she wanted to see his eyes again in the faint light.

"Viola," he muttered, his voice dark with longing, caressing her breasts. "We need to get out of this bloody closet."

His large hands had shaped her entire body into a shrieking mass of nerves. Her nipples were standing against the fabric of her bodice.

"I know you are marrying another woman," Caitlin said. "I know . . . I know I don't belong in your parish. I shall find some other—"

The sentence broke off.

"Finally kissing her," Devin growled.

"You—we mustn't," Caitlin cried. "I shall attend the performance of the Noah play tomorrow night. But I will not bother you again."

"That's sad," Viola gasped.

Devin pushed back the curls he'd disarranged and kissed her cheek. "I'll solve it for you, Viola. If they would just leave the bloody room."

"I can be silent," Viola said, hoping she was right. She couldn't hold back much longer.

"You see," Caitlin said clearly, "my deadly sin is envy. I cannot stay here and watch Miss Harriet Pettigrew take what I want most in the world." Her aching words fell softly into the room.

"Caitlin." Mr. Marlowe's voice was unsteady. "If your sin is envy, mine must be lust. For I want you more than anything I have wanted in my life."

"Damn, he came through in the end," Devin muttered.

Caitlin did not answer.

There was the sound of swift footsteps, and the door opened and shut. A moment of silence, and the vicar—Mr. Marlowe, who never raised his voice!—snarled, "Bloody hell," and the door slammed behind him.

"Thank God," Devin grunted.

He thrust up at the same moment that Viola ground down on him, a cry escaping her lips.

"Not too loud," Devin said, thrusting again and again.

"I can't be still," Viola gasped, just as he sealed his mouth over hers. Fire washed over her and he took her cry. Kissed her hard and let himself go, with such a powerful thrust that she felt his entire body shudder.

For long minutes afterward, she lay against his chest, his shaft still thick within her, his heart still pounding against her cheek, his harsh breathing telling her of his pleasure.

At length, she said, drowsily, "I think that if I stand up, there might be a mess. On my legs, I mean."

"There will be," Devin said. "I've never come so hard in my life."

Viola didn't answer, storing up his words to think about later.

Strong hands gripped her hips and lifted her carefully up and away from him.

She sucked in a breath: She was a little tender, but mostly her body tingled with remembered pleasure.

"I'd like a bath," she murmured.

Devin handed her a snowy white handkerchief, embroidered with the ducal crest. "For the mess," he said, a note of apology in his voice.

Viola busied herself with doing what was necessary, but she couldn't stop herself from giggling.

"What is funny, Duchess?" her husband asked, coming nimbly to his feet and holding out a hand to her. "Let's go home. I have plans that involve a bed."

"A bath," Viola said firmly, as he eased open the door. Light streamed into the closet. "Just look at my skirts." They had been pale yellow, but now they were streaked with brown dust.

Her husband's mouth curled. "Agreed." He began walking toward the door, but Viola caught his hand and pulled him to a halt.

She pointed to the back of a sturdy chair. He popped her on it, seeming to love picking her up as much as she adored his hands around her waist. She slung her arms around his neck and pulled him closer.

Her love for him felt as if it was simmering under the surface. "You said that you have an estate in the country," she said.

He nodded.

"What if we went there the day after the play?" she asked. "Just the two of us."

"I haven't had time to clear out the wheelbarrows."

"I'm sure that you could think of some way to make a wheelbarrow amusing."

He leaned forward, cupping her nape with a large hand. "Just the two of us? You'd miss the rest of the Season. My uncle is giving a ball for Hazel in our townhouse."

"I needed Joan's support, not the other way around, and we could return for the ball. Sir Reginald wants no assistance from either of us."

Devin frowned. "Your sister is reckless. It might be better if you were here for the rest of the Season."

"My mother and Aunt Knowe are her chaperones," Viola said. "Besides, my stepfather is having Daisy and Cleo sent to your estate, just as soon as I am certain that your cowshed will keep them comfortable. Why are you laughing?"

"Because my cowshed is more like a cow mansion, and the king of it is a sturdy fellow called Rex. Who will make Daisy and Cleo *very* comfortable."

"Comfort is good," Viola agreed, her voice husky. She leaned forward and eased her mouth onto his, unable to stop herself.

"Bath," Devin said later. "Bed. Are you certain that you want to see the play? We could leave for the country now."

"Yes, because you're going to save Mr. Marlowe, remember?"

"I could do that by eight in the morning and we could be on the road out of London."

"I can't miss the play," Viola said. "It was my idea. What if there is a fuss over that drunken Noah? You should be there."

For a second, Devin got the calculating look he had when he worked with his equations. Then he scooped her up and carried her out of the room.

"My wife twisted her ankle," he told the vicarage housekeeper, as Viola hid her face against his chest to hide the fact that she was shaking with laughter.

"Your Grace! I had no idea . . ."

But the housekeeper's voice trailed away as Devin strode out of the vicarage and straight into their waiting carriage.

Chapter Thirty-one

*I*n retrospect, Devin realized that he should have guessed everything would go wrong. It was too good to be true.

Making love to Viola in the dusty closet, she'd blurted out that she loved him.

Loved him!

He didn't have much faith in the emotion, or belief in it. But he recognized the statement as a landmark.

Viola had thought she was in love with Marlowe; now she thought she was in love with him. He told himself that love was an illusion, but the sentence warmed him nonetheless.

The next day, Binsey entered his study looking flustered. "We are removing the last of the chamber pots, Your Grace. You do want all of them to go to Oxford? Even this one?"

Devin looked up and realized the butler was carrying the burnished one that had supposedly been used by King Henry VIII.

"Did you remove that from Her Grace's desk?" he asked. "I believe she was making use of it."

Binsey nodded. "You said the entire collection, Your Grace."

"Here, give it to me," Devin said. "I'll ask her if she still wants it, and if she doesn't, we'll send it to the Ashmolean on its own."

The butler brought over the pot and set it on Devin's desk, bowed, and left.

Devin opened it. Like Pandora's box, he thought later. It held an unfinished letter, and the greeting leapt out at him.

Dear Mr. Marlowe.

Viola was writing to the vicar.

She was corresponding with one man while married to another . . . while married to him. His duchess was—

Without realizing what he was doing, he plucked the small sheet of paper from the chamber pot.

Dear Mr. Marlowe, Viola had written, *I wish to congratulate you on the perspicuity of your recent sermon on marital harmony.*

What the bloody hell? He cast his mind back to Marlowe's most recent sermon, but frankly, he hadn't paid attention. Attending church was more interesting now that he had a duchess beside him, but he had never seen any reason to accept advice from a vicar.

His wife clearly had a different point of view.

She not only listened, but apparently she was sharing details with Mr. Marlowe about their marriage. Confirming whatever it was he said by reference to their private life.

I shall take to heart your point as regards avoiding using another human being as an instrument for one's own pleasure, thus making a spouse an object of indulgence.

His hand crumpled the page, and rage filled his chest.

For long moments, he stood stock-still, letting the anger course through him. It was a trick he'd taught himself, thanks to Annabel's betrayal. All those years ago, when she tried to trick him into marriage, he had lost control.

Since that moment, at the slightest anger, Devin shut his mouth and simply breathed, no matter how long it took, or how peculiar it seemed.

When he was certain that he was in no danger of shouting at his wife, he walked upstairs. He shouldn't have read Viola's letter, but the crime was inadvertent. She shouldn't share details of their married life with a vicar or anyone else.

That crime was not inadvertent.

His heart was thudding in a jerky rhythm because even though he was in control of his words, his body didn't agree. His body felt betrayed, the way he felt every time his mother fled the house without a backward glance.

No matter how much he told himself that there was no parallel, his body wasn't convinced. His hands were unsteady. Every breath he took burned in his chest.

He found Viola in her chamber, sitting by the fire. Her hair fell over one shoulder, a waterfall of bronze strands.

He couldn't say anything.

Who had committed the greater crime, he or she?

He still had to tell her who he was. He still had to confess his secret, and discover whether her love was strong enough to forgive him. Every day he woke up, telling himself that today would be the day, but somehow it never was.

How could he tell her that *he* had ruined her life? Her future husband had frightened her until she spent years in purgatory, living in the country, hiding in a cowshed, terrified of men? He opened his mouth, but no words emerged.

She would leave him.

She would take everything that mattered in his life and leave him.

For the first time in their marriage, he seduced Viola not because he was blind with lust but because he wanted to see *her* blind with lust. He made love to her expertly, caressing her, kissing her, turning her this way and that, showing her new sensations and building her to such a shattering climax that she brought him with her.

Afterward she lay prone on the bed, her hair spilling around her in kinks and curls, her creamy hips showing the ruddy imprint of fingers where he had deftly held her at just the right angle until she could feel every bit of his shaft.

He felt a surge of satisfaction.

Viola rolled over and pushed a thick lock of hair out of her eyes.

He smiled at her. "How are you?"

She sighed. "What was that?"

"What?"

"*That*," she said. "Not that I didn't enjoy it, because I did. But I liked it better in the closet."

He stared at her, astounded. "Because there was someone nearby?" His mind spun. He could think of any number of public places where he could make love to her if that's what she wished.

"No!" she said, wrinkling her nose. "I wouldn't want to do it again. I liked the closet because you were tender."

Tender?

He tried the word out and decided he wasn't sure what she meant. His eyes went back to his fingerprints on her hips but they had faded. "I should have been more gentle," he said. "I apolog—"

Viola clapped a hand over his mouth. "No!"

He blinked at her and opened his lips enough to nibble on one of her fingers.

"Come here," she said, wrapping her other arm around his neck and tugging. "Here."

They lay together, and she tugged and pushed and pulled until she had their bodies in just the right position for whatever she wanted to demonstrate. Her slender knee was between his and her arms were around his neck.

She leaned forward and his body rejoiced. He was thoroughly in favor of his wife teaching him the meaning of every word in the English language, as long as the lesson was conveyed when they were naked.

She didn't kiss him.

Instead, she rubbed noses with him, her eyes looking into his.

"Tenderness," she said. She pushed at him again, and he rolled onto his back. She pressed a kiss on one eyelid and the other. Eyes shut, he let himself experience tenderness, which turned out to have nothing to do with his demanding cock, or his thumping heart.

Perhaps it had something to do with his heart.

When she kissed his chest and murmured "tenderness," he had the feeling it might break.

Chapter Thirty-two

$\mathcal{T}$he cloister of St. Wilfrid's was a long, narrow space, lined with fantastically carved stone windows that seemed to be made from wood, not stone, since the casements curled into arresting shapes, complete with sprouts and tiny leaves. The high ceiling was formed of arches made from the same beautiful cream stone.

Devin walked down the chamber, noting with interest that footmen in Wilde livery were arranging chairs in long rows down the cloister, preparing for the play that would be staged in the evening.

A boy was trotting up and down the room. "You must fit in at least thirteen more chairs," Erik shouted. He had all the force of a Wilde, and footmen scurried to do his bidding.

A neatly built stage filled nearly the entire width at the far end of the chamber. As Devin neared, Lavinia clapped her hands. "One more time with the flood, if you please!"

"Right you are," shouted a voice that Devin recognized as that of his coachman. On the opposite side of the arch a man in Lindow livery was peering down. "Ready, Hollyburn?" The two men nodded to each other.

Shimmering blue silk unfurled from the arch high above, fell down to the back to the stage, and flowed forward, more slowly, falling off the front.

"Magnificent," Devin said, strolling forward.

"Not quite," Lavinia said, sparing him a glance. "See the right edge? Mr. Hollyburn, you forgot to give a last flip to the string."

"Sorry, me lady," a voice bellowed back.

"Again," she directed. The cloth began gathering into folds.

"How does that work?" Devin asked.

"String runs through small brass hoops sewn underneath the cloth," Lavinia told him, watching closely as the cloth began slowly making its way back to the heavens. "Where's Viola?"

"At home, napping." Devin had left her behind, a cloud of silky hair spread over the pillows, her cheeks still high with color, her eyes shut. He had to fulfill his promise to her as regards Mr. Marlowe, and he had a good idea how to do it.

Lavinia looked at him with a wry smile but said nothing.

The second time the flood spilled from the sky seamlessly, rolling forward and flowing over the edge of the stage.

"Perfect!" Lavinia called.

A whiskery face peered down from the arched roof. "I have it now, me lady," Mr. Hollyburn said.

"Where are the actors preparing themselves?" Devin asked.

"They're in the library," Lavinia said absentmindedly. "Rogers, can you roll out the ark, please?" she called.

Devin strolled on, taking in the brightly painted wooden ship, a frontispiece that had clearly been painted by children. The lines weren't straight and the colors merged, but it was a magnificent piece of art, all the same.

"A larger chair for the bishop," Erik shouted from behind him.

The front row would hold ecclesiastical dignitaries. The second row was for peers and their spouses, creating an interesting collision of two powerful worlds that rarely found themselves in the same audience. Without question, Bishop Pettigrew had never watched the outrageous play *Wilde in Love*, which had transfixed London audiences for weeks.

"I think we may have sold too many tickets," Viola had told Devin that morning, her eyes shining.

Gentlemen could stand along the walls. The important thing was that his wife's idea was coming to fruition. All of this came from an idea that Viola quietly—but persistently—brought into being.

The truth was that his duchess, his small, funny, shy, brilliant wife, was formidable. She was like a tidy hurricane. She came into his life . . . and now everything was changing. Mathematics was falling behind him, reminding him of the passionate way he used to play war with his wooden soldiers, until the day he put them away for good.

These days, he spent his days and evenings with the Wildes or Murgatroyds, surrounded by people who didn't show any particular interest in his behaving like a duke. In fact, he had the feeling that ducal behavior was strongly discouraged among the Wildes. There were too many strong men.

They had to lay down their weapons and their dignity in order to enjoy each other.

Behind the stage was a curtained area, a sign indicating it was intended for costume changes. Next to it was what seemed to be the staging ground for Noah's animals—given that a pensive-looking goat was tied to a stone railing.

Two things occurred to him on the way to the vicarage library. One was that his parents had never enjoyed anything, including time together. The other was that he wanted more than anything in the world to spend his life enjoying Viola.

One errand and he could return home to her. His quickened blood beat in a rhythm that had to do with—

Love.

He wasn't a fool. Men who felt the way he did announced they were in love. They wrote poetry, painted portraits, generally made fools of themselves.

He loved his wife.

The Wildes loved their spouses; his uncle had loved his wife; someday Otis and Hazel would love their spouses.

He loved Viola. He'd thought as much before, but now the truth of it settled into his bones.

Through some miracle, he had been reformed into a new person, a strange man who knew instinctively how to love. Who recognized the emotion in other people's eyes. Who had become part of a fellowship that he hadn't truly believed in: people who loved others.

He did his errand and went back home, finding Viola in the bath.

His skin prickling with this new emotion, Devin nodded to her maid, who whisked out, giggling. He sat down on a stool and played maid for his wife, washing her long hair.

The bathing chamber pulled the world snugly around them. It was such a safe, warm space that for the first time in years, Devin allowed himself a glimpse of the freezing, black fear that he had grown up with.

He had been gently combing her wet hair, but he put down the comb.

Viola turned her head. "Devin?"

He dropped a kiss on her ear and said, stunned, "I was afraid for a long time as a child."

She turned around completely, a wave of water following her motion, threatening to pour over the tub like Noah's flood. She rose on her knees, wet hair covering her breasts.

"You look like a naiad," he said. "You're beautiful, Viola."

She ignored the compliment. "Being afraid is exhausting."

Devin considered her point and realized she was right. Some part of him had wound tight in childhood and spent years vibrating in a high wind. He nodded.

She leaned forward and put wet hands on his cheeks. "There's nothing to be afraid of now."

She was wrong.

Was it possible to be terrified of losing love one has only known for a short period of time? He knew the answer. It was *yes*.

"Are you afraid that you might become your father?" Viola's eyes searched his and she gave him another sweet kiss.

"If I lose my temper, I might turn into him," he said, forcing the words out of his mouth. "I might hear his shouts emerging from my mouth. I might become him."

Viola sat back on her heels. A few strands of wet hair slid around her right breast. He was instantly hard. She shook her head. "You won't become him."

Her voice held complete certainty.

"Devin," she said, crinkling her brow. She stood up and got out of the tub, paying no attention to the water that came with her. She stood in front of him, an exquisite, very wet water nymph.

Then she knelt in front of him. "Devin," she said again, and opened her arms.

The look in her eyes was intolerable. Pity. He loathed pity. His male pride snapped around him like the suit of armor up in the attic, the one that had belonged to his great-great-grandfather.

"There's nothing wrong with me, Viola." He stood, catching one of her hands and bringing her to her feet. He turned and caught up a sheet of toweling, wrapping her in it until her back was to him and she couldn't see his face.

What in the bloody hell was happening to him?

Chapter Thirty-three

$\mathcal{V}$iola walked into the cloister on Devin's arm that evening, her heart beating quickly with excitement. She was tired—the day had been nothing if not emotional—but also thrilled. She had first had the idea of putting on a cycle play when they studied them in school, years ago.

And now . . . here it was.

Not that she could take credit for it. Otis and Joan had managed casting and rehearsals; Lavinia and a crew of seamstresses had created the costumes. Caitlin had overseen the sets, painted by the children in the Sunday school and orphanage. Erik would prompt the actors.

Still, it had been Viola's idea.

The cloister was crammed with elegantly dressed aristocrats. Every chair was occupied, and gentlemen stood along the back and sides of the room.

"Our seats are reserved in the second row," she reminded Devin. "It will go well, won't it?"

He looked down at her, heavy-lidded eyes calm and confident. "If the play is boring and the ark falls over and the flood doesn't work, the orphans won't care.

They'll just be happy to be warm and fed and off the streets. It has already gone well."

She took in a deep breath. "Caitlin said the children are wildly excited to see the performance tomorrow. They painted the sets, you know. Every single one of them had a hand in the ark."

"I could tell," Devin said, his eyes crinkling as he smiled.

That smile was so beautiful that her mind fogged. By the time she pulled herself back together, they had reached the front of the cloister, and Devin was bowing before Bishop Pettigrew and his flock of soberly dressed clerics.

Miss Pettigrew had made a special effort this evening; she was wearing a ruby-colored dress trimmed with orange satin leaves around the bosom. The color suited her dark hair and coloring, Viola thought, determined to be kind.

"The Duke and Duchess of Wynter," Miss Pettigrew said. "My father, Bishop Pettigrew. And my father's archdeacon, Mr. Bell."

Mr. Bell was a splendidly bearded man who appeared to great advantage in clerical garb. He looked like a plausible bishop, in fact.

"We are somewhat concerned about this entertainment," the bishop said ponderously. "I gather this is your idea, Duchess. The cause is an excellent one, though I feel compelled to point out that the Anglican Church has frowned upon the cycle plays since the days of Good Queen Bess."

"I believe the Elizabethans felt that the appearance of our Heavenly Creator on stage was particularly abhorrent," Mr. Bell remarked, leaving no doubt about where his own feelings lay.

Miss Pettigrew rushed in before Viola could say a word. "I am quite certain there will be no such desecration in this play," she said importantly. "We might hear a voice, perhaps, but there is no reason for someone to actually impersonate the Divine. Mr. Marlowe would *never* allow it."

"We should make certain the preparations are proceeding satisfactorily," Devin said, while Viola was trying to remember whether God appeared on the stage in the Noah play or not.

"Please inform Mr. Marlowe that his seat is waiting for him," Miss Pettigrew said, indicating the chair beside her.

Viola saw Caitlin as soon as they entered the makeshift dressing area behind the stage. She was laughing with a plump man dressed in what looked like two white sheets with a wobbly halo suspended over his head.

"Maybe he's an angel," Devin said.

"I hope so," Viola said.

She and Devin walked over, and Caitlin introduced Mr. Brisket.

"I do know His Grace, but I'm pleased to meet my lady duchess. I'm a butcher by trade," Mr. Brisket told Viola. "Many a pork chop on Your Graces' table came from my shop."

"I am doubly pleased to meet you," Viola said, smiling.

"Do you think your costume is quite secure, Mr. Brisket, or would you like a few more pins?" Caitlin asked.

"Goodness, my lady, if you put any more pins into my gown, I'm likely to clank as I walk," Mr. Brisket said. Caitlin nodded and slipped away to help fix the tail on a young squirrel.

"What part are you playing, Mr. Brisket?" Viola asked, holding her breath.

"Well, I'm a lucky one, I am," the butcher replied. "Can't you guess?" He beamed at her. "I'll give you a bit o' my lines." In a fine, plummy tone, he intoned: *"Behold, I will destroy them with the earth."*

"You're God," Viola said hollowly.

"Trust you to catch it!" Mr. Brisket said. "I'm a bit worried about forgetting the bits about the length of the ark: three hundred cubits, it is, the breadth of it fifty cubits, and the height of it thirty cubits. Lady Caitlin has coached me on it. She's a splendid young lady, she is."

Viola nodded, looking around. Lavinia was across the room, pinning a large bow onto the bosom of a curvaceous woman.

"That's Mrs. Noah. She's a bit of a shrew," chuckled Mr. Brisket. "This is a right lively play, Your Graces. These medieval people must have been a spirited bunch. No doubt but it'll be a success. We're having a second performance tomorrow night, did you know that?"

Devin nodded.

"All the tickets tonight were bought up by the gentry, which is good for those poor orphans. But our relatives will see it as well. Tomorrow night's performance will be half-price, just for people like meself. Now isn't that a splendid thing?"

"Absolutely," Viola managed. God was a butcher in a sheet; Noah was a drunkard; Noah's wife was a curvaceous shrew.

The audience was full of the worst tattlemongers in all London, people who could stir up a scandal-broth without the slightest encouragement. Lord knew what they would do when a bishop and an archdeacon left the performance in a fury.

Devin drew her to the side. "Don't worry," he advised.

"You're laughing," Viola accused.

"I'm not even chuckling."

She shook her head at him. "You're laughing inside."

"Perhaps."

"It's going to be a disaster," Viola moaned.

"Remember, the tickets are sold," her husband said. "No one can get their money back. Besides, look at that."

Caitlin was hugging one of the orphans, who was holding up his finger and weeping. Mr. Marlowe walked directly to her. "What seems to be the matter?" he asked.

"Come with me," Viola whispered to Devin, walking in that direction. When they were close by, she swerved and stepped behind the curtain that served as Noah's tent, pulling her husband with her.

"What is this affinity you have for hiding?" he asked, his hand sliding down her back and shifting to her bottom. "Why are we always eavesdropping? I'm sure Aunt Knowe wouldn't approve."

"Devin!" Viola protested, moving her hips away from his caress.

"If you're making me hide behind a curtain, you must expect a certain level of intimacy," her husband said. But he pulled her in front of him and contented himself with wrapping his arms around her.

"Freddy was nibbled by the calf," Caitlin said. She was staring intently at the child's finger, and not looking at Mr. Marlowe.

"The *calf*?"

At that, Caitlin did glance up. "Surely you remember there are live animals in the performance? As you will recall, the Duke of Wynter overruled Miss Pettigrew."

"I'm a sheep!" Freddy piped up.

"Why don't you go find your tail?" Caitlin told him, and he ran away.

"I recall there was a rat," Mr. Marlowe observed. "I didn't realize that St. Wilfrid's was welcoming true livestock."

"Only a few," Caitlin said. "Mr. Brisket kindly brought two rabbits and a calf from his butcher shop. Oh, and some chickens."

"Where are the animals?"

"Miss Pettigrew is going to hate this," Viola murmured.

Surprisingly, Mr. Marlowe didn't look angry.

"Behind the stage," Caitlin said.

At that moment they all heard a distinct lowing noise.

"My fiancée detests animals and has strong views about their rightful place," Mr. Marlowe remarked.

"We all know that," Caitlin said, her voice perfectly even. "You'll be glad to know that Sam the rat has not joined the cast. I didn't want to upset Miss Pettigrew."

"Too late for that," Devin said in Viola's ear.

"Everything seems to be quite well here," Mr. Marlowe said, smiling at Caitlin.

"Do give Miss Pettigrew my best wishes," she said. "I hope she will not be scandalized by the animals."

Mr. Marlowe bowed. "To be honest, Lady Caitlin, I fear the worst."

She blinked at him.

He dropped a kiss on her cheek. "I will join Miss Pettigrew in the front row." Mr. Marlowe walked away.

Caitlin looked like a teakettle on the boil.

"Hello!" Viola cried, popping from behind the curtain.

"Did you see that? I will never darken the door of this church again," Caitlin said in a low, furious tone. "He kissed me, as if I were a light-skirt, and strolled off to sit beside his betrothed." She scowled at Devin. "St. Wilfrid's deserves better."

"I have no doubt," Devin agreed. "Should I cut him off without a penny?"

Caitlin gasped. "No!"

"He shouldn't have kissed you," Viola observed.

Caitlin wound her fingers together. "It's no matter," she said, her eyes shining with tears that she determinedly blinked away. "A more important problem is that we've had two dress rehearsals and we haven't managed to get through the play either time. At least Mr. Higgins seems to be fairly sober tonight."

"Sober?" Viola echoed. "I know the character of Noah is tipsy in the play, but do you mean in real life?"

"Where *is* Noah?" Devin asked, laughter running through his voice.

Caitlin turned around. "There he is—oh, dear."

Mr. Higgins was a large, red-haired man wearing a flimsy tunic, the sewing circle's idea of biblical garb. As they watched, he hoisted a great bottle of ale in the air and drained half of it.

"He takes his role very seriously," Caitlin said.

"I know him; I'll just have a word," Devin said, striding away.

Viola watched her husband stop to exchange greetings here and there. He reached Mr. Higgins and ushered him out of the room. "Devin is a problem solver," she told Caitlin. "Likely he'll take him upstairs to sober up."

Caitlin looked at her, eyes brimming with tears. "Oh, who cares, Viola?"

"You've worked hard on the play, and for the orphanage as well," Viola said. "*You* care, Cat."

"Not any longer," Caitlin said miserably. "I shan't be able to help the orphans after tomorrow, Viola. My father is furious."

"Because of the play?" Viola asked.

"No, no," Caitlin said. "He doesn't care about the play; he thinks this is merely a benefit for orphans. Can you imagine if he knew that Noah is drunk?"

Viola winced. "I didn't remember that part of the play. I had originally suggested *The Second Shepherd's Play.*"

"People must have become more sensitive over time," Caitlin said. "I can assure you, Viola, that the outrage that a drunken Noah might cause would be nothing to the outrage if we had staged the Lamb of God sequence in *The Second Shepherd's Play*. If you remember, one of the shepherds had *stolen* a lamb and planned to cook it for supper."

"Clearly medieval plays are more lively than I remembered."

"It doesn't matter," Caitlin said, a tear rolling down her cheek. "This is the last time I'll attend St. Wilfrid's or be around the children."

Viola wrapped her in a hug. "Don't cry, darling. Devin will fix everything."

Caitlin sniffed and pulled out a handkerchief. "He can't fix my life," she said wearily. "My father threatened to pack me off to the country unless I agree to marry the earl, and I won't. I refused him this morning."

"Not the gargoyle-loving earl?"

Caitlin nodded miserably. "I won't. That's that, and I'm being sent to the country to become a companion to an aged aunt. She's very devout. Perhaps her vicar will be interested in starting a Sunday school."

"Give Devin a chance to fix things," Viola said, wiping away Caitlin's tears. "I trust him."

And she did.

Deep inside, she was utterly convinced that Devin would make certain that Mr. Marlowe didn't marry Miss Pettigrew.

"We've saved you a seat next to us in the second row," Viola said. "Shall we go there now?"

The chaos was settling down. The lambs, squirrels, and piggies had tails. Mr. Higgins was back, though to Viola's inexperienced eyes he didn't look much more sober. He was grinning at Devin.

"All right," Caitlin said miserably. "As long as I don't have to speak to Miss Pettigrew. It hardly needs to be said, but she won't enjoy the performance."

"I'll protect you," Viola promised.

Chapter Thirty-four

At first, *The Play of Noah* appeared to be going remarkably smoothly. The curtain opened promptly at eight-thirty, and the audience declared the little girl who lisped a welcome to be adorable.

Mr. Marlowe climbed onto the stage, and thanked everyone for their kind support of the new orphanage.

Once he returned to his seat beside Miss Pettigrew, Otis thanked the Duke and Duchess of Lindow for the refreshments to follow; the Duke and Duchess of Wynter for hosting the play in St. Wilfrid's cloister; Mr. and Mrs. Parth Sterling, who had provided fabric for the costumes and the flood; and the parish sewing circle, who had ably taken on sewing everything from piggy tails to God's halo.

In the seat directly in front of Viola, the bishop's back stiffened at the mention of God's halo, but his daughter talked to him in a low voice until he settled down.

The play proper opened with God's visit to Noah, who behaved very well during the encounter. Anyone would have been surprised by such a visitor, and only the most exacting of critics could say that Noah overacted by swooning.

True, God's fluffy halo (fashioned out of a quantity of cotton batting) fell to the side at one point and swung from an ear, but Mr. Brisket discovered it soon enough and put it back with a chuckle. More importantly, he remembered every one of his lines, even the difficult ones enumerating the ark's cubits of length.

Great shouts of laughter swept the room when Noah's wife scolded him for wasting his time building a ship (*"You're as thick as Tewkesbury mustard and I rue the day I married you!"*). And scolded him for bringing messy animals into the house (*"You fat-guts, stewed-prune brained ruffian!"*). And scolded him for being a worthless husband (*"You bull's pizzle, you three-inch fool!"*)

"'Pizzle'?" Viola asked Caitlin, and then giggled, figuring it out for herself.

"Mrs. Noah has left the script," Caitlin moaned.

There was an unfortunate moment when the calf shifted all her weight to Noah's foot. But while purists—or bishops—could wish that his language were not as colorful, the audience greeted his explosion with great delight.

Viola noticed, though, that the line of black-garbed persons in the front row showed no signs of enjoyment. They were completely silent, shoulders twitching during the more exuberant lines and not even a chuckle greeting the hilarious bits.

At just the right moment, a sea of blue silk flowed from the heavens and rippled across the floor and over the edge of the stage.

The cast made it through the ocean journey with great aplomb. By that point, the audience was roaring with laughter every time Mrs. Noah opened her mouth.

The dove (a cleverly fashioned piece of pasteboard) hopped onto Mount Ararat; the ark landed; the animals were escorted off the stage. Noah was drinking from a hip flask with great abandon, Viola noticed with some alarm. Of course, the Bible did say that Noah drank too much wine. But did he have to be quite *so* drunk?

Even worse, on the way out of the ark, Noah tripped and tossed the chicken he was holding into the front row. He ambled forward to retrieve it, but somehow the goat had freed itself as well and fairly leapt off the stage. Faced by a solid line of bodies, he panicked and charged forward, head lowered.

Viola heard a scream, but she was too short to see what was happening; next to her, Devin was shaking with laughter, and down the row, the Wildes were on their feet.

"Where did the chicken go?" Caitlin whispered.

"I can't see!" Viola said.

Thankfully, Lord Erik Wilde leapt from his prompting corner and retrieved the chicken.

The play began again, and Noah retreated into his tent, upending the flask into his mouth as he did so. His son Ham entered and retreated in horror, shouting. Noah seemed to be having a hard time remembering his grandson's name in order to curse him—poor Canaan kept hissing his name, while Noah stumbled about calling him Caner and Cabit and Calus.

It was a huge relief when God reappeared and announced, *"And the years of Noah were nine hundred and fifty years, and so he died."*

To her dismay, Viola saw that Mr. Higgins, playing

Noah, had decided to interpret God's last lines; he heavily collapsed on the floor. But the cast very properly ignored his prone body as they took their bows.

The ecclesiastics in the front row ostentatiously did not applaud.

Mr. Marlowe climbed onto the stage and thanked everyone again for guaranteeing that the orphanage would be sustained for an entire year.

Viola watched the vicar curiously. He certainly was beautiful, with his gentle eyes and scholarly voice. By way of comparison, she glanced up at Devin. Her husband's strong chin was set, and he had an expectant look; he was watching the bishop furiously speaking in a low voice to Mrs. Pettigrew.

She had angry red spots in her cheeks and yet a satisfied look, as if she took pleasure in the fact that her worst predictions had been confirmed.

Around them the audience began gathering their wraps, looking both cheerful and expectant while preparing to partake in the Duke of Lindow's excellent refreshments. His Grace had dispatched most of his kitchen servants including his French cook to the vicarage that morning, and they had spent the whole day preparing splendid confections.

The cast poured out from behind the stage and was surrounded by laughing groups offering compliments.

Not everyone was happy.

Miss Pettigrew surged to her feet. Over the chatter from the crowd, Viola could hear how shrill her voice was, but not what she was saying.

Caitlin and Viola rose and walked with Devin to the end of the row of chairs. "I knew she would hate it," Caitlin said in a small, unhappy voice.

"It was the chicken, me lady," a deep voice said.

"That dratted bird flew straight at Miss Pettigrew. I think it landed on her shoulder. I couldn't see clearly because of my halo."

Devin nodded to Mr. Brisket. "I must congratulate you on a masterful performance of Divinity, Brisket. Not an easy role, and I fancy that not everyone could carry it off, especially given the small problems with your costume."

The butcher lowered his voice to a low rumble. "I reckon you couldn't see the bishop's face, Your Grace, but up on the stage one couldn't help but notice that his ilk weren't enjoying the performance. I just thought I'd give you and Lady Caitlin here a heads-up in case they kick up some dust."

Devin grinned at him. "It's very kind of you to warn me, Brisket."

In the front row, Miss Pettigrew had turned to Mr. Marlowe and was shouting at him, her face twisted with rage.

"Hopefully she's giving him the mitten," Mr. Brisket said. "My missus has said as how we would find another parish if the rector marries that one. She's a tartar, and only going to get worse as she ages."

Viola opened her mouth to defend Miss Pettigrew, but Devin slung an arm around her and smiled. "No point, love."

Love?

Did he just call her—

"Just one more moment," Mr. Brisket said with deep enjoyment. "Yep, that should do it!"

Caitlin gasped.

Despite herself Viola looked back at the front. Mr. Marlowe's face now sported a red patch high on one cheekbone. "She struck him!"

"A solid blow," the butcher said in a tone of deep satisfaction. "Welp, I'd better join the others. The cast is having its own party, you know. That way we won't put the swells to the blush."

"No, you are not!" Caitlin cried. "That is an absurd idea, as I told the sexton when he mentioned it to me. You will all be joining us."

Mr. Brisket looked down at her with a broad smile. "You're a right one, you know that, me lady?"

En masse, the ecclesiastics swept out of the room, Miss Pettigrew clinging to the archdeacon's arm while Bishop Pettigrew led the way.

"Like Moses parting the Red Sea," Devin remarked.

Viola shook her head at him; the mischievous version of the Duke of Wynter was in full sight tonight.

Caitlin asked, "Mr. Brisket, do you think something could be done about Noah before he joins the party?"

"Absolutely," he said promptly. And: "Hello, there, Vicar!"

"Evening," Mr. Marlowe said absentmindedly, his eyes on Caitlin.

"Reckon you've got something to say to this young woman," Mr. Brisket said in a tone of high pleasure. "I'll just have a word with Jeremiah Higgins. Reckon we'll have to make a trip to the water pump and pour a pail of water over his head. I just don't understand how he became that foxed on a few bottles of ale!"

"That would be most kind of you." Mr. Marlowe extended his hand. "You made a splendid deity, Mr. Brisket. I was proud to see you play the role."

Mr. Brisket went rosy all over his face. "That means a lot, sir. Means a lot, coming from you. Well, I'll go and take care of Higgins."

Viola noticed that Mr. Marlowe's right cheek was still red.

He rubbed the spot. "Miss Pettigrew has a strong right arm."

"I am very sorry," Caitlin began.

But she was pulled into an embrace—and kiss—so tight, fierce, and brazen that Viola took a quick look to make sure that the bishop had left the premises.

"Caitlin," Mr. Marlowe said hoarsely. "I love you. I want you to marry me, and put on irresponsible plays, and teach the orphans how to speak to animals."

She opened her mouth to answer, but he pulled her close again and his mouth closed hungrily over hers, and she melted against him.

"Nearing the end of act five," Devin said cheerfully.

"Lust is a sin, Caitlin, but this isn't lust," Mr. Marlowe said. "Not only lust."

"Good thing he clarified that," Devin commented.

"I will marry you," Caitlin said.

Mr. Marlowe blinked and apparently thought better. "I shouldn't ask you. I'm not worthy of you. Not at all."

"This morning I turned down an earl," Caitlin said, tracing his lips with her finger. "I rejected Baron Tibblesfoot last week."

"Exactly," Mr. Marlowe said, clearly struggling to hang on to his common sense.

Viola tugged on her husband's arm. "We should probably allow them some privacy," she whispered.

"Not before the curtain falls," Devin protested, his eyes full of laughter.

"There's only one eligible duke left on the market this year," Caitlin said thoughtfully. "Perhaps I should marry him."

Silence.

"Except that I want to marry you," Caitlin stated. "I want to marry David Marlowe and live in his vicarage."

"I don't have the income to support you properly." His voice was strained.

"Even if my father refuses to pay my dowry, my mother left me her jointure," she replied cheerfully. She tipped back her head and looked into her future husband's agonized eyes. "You haven't any choice, darling."

Mr. Marlowe's jaw tightened. "One always has a choice to do right or wrong."

"Not this time. You've ruined my reputation. No gentleman will ever marry me now." She giggled again.

Mr. Marlowe gaped.

And slowly turned around.

There, looking on with enormous interest, was a good portion of the London *ton*. It seemed that they had glimpsed something more interesting than the refreshments offered in the next room.

"What I don't understand," broke in a complaining, huffing voice, "is how Higgins got hold of the vicar's best brandy? When did he take it from the study? For that's the situation, sir." Mr. Brisket emerged out of the crowd, looking aggrieved. "I'm afraid that I've had to send Higgins home. He simply is not fit for company. He won't be feeling any too chipper tomorrow either," he added.

Mr. Marlowe had apparently decided that since the damage was done, he might as well continue; he started kissing Caitlin again.

"It's the vicar's best brandy, Your Grace," Mr. Brisket said. "Someone gave a whole flask of it to Jeremiah

Higgins, and it was the brandy made him bosky. Too fuddled to keep hold of the chicken, not to mention generally acting like a bufflehead during the play."

Devin smiled and tucked his arm around Viola. "Thank you very much for your help, Mr. Brisket. As for the brandy, we'll think no more about it."

Viola gasped as she looked up at him. "You did it! Brandy, hmmm?" She grinned at him. "Did that come from the vicar's private stock—or the duke's?"

"Prudence is a cardinal virtue," Devin announced severely. And he gave her a hard, swift kiss, to the gathered delight and shock of the audience.

Chapter Thirty-five

 $\mathcal{W}$ e're going to the country," Viola sang to herself, waking up early the next morning and turning to wake Devin—

He wasn't there.

She sat up, pushing mounds of hair out of her eyes, and discovered that her husband was seated at her desk. He was fully dressed, looking every inch a duke, from his exquisite coat to his burnished shoes.

"What on earth are you doing up already?" she asked. He didn't smile at her, or even wish her good morning. His face was utterly composed, with a stillness that she hadn't seen in weeks.

"Devin?"

He was rubbing his finger on the gilded sides of that silly chamber pot she kept on her desk. They'd ended up in her chamber last night because she had to change into a nightdress, and he didn't want to separate.

"What's the matter?" she asked.

"I have several things to confess." His voice was toneless.

Her heart skipped a beat, or several beats. "Could you please come here?" She was wearing one of Lavinia's frivolous nightdresses made of silk and lace. She felt at a terrible disadvantage, faced by an aristocrat wearing a formal suit, not to mention a snowy wig.

"No." Devin's gaze was entirely impersonal. "I think it's best I stay here. After telling you, I will leave, Viola. If you'd like me to return, you could send me a message. Or you could go to the country by yourself, or to your parents, and I would accept that."

"What are you talking about?" Viola asked. Her voice rose from anxiety. "Why? Why would you leave?" She narrowed her eyes. "Do you have that disease, what's it called?" She raked her brain. "The pox?"

"No. I am not ill. Obviously, I hope you won't leave, but it is within your purview," Devin said politely. He looked completely indifferent.

Viola had the sudden thought that perhaps she was still asleep. But no. The sun was coming in the window. The ribbon on her nightdress was tangled, and there was a muscle ticking in Devin's jaw.

This was real.

"Right," she said, her voice emerging in an irritating squeak. "Please tell me whatever you wish." She paused and added, "It won't make any difference to how I feel about you, Devin. I won't leave you."

"Please do me the courtesy of not referring to my mother," he said. "I am no longer a child. In fact, I haven't been a child for longer than you have been alive."

That was a low blow. It was true that there was a decade between them, but Viola never considered it a problem. Apparently, he did, since she was about to be lectured like a child.

"Right," she said, swinging her legs out of bed. "I will listen to your confession later. First I shall take a bath and dress."

For the first time, she saw a flash of emotion in his eyes. Devin wanted to get it over with, whatever it was. He didn't say anything, though, just watched as she walked across the room and pulled the bell cord for her maid.

When he opened his mouth, she held up her hand. "No."

"Viola." Temper growled under the word, but he had himself well in hand.

Viola couldn't say the same for herself. "I woke from sleep, expecting to leave for the country with my affectionate, loving husband. Instead he's decided that he must inform me of some vague sin this very moment."

He nodded. "Before we leave for the country."

"I am resistant to dramatic statements before eggs and tea," she told him, pulling on her dressing gown and tying it tightly around her waist. "I am also extremely resistant to being held hostage by my husband's penchant for drama."

He looked shocked, even horrified. "Penchant for drama?"

"Exactly. Apparently you woke in a foul mood and decided, for whatever reason, to share a secret you'd been nurturing. You can save that secret until I feel ready to hear it. Which will not be until I've had breakfast and at least a pot of tea, and likely two."

Devin was giving her a look that might have sent chills down the back of a constable, but Viola was unmoved. He loved her. He was overlooking that fact at the moment, too caught up in glaring at her to remember.

He loved her.

This sort of thing would probably happen every now and again in their marriage, she decided, given his unhappy childhood.

Her maid opened the door and curtsied. "Your Graces."

"The duke is just leaving," Viola said, not looking at him. "I wish to dress. His Grace will wait for me and we shall breakfast together. I shall put on a traveling gown, obviously, since we are leaving for the country after the meal."

She flicked a glance at Devin's shoes, meant for London and not for travel.

Her husband walked out with his icy veneer intact, which probably made him feel more comfortable. Her maid retired into her dressing room and began gathering her garments.

Viola's eyes rested on the chamber pot, gently glowing in the morning sunshine.

She walked over and plucked off the top. Inside was a crumpled sheet of paper. "Crickets!" she exclaimed.

"Your Grace?" her maid called from the dressing room. "Did you say something?"

"No. Thank you," she replied.

Smoothing out her silly letter, she actually found herself smiling. What a little fool she'd been, with no idea at all about what she was talking about with regard to marital harmony. Marlowe didn't know much either, though presumably Caitlin would teach him about spousal pleasure.

She ripped the paper into shreds and threw it

down on the desk. She should have done that the moment she realized that the unfinished letter had been moved with her belongings from the Lindow townhouse to her new home. Instead, she had stuck it in the chamber pot with the vague idea of making Devin laugh by showing him that her ignorance of marital beds extended to more than male nipples.

Devin had been holding the chamber pot. Could he have read that foolish letter?

It seemed unlikely. He was angry about something related to a confession he wanted to make. No marriage foundered on a girl's silly scribblings to a vicar.

Her traveling costume was made from green striped bombazine, worked around the hem with a border of exuberant flowers and trimmed in cherry. The exquisite lace at the neck was cleverly gathered, enabling the wearer to tighten the bow in front and cover her cleavage.

Or not.

Viola pulled the ribbon out entirely. She moved in front of the mirror to adjust the cherry-colored ribbons in her hair, and glanced down to see that her nipples were covered.

Barely.

She leaned forward and rubbed another layer of lip salve on her lips and tucked the case in her pocket for good measure.

"I'm ready."

"You are exquisite," her maid cried, hands clasped.

"Good," Viola said, smiling at her.

She took a deep breath, calmed the sparks of nervousness in her stomach, and walked down the stairs. She meant to eat everything on her plate because she'd be damned before she'd let Devin think that fear of him had gone to her stomach.

That was crucial.

No matter what he was about to confess, he was her husband, and she had no fear of him.

After breakfast, eaten in polite and punctilious silence, they repaired to Devin's library. Without the forest of Greek statues, it had turned into a looming room that desperately needed refurbishing. Like the rest of the house.

Viola deliberately reapplied her lip salve at the mirror in the corner over the fireplace, sauntered back to the settee opposite Devin, and sat down, making certain to discreetly tweak her bodice to reveal the maximum amount of bosom.

He leaned against his desk, managing to look twice as tall as he usually was. But there wasn't even a twinkle of fear in Viola's heart and she waved her hand at him carelessly. "I am ready."

A moment later, she found herself staring at him, her mouth open.

Incredulity was her primary response.

"*You?* That was you? I wondered . . . But you said you hadn't been to Lindow Castle in years!"

"That *was* years ago."

"Who was the woman in yellow shoes?"

His brows furrowed. "Her name was Annabel. She was my mistress and I'm afraid that I misjudged her. As you will recall, at the time I chided her, thinking that you were assigned the role of witness, allowing Annabel to try to force me into marriage. I say 'try' because I would never have married her."

Viola's gut twisted for the first time and she noted that there was one thing that still frightened her. "Did you love her?"

"God, no," Devin said impatiently.

Viola smiled.

"I was unfair to her. I misjudged her. She wrote to me several times, and I tossed her letters in the fire. I would offer her an apology now, except she married and moved abroad."

"I would take extreme exception to your contacting her for any reason," Viola told him.

"I'm not interested in her," Devin said harshly. "What I am telling you is that I was the man who terrified you to the point of causing you to hide in a cowshed rather than debut at the proper age." He was obviously wedded to the idea that he had to drag out every detail of her embarrassing shyness. "I bellowed at Annabel, threatening her with—"

"But she *did* mean to trap you," Viola interrupted.

He froze.

"A matron came in directly after you left, and Annabel screamed at both me and the woman, saying her witness had ruined everything by being late. I threw up."

She was watching him closely and she saw that his veneer was cracking. He was coming back to himself.

"Some of the vomit splashed on Annabel," she added.

His eyes frosted over again. "I am still the man who terrified you."

Viola crossed her arms over her chest and frowned at him. "I suppose you're telling me, because you're afraid that someday you'll lose control and shout at me, and I'll vomit on your shoes."

"I'm not afraid you'll throw up on me!"

She smiled at him. "Let me ask you this. Did you read the letter that I wrote to the vicar about the marriage bed? Which, by the way, he would have known absolutely nothing about."

He nodded. "It was inexcusable of me, but inadvertent, I promise you."

"I wrote it months ago, back when I was trying to respond to Marlowe's sermons in a failed effort to convince him that I'd be a good vicar's wife. I couldn't think of a thing to say about that one, for good reason."

She saw a lightening in his expression. "You wouldn't have been a good vicar's wife."

She didn't get up, because he had to come to her.

"I don't know," she said meditatively. "Mr. Higgins said that he's ready to take on *The Second Shepherd's Play* next year. *The Fall of Lucifer* would surely collect a large audience."

Their eyes met.

"I love you," Devin said. His voice was quiet. It wasn't an excuse or a justification; it was simply the truth.

She grinned at him. "I know."

"I'm jealous of Marlowe."

She nodded.

"I want a different vicar."

She shook her head. "What I felt for Mr. Marlowe was as empty as my reaction to a sermon about marital intercourse when I didn't even know that men had nipples. My love for you is in every part of my being. It will never go away. If you do lose your temper and threaten me with life in the country, I'll laugh at you, Devin."

He started making his way toward her now, slowly. "You would?"

"There's no country house in which I might sleep, where you wouldn't sleep next to me. You are my safety, and you're my life. I know you, Devin. And I know you love me."

He was close enough that she heard his shaky breath. "You aren't leaving me, are you?"

She shook her head. "Never."

"We're going to the country together." He sat down beside her.

"Daisy and Cleopatra are waiting," she reminded him.

"How can you so easily forgive me, when I was the man who terrified you?" He sounded truly mystified.

Viola leaned toward him. "You are the man whom I inadvertently interrupted in an intimate moment when I was a young and callow girl. You are also the man who makes me feel safe wherever I am. Who makes me feel as beautiful as any Wilde, and more important than any duke's daughter. Who has taught me what it means to love a man and to be married."

Devin cupped her face in his hands, and his dark eyes searched her face. He kissed her, and both of them knew that he didn't need any more lessons in tenderness.

"I love you," he said a while later, his voice raw with the truth of it.

"And I love you," Viola promised him. "Always."

Epilogue

Viola was coming down the corridor to the nursery when she heard her son's voice floating out the open door.

"I'm sorry I did it," five-year-old Otis said earnestly. "I shouldn't have done it, I know that."

"Why did you do it?" Devin asked. "It wasn't the act of a gentleman, Otis."

Viola shook her head. That realization she had had long ago—that given a happy childhood, Devin would have been a very naughty boy—had bred true in his son.

"I did it because I wanted to," Otis said, with inescapable logic.

"But now Mama's favorite chamber pot is dented," his father pointed out.

Viola winced, and walked into the room.

Sure enough, Otis was drooping on his father's knee, and beside him was a gleaming, slightly dented chamber pot once used by King Henry VIII.

"I'm sorry, Mama!" Otis cried, scrambling down and running to her, throwing his arms around her knees. "I'm sorry about your piss pot, I truly am! I didn't mean to."

Viola stooped down and put him on her hip, knowing that in a month or two, he'd be too heavy for her to pick up. He was his father's child in height as well as character. She met Devin's eyes over Otis's head. Sure enough, her husband was on his feet and coming to take their son away.

"He's too big for you to carry these days," Devin said, his caressing smile telling her that he was as excited as she was about the baby who would join the family in a few months. He set Otis on his feet and said to him, "It wasn't right to take something from your mother's room and use it for any reason, son."

"Mama doesn't piddle in it," Otis pointed out. "I didn't either," he added.

"I keep precious things inside instead," Viola told him.

"That's just be-culiar," Otis said. "Tommy said that you'd be mad at me." He looked up at his father. "He said that you might be mad enough to send me away to school."

Viola knew with unshakable faith that she had married the right person.

She knew that she would love Devin till the grave and beyond.

But that didn't mean that there weren't moments when her heart practically burst with the emotion. Say, for example, when His Grace, the Duke of Wynter, crouched down in front of his young son and told him that he would never, ever send him away. And he would never be angry with him either. "Cross, perhaps," Devin said, kissing his son on his forehead. "But you're working on being less naughty, right?"

"I'm trying," Otis said earnestly. But he paused, because their son was nothing if not honest. "I'm not sure it's working, though."

"That's all right," Devin assured him. "Mama's working on not being afraid of horses, isn't she?"

"It's not working," Viola confirmed with a sigh.

"What are you working on?" Otis asked his father.

Devin stood up again. "Loving your mother." He leaned in and gave Viola a swift kiss.

"That's silly," Otis said.

"Why?" Devin asked.

Otis raised a tiny eyebrow. "Because that's easy. It's *hard* not to be naughty!"

When his parents didn't stop kissing, he made his way out of the nursery as quietly as he could. He had to go to the cowshed, where his best friend Tommy was looking after the new calves, and tell him that everything was all right.

Otis had an idea that would make a better target for his slingshot than the chamber pot.

If he could just find a goose egg . . .

A Note about Cycle Plays and Shakespearean Insults

 $\mathcal{I}$ hope you enjoyed my rendition of a medieval cycle play! In the Middle Ages, individual play cycles were performed annually in the streets of 127 different towns in the British Isles. The plays instructed parishioners about the major events of the Bible and liturgical year, and subject matter ranged from the fall of Lucifer, to the creation of Adam and Eve, all the way to the Assumption and Coronation of the Virgin Mary. They were performed on wagons that moved through each city, allowing an audience standing in one place to see all the plays, one after another. A given cycle could include well over thirty plays (the York cycle has forty-eight). Each play would have been assigned to a guild, or group of craftsmen; the baker's guild, for example, would have performed the Last Supper. Scenery was minimal, but costumes were elaborate.

My version of *The Play of Noah* is a loose interpretation of several plays in the York cycle, including the *Building of the Ark* performed by the shipwrights. Noah's irritable wife comes from *The Flood*, originally performed by "fishers and mariners," and written by a playwright now known as the York Realist. I should add that while medieval performances did include impromptu riffs, Noah's wife would not have hurled Shakespearean insults hundreds of years before that playwright's birth. Another note: Caitlin and Viola briefly discuss *The Second Shepherd's Play*, the most famous cycle play. It comes from the Towneley sequence and was written by a playwright now known as the Wakefield Master.

I made up St. Wilfrid's, but based its cloister on that of St. Bartholomew the Great in London, which hosts refreshments after Eucharist as well as the occasional medieval banquet and a Michelin-starred restaurant, Club Gascon. The York cycle was last performed in 2016 in the streets of York; I like to think that St. Wilfrid's would welcome a rakish medieval play to go with their medieval banquet.

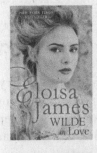

Do you love historical fiction?

Want the chance to hear news about your favourite
authors (and the chance to win free books)?

Mary Balogh
Lenora Bell
Charlotte Betts
Jessica Blair
Frances Brody
Grace Burrowes
Evie Dunmore
Pamela Hart
Elizabeth Hoyt
Eloisa James
Lisa Kleypas
Stephanie Laurens
Sarah MacLean
Amanda Quick
Julia Quinn

Then visit the Piatkus website
www.yourswithlove.co.uk

And follow us on Facebook and Instagram
www.facebook.com/yourswithlovex | @yourswithlovex

piatkus